The Dog Hunters

by David Bell

The Adventures
of Llewelyn&Gelert
Book One

All rights reserved. No part of this publication may be reproduced or transmitted by any means, digital, mechanical, photocopying or otherwise, without the prior permission of the author.

David Bell has the right of attribution – the right to be identified as the author of the work, and asserts this right. The author has the right of integrity – the right to object to and prevent derogatory treatment of the work. Derogatory treatment is treatment (by distortion, mutilation or otherwise) that is prejudicial to his honour or reputation. He also has the right to accurate attribution – the right to be accurately attributed as the author of the work and not to have the work attributed to someone else.

Copyright Text David Bell 2013
Copyright Cover and all Illustrations David Bell 2013

ISBN-13: 978-1491009314 Paperback

Set in Baskerville. So you could say Baskerville of the hound.
Printed by CreateSpace

Also available on Kindle and other devices

PRAISE FOR 'THE DOG HUNTERS'

☆ ☆ ☆ ☆ ☆ *I loved it. Brilliant for young adults and their grown ups!, - I am a teacher so I read this book originally thinking of it as a book for teenage boys. However, I quickly got sucked into it, and loved it as an adult. It is beautifully written with both good language and great colloquialisms which make it fun, and personalize the characters. It is an adventure of boy and his dog , with elements of medieval history, loads of geographical references and just enough science to keep us curious. Can't wait for the sequel!*

Katrina Nicosia August 8, 2013

☆ ☆ ☆ ☆ ☆ *My 11 year old couldn't put it down!, This book is great for a wide range of ages. Lots of twists and turns and completely unpredictable. I downloaded it on a recommendation but didn't get to read it first as my 11 year old boy had his 'head in the book' until he had finished it! He loved it, as did I and can't wait for the next one from this author!*

Emma Gardiner July 25, 2013

☆ ☆ ☆ ☆ ☆ *A Rip Snorting Read. - I'm not keen on dogs - they smell and they slobber all over you - but I loved this! It's unlike anything else I've ever read before. For sure it's a familiar genre of action adventure with a couple of teenagers as the heroes but the characters are fresh and exciting and the plot revolves around believable exotic breeds of dogs rather than easy magic worlds and hobgoblins. It's very visceral; there's plenty of gore, vomit and other bodily mess to satisfy the most ghoulish young reader and set in the 1200's it's brings to life a period of time which rarely appears in fiction - let alone childrens' fiction. 10/10 for originality and well crafted imagination.*

Kelvin Johnston 4 July 2013

☆ ☆ ☆ ☆ ☆ *A cracking good read. This isn't really the kind of book I'd normally go for, like Harry Potter wasn't, but I found this as addictive. It rattles along and I like the juxtaposition between traditional telling of the tale and the use of 'today talk'. The author uses it brilliantly to lighten the tone and introduce humour. And I love the first sentence of Chapter Two, no twelve-year-old would be able to resist reading on... All the time I was reading, I was running the film in my mind. In colour. The only other writer to do that to me is Nicholas Evans (The Horse Whisperer). A cracking good read.*

Redacteur 31 July 2013

☆ ☆ ☆ ☆ *Great book for young adults-, or even younger! I'm not in this category, [more into the Jane Austin genre] but downloaded it on my Kindle out of curiosity, and loved it. It's just great fun, with medieval history given a new slant, and enough gruesome stuff to appeal to those who like this sort of thing. I was so happy for Gelert - I always hated the thought of him being undeservedly slain, and have been known to sob at his grave... this lovely wolf hound certainly had a very complicated later life!*

Willia 27 July 2013

Most thanks to Jeneal for waiting so long, and Frank for being Llewelyn. Also to my Mum, Tony & Fiona, Dan & Kate, Dean & Caroline, Sarah & Paul, and all my other good friends for your encouragement, and to my copy editor Deirdre Coleman and proof reader Helen Greatrex.

Special thanks to Reilly the wolfhound and Sandy and Donna – indeed to Wolfie owners everywhere; only very special people can share their lives with such wondrous animals.

And their farts.

PREFACE

By Gelert

The story goes that the King left me in the nursery to look after his son, Llewelyn, as he'd done a hundred times before.

He then went off hunting.

And when he returned, he killed me.

You'd have killed me too if you'd seen what he saw as he stepped into the nursery; me, alone, my muzzle covered in blood, the room turned upside down, the crib on its side and no sign of the baby.

The King thought I'd eaten his only child, so he whipped out his sword and stabbed me.

Three times.

The first stab, his aim was off, and he only managed to slice the top off my left ear. The second one got me in the shoulder and broke my collarbone. By the third go, his eye was in, and that's the stab that saw me off. There I lay, heaving my last breath in a steaming pool of blood.

Then the King heard Llewelyn crying under the overturned crib.

Next he found the corpses of the two wolves, their throats ripped out. I did that. I'd killed them, saving Llewelyn.

That's when the King realised the tragedy of his mistake.

And so did everyone else.

Especially the bards, who knew a good story when they saw one. Straight away they were singing about how the King never smiled again, and how he laid my corpse to rest in a magnificent tomb that would 'forever be a memorial to man's best friend', their songs spiked with the not-so-subtle subtext of the dangers of jumping to hasty conclusions.

Oh yes, the bards' tales were sad, full of nobility and spattered with lashings of blood and guts. Everyone who heard them wept and told their friends, who in turn told theirs.

And so the tale of my death was passed on, and travelled around the world in just a few years, which was pretty fast eight hundred years ago.

(Today, of course, it would have gone viral in a nanosecond – there's always some spotty snot-nose with a Samsung and a Twitter account lurking in the background. But, believe me, back then a story going around the world in just a few years was as fast as it got.)

Well, here I am, alive and telling you that you shouldn't believe everything you see on the internet, or in storybooks, or the papers, or on the telly. The truth is: the King didn't kill me.

Oh, he had a proper go at it. But, just in time, he heard baby Llewelyn crying, and in the middle of his third stab, he managed to pull his sword.

That fraction-of-an-inch-less blade in my guts saved me.

Of course, with a brace of enormous dead wolves as proof of my 'noble fearlessness and heroic dedication', from then on in it was all 'O faithful hound!' and 'which idiot left the front door open when we went out this morning?'

But, let's face it (and in their defence, I suppose), the bards wouldn't have made much of a living telling a story about a king who doesn't kill his faithful wolfhound and everyone goes off for breakfast. That's why they embellished the facts, turning a nearly nasty mistake into the crowd-pleasing load of old cobblers that became what everyone knows as The Legend of Gelert the Faithful Wolfhound.

That's show business.

How the bards would have spun 'Emperor of China Sends Vast Fleet To Buy Dog', or 'Fourteen-Year-Old Boy Slaughters Entire Pirate Fleet, Braves Typhoons, and Falls In Love' is anyone's guess.

They'd have certainly made a meal of anything that included flying dogs, men who live for a thousand years, and scenes of rabid apes surfing tidal waves.

Mercifully for the truth, the bards weren't around to see what happened a few years later.

So, extraordinary though everything that follows might appear, trust me, it's true. I remember it all as clearly as I remember my dinner last night, which, if you're interested, was two cans of Pedigree Chum mixed with leftover Fray Bentos steak and kidney pie, covered with melted Vienetta.

PART I: THE BARGAIN

Chapter 1. Fire

—————————————

Sieges are boring, thought Llewelyn.

He sat at his desk, squinting at his slate in the glum glow of a single rush light. Gelert the wolfhound lay snoring at his feet. The huge dog's scarred nose twitched in a dream.

What can you smell, old mate? Llewelyn wondered. *A stag? A hare? Another dog's bumhole?*

Gelert's fur was a thinning blondish grey with bare patches of crimson scabs showing through. Plum-sized lumps bunched along his flanks and haunches, wobbling as his legs twitched and began to sketch a sleepy run. Whatever he'd smelled in his dream, he was now chasing it.

At least your dream is getting you out of the castle.

No-one had left the stronghold for six months, not unless they were dead and being thrown over the battlements or chucked into the ebbing tide.

Llewelyn recalled the early days of the siege. Once the drawbridge had been pulled up and the portcullis slammed down, the castle had buzzed with the thrilling notion that you might shortly find an arrow in the back of your head. Schoolwork had been forgotten. Just making it through the next few days was all that mattered.

Gradually, everyone inside, and the English army outside, settled in for a long siege. Shortly afterwards, Llewelyn's father, the King, remembered that he was paying Friar William 'a bloody fortune' for tuition. So now, five and a half months on, Llewelyn found himself wishing the English would pull their fingers out and do something.

Anything would be better than schoolwork. Anything would be better than learning how to be a Prince of Wales.

Gelert carried on snoring and twitching.

No Latin verbs for you, lucky old bugger, Llewelyn sighed and returned to his books.

The castle grew quiet for the night.

The young prince's dank quarters were high in its tallest

tower, safe from the fighting while he studied what? Plutarch and Plato. What use was Archimedes in a siege? Shouldn't he be practicing his swordplay and archery? Why wouldn't his father let him train with the men? His older brother Prince Dafydd was a warrior, why couldn't he be too?

Miserable, he scratched out a few more words on his slate. In the still of night, the screeching of his chalk was all the more jarring. It must be nearly midnight, and here he was, still sweating over the same stupid, useless passage he'd been working on since sunset.

Suddenly, Gelert leapt to his feet barking. Llewelyn jumped, knocking his slate from the table. Three hours of translation shattered on the stone floor. He put his hands to his head. Friar William would give him a beating tomorrow morning.

"AAARG! You. Stupid. Dog!"

Gelert looked hurt, but padded over to the door and sniffed the gap beneath it. Then Llewelyn heard the racket from the courtyard below. Shouting, which quickly grew louder; the frantic ringing of a bell, then screams. Squads of soldiers running through the castle.

A faint smell of burning pricked at Llewelyn's nostrils. Fresh smoke, not the bitter stink of long-dead fires.

"Something's burning!"

Gelert looked back at him with his 'told-you-so' look.

Llewelyn's first impulse was fear, but then he smiled to himself. He had an excuse to stop doing homework and for his broken slate. He grabbed his longbow and arrows, snatched up the rush light, and ran across the room.

Gelert edged backwards as tendrils of smoke seeped under the door.

Llewelyn tugged it open, pulling in a swirling curtain of thick smoke that made his eyes smart. He breathed through his mouth, which started him coughing, and ran, taking the gloomy spiral stairway three steps a time. Gelert was behind him, cautious of the smoky gloom and the steep pitch of the uneven stairs. Llewelyn knew every one of the two hundred and seventy steps to the ground floor and he raced ahead.

Moments later, he careered through the doorway at the bottom of the tower and into a nightmare.

The castle's courtyard was a confusion of shadows cast by the flames of a hundred fires. Soldiers lumbered across the open space, blundering into each other in the smoke. Officers bellowed orders heard by no-one.

The night sky beyond the castle walls glowed brighter. Llewelyn looked up as a whirring sound rose above the crackling fires and shouting men. A swarm of flames arched over the battlements, cascading into the courtyard. *Fire arrows!*

One was heading towards him. Llewelyn took two steps back. The thick-shafted arrow smacked into the earth in front of him, spattering gobbets of blazing tar at his feet. The rest of the volley smashed around him. Most of the arrows sparked against stone or thudded into the packed earth, but some hit timber, cloth and straw. Still the fire arrows came, volley after volley shredding the dark sky.

Llewelyn winced as he saw a soldier hit from above. The flaming arrowhead lanced into the man's shoulder, extinguishing itself as he tumbled like a sack of beets thrown from a cart.

Llewelyn wondered where his father was and looked around the ramparts. The King would be up there somewhere, directing his men. He must be; Welsh archers were finding targets beyond the castle walls and the rain of fire arrows withered. English curses and screams faded into the night.

But a lean-too shed was fully ablaze, threatening the walls behind. If the fire got too hot, the old mortar would crumble and the patched masonry might collapse.

The fire was terribly hot. Even from twenty yards away, Llewelyn felt the skin on his face and hands prickling. The closest fire fighters backed away from the growling flames.

Then his father's voice cut through the turmoil.

"You lot, stop scratching your arses and form three bucket chains from the well! Owain, why aren't your boys out here helping?"

The King emerged from the stairwell of the western tower and strode through a bank of smoke. His armour flashed from the flickering fires and his great cloak steamed as he stood silhouetted against the inferno, pointing and shoving his men to where they should be.

Instinctively, Llewelyn shrank into the shadows.

The King marched towards the burning outhouse, his beard beginning to smoulder, but even he had to step back as his armour grew too hot to bear.

"Bugger and damnation!"

Still bellowing orders, he unbuckled the metal plates and his chainmail tunic, tossing them carelessly around him.

"Do I have to do everything myself?" he shouted and saw Llewelyn's big brother running across the courtyard, sword in hand.

"Dafydd! Why the sword?"

Prince Dafydd stopped and shrugged. He thought anything not involving using a sword was a waste of sword swinging time. In his shadowed hideaway, Llewelyn shook his head at his brother's gormlessness and saw his father do the same. The King sighed, then gathered himself before shouting at Dafydd.

"Do something useful. Have those men above the portcullis drag that cauldron of water above the fire! And get a bucket chain going here!"

Soon, lines of soldiers and lads were handing slopping buckets from the well to the shed. The lead men ran in to throw their feeble splashes of water onto the roof. The spray streaked the wall of flames black for a few seconds, but the fire rushed back brighter.

Then the soldiers from the portcullis tipped their cauldron. The fire flared and belched hissing steam, and an explosion of flaming tar and firebrands shot upwards in a ballooning fireball that knocked three soldiers from the battlements. They crashed through the open roof of the shed, splaying scraps of burning timber and thatch across the courtyard.

"Keep at it!" roared the King, "You lot on the seaward ramparts! Down here, now! Get flails! Flog the fire to death!"

Llewelyn knew he had to help. He slung his bow over his shoulder and ran into the stream of soldiers pouring into the courtyard, quickly getting caught up in the mass of chainmail and muscle.

In the bustle, no-one knew he was their prince. Someone shoved a heavy flail into his hands.

"Get to the front little'un!"

Llewelyn was small enough to squirm forward, but his

longbow kept snagging him in the heaving crowd.

Oh Mother of Jesus, don't let it break! If he fell, he'd be trampled.

Suddenly he broke through the forward ranks and the fire sucked the air out of his lungs. His throat felt like he'd swallowed a pound of boiling barley chaff and his eyeballs began to fry. As he tilted the top of his head towards the flames, his hair began to singe.

Llewelyn ignored the pain and raised his heavy flail. The scorching heat rasped at his exposed hands, but he felt elation coursing through him; he was fighting alongside his father's men! He was helping out!

I'm actually doing something useful!

Then the shoving of men behind eased, and he felt a sharp tug at his belt. He fell, spread-eagled, dropping his flail as he was jerked backwards, his face in the dirt. The tips of his longbow scoured two jagged lines either side of him. The throng of men parted to let him pass. Some of the soldiers were laughing.

Llewelyn twisted to see who had hold of his belt. It was Gelert. The old wolfhound was dragging him as easily as if he was pulling a badger from its set.

"Gerroff!" he yelled, reaching back to biff at Gelert's head. The men's laughter grew louder.

"Leave me be!" he cried. But Gelert kept dragging.

"Let him go, Gelert." It was the King.

Gelert dropped Llewelyn. More laughter rippled through the watching ranks.

"What are you lot looking at?" the King bellowed. "Get to work!"

The soldiers threw themselves back into the fire fight.

Llewelyn sprang to his feet, furious with Gelert.

"You idiot!" he screamed, and kicked out at his old friend. He might as well have tried kicking a cow.

"No. You're the idiot," said the King, grabbing Llewelyn by his hair.

"Ow! That hurts!" he squeaked.

"Not as much as being burned alive!" spat his father. "It's not your place to be with the men, you hear me?"

"I was helping. I was doing something!"

"You're thirteen. You weren't helping anyone."

"They laughed at me!"

His father threw him down. "Better than them crying at your funeral. Go back to your chambers and get on with your studies."

He turned and walked back towards the fire.

Llewelyn's guts turned inside out and his brain froze. Gelert saw his anger and went to nuzzle at his face, but the young prince shoved him aside and sprinted after his father.

He'd had enough. *I'll show you what a thirteen year old can do!*

Just as he was going to take a flying kick at the soft back of his father's knee, right where it really hurts, a frightened-looking foot soldier came running from the far side of the courtyard.

"Sire! Sire! Sire!"

The King stopped and Llewelyn crashed into his back.

"What is it?" the King asked, ignoring his son.

"Sire! There's something you need to see, Sire! Lights, sire! Lots of lights sire, out at sea, sire!"

The King's face turned pale in the flickering firelight and he glanced nervously at the harbour gatehouse, then up at the seaward battlements.

The Welsh castle had proved itself impregnable by land, but lights out at sea could mean only one thing; a fleet of ships. If they were English warships, the castle was in trouble. The King looked back at the fire. His officers were in control and the teams of soldiers were on top of the conflagration.

"Follow me," he ordered, heading for the doorway of the seaward gatehouse. The foot soldier jogged after him.

Llewelyn knew his father hadn't meant the order for him, but he followed anyway. Old Gelert loped wearily behind.

🐾

The twisting stairway was steep and narrow and filled with smoke. By the time they reached the top, everyone was choking and winded by the climb. The King flung open the door onto the platform and hurried over to the seaward side of the gatehouse battlements.

"There, sire!" wheezed the foot soldier, pointing needlessly.

"By the bones of Saint David!" thundered the King.

Llewelyn pulled himself up into an embrasure alongside his father.

The King finally noticed him and scowled.

"Well, now you're here, make yourself useful," he sighed. "What d'you make of that lot?"

Llewelyn's breath caught. A string of orange lights at least two miles wide shimmered across the dark horizon, a beautiful yet chilling sight. As his eyes grew accustomed to the dark, the array of lights seemed to grow bigger and multiply.

"There's hundreds of them!"

The King said nothing and dismissed the foot soldier with a gesture.

Llewelyn had never seen him so worried. He felt sick in his soul, sensing what was going through his father's mind: *What if it* is *an English fleet?*

He tore his gaze from the lights and looked landwards. The surrounding hills bristled with the besieging English army, who outnumbered the Welsh defenders two hundred to one, spreading up the slopes facing the castle and along the beaches on either side. Countless campfires shimmered through the heat haze rising from the courtyard, like the glowing red eyes of an immense pack of wolves waiting to pounce.

Until now, the English army had been a neutered force. The Welsh castle stood at the end of a narrow causeway jutting into the deep sea. This sliver of land and the surrounding waves had held the English at arm's length for half a year. Again and again the roadway had been strewn with fresh layers of corpses killed by volleys of Welsh arrows.

Llewelyn looked back to the orange lights on the horizon. Warships could attack the rear of the castle through its enclosed but poorly defended harbour. The sea that had both protected and kept the Welsh resistance supplied would now deliver death and destruction.

Wales might be lost.

But then, the lights sank into the sea, winking out, like candles burning to their wicks.

"At least they won't approach the coastline in the darkness," the King muttered miserably, "Tomorrow though …"

"They might not have been English," ventured Llewelyn.

"Who else could it have been? Now King Henry's dead, Edward's off the leash. He'll be wanting to sort us out once and for all ..."

"Maybe it's a Scottish or an Irish fleet. Maybe they got your messages and they've come to help us."

The King paused, looking at Llewelyn sadly.

"That's what your mother would have said. She always saw the positive. But she knew Wales couldn't beat the English without allies."

He stared out to sea, lost in thought. After a while he turned back to Llewelyn, a yearning passion in his eyes.

"You see, son, this is why I want you to study. You're clever, like your mother; you need to learn how to do smart things like making alliances, talking to people, working together. I'm like your big brother, Dafydd, God bless him. All we know is fighting, but the world's changing. Now it's all about diplomacy. A king needs to be wise, not strong. Which is why I have to keep you from harm. Dafydd, God bless him, well Dafydd might not be the right man for the job."

Llewelyn heard Gelert at the doorway behind them. The old dog stood stiffly on his hind legs, resting his huge front paws on the cold granite ledge and sniffing the night air. The King stroked the fur at the stub of the wolfhound's mangled ear.

Gelert turned and slobbered his face.

"Isn't that right my old friend?" said the King fondly. He sighed and turned back to Llewelyn, "The Good Lord knows he's done a better job of looking after you than I ever did."

Llewelyn rolled his eyes, angry that his father thought he needed Gelert to keep him safe. "I can look after myself!"

The King sighed. "Don't you see, Llew, it's Wales you need to look after. Now, do what your mother would have wanted you to do; go back to your chambers ..."

"I'd be of more use to Wales if you didn't keep me in my room!"

Frustration snapped the King's patience. He looked around his castle, angry eyes slitting as he thought about his reply.

"So, you want to be more useful?"

Llewelyn heard a slyness in the question. "Yes. I want to help you fight the English," he countered, "Like Dafydd."

The King rolled his eyes, exasperated. He thought for a moment, then pointed toward the courtyard.

"We can't fight the English without arrows, and we used up a couple of thousand of them tonight. But there are a lot of dead English fire arrows down there that we can use. First thing tomorrow, you can pick them all up."

"But there's millions of them!" Llewelyn yelped. Picking up arrows wasn't how he'd imagined himself helping the fight.

"Millions of ways to beat the English…"

"But they'll all be broken, and burned!" interrupted Llewelyn.

"That's why you have to pick them all up and, as I was going to say, take them to Owain in the armoury."

The King fixed him with an icy glare. "Unless, that is, you don't really want to help."

Llewelyn floundered.

His father's eyes narrowed.

"Or maybe you think it's beneath you?"

Llewelyn gulped. That was precisely what he'd been thinking.

"What about my schooling?" he blurted, remembering that Friar William was due another day of classics, politics and logic.

God, I must be desperate if I'm using Friar William as an excuse.

The King shrugged.

"Make your mind up, Llew. It's either the arrows or Friar William. What's it going to be?"

Llewelyn hung his head. "Pick up arrows," he mumbled.

"Good lad. I'll tell Owain to expect you. And when they're ready, you can take them up to the archers on the ramparts. You'll be more useful than Dafydd and his sword will ever be," he concluded, and went for the doorway. He hesitated, framed in the black hole of the stairway, and called back.

"If Friar William has a problem with my orders, send him to me. If the English fleet comes, arrows will be more important than algebra. Now, get back to bed; you'll need an early start."

With that, the King headed back down to his soldiers.

Llewelyn stood on at the battlements and sighed. No lessons and no Friar William would be good, *but picking up arrows?* He knew his father had out-manoeuvred him.

Gelert was still sniffing the sea air.

Gelert's dawn farts were cruel reminders of nature's darker workings.

Llewelyn sometimes wondered if his old dog was rotting from the inside out. Or perhaps dying rats had taken to crawling up his old friend's bum.

Whatever, his farts seemed to be triggered by the rising sun, or maybe it was the sound of the cockerel crowing.

Gelert was oblivious to the stench of his gift to the new morning, and barked happily from the foot of his bed, watching Llewelyn stagger into his clothes.

The prince flew down the stairwell, skidding out onto the courtyard where he stood and stretched, waiting for Gelert to join him.

Everywhere was a mess. The charred shed was a sullen tangle of blackened timbers. They still radiated a heavy heat that curled the air. He smelled the depressingly familiar odour of roasting meat – the smell of bodies baking in the embers. Then Llewelyn noticed sprays of black on the ground. The rest of the dead had been cleared, but their spilled blood remained, puddles of lost lives drying to a crust.

His father was right. Hundreds, no thousands, of arrows lay around, studding the earth and woodwork. He picked one up. Its shaft was scorched in places, but was still true and strong. Llewelyn brushed away the remains of burnt rags from the hefty broadhead. Its ugly sharp blades glistened in the dawn light. He smiled at the thought of this English arrow in an Englishman's guts.

But first he had to pick the rest of them up.

Gelert emerged from the doorway, sniffing the air. He paused at one of the drying pools of blood and started to lick at it.

"Oye! Gerroff!" yelled Llewelyn. Gelert looked up and growled.

"Don't you growl at me, you filthy old fleabag!" laughed Llewelyn, and too late he smelled a new stench.

He drooped; it was Friar William.

"Ah, there you are, boy!"

Before Llewelyn could turn, a hand gripped his shoulder and pinched, making him squeal with pain and forcing him to his knees.

Gelert snarled, but Friar William ignored him. The priest was the only person Llewelyn knew who wasn't intimidated by the huge dog.

"Tell me, boy," breathed Friar William into the back of his ear, spackling him with rancid spittle, "Why are you not in your chambers for today's lessons?"

"Sir, I'm helping with the arrows," he gagged. His tutor stank as if he'd sucked up one of Gelert's choicer farts, reworked it through his guts, and was sweating it out through his greasy skin.

The priest released his grip. Relieved, Llewelyn rubbed his bruised collarbone, but Friar William had let him go only to cuff him a slap to the side of his head that sent him scrabbling to the floor.

The priest stood above him, swaying slightly.

Pissed again. Llewelyn knew all about Friar William's secret stash of black bottles and was used to his mood swings.

Gelert barked half-heartedly at the priest.

"Silence," said Friar William. The huge wolfhound instantly shut up and backed away.

How does he do that? Gelert had always been if grudgingly obedient to Friar William from the moment he'd turned up at the castle just three years ago.

Maybe it was because Friar William was so very ugly. His face resembled a pig's bladder stuffed with rocks, his bloodshot, rheumy eyes buried in folds of drooping sallow skin. His mouth was a dripping hole filled with jagged stumps of rotting teeth.

Even Gelert must find that face intimidating.

Now Friar William sneered down at Llewelyn.

"I care not what you are doing, boy," he slurred, "I asked why you are not at your lessons."

Llewelyn stood up and dusted himself down.

"I am here because my father ordered me collect all these arrows and take them to Owain to be fixed," he said as formally as he could. "Father said if you have a problem with that to see him personally."

Friar William eyed him blearily. His hooded eyelids flickered; it was a curious facial twitch that usually meant the old goat was thinking evil thoughts.

"Well I do have a problem with that," he sneered. "Where is he?"

"I don't know sir," said Llewelyn truthfully. The King could be anywhere in the castle. Inside, Llewelyn quite liked the idea of the wheezing old priest having to haul himself up and down any one of a dozen spiral staircases looking for him.

"Well, isn't that just like you to not know anything important?"

"He'll be readying the castle for the attack by that fleet of ships we saw last night. I know that's important!" blurted Llewelyn.

Friar William went goggle eyed and his jaw dropped. His face flushed and he grabbed Llewelyn by his sore ear, yanking him closer.

"WHAT fleet of ships? Tell me boy!"

"Last! Nnng! Night!" grunted Llewelyn, determined not to cry out. "Lights! Hngch! Horizon! Hyrg! Hundreds! Oytch!"

Llewelyn knew that word of the lights would have spread quickly throughout the rest of the castle, *but you were getting drunk in your room.*

Friar William grew redder and angrier. He let go of his ear, readying to slap him again, but Gelert had had enough. He snarled and stepped forward, fur bristling. For once, Friar William took notice. He glared at Gelert, then at Llewelyn, and stalked away.

Thank God he's gone!

Then Llewelyn remembered the thousands of arrows he had to pick up. It would be hours of dirty, back-breaking work, so he allowed himself a moment to wallow in the thought of his father having to contend with Friar William on the warpath.

The day's not turning out so bad after all, he sniggered to himself as he set about his task.

❧

At noon, Llewelyn stumbled sweating into the armoury, a huge bundle of spent arrows under each arm.

The armoury was deep in the castle's cellar. It was where all the weapons were made and fixed, and he liked coming here. The clamour of hammers on metal was the nearest he got to the sound of battle.

Fifteen or so apprentices worked in the dank depths of the armoury. They were scrawny boys, few more than ten years old. All were pale beneath layers of filth. Theirs was an endless grind, sharpening swords and spears, repairing armour, and forever making new arrows. Always new arrows.

The apprentices stopped working and watched sullenly from their workbenches as Llewelyn stumbled past with his bundles. They seemed grimly glad that he too was doing menial work.

Gelert loped in through the doorway and was greeted with a collective gasp. All the boys were in thrall of the huge wolfhound.

Llewelyn dropped his arrows, the clattering sound breaking the silence.

Owain the armourer came stumping over. He was a leathery old bag of wrinkles, the King's right-hand man and his former commander of archers. He'd lost both legs at the knees to English crossbow bolts two months ago. That was the end of his life as an archer, but such was the old warrior's tenacity, he'd simply bound up his bleeding stumps with hoops of iron and shouted at his legs to just damn well get walking again. Shouting usually got Owain what he wanted.

"Out of the way, maggots," he yelled at the cowering boys, who scattered as he waded through them. His metal-shod stumps clanged, sending up sparks from the granite floor.

He took one of Llewelyn's arrows, and wiped soot from the shaft.

"These are bee-yooties, Your Highness!" he laughed, "Even more beautiful once we've fixed them up and they're decorating some English skulls."

He went still, and cocked an ear upwards.

"Hmm. Though the buggers are very quiet, don't you think?"

Llewelyn listened. *Yes, I haven't heard a peep from them all morning.*

"Maybe they're packing up to leave," he half joked.

"If only. More likely they saw those lights out to sea last night. If they were English ships like your father thinks, our chances of fighting them off are about as good as Gelert's chances of learning to play the flute while riding a two-legged donkey falling off a waterfall."

Gelert heard his name and woofed happily, his tail cuffing a couple of apprentices to the floor.

"Whatever the reason, they're too damned quiet out there," continued Owain, "and in my experience, a quiet Englishman is never a good thing – means he might be using his fat pig brain to think with, God forbid."

He picked up a fistful of arrows and held them up to the light.

"No point fretting though, if they're quiet, it gives us time to fix this lot. MAGGOTS!"

His boys looked up from their workbenches, eyes wide with fear.

"When your Prince comes back, I want these ready." He gestured to the pile of arrows. 'Well? What are you waiting for?"

The boys bustled forward, grabbing at the tangle of shafts.

"Come on then." Owain gestured for Llewelyn to leave.

"No, I think I'll stay here."

"Why on earth would you want to do that?"

"I thought maybe I could help," offered Llewelyn.

Fixing arrows might be fun. Better than going back to my lessons.

Owain stared at him, baffled.

"*Here* is not your place. Your place is in your room, with your books and learning, and ruling and what not."

"You sound like my father," retorted Llewelyn without thinking.

"I'm flattered," Owain said evenly, "but maybe it's time you started behaving like him."

Llewelyn felt slapped by the flat observation.

Owain turned and stumped up the stairs and out into the courtyard. The clanging sound of his iron stumps disappeared around the corner.

Gelert nuzzled his young master's ear, trying to comfort him.

"Oh leave me alone!" Llewelyn muttered, and looked around the armoury. The apprentices were chattering, busy at their work. As he watched them, they fell into an uneasy silence, each boy observing him, waiting for something to happen. Llewelyn realised he didn't know what that something was.

"Anything I can do?" he asked brightly.

There was no reply, but he heard a stifled snigger. He saw scorn in some faces. Owain was right; this wasn't his place.

But where is it? Not stuck in a tower, surely?

"Carry on," he muttered to no-one in particular, but none of the apprentices moved or said anything.

"Come on Gelert!" he said, and with as much dignity as he could muster, he made for the door.

He flushed when he heard the boys burst out laughing as he left.

🐾

As he emerged into the sunlight, Gelert growled and Llewelyn's cloudy thoughts snapped into reality. The atmosphere had changed.

The courtyard throbbed with urgent sounds and movement. Everywhere archers and men at arms were hurrying towards the stairwells to the ramparts, pulling on their armour and helmets and tripping each other up in their haste.

Llewelyn heard stray arrows clatter against the outside of the castle walls. The besieging English army had woken up.

But a scattered volley was nothing new. *Something else must be happening outside, something big.* He saw his father on the battlements, ignoring the last of the twittering English arrows.

"What's going on?" yelled Llewelyn, but the King was too preoccupied to notice him. He was deep in conversation with Owain and Prince Dafydd and his lieutenants. Everyone was pointing at something inland, something past the siege lines. Naturally, Dafydd was pointing with his sword.

At least they aren't looking out to sea.

Llewelyn sprinted up the nearest stairwell, joined the flow of men running to their positions and nipped between them, overtaking them. He quickly reached the upper walkway and leaned out through an empty embrasure.

What he saw sent a cold shiver up his spine, which then jumped into his stomach before tumbling down to his bowels.

Twenty miles beyond the sprawling English encampment, past the forest, lay a ridge. A rhythmic flickering of lights poured over the ridge, reflections from thousands of spearheads and hundreds of ranks of polished armour.

The English had sent a second army.

Then Llewelyn saw great rickety shapes emerging through the haze above the ridge. They were gaunt structures clothed in hides and festooned with swaying ropes. They straddled the horizon like the skeletons of headless giants rising from the grave. Behind them rolled squat wagons bearing angular timbers, crude cross-frames and stout throwing arms. They reminded him of a madman's version of a hangman's gibbet, only far more sinister because they were huge and they were moving towards him.

"Siege engines!" he yelped.

The King heard him, and looked over, alarmed.

"What the HELL are you doing there, boy?"

He stomped towards Llewelyn, archers squeezing up against the battlements to let him pass. A hopeful volley of English arrows clattered against the stonework in his wake.

"Are you alright? No scratches?"

Llewelyn lowered himself back onto the walkway.

"I'm fine!" I'm not a child!"

The King's concern turned into anger.

"You're stupid, that's what you are, or you wouldn't be hanging your arse out over the walls so anyone can take a pot shot at you!"

Just then, Gelert made it onto the battlement, panting and wheezing from the stairs. The King threw his hands up in annoyance.

"And why did you bring him up? Poor old thing. What were you thinking?"

Llewelyn's temper flared, feeding off his father's growing fury.

He pointed at the siege engines. "I was thinking you've got trouble!"

"Don't get clever with me, boy!" snapped the King. "Get back to your room. Things are going to get bad soon."

"Soon?" Llewelyn snapped back. "They're bloody miles away!"

That earned him a vicious clip around the ear, the one that Friar William had cuffed and mangled earlier. He winced and staggered.

The King pointed down at the army at the far end of the causeway.

"Yes, but they'll put heart into that lot down there. Now, go to where it's safe."

"Let me fight! I know I can do it!"

"Not till I say you can!" The King's anger was mounting.

"But I can help! I can fire a bow!"

"Ptcha! You didn't even bring your bow with you! You'll do as I say, and what I'm saying is get back to your room!"

Owain clunked towards them, sparks flying from his metal stumps.

"You can't hide the boy from siege engines ..."

The King turned to the old armourer, coiling up his rage, readying himself to really start shouting. But then he abruptly deflated, taking deep breaths.

"How long before they get here?" he sighed, rubbing his hand across his eyes and pinching the bridge of his nose.

"The siege engines? Two, maybe three hours to get here, and one more before they get going."

"Four hours to lose the kingdom," said the King miserably.

Just then, a man-at-arms appeared panting in the doorway of the tower. It was the same sentry from the seaward gatehouse.

"Sire! Your Highness! Sire!" he shouted, his voice warbling.

"You again? Stop blithering and get over here!" snapped the King.

The soldier lumbered up breathlessly. His heavy armour made him clumsy and his scabbard caught Gelert on the rump. The old dog gave a low growl, unnerving the man, who jumped two feet backwards.

"Well?" asked the King patiently.

"Oh, yes, sire! The message, sire!" stuttered the soldier, composing himself. "Your Highness, sire!" he shouted. "Sire, there's a strange boat coming, sire! From out there, sire. From the sea, sire!"

_____

The King, Llewelyn and Owain hurried their way back over the battlements, down through the eastern tower, across the main courtyard, and back up the spiral staircase of the western tower. Gelert quickly fell behind.

"We'd get there faster if we went around the battlements!" urged Llewelyn.

"You'll get another clip around the ear," said the King, "I'll not have some lucky English bowman picking you off."

Owain stomped and clattered behind them muttering something about mollycoddling and kids today.

Father and son finally reached the lofty heights of the keep. The sentries were whispering nervously, transfixed by the view out to sea. They shut up and jumped to attention as their king and prince arrived.

Llewelyn held himself up in the embrasure next to his father. They squinted into the softening afternoon sky.

Close in, less than a mile away, lonely and tiny in the greyness of the Irish Sea, a single ship was sailing directly for the castle's harbour.

It was strange looking, quite unlike anything Llewelyn had ever seen. Its two red sails were square and ribbed.

"They look like a fish's fins!"

"I don't know much about boats," said Owain, catching up and wheezing from the exertion of the climb, "but that's not English."

"And it's too small to be a threat," said the King gratefully.

Gelert, panting hard, joined them. He clambered his front legs up next to Llewelyn, his old joints creaking. When he saw the ship he bristled with suspicion, his tail hanging still.

"It's only a boat, old friend," soothed Llewelyn, but Gelert's growls grew more guttural and threatening.

"Holy Mother of God! Look!" rasped the King.

Beyond the small ship, the hazy horizon started to break up. Red sails rose from the shimmering water. Slowly, a line of huge, slab-sided hulls appeared beneath them. The distant vessels were fuzzed, making them hard to count, but the line stretched two miles wide from wing to wing. Llewelyn guessed the ships numbered in the hundreds.

Then, as one, every sail dropped, leaving a forest of naked masts. The cliff of hulls lay impassively hove-to, waiting.

Everyone on the battlements began babbling.

"Quiet!" yelled the King. "They're not English, so stop filling your pants!"

Llewelyn watched the closest ship tacking to enter the harbour. *They've come to parley,* he thought. *They've sent a small ship so as not to frighten us.*

Soon, the boat was close enough to make out the people on board.

A short, almost spherical man, stood on the foredeck surrounded by men at arms. He was dressed grandly in shining robes of intense black, bright white, radiant blue, shimmering green and glowing red. He was so fat, the colourful folds of material stretched tightly around his waist. From his high angle on the castle walls, Llewelyn couldn't see his feet. He looked like a gaudily painted inflated pig's bladder.

"Colourful little butterball!" said the King. "Must be silk he's wearing."

"What's silk?" asked Owain.

"It's very expensive cloth made from caterpillar crap," said his father confidently. "He must be important."

By now they could hear the oddest sounds coming from the boat.

"Are they strangling donkeys down there?"

"It's music," said Llewelyn. "They're showing us they're friendly."

"Shows me they can't play their instruments!" said the King as he turned to the sentries. "Find Prince Dafydd. I want an honour guard for our visitors. Fully armed, mind; it could still be an English ruse."

The strange ship was taking in its sails, slowing as it passed the end of the mole. The King made to go.

Just then, a slobbery voice boomed from the darkened stairwell.

"You! I would have words with you!"

It was Friar William. Owain spat in disgust as the loathsome priest wheezed onto the keep's platform.

Llewelyn tried to shrink from sight before realising, to his great relief, that it was his father who was the centre of Friar William's attention.

"What's this I hear of a fleet of ships last night!" seethed the priest, his baggily angular face blubbering. A haze of stench floated round him. The King coughed, squinting with incomprehension.

"I'm sorry?"

"This morning," he replied, glancing at Llewelyn. "Your offspring here told me. On the horizon. Last night. Why was I not informed?"

The King's bewilderment lasted a few more moments. "Why should I have to tell you ...?" he started before growing cross. He pointed out to the sea. "See for yourself, you filthy old goat."

The priest glared at him, but couldn't help glancing over the parapet.

His eyes popped when he saw the smaller boat, then grew wider still at the sight of the huge fleet on the horizon. He collected himself, and Llewelyn thought he detected a brief smile. The moment passed, and the priest's face recomposed itself into its more familiar sack of frowning creases.

"It is an Imperial Chinese fleet," he said matter of factly, almost as if he'd been expecting to see it. "And the junk below is a Grand Admiral's yacht, if I'm not mistaken, which I'm not."

For a few moments, the King didn't know what to say.

"I can see it's a fleet!" he blithered. "But ... but ... but! Chinese?"

"Chinese. As in 'of China'. Or you may know it as Cathay. It's a land far to the east. A magnificent empire ..."

"Yes, yes, yes! I've heard of China, but a Chinese fleet ...?"

"An Imperial Chinese fleet," repeated Friar William, almost, but not quite, patiently. "And that man down there will be a Grand Admiral, the representative of the Emperor of China."

"But? But? Why has an Imperial fleet from China come here?"

"I venture to suggest that you will find out why in due course if you are wise enough to avail yourself of my prodigious linguistic services."

The King bridled at Friar William's condescension, "What?

You're telling me you can speak Chinese?"

"I am fluent in all five extant forms of Chinese, as it states, unequivocally, on page thirty two of my Curriculum Vitae."

"I bet you are," said the King, who'd stopped reading Friar William's credentials at the words 'Curriculum Vitae'.

"An Imperial junk, you say?"

"You can 'bet' on that also. Your Highness."

"Well then, Friar William," said the King, ignoring his sarcasm, "It is my great honour and privilege to reward you with the official title of 'Interpreter Royal to the Court of the Sovereign Kingdom of Wales', salary yet to be agreed. Now, let's see if your Chinese is as good as you claim."

❧

Soon, an impromptu but sufficiently regal retinue gathered inside the seaward gatehouse. Soldiers lined the battlements looking down. Everyone quivered with curiosity, the siege briefly forgotten. The junk had pulled alongside the dock and its sailors were busily tying it up.

"Open the gate!" said the King.

Closer to, the boat was even stranger, very different to anything Llewelyn had seen. It looked sleek and fast despite being squarer and more high-sided than any ship he knew. It had seen some rough sailing; the flat-sided black hull was battered, and was thick with barnacles and weed below the waterline. The oddly slatted red sails were stained and faded, torn and patched.

"Raise the portcullis!"

Together, the King and Princes Dafydd and Llewelyn strode forward from the shadows of the gatehouse, Friar William shambling alongside.

Grey old Gelert ambled casually after them through the gate.

Instantly a clamour of excited voices erupted from the Chinese ship.

Llewelyn was puzzled at this childish reaction. It was led by the gloriously robed Grand Admiral, who pointed down at them, smiling, laughing and shouting with unconcealed glee. His entourage of officers was no better, squealing like five year olds, and by now, all of the crew were at the ship's railings adding to the commotion.

No, not all of them, Llewelyn saw.

One man, a senior-looking officer next to the round Admiral, stood stock-still. Here and there among the clamouring crew were other equally motionless men. Together, their unblinking gazes were fixed in one direction.

They're staring at something behind me, thought Llewelyn, and stole a glance over his shoulder, but there was only Gelert.

The old wolfhound had flopped down and was meticulously licking his hairy testicles, oblivious to all the excitement on the boat.

Meanwhile, Friar William was straining to pick out words from the babble. He seemed oddly relieved by what he heard.

"What are they saying?" asked Llewelyn.

"If you must know, it's 'the dog is here. The Great Dog is here!'"

"Gelert? They've come to see Gelert?"

Hearing his name, the old wolfhound hauled up his battered body and padded over to Llewelyn. A sudden hush descended over the Chinese visitors, followed immediately by a soft cry.

"OOOOOH!"

Gelert jumped up and placed his huge paws on Llewelyn's shoulders. Standing on his hind legs like this, the massive wolfhound towered over him, and was almost as tall as the King.

"AAAAH!" responded a Chinese chorus. "Da gou! Da gou!"

Gou, thought Llewelyn. *Is that their word for dog?*

Puzzled, he looked into Gelert's amber eyes.

What's so special about you, old mate?

Gelert flopped back down onto all fours, shedding a shower of scabby skin flakes.

"So they like dogs," said the King. "What happens now?"

Friar William took a while to reply. He seemed oddly detached, another faint smile playing on his blubbery lips.

"We, or should I say I, talk."

The Grand Admiral had composed himself, and behind him the silent senior officer had broken free of his Gelert-induced trance. A gangplank was run down to the quayside and the Chinese delegation descended onto Welsh soil. The King motioned Llewelyn to step forward with him.

"Come on, son, let's put some of your education into practice."

Standing behind his father, Llewelyn could gawp without embarrassment.

He was most struck by the shape of the Admiral's eyes, which appeared as slightly sharpened ovals. They were a deep, dark brown.

The other officer, the one who'd stood so still watching Gelert, had startlingly light-green eyes. He was thick set, broad faced and middle-aged, but his face had an ancient leatheriness to it. He looked as if he'd been sewn inside the pickled hide of a far older man.

Llewelyn shifted his attention to the soldiers in the rear ranks. Their armour was made of overlapping plates of shimmering blue steel, like fish scales. They carried stubby spears, gently curved swords and small oval shields, and their cone-shaped helmets sported horsehair plumes.

Most odd were their bows, which were quite unlike his simple longbow. They were shorter, with two delicately curved staves sprouting from an elaborately shaped grip. *Girls' bows.*

He looked at the men's faces. Everyone had pointed brown eyes. *But no*, here were a couple whose eyes sparkled with the same luminescent green as the enigmatic senior officer's. They also had the same aged-but-not-old look about them. *And there's three more of them.* Llewelyn quickly counted a dozen or more green-eyed men among the assembled soldiers.

Then his thoughts were dragged back to the greeting ceremony; Friar William had begun to talk to the Chinese.

The blabberings coming out of the priest's mouth were a jumble of sharp twanks and half coughs, not at all like lilting, rolling Welsh. The King turned to Llewelyn with a look of bemusement. Both had to hold back fits of sniggers. Prince Dafydd guffawed, earning a kick from his father.

The Admiral replied and Friar William translated.

"I have the honour to introduce you to their Excellencies and humble servants of the Emperor of China, Grand Admiral Kwan See, and Captain Chang, commander of this Imperial vessel."

The two Chinese officers bowed deeply.

So, the green-eyed one is the ship's captain, thought Llewelyn. *'Chang'.*

Sounds like a sword being sharpened.

The King bowed back, then pointed around the castle's battlements and the obvious signs of siege.

"Tell their Excellencies they are welcome, but as they can see, our castle isn't a safe haven for them in their travels."

"His Excellency, the Admiral indicates that he has appraised the formidable extent of our enemy's forces," translated Friar William. "Furthermore, he has observed the magnitude and irresistible threat of their approaching reinforcements and recognises that, indeed, the defence of your fortifications is at a very precarious juncture."

The King scowled, trying to retranslate the priest's torturous string of fancy words into something approaching ordinary Welsh.

"He elucidates, however," continued Friar William, "that he has not come as a tourist, but that he wishes to trade with you."

The King was surprised. "Can't he see we're a little busy here? It's really not the time or place for trading. Tell him, tell him …," he fumbled to articulate a suitably phrased response, "Dammit! You're the translator. Tell fatty to go set up shop somewhere else! But tell him nicely."

Friar William scowled, but translated.

The Admiral grew serious before hawking up his reply. Friar William smiled before translating, and when he turned back to the King he looked smug. "His Excellency, the Grand Admiral Kwan See, says he admires your formidable negotiating skills but proposes that in return for what he wants he is in a position to offer you sufficient arms and personnel that you may vanquish your enemies in perpetuity, and return your glorious Kingdom to a peaceful and prosperous harmony."

"What?" barked the King.

The priest rolled his eyes. "The Grand Admiral says he will destroy the English if you give him what he wants!"

"Aaah! I see!" The King scratched his head, hooked by the offer, but suspicious. "Inform His Grandity that this is indeed a very generous proposal, but ask him what he wants in return."

Friar William translated. "Why, it is nothing!" said the priest dismissively.

He pointed at Gelert.

The old wolfhound lay at Llewelyn's feet, gnawing at a particularly tasty tick he'd found stuck between his toes.

"Give the dog to the Emperor and in return he will give you your kingdom."

"He wants the dog?" laughed the King, "Why would the Emperor of China want ... that ...?"

Gelert was now sniffing at his bumhole.

Meanwhile, blood pounded in Llewelyn's ears. His vision closed down, tunnelled by deep red circles. He felt dizzy, and fell to his knees, pole-axed by the thought of losing his old friend. He grabbed Gelert round the neck for support. Sensing his misery, the old hound stood up, dragging Llewelyn onto his feet.

The Admiral gave a high-pitched laugh and blabbered enthusiastically.

"Believe it or not," Friar William rolled his eyes, "His Excellency says the 'Great Dog' is all he had hoped for; that he truly is the finest dog in the world, a wonder in his own right, a marvel to behold ..."

Gelert farted.

The Grand Admiral and his retinue roared with laughter.

Friar William, now puce with embarrassment, continued.

"He adds that, such is the Emperor's appreciation of the stories of Gelert's courage and loyalty and gracious nobility, that he wishes him by his side so that both he and his subjects may be enriched and illuminated by this magnificent animal's presence."

The King was still baffled. "How in God's name does the Emperor of China know about Gelert?"

The priest rolled his eyes again. "You of all people should be familiar with The Ballad of Gelert. It is sung even in the civilised world, far beyond this damp backwater of yours. So of course the world's most powerful man has heard of 'the world's greatest dog'."

The King was scornful. "The ballad says I killed Gelert! The ballad is rubbish. Nonsense made up by idiots who can't get a proper job!"

The castle had gone quiet. Everyone was looking at their shoes. They knew the King didn't like to be reminded of his 'one tiny lapse of judgement'.

Friar William had no such qualms. "Well, let's just all be grateful that the Emperor also heard that Gelert survived your inept attempt at wolfhound slaying. The dog saved your boy, and now he's saved your kingdom ..."

The King interrupted him, angry. "Not yet he hasn't, you cankerous, conniving scumbag! You think I'd give my boy's dog away? Tell blubberguts we can handle the English ourselves, then tell him to sling his hook!"

❧

Unable to believe what he'd just heard, Llewelyn's heart leapt.

He jumped up to hug his father but Friar William, a picture of angry indignation, pushed him aside.

"You'd pass on your one chance to save your kingdom because you don't want to hurt this brat's feelings?" he hissed at the King. "Edward will have your bowels strewn across London. Your little boy? If he's lucky, he'll live the rest of his short life as a kitchen slave. Your precious Wales will be a distant memory. All for what?" he added viciously. "A dead dog. Half-digested bones on a dung heap! That's what your guilty conscience and your maudlin ideals of loyalty will have got you!"

It was an unexpectedly long tirade; Friar William never got this passionate.

"He's got a point," said Owain reluctantly.

Llewelyn wrapped his arms around Gelert's thick shaggy neck. Owain was right; a dog should never be more important than a kingdom. He stood and addressed the King formally and calmly, but with tears running down his cheeks.

"Father, I'd rather Wales lived on, and I think so would Gelert. Better he's with the Emperor of China than dead on a dung heap."

He'd hoped his words of noble self-sacrifice would lift his spirits, but they only made him feel like puking.

"Aye, the boy is right," chimed Owain, "especially if the old dog ends up next to the fat priest's stinking corpse."

Friar William glowered at Owain, but drove his point home.

"See, both your brat and your trained monkey see the sense in this offer."

Llewelyn saw the anger in his father's eyes but still the King shook his head.

"This is stupid," he said crossly, pointing at the junk. "A few Chinamen can't save Wales. Not in a month of Sundays."

The junk did look very small, hardly big enough to hold fifty men.

Friar William glowered at the King, florid with rage. "Idiot!"

"Idiot? Idiot? ME?" roared the King, whirling on him.

"The Imperial fleet!" screeched Friar William jabbing his finger at the far horizon. "There's more men cleaning the privies on one of those ships than you have in this pile of stones you call a castle!"

The King recoiled as if he'd been slapped. His chest heaved and his fists clenched and unclenched furiously. He looked at Llewelyn, and squeezed his eyes shut, forcing himself to be calm. Then he spread his hands in a placatory sort of way and turned, smiling, to the Grand Admiral, who smiled back.

Llewelyn's heart sank again, knowing what was coming.

"Very well, let's hear them out."

The priest huddled with the Admiral, who took some time to give an answer. He gesticulated wildly, his pudgy hands miming a terrific battle. Friar William waited until the end before translating. Now he was getting his way, he had become surly and abrupt again.

"It's a good offer. Accept it and we'll be done."

"Details please, priest," hissed the King, his patience still strained.

"Very well," snorted Friar William before carrying on.

"The Admiral solemnly swears to engage with the besieging English forces and annihilate them to the last man. Evidence of this will be supplied in the form of the heads of the slain enemy, which will be displayed in piles of one hundred for ease of calculation ..."

The King's eyes grew wide.

"That would be handy," muttered Owain.

"Further to this," continued Friar William, "on completion of the battle, he promises to sort and deliver all salvageable enemy armour and weaponry, including siege machinery, all horses and other draught animals, plus any treasures, sundry articles and chattels found in the enemy's baggage train."

The King turned to Owain, a smile cracking his hard-set mouth.

"They must really want that dog!" he laughed.

Llewelyn drooped.

"Finally," Friar William took a huge breath and pointed directly at Gelert, "on completion of said services, in return, you, his Highness the King of Wales, agree and swear on your oath to deliver this dog, Gelert the Wolfhound, safely to this Ambassador of The Exalted Mighty Emperor Of China, Shining Centre Of The Universe, Conqueror Of The Mongol Hordes, Destroyer Of … well, the rest isn't important … who will take Gelert the Wolfhound unto the comfort of his bosom, and lavish said animal with all the luxuries and privileges attendant to being the Emperor's boon companion."

At that moment, a great wave of cheering rolled and echoed through the castle. It came from the English army outside.

The King looked up to the battlements. "What's going on?"

"The first of the English reinforcements have arrived, sire," a sentry called back. "Five hundred knights just came charging into their camp, so they have, sire. The buggers are all going mad so they are, sire!"

"That was quick," muttered the King. He caught Llewelyn's eye and shrugged.

Llewelyn felt his throat closing up and tears threatening. He swallowed and nodded once to his father, who turned to Friar William.

"Tell the Admiral we agree."

❧

The oaths were soon taken and the contract completed. The Chinese cheered and their musicians blared out celebratory noises.

Llewelyn watched word of his father's decision spread among the onlooking Welshmen. It was sadly consoling to see that the news was being greeted with excitement and relief.

Gelert sat oblivious to the import of everything that was happening.

The Admiral beamed happily and waddled towards him, hands outspread. Llewelyn felt himself choking up again. *Come to examine the goods.*

But Gelert wasn't having any of it. He jumped up, growling his most intimidating 'keep away from me' growl. The Admiral flinched, his fat frame shaking. He laughed a nervous, embarrassed laugh. Gelert continued to growl defiantly as he backed off.

That's right mate, thought Llewelyn spitefully. *Tell him you're not his yet.*

Just then, three Chinese soldiers ran to the centre of the open ground of the harbour carrying a two-foot pointed red tube attached to a six-foot-long pole. They planted it firmly into the dirt, and one of them tested the wind's direction. Satisfied, he applied a match to the bottom of the tube, which suddenly exploded, and with a deafening roar shot vertically into the late afternoon sky. It carried on climbing, a column of smoke and flames pushing it higher and higher. Among the Welsh, the effect was stunning.

"OOOOOOOOOOOOH!"

Necks craned as the projectile rose until it was almost beyond sight. Abruptly, it exploded into two impossibly bright balls of spinning light – one blue, one red. As they tore apart, clouds of coloured smoke blossomed around them.

"AAAAAAAAAH!"

A second later, they heard a cracking boom.

"OOOOOOOOOOOOH!"

"Now that's what I call a fire arrow!" said Owain.

Amid the din, Llewelyn noticed a furtive movement at the back of the Chinese contingent. He was surprised to see Friar William whispering to the green-eyed Captain Chang, who nodded in reply.

Odd; it's as if they know each other.

But it was the briefest exchange, and Friar William quickly shuffled back into the castle, looking very pleased with himself.

Then the sentry called down again, distracting Llewelyn.

"Sire! On the horizon! The Chinese fleet, sire! It's setting sail, so it is! Looks like, yes, it's moving towards us, sire! The whole bloody lot of 'em, so they are, sire!"

A wild cheer rang around the Welsh soldiers lining the battlements.

"That fire arrow was a signal," said the King.

For the Chinese delegation, the fiery display had been the finale to the exchange. They quickly re-boarded their junk, their soldiers marching smartly after them and raising the gangplank.

The Welsh courtiers, seeing their part of the job was done, were returning to the safety of the castle, and Prince Dafydd, swung his sword to order the men back to their posts.

The bustling moments passed into silence.

The King stood, hands on his hips, gazing at the Chinese ships.

"They're enormous! But slow. How long till they get here?"

"Search me!" cackled Owain, "I'm an archer, not a sailor."

Llewelyn had already figured it out. Beating into the wind, the huge fleet would have to make several ponderous tacks, which would take some time. It was a simple problem of geometry with a bit of algebra thrown in.

"A couple of hours at least, more like three," he said confidently.

The King raised an eyebrow. "How did you work that out ...?"

Llewelyn just shrugged. *Isn't it obvious?*

"Three hours!" gulped Owain. He pointed landward, "The English won't wait three hours ..."

"Exactly," frowned the King, "It's not over yet," he sighed, and turned for the castle.

Llewelyn hurried after him, Gelert trotting on behind.

"And you two can get back to your quarters!" his father ordered, without looking back.

Llewelyn stopped in his tracks.

"When will you ever stop worrying about me?" he shouted.

The King barely broke his stride.

"It's Gelert I'm worried about. Don't let anything happen to him."

Hours passed. The sun began to fall westward into the evening sky.

The Chinese fleet made slow progress.

High in his room, Llewelyn looked on in frustration as the castle prepared itself for a new assault from the land. He watched his father cross the courtyard below, his armour clanking, Prince Dafydd tagging along, waving his sword.

Well, I'm not staying up here, whether he likes it or not.

He reached for his chainmail shirt and jammed on his helmet. Gelert woofed uneasily, not used to seeing Llewelyn dressed like this. He whined as Llewelyn strapped on his sword and gathered up his longbow and quiver of arrows.

"Don't worry, old mate," said Llewelyn, stroking his head. "No matter what happens, it's a life of luxury for you – either with a Chinese Emperor or an English King. But promise me you'll do something for me, whoever you end up with?"

The big dog looked up at him quizzically, his one ear cocked.

"Promise me you'll crap in his slippers?"

Gelert woofed happily.

"Good boy. Come on, let's go see what's happening."

🐾

They sneaked down the tower, along the corridors and through the echoing banquet hall. The outside sounds of battle preparations faded as the gloom of the inner fort enveloped them.

Llewelyn looked round the great room, its high ceiling lost in the dark. Memories of dim smoky evenings washed over him, of the drunken feasts where he'd listened to the King and his warriors telling their tales of terrible battles, and the bards singing their songs of Wales's glorious past, and Prince Dafydd waving his sword.

They made their way up through the back stairs of the furthest tower of the western walls. His father wouldn't see him up there.

A pair of oyster catchers flew by as they stepped onto the windy ramparts. Silhouetted against the orange and violet sky, their soft panting whistles sounded mournful.

The battlements were deserted except for two guards who moved to one side as Llewelyn leaned into an embrasure to peer out to sea.

He shivered when he saw the Chinese fleet.

It seemed to fill the sea, a mass of hulls, towering masts and huge red sails glowing against the sunset. The ships turned and tacked silently towards the castle.

He counted the masts on one of the ships.

Nine? That's impossible! No ship built had more than two masts.

These were unworldly vessels that made even his father's castle look small. Who could resist them? Llewelyn felt a balloon of joy swell in his chest. After six months of siege, it felt odd to be confident again. Then he looked back across the castle to the landward side and his buoyant thoughts dissolved.

The rest of the English reinforcements had arrived.

Their army now spread far beyond the boundaries of their old camp and onto the hills surrounding the bay. It heaved darkly across the land, a swollen prickly press of armour, swords and spears.

The ugly siege engines and towers were arrayed at the end of the causeway, just beyond bow range. Two trebuchets and four mangonels loomed above the mass of soldiers. Llewelyn tried not to think of the destruction they would cause once the deadly catapults began hurling their projectiles at the old castle.

He looked back to sea. The Chinese were at least half an hour away.

The bombardment will begin before the Chinese fleet get here!

There was no way it could fit into the small harbour. The mighty ships would have to enter in twos at best. Then it would take hours to disembark the troops. The English could take the castle first. Llewelyn's feeling of elation drained, and his soul refilled with the thick mud of despair.

He saw his father stride onto the ramparts on the far side of the castle, his red cloak floating gloriously behind him.

The enemy army stirred as if they'd been expecting him. A single trumpet blared, and the sound picked up and repeated across the massed regiments. Then a drumbeat sounded and the Englishmen began to cheer. A column of armoured cavalry was making its way down from the upper reaches of the camp; dozens of noblemen in burnished armour astride their huge prancing warhorses, surrounded by phalanxes of bannermen carrying colourful flags.

Here come the nobs.

The King, knew the right time to draw his sword, and the setting sun flashed on its four foot blade as he held it, two handed against the sky. A defiant cry rang around the castle, strong Welsh voices answering the English rabble. Tears blurred Llewelyn's vision, welling up and pouring uncontrollably down his face. Pride in his countrymen's bravery mingled with a sense of hopelessness.

Too late! he thought.

Then Gelert growled and he heard footsteps behind him.

"It'll soon be over, boy," croaked a familiar voice, "Just be patient."

Friar William shuffled onto the platform. He seemed serene and even smiled at him. Llewelyn wiped his eyes, angry at the intrusion.

"If your friends don't get a move on, nobody's going to get Gelert," he said, expecting a slap around the face, and not caring.

Friar William merely shrugged, still smiling. He reached to the wolfhound as if to pat him. Gelert growled and, wisely, the priest withdrew his hand, shrugging.

"You're angry, and you're scared," he said to Llewelyn, "But fear not, boy; the King will win the day and my life's work will endure."

Llewelyn was side-swiped by the priest's kindly words.

I've never thought of myself as Friar William's life's work!

Friar William beckoned him to the seaward battlements.

"Come, watch. It will be an education."

The approaching wall of huge black Chinese ships seemed to have tripled in size and number.

Llewelyn tried to count them, but lost his place at ninety with still more than two thirds to go; the fleet was so immense it spread beyond his restricted view.

The two biggest ships headed directly for the harbour, while the rest of the armada divided, the two wings cruising by either side of the harbour entrance.

Llewelyn knew he had to tell his father. He ran to the battlements overlooking the castle, searching for him among the milling Welsh soldiers. There he was, on the ramparts of the gatehouse facing the causeway.

"Father!"

The King looked up, alert to the sound of his son's voice.

"The Chinese ships are here!" cried Llewelyn pointing westward.

"What?" shouted the King, distracted by the more immediate threat of the gathering English attack. Llewelyn filled his lungs and, turning purple with the effort, screamed once more.

"Chi! Nese! Ships! They're here!"

The King gawped for a moment and quickly gathered himself. "Meet me at the sea gate!"

Llewelyn reached the foot of the stairway just as his father arrived winded and sweating with exertion.

"Open the Judas door!"

Guards shifted the locking beam and opened the door within a door. Blood-red light silhouetted the bars of the portcullis beyond. The King and Llewelyn stood with their foreheads pressed against its cold bars. Gelert arrived, wedging himself between them.

"My God, I really hope they're on our side!" gasped the King.

The two biggest junks sailed directly towards the harbour entrance, their tall hulls glistening in the sun. Each had nine ranks of tightly ribbed slatted sails that flapped and shivered like great leathery wings as the ships came about.

They lined up and passed through the gap in the mole.

Once inside the calmer waters of the port, they moved apart, dropped their sails, and pirouetted serenely so that their prows faced either side of the Grand Admiral's junk. Then they slowly side-slipped towards the harbour side, and Llewelyn felt the deep thud of the impact as they stopped dead, each hull perfectly parallel with the dock. Their railings bristled with hundreds of armoured men and sailors and Llewelyn could hear the distinctive sound of whinnying and snorting drifting across the dockside. *Horses. Lots of horses.*

Dozens of sailors leapt down to the ground and expertly tied up, hauling their ships flush to the harbour. Their square sides presented as massive timber walls, as solid as any building, and towered above the Admiral's vessel, which now looked insignificant and vulnerable.

Then the green-eyed captain appeared at the bows of the smaller junk. He shouted orders at the huge ships on either side. A shiver ran through the ranks massing on deck; everyone seemed impatient to disembark. Grand Admiral Kwan See joined the captain at the railings.

Noticing the King watching through the portcullis, he waved happily, then pointed at the portcullis with one hand, making lifting gestures with the other.

Friar William appeared from the gloom, sweating and panting from his descent from the roof of the keep.

"Well, what are you waiting for?" he hissed.

"What?" replied the King, still overwhelmed by the behemoth junks.

"They can't walk through wood and iron bars. Raise the portcullis!"

The King jumped, startled from his trance-like state.

"Er ... Yes. Right. Open the gates. Raise the portcullis!"

Llewelyn found himself hopping from one foot to another, his heart hammering with curiosity. As the rusty portcullis rose, he squirmed underneath and sprinted to touch the sides of the nearest giant ship.

"Get back, boy!"

But he ignored his father's anxious shouts, drawn by the stupefying size of the nearest junk. He stopped, forced to turn his whole body to take in the length of the vessel. His neck hurt from looking up at the tallest masts, which appeared higher than the castle walls. The ropes binding it to the quay were as thick as his legs.

Gelert loped after Llewelyn. The sailors and soldiers lining the railings pointed at him and chattered excitedly. Captain Chang yelled at them and they were instantly quiet.

Llewelyn reached out and ran his hands across the colossal hull. The black planks were cold and smooth; the grain of the timber was finer than any wood he knew, yet harder, almost as hard as iron. He felt dull vibrations from within, the movements of many men and horses.

Gelert sniffed and snorted and barked, which set off a wave of neighing and hoof clattering from inside.

A sharp cry from above made Llewelyn look up. Captain Chang motioned angrily to him to step away from the huge boat.

"Come on, boy," he said to Gelert, "he looks serious."

They shuffled back a couple of feet, but the captain kept shooing them until he was satisfied they were far enough away. Then he shouted again.

A moment later, three sections of the side of the ship seemed to fall off, collapsing outwards onto the quayside with a cackle of chains and a triple thumping crash. Seconds later, the side of the other ship peeled apart in similar fashion.

The King gasped. Llewelyn stepped backwards, awestruck, unable to tear his eyes from the spectacle.

The sides of both ships had opened into six gangplanks, each fifty feet wide. Inside were ranks of footmen, spearmen, archers and mounted cavalrymen, all standing smartly to attention. Their numbers were lost in the cavernous gloom of the ships' exposed holds.

"There must be a thousand men in there!" whispered the King.

"Thank Dog!" hissed Friar William.

At a command from within, the Chinese soldiers presented arms in an immaculate display of discipline. The hissing sound of rattling armour echoed from the castle walls.

Meanwhile, smaller, longer gangplanks were being run down

from the upper decks, enabling more men to disembark.

"By the Bones of Saint David!" muttered the King, "I really, really do hope they're on our side."

They walked towards the ships. The Grand Admiral called out.

"What's he saying, priest?"

"He's requesting your permission to land his troops," Friar William replied, "and begs that you retire to the highest parts of the castle."

"Wait a minute! Doesn't he want us to help in the attack?"

Friar William translated. "The Grand Admiral says he is grateful for your kind offer of assistance, but politely suggests that should your men go into battle with his soldiers they might be confused with the enemy in the chaos of the fighting."

"Makes sense," pondered the King. "We probably all look the same to them – I know they do to me!" he laughed.

Friar William shot him a contemptuous glance, his left eye twitching. "He also requests that you wait for his signal before opening the main gate, prior to the assault."

"Very well. Ask him what the signal will be."

Friar William conferred with the Grand Admiral.

"He says, 'When a single arrow blossoms red against the setting sun, then, and only then should the main gate be opened.'"

"Very poetic," grumbled the King, not knowing what to do next.

"Meanwhile, I am to remain with the Admiral," said Friar William superciliously. "He values my input."

"He doesn't value his sense of smell," muttered Llewelyn.

If Friar William had heard the comment, he ignored it. "Well? Go on …," he said, shooing his hand in the direction of the nearest tower. "Off you go!"

The King narrowed his eyes, considering a riposte, but instead turned to Llewelyn. "We'd better do as we're told then."

"There's good boys," said Friar William, oozing condescension.

Llewelyn expected his father to explode, but he just glared at the priest.

"Basdithmuthfinarrsnbludifummpriest," he muttered and turned to the Grand Admiral and bowed. Kwan See bowed back.

"Come on, Llew, come on Gelert, let's go find some fresh air."
Together they trudged for the nearest stairwell.

From the top of the keep, a glance lifted their spirits.

The panoramic view showed the rest of the Chinese ships grounded sideways onto the shallow beaches facing either side of the castle.

The falling tide had left them brooding and silent in the dusk, like gigantic beetles carved from a mountain of coal. Their masts swayed as the huge junks shifted in the retreating surf, casting shadows up the wet sand, black elongated fingers clawing at the land.

The arrival of the fleet had thrown the English army into turmoil.

The core of their forces was boiling with hesitation and confusion. Sergeants-in-arms angrily stalked their lines of men, kicking and shoving them to pay attention, but the thousands of soldiers couldn't help scanning the beaches on either side of the castle. A hubbub of worried whispers slipped and seethed above the throng.

"They're already in a lather," said the King rubbing his hands together. "Wait till they find out what's inside those ships!"

By now, divisions of English soldiers were being hurriedly marched from their positions opposite the castle towards the threat on the beaches. The manoeuvring was a shambles. Agitated messengers on horseback hurtled between the ranks, only adding to the chaos.

Suddenly, fanfares blared from the junks at the quayside. Deep booming drums started up, sounding a slow marching beat. Llewelyn and the King ran back to the western parapet to see what was happening.

The first ranks of Chinese soldiers were filing down the gangplanks from the two huge ships. They marched with rigid precision to the beat of the drums, hundreds upon hundreds of men forming up in two perfectly squared-off, knife straight columns.

Another fanfare sounded and the drum tempo suddenly increased. Then Chinese cavalry trotted smartly out of the junks, taking position ahead of the foot soldiers. Their mounts snorted great clouds of steam in the chilling air, hooves kicking the ground with excitement.

Meanwhile, the Welsh garrison had assembled on the ramparts. Some cheered the Chinese force, most just stood slack-jawed at the spectacle.

Owain arrived with a couple of other officers, stumping over to join them on the battlements. He whistled when he saw the army below.

"They look smart enough. Hello, what's this now?"

The drums grew faster still, and twenty wheeled mechanical crossbows clattered down the gangplanks, each pushed by five-man teams. They were five yards long with bows twelve feet across and mounted with tall racks of five-foot-long crossbow bolts. Each bolt was as thick as a man's arm and tipped with cruelly barbed spikes. The crossbowmen ran their bulky weapons through the gap between the foot soldiers and horsemen and took their place in front of the cavalry.

"Very impressive!"

Another fanfare, and the drum tempo became faster still. The huge maws of the two ships spat out new oddities.

"What on God's earth are *they?*" squeaked Owain, gawping at the thirty pairs of men trundling forward barrow-like contraptions. Each box held dozens of the fire arrows they'd seen earlier. The soldiers took their place ahead of the mechanical crossbows.

A final fanfare squawked, and the drums resumed their slow monotonous beat. This heralded the appearance of the Grand Admiral, who strode pompously down the gangplank of the small junk. A soldier led a gleaming chestnut horse to him and helped him into the saddle, where he sat, his short legs splayed almost horizontal by the girth of his huge horse. He looked ridiculous as he dug his heels in, and his fat wobbled as the horse walked between the columns of soldiers. A dozen or so mounted officers and twenty heralds carrying huge flags on tall poles followed.

Llewelyn watched Friar William trot up to the Admiral's side. From this high up he looked like a bundle of dirty rags being blown in the wind. The Admiral's horse shied away from the priest, and a few of the Chinese retinue recoiled from his stench.

He swaggered alongside the Admiral as his party reached the head of the compact army.

"Stinking fat pig," muttered Owain.

Llewelyn laughed, but shut up when he saw Captain Chang stroll casually down the gangplank at the rear of the Imperial command. He wore no armour and hung back from the others. *Why's he leaving the ship?*

By now, the head of the Chinese column had reached the barbican on the opposite side of the courtyard. It halted, standing straight along the central axis of the castle. All that lay between them and the English army were the portcullis, the main gates and the drawbridge.

The fanfares ceased and the great drums stopped booming.

Gelert woofed.

Several dozen Chinese soldiers looked up at him, pointing and chattering. Llewelyn saw that the green-eyed captain was also gazing at Gelert.

Creepy, he thought.

He turned his attention to the fleet of giant beached junks.

The wind had dropped to a gentle breeze. The sun clipped the western horizon, bathing the scene in a thick orange light. Silence fell. Now the Chinese Admiral was consulting with Friar William. The priest stepped forward and, cupping his hands, shouted up to the King.

"The Admiral asks that you lift the portcullis. Then be ready to open the main gates and drop the drawbridge when the signal comes. You do remember the signal don't you? The single red blossom!"

The King huffed at the priest's harping tone, but waved assent.

The slow clanking of the portcullis punctuated the atmosphere with its jarring rhythm. Every Welshman held his breath; this was the first time it had been lifted in six long, harrowing months.

In the courtyard, a couple of Chinese soldiers planted a new fire arrow and, at the Admiral's command, set it off. It flew into the air and exploded with a bright bang, spreading petals of red smoke.

"Open the gates and drop the drawbridge!" roared the King.

The gates swung inward revealing the thick slab of drawbridge. Welsh men at arms leaned into the spokes of the capstans that wound the drawbridge chains, and a sergeant struck his sledgehammer at the thick iron pegs locking them in place.

"Heave!"

The soldiers pushed and grunted, and nothing happened.

"Oh bugger!" said Owain.

The chains have rusted into place!

After six months shut up fast, the drawbridge wouldn't budge.

Suddenly, something huge crashed into the outside of the drawbridge, nearly knocking it off its hinges. A thick rim of dust billowed around the frame of the hefty door, and then the drawbridge chains loosened. The men at the capstan sprang back as the great wheels unwound in a spray of whirring, rusty flakes. The drawbridge fell, smashing down on the massive boulder that had unloosened it.

The shattered boulder was a missile from one of the siege machines.

The English had opened the door to death, and now the Chinese brought it out to them.

The front rank of four Chinese arrow barrows shuddered once, then spewed forth their contents.

A hundred fire arrows smashed into the English forces standing opposite, exploding against the massed ranks, punching men down and spraying flames and sparks throughout the shocked soldiers.

A few were killed, many were burned, but most just turned and ran.

Already, the leading arrow barrows had pushed out from the castle and now stood on either side of the gatehouse reloading. The next in line rushed forward, stopped, and fired another death-dealing volley, followed quickly by the third rank.

It was a withering display of disciplined efficiency that sent a torrent of exploding arrows into the unsuspecting enemy. A rolling bank of smoke drifted slowly through the English army, creating further disorder.

Then the twenty mechanical crossbows moved forward. The bowmen cranked their handles, shooting their heavy bolts as they advanced. Thonk! Thonk! Thonk! A fresh barrage of death ripped through the dissolving ranks.

"Dear God!" croaked the King, lost in shocked appreciation, his eyes glittering and his hands gripping the stonework of the parapet.

Owain was stumping a sparky gig, the other officers were laughing, punching the air, and Gelert woofed, glad everyone was happy.

The onslaught continued below.

The end of the causeway was a maelstrom of suffering. Shockwaves of confusion rippled through the already bewildered soldiers. Llewelyn knew they were on the point of breaking.

The crossbows moved aside. Now it was the Chinese cavalry's turn. The horses leapt from standing to full gallop and tore onto the causeway. Even as they accelerated, the horsemen were loosing their bows, reloading, pulling back and letting go again with such speed that Llewelyn could scarcely see any pause in their actions.

"Now that's what I call good shooting!" yelled Owain gleefully.

The riders ploughed great gaps through the fleeing English ranks, bowling men down, their horses' hooves crushing skulls and snapping limbs. More cavalry careered up the causeway, flowing through the gaps, pushing deeper and deeper into the shattered columns.

Llewelyn watched with something approaching horror as his enemy fell like a field of barley to a huge, many-bladed scythe. The torrent of Chinese horsemen swept around the now abandoned siege engines.

Then he heard a distant roaring of men and the clash of metal on metal. Gelert lolloped to the northern wall, barking madly.

The beaches! Llewelyn ran to join him.

🐾

"You might want to see this, father!" he croaked.

The rest of the junks had lowered their sides, disgorging thousands of soldiers and hundreds of horsemen who swarmed across the hard-packed sands, hooking around towards the castle.

If the slaughter on the causeway was bad, on the open beaches it was terrible. The sand and dunes became slick with blood and the sea turned pink as the cavalry slashed through the battalions sent to intercept them.

Then the Chinese foot soldiers arrived to finish them off.

Englishmen fell by the hundreds, swiftly whittled into smaller and smaller knots of shocked survivors.

The Chinese rolled up the English as the sun dipped below the horizon, herding the retreating masses into the killing ground in front of the castle. The doomed army drew in on itself, its perimeter shrinking even as the centre of the army was eviscerated from within.

At this rate, the fighting would be over in less than an hour.

"By God, son!" yelled the King, "It's a miracle!"

He paced from one battlement to the next in a state of steely astonishment, roaring encouragement at his new allies. He thrashed his broadsword in the air, as if trying to join in the fight from afar. Gelert ran from side-to-side, not knowing what to bark at next. Prince Dafydd waved his sword and Owain and the other officers were already hoarse with cheering.

Llewelyn looked down into the courtyard. The tail end of the Chinese ranks was double marching through the gatehouse, watched happily by the Grand Admiral and his retinue.

Friar William was pacing to and fro. He seemed impatient, and kept looking over at the green-eyed captain standing in the shadows a few yards away.

Llewelyn saw the Grand Admiral beckon the priest to him. They talked earnestly for a few minutes, glancing up at the battlements. Gelert was still barking excitedly at all the noise and fuss outside. The Admiral pointed up at him, and Friar William nodded.

Llewelyn gulped and stepped back from the battlements. In his heart, he knew that the discussion below was to do with his father's deal with the Chinese.

"Shut up, Gelert!" he whispered hoarsely.

The King saw him and stopped his celebrating.

"What is it, son?"

Llewelyn just peered back over the stonework. Friar William bowed deeply to the Admiral and headed for the entrance of the keep.

This isn't looking very good.

Llewelyn saw the green-eyed captain following the priest.

This is now looking very bad.

He called Gelert over, his heart thumping in his chest, the saliva suddenly cold in his mouth.

The King had seen everything. His shoulders slumped guiltily and he avoided Llewelyn's gaze. But then the thrill of victory and all it meant swept him back into his exalted mood.

"Don't be glum, Llew," he beamed, putting on his encouraging face. "Gelert has saved Wales! The bards will be writing new songs about him! Proper songs that tell the truth!"

Llewelyn knew tears would change nothing but still they came.

The clamour of the battle receded as the fighting pushed further from the castle, which suddenly felt very empty.

The King glanced back over the parapets into the courtyard. The Admiral and his retinue were riding through the gateway.

"Looks like they're going to take a closer look at the fight," he said cheerily. The joy of the victory had erased his discomfiture with Llewelyn. "Do you know, I've half a mind to join them!"

"The Admiral said to stay up here," sniffed Llewelyn, glad for the chance to have something to take his mind off Gelert.

"Ptcha! That was before."

Llewelyn forced himself to stop blubbing.

"Can we come?"

"Absolutely not! What's safe for me is not safe for you."

Blood roared in Llewelyn's ears, his sadness turning to hurt. "But …"

"No buts, son. You. Stay. Here."

Just then Friar William walked up onto the platform. Llewelyn, still snivelling, hardly noticed the Captain wasn't with him.

"Ah! Priest!" said the King. "Good! I want to join in the mopping up, maybe knock off a dozen or so English myself." He laughed. "That's if there are any of 'em left by the time we get there!" Friar William seemed relieved.

"What a pleasant coincidence," he smiled. "I had only just suggested to the Grand Admiral that you might crave his exalted permission to join the fray, and he very kindly agreed …"

"Then we're all happy," beamed the King, slapping Friar William on the back. "Oh," he added, "you'd better come too."

Friar William hesitated. "A battlefield is no place for a man of God," he said aloofly.

"You'll do as I say!" said the King, becoming irritated.

"No. I shall remain here and attend to the Great Dog."

"Nonsense! Gelert is fine," scoffed the King, now with an edge to his voice. "But I'll need you down there. Translating. Come. Now."

He had raised his broadsword and now held it horizontally at hip height, the point slowly swinging towards Friar William's belly. The action was subtle, hardly even half a threat, but the priest couldn't ignore the growing anger on the King's face.

He paused, then shrugged. "Very well, but," he turned to Llewelyn. "remember boy, the dog's the Emperor now."

The King prodded the priest with his sword. "Ignore him, Llew," he said kindly. "It'll take days to sort everything out once the battle is over. There'll be all those heads to count, never mind all the banquets and speechifying, and all that nonsense."

He patted Gelert's head.

"I promise we'll keep the Chinese here as long as possible, so you two will have plenty of time together."

Llewelyn sniffed. It wasn't much consolation, but it was better than nothing. "Thanks," He hugged Gelert and forced a smile, but his voice was still cracked. "We'll have lots of fun before, before …"

Gelert slobbered him full on the face. "Gerroff!"

"Good lad," whispered the King, rising briskly.

He turned to Prince Dafydd and Owain and the other officers and sentries. "You lot!" he roared, "come with me. You'll do more good as my escort than you will counting seagulls up here!"

Owain didn't need to be told twice. He rubbed his hands at the idea of joining the battle, and Prince Dafydd swiped his sword at the heavens like a true warrior should. The King shoved Friar William ahead of him.

"Have fun, Llew," said the King, looking back. "I'll see you in an hour or so."

♘♞

Despite his father's assurances, Llewelyn felt very lonely. He still had Gelert, but for how long?

He reached for his old dog's neck, but the wolfhound pulled away, a warning growl in his throat.

"What is it?" Llewelyn walked the perimeter of the stone works, looking for a threat. The echoing screaming metal sounds of the distant battle rolled back and forth in the night air, but there weren't any dangers up here.

He leaned over the battlements and watched the King stepping into the courtyard with the others. They passed beneath the portcullis, walked along the causeway, then broke into a trot. Even Owain kept up, his iron-shod knees clanking twenty to the dozen.

They were all eager to get to the fight, all except Friar William who lagged behind, looking back at the castle. Prince Dafydd stomped back to gee him along, encouraging him with the flat of his sword.

Then Llewelyn heard a footstep.

Captain Chang emerged from the shadows of the doorway.

He glanced at Llewelyn, and drew a quick breath when he saw Gelert was with him. Then he checked out the empty battlements. He seemed relieved they were alone, his eyes shimmering green and black in the orange sunset as he stepped forward.

Gelert growled and advanced on him, his fur bristling.

The captain checked himself, understandably nervous. He pointed at Gelert, and gabbled at Llewelyn sounding demanding, almost haughty.

Llewelyn recognised the word for dog and shook his head.

"No!" he said fiercely, "No gou, not yet!"

Hearing the Chinese word, the captain raised an eyebrow.

"Yes, I know your stupid word for dog," said Llewelyn, "and no, you can't have him. Not yet."

Chang grew annoyed. He gestured angrily towards the battle, then back at Gelert, then at his junk in the harbour. Llewelyn knew precisely what he was saying and shook his head in reply.

"No gou. We wait for my father," he said firmly, surprising himself with his assertiveness.

The captain glowered and his hand drifted to his sword's hilt.

Gelert growled even more menacingly and advanced. As he moved closer, Chang stepped back, slowly withdrawing his hand from his weapon. Gelert stopped, but remained growling on guard.

Momentarily flustered, the captain regained his composure. He looked at Llewelyn, pointed to his mouth and shrugged apologetically.

You can't speak Welsh, thought Llewelyn. *Tough!*

Speaking again in Chinese, and sounding more conciliatory, the captain knelt and took something from his pocket.

He held it out to Gelert.

Llewelyn half expected to see a scrap of meat, but there was nothing there. The old wolfhound sniffed deeply at the empty hand and his tail began to wag happily. Then, to Llewelyn's astonishment, he began slobbering the captain's face. Chang smiled to himself, as if he'd known he could befriend the huge dog so easily.

A pang of jealousy struck Llewelyn. Gelert usually took a while before he'd let someone bribe him so easily. But then he softened; if Gelert liked the captain this quickly, when the time came to go, saying goodbye might not be so unbearable.

Maybe old Green Eyes isn't so creepy after all.

He smiled at Chang, who got up, smiling back. Gelert yapped, still sniffing eagerly at his empty palm.

They stood for a few uneasy moments, each muted by a lack of common language.

Then the captain rubbed his belly and pointed at his mouth.

Llewelyn realised he hadn't eaten since first thing that morning. Neither had Gelert. *You're hungry? Me too! I'm bloody starving!*

He laughed, and rubbed his stomach too.

Captain Chang laughed back, and mimed stuffing food into his mouth and chewing hungrily. Then he gestured to Llewelyn that maybe they could all go down to the courtyard and to his ship. It seemed like a spur-of-the-moment suggestion.

Llewelyn thought about it. *Why not? What's the harm in a bit of grub?* In the distance, he saw that his father and the others were catching up with the Grand Admiral's retinue. That made his mind up. The King need never know he'd left the keep to go raid the kitchens.

"All right, then," he said brightly, "let's go!"

Captain Chang gestured to the doorway and bowed low to Llewelyn. The young prince was flattered.

I could get used to having some respect.

Llewelyn picked up his longbow and arrows. The captain patted Gelert's head, and the old dog barked back, still sniffing his hand and bounding with happiness.

Slut, thought Llewelyn.

Together the three new friends went down to the harbour.

❧

After the chaotic carnage on the beaches and the causeway, the quayside was eerily quiet and still.

Llewelyn peered up the open ramps of the nearest giant junk as they walked by. The exposed holds were cavernously empty, poorly lit by round lanterns. One or two sentries paced the railings above and he saw only a few sailors in the rigging.

Most of the crew must be out there fighting.

Gelert trotted behind Chang, nose in the air, as if he was on a leash as long as the trail of scent wafting from the captain's hand.

The captain paused at the foot of the narrow gangplank and grinned back at Llewelyn. Again he mimed eating food, finishing off by sticking out his belly and rubbing it happily. He pointed up at the deck and beckoned, smiling all the while.

Llewelyn was having second thoughts. Never mind disobeying his father, there was a big difference between leaving the keep and going on board this Chinese ship.

But he was hungry and curious. He'd never been on board a ship like this. *It's not as if he's going to sail off with me.*

And I'm bloody starving!

Meanwhile, the captain called softly to the deck of the junk. A sailor came to the railings and did a startled double-take when he saw Gelert. Chang whispered a few sentences, and the crewman nodded vigorously. Two more men joined him, and when he told them what the captain had said, they nodded excitedly, and disappeared from sight.

Gone to get the grub, thought Llewelyn.

Chang smiled and winked at him, then strolled casually up the gangway, his hand trailing behind him. Gelert followed eagerly, sniffing at the captain's wiggling fingers.

Llewelyn stepped up to the gangplank. It was only a few feet wide.

Ahead, Gelert stopped halfway and looked back at him, waiting for permission to go on.

Well, laughed Llewelyn to himself, slightly relieved. *At least he's still thinking about me a little bit!*

"Go on then!"

The old wolfhound yapped once and bounded after the captain.

Llewelyn looked around the silent dockside; everything was safe and quiet. Black waves pushed and pulled the boat to and from the dock, making the flimsy gangplank sway and creak. He slung his longbow across his chest. It wasn't the best way of carrying it, but the narrow gangplank had no handrails and the junk swung freely at its moorings. He'd need his hands free for balance.

Gelert was already on board, standing silhouetted against the dark-red sky wagging his tail and barking encouragement.

Llewelyn stepped onto the gangplank. It was made from hard, shiny, yellow poles lashed together. They felt curiously springy underfoot, quite unlike the solid feel of proper wooden planks and the gangplank began to bounce from the rhythm of his footfalls.

Suddenly, the wind combined with a bigger swell and thrust the junk towards the harbour wall. When the hull smacked into the solid granite, the gangplank leapt upwards, sending Llewelyn sprawling forward onto the yellow poles.

As the junk rebounded from the harbour wall, his helmet fell off, tumbled down the gangplank and rolled to a stop on the quayside.

Llewelyn grasped hastily for the lashing ropes and looked up.

Gelert was barking frantically; the captain was shouting orders.

The junk continued its drift away from the quayside. The gap widened and Llewelyn could feel the end of the gangplank dragging towards the edge of the harbour. In a few seconds, it would fall off and he'd drop into the churning water where he'd drown, dragged down by the weight of his armour.

Terrified, he looked up again. Four sailors had grabbed the ship end of the gangplank; several more were unfixing it so they could pull him on board. But he also saw other sailors casting off the ship's lines.

Hey! Won't that let the boat drift away even more?

All at once, the red fish-fin sails were being hauled up. They flapped and banged noisily in the breeze, jerking the junk seaward.

"No! Just pull the boat closer in!" Llewelyn yelled, but the heavy mooring ropes had already fallen into the sea.

Up on the deck, Gelert was beside himself. He ran to and fro, barking and jumping up to see over the railings.

The sails filled and the junk continued to draw away from the dock. The four sailors started to haul the gangplank on board

– just in time. The far end scraped over and off the edge of the quayside, and Llewelyn dropped a couple of feet. The sailors grunted with the sudden strain, but held the gangplank firmly and began dragging it on board. *I'm safe.*

The captain shouted new orders, and to Llewelyn's horror, the sailors stopped pulling. The junk was now fully adrift and turning slowly to face the sea. The gap between it and the harbour was ten yards wide and growing. Llewelyn clung, knuckles white, twenty feet above the swirling water.

Chang walked to the ship's side next to Gelert, who howled uncontrollably. He looked down, his green eyes cold.

"Help!" pleaded Llewelyn hoarsely, sending Gelert into an even greater frenzy. The huge dog bustled past the four sailors and into the open gangway, preparing to go to his master's aid.

Startled, Captain Chang wrapped his hands around Gelert's neck and heaved him back onto the deck. As he struggled to hold the dog down, he shouted a new command to the sailors holding the gangplank.

They seemed shocked by his order, and looked at him pleadingly. But the captain just glared at them and repeated his command. The sailors looked back at Llewelyn. They seemed sad but helpless.

Then they pushed the gangplank away from the junk.

🐾

Llewelyn was so surprised he forgot to scream.

His breath was knocked out of him as the gangplank slapped hard onto the waves, jarring him with the impact.

Miraculously, it didn't roll over. Whatever the yellow poles were made of, they floated, but the gangplank was unstable in the choppy swell. Llewelyn's armour and his heavy sword threatened to tip him into the water. His longbow and quiver were awkward encumbrances. It took all of his panicked efforts not to overbalance as the gangplank twirled around.

Behind him, he heard Gelert snarling and a growing clamour of men shouting. It was a terrifying sound, but Llewelyn dared not turn to look for fear of upsetting his makeshift raft. Paddling with one hand, he slowly circled the gangplank around, bringing the junk back into view.

What he saw was horrifying, but grimly satisfying.

Gelert was berserk with rage. His hackles had risen, making him appear twice as big and fierce, and he was trying to throw himself out of the junk. The entire crew was struggling to keep him on board, and had formed a circle around the furious dog, shouting and jostling, terrified of his snarling fangs. A few were holding out ropes, trying to loop them around Gelert's neck and legs. Some were jabbing him with the blunt ends of pikes, while others tried to club him back, anything to keep him away from the railings.

Then Chang stepped into the ring. Blood poured from a wound on his cheek. He waved his smelly hand at Gelert, but that trick no longer worked; the wolfhound almost bit his fingers off. The old dog lunged at the railings again, only to be beaten back.

The fight was a terrifying stalemate. Gelert snapped viciously at anyone who came close and the sailors could barely keep him at bay.

Then a big man threw himself onto the wolfhound and wrestled him to the deck.

A moment later Gelert sprang back up, his jaws dripping red.

He'd ripped out the sailor's throat.

The doomed man writhed, clawing at his wound. Gouts of blood spurted through his fingers and sprayed his crew-mates.

Terrified, they backed away from Gelert, then, incensed by the death of their friend, jumped back in, beating at him in retaliation.

The captain screamed at his crew to stop and drew his sword, forcing them to back off.

Gelert, bloody but not broken, saw his chance. He leapt and grabbed hold of Chang's sword arm, shaking and tearing at it, forcing him to drop the weapon. Then Gelert dragged him running through the ring of men and together they crashed through the railings, plunging into the sea below.

Gelert bobbed to the surface.

"Here, boy!' shouted Llewelyn. Seeing him, Gelert put his good ear back, and started up a ponderous doggy paddle toward him.

The captain broke surface a yard from the junk, spluttering with panic. He caught hold of a dangling mooring rope and three sailors pulled him back on board.

"Hurry, Gelert!" spluttered Llewelyn, swallowing a mouthful of salt water. The old dog was only twenty yards from the junk.

Chang screamed more orders and the junk slowly turned to follow. It quickly gained headway and bore down on Gelert.

"Hurry, boy!"

The captain glared at Llewelyn, wiping blood from his face. Then he ran to the junk's bow, gathering some of his crew as he went. In moments, they'd lowered a rope ladder down the side of the ship. Others wrapped a length of rope around a cleat and looped the free end around Chang's chest.

Llewelyn watched the captain step out of the gangway. His men paid out the rope, letting him walk backwards, hands free, to the bottom rung of the rope ladder. He hung out, parallel with the sea, feet against the hull, holding onto the rope with his good hand and reaching out with the other. Passing wavelets splashed up at him and spray smeared his bleeding face. All the while he shouted orders, guiding the junk closer and closer to Gelert.

Llewelyn looked up at the towering bows of the junk as it neared. He reached uselessly for his old friend who was still a few feet away.

"Faster, boy! Faster!"

The captain leaned out over the wolfhound, but rather than grabbing him, he planted his hand on Gelert's shoulders and shoved him firmly under the water.

Gelert disappeared in a floundering of limbs, resurfacing seconds later, blinded by his own splashing and coughing seawater.

Now the junk was slowing. Its mainsail had been lowered.

Chang leaned out to grab Llewelyn.

"Piss off!" he cried, desperately trying to paddle out of reach.

He felt the captain grasp him by the scruff of his chainmail. Suddenly, the two of them were flying through the air, hauled up the side of the ship by the sailors. Gelert howled forlornly and paddled furiously to catch up with the junk as it halted, dead in the water.

The sailors dragged them aboard and the captain dropped Llewelyn heavily. Blood streamed from the savage wounds on

Chang's face and hand, washing the deck pink. He fumed at Llewelyn who lay at his feet, wet, fearful and confused.

Bugger you! thought Llewelyn. "Wait till I tell my father about this!" he yelled angrily.

Gelert heard his voice from below and howled.

Captain Chang scowled at Llewelyn before stripping him of his weapons and throwing them to a crewman. Then he grabbed him by his shoulders and manhandled him to the railings, shoving him out for Gelert to see.

The old dog was splashing around the bottom of the rope ladder, his paws scrabbling uselessly against the ship's sides. He barked plaintively, desperately searching for Llewelyn.

The captain shouted to catch his attention, and held Llewelyn further out. The young prince yelped with fear and, hearing him, Gelert looked up and his panic subsided. He barked happily, his great tail thrashing the sea.

Relieved, Chang pulled Llewelyn in, still holding him in sight of Gelert, and ordered a man down the rope ladder to fetch the dog.

The sailor gulped. He was a giant of a man, but he'd seen what Gelert could do to someone. Discipline took over and, warily, he climbed down the ladder, glancing back over his shoulder.

The wolfhound grumbled, but didn't resist when the sailor hooked his arm around his shoulders. Grunting, the man got a grip of his long shaggy belly fur, and lifted him out of the water. Gelert mewled, but with Llewelyn in sight, he stayed calm.

Strong as the giant sailor was, Gelert was too wet and heavy for him to carry up the ladder. Six crewmen grabbed the ladder and heaved man and dog up.

Meanwhile, Llewelyn twisted free of the captain's grasp and leaned over the bulwarks. He shouted encouragement to Gelert, who squirmed and yelped with delight. As they reached deck height, the big sailor could no longer hold him. Gelert flew from his grasp and bundled Llewelyn to the deck where he slobbered and snuffled his face, whimpering joyfully.

Captain Chang and his crew stood around them, silent and angry.

The body of the dead crewman lay against the railings,

drained blue-white.

Tough! thought Llewelyn.

He pushed Gelert aside and got up, angry. Now he knew why he'd been saved; only so that the Great Dog could be tamed. He reached for his sword, remembering too late that it had been taken from him.

He had to get off this boat; to get back to his father and tell him what had happened. Bargain or no bargain, this was an outrage and these Chinese would pay.

The captain glowered, fingering the bleeding gash in his cheek. He turned on his heel and stalked aft, shouting new orders to his crew who hauled up the mainsail. The junk moved forward again.

Llewelyn stood, ignored and helpless as the ship came to life around him. Gelert looked up at him quizzically, shivering.

You know as much as me, mate!

Looking around the deck, Llewelyn saw a white-haired old man sitting in the ship's cockpit, pushing hard against a long black handle.

That must be the tiller.

The rudder bit and the junk heeled to port. As the deck tilted, Llewelyn staggered and reached for the railings. Something bumped into his leg. He looked down. It was the corpse of the dead sailor, sliding in a slick pool of thick blood.

As if in a dream, Llewelyn watched the body slowly slip through the smashed gap in the railings and silently disappear overboard.

🐾

Spooked, Llewelyn looked around, wondering if anyone else had seen the body go. No, they were all busy working the ship.

He was amazed to find that they were still only a hundred yards from the dockside. The glow of the distant battle had thinned to an orange smear against the now black sky.

The pair of huge nine-masted junks sat impassively either side of the space they'd only recently left. Scores of sentries lined their railings, shouting after them. Some of them ran to and fro, as if in panic.

A lone figure stood on the dockside waving his arms wildly.

Odd, thought Llewelyn briefly, but already he was thinking ahead. The junk was still within the confines of the harbour. He was still close to land. But they were heading for the harbour entrance, sailing away from the castle, his father, his home and his country.

He ran to the stern, Gelert limping behind him.

"Help! Father! Guards!" he yelled at the castle.

Gelert stood next to him. He howled plaintively, but his voice seemed broken.

"Don't you worry, mate!" he said, "We'll swim for it!"

He struggled to pull off his armour. The breastplate fell with a dull twank. By now, the junk was passing the harbour entrance. The stone works on either side were only a few yards away. We'll make it!

But as Llewelyn squirmed out of his chainmail tunic, Captain Chang walked up, grabbed him by the neck and shoved him to the deck.

"Let! Me! Go!" screamed Llewelyn, trying to squirm away. "Gelert, get him off me!"

But the wolfhound just flopped down heavily. He lay, chest heaving, whimpering plaintively in a spreading dark pool.

Llewelyn writhed and kicked helplessly in Captain Chang's strong grip. He yelled out, hoping his father might hear him, but his boy's voice was small in the vast emptiness of the sea.

The junk was now in open water, rising against and falling back into the choppy Irish Sea. Chang released Llewelyn and walked away.

Llewelyn scrambled over to Gelert. He stroked his hand through his wet fur. It felt sticky. He sniffed his dripping fingers, then tasted them. He smelled copper and tasted salty iron.

Llewelyn's hand was drenched in Gelert's blood.

~~~~

Four thousand miles away, the sun had just fallen behind the stinking, dusty, brown-baked city. The girl dragged Shoon's skeletal remains to the sampan's railings. Three crew dogs helped her, tugging at his puke-and-shit-fouled clothing.

The first body she'd had to drop overboard (was that really only a month ago?) had floated for a week, forever bumping against the hull before the crabs and rats and fish had eaten their fill. She'd learned to weigh the rest of the corpses with something heavy before she tipped them into the harbour. She looked into Shoon's face as she stuffed rocks into his pockets. His transparent yellow skin was stretched thin and white over his skull and the sharp edges of his cheekbones and eye sockets. His dead eyes, pasty green, stared back at her. If she hadn't known it was Shoon, she wouldn't have recognised him.

Surprisingly, he had been the last to die. Surprising, because he'd been the first to fall ill; but not surprising because Shoon had been the strongest man in the crew. Everyone had watched in horror as his armpits and groin had erupted in bursting purple pustules. When he began vomiting black bile and voiding his bowels, the men had edged away as he screamed and writhed and sweated himself into unconsciousness.

Then, one by one, they had each gone the same way.

Everyone but her.

Shoon's lice dog snuffled out from his tunic. She picked it up and put it in her pocket, wondering why none of the crew's lice dogs had died, nor hers. All the sampan's crew dogs were fine, thank Dog.

Then she heaved Shoon's bag of bones over the railings. It tumbled into the scummy sea with a thick splash. One of the crew dogs howled softly as the body sank in a haze of brown bubbles.

The oily water in the harbour glowed a bleary orange, its surface blackened by a blanket of buzzing flies gorging on floating sewage and unidentifiable rubbish.

The girl spat. Everything reeked of shit and decomposing flesh; the port, the city, this whole stinking, filthy, rotting country.

It was the water, she knew. The milky water Shoon had brought back from one of his foraging trips into the city. Or maybe it was that dead goat they'd traded rice for. Or that tray of eggs, or those cabbages. Oh it could have been anything.

The men had laughed at her for sticking to the stale supplies in the hold of the sampan, but now the men were all gone, and she was left with just the crew dogs and her lice dog for companionship.

There was no satisfaction in surviving, just as she held no regrets for having stowed away in the first place. All she felt was the loneliness of knowing that there was nothing she could do now but wait.

PART II: THE ESSENCE

Chapter 9. Lice dogs

The junk's bows cut across short waves, shattering them into rainbowed mist that flew back along the deck. In the sunset's final rays, the spray shimmered golden and warm, but was icy cold.

The puddle of bloody water oozing from Gelert's trembling body was spreading.

Llewelyn stood up, searching for the captain.

"Oye, you!" he hollered. Chang looked up. "Look what you did to my dog!"

A few sailors approached, and the sight of Gelert made them groan and also call urgently to the captain.

Grunting with effort, the injured wolfhound tried to stand. His movements further opened his wounds, and a fresh splatter of deep-red gore drenched the deck.

Captain Chang pushed through the crowd of crewmen that had now gathered. Horror creased his face when he saw Gelert's broken body.

"Help him!" fumed Llewelyn.

"Kung!" called the captain.

A hatchway near the junk's bows banged open and a man's head appeared.

Gelert swayed unsteadily then collapsed heavily onto the deck leaking blood. The circle of sailors stepped forward with a collective gasp of anguish as Llewelyn knelt to hold the old wolfhound's head.

"Don't worry, old boy. I'm here; you're safe with me." He glared at the captain with hatred.

Chang stood silently chewing the back of his knuckles. Lights were brought, and a moment later, Kung arrived carrying a large bag, shoving impatiently through the crowding crew and pushing the captain aside.

He was a thin, nervous-looking man whose skeletal face was made more pinched by his hair, which was scraped into a tightly plaited ponytail. Squatting next to Gelert, he ran his hands expertly over the great hound's trembling body and along his quivering legs. As he examined the cuts and gashes, he made soft cooing sounds to comfort Gelert.

Llewelyn watched his face intently, looking for reassuring signs. But Kung was far from happy and grew increasingly concerned. Gelert's wounds were bad enough, but he also tutted at the ugly growths and patches of scabby skin all over his torso.

Kung asked accusing sounding questions, concern replaced by anger. His green eyes flickered with an odd twitch. Llewelyn blinked. *Who does that remind me of?* But then the look was gone.

The captain held open his arms in an 'it wasn't my fault' gesture and pointed to where Gelert had killed the sailor. He gawped when he saw the corpse had disappeared. Only the smear of blood remained.

Kung snorted and dismissed the captain with a contemptuous wave, scanning the crew with undisguised hostility. He turned back to Gelert and reached into his bag, which was filled with oddly shaped jars and bottles. Digging deep, he found an earthenware pot from which he scooped a handful of viscous green paste. It looked and smelled disgusting, but Gelert sniffed and his ear pricked up. He flinched as Kung began to smear the ointment onto his wounds, but then closed his eyes blissfully and wagged his tail feebly.

"Aaah!" chorused the crew, but their relief turned to anguish when the old wolfhound's eyes rolled back and he slumped into unconsciousness, twitching and whimpering.

"What's the matter?" cried Llewelyn. "Is he all right? Is he going to die?"

The junk suddenly whacked into a bigger wave and a cloud of chilling spray slashed the exposed deck, drenching everyone.

That was enough for Kung. He stood and ordered two sailors to pick Gelert up. The men lifted his limp body over to a hatchway near the stern. Kung trotted ahead to open it, and the crewmen gingerly descended the ladder then carried the old dog into the hold of the junk.

Ignored by everyone, Llewelyn, climbed down after him.

The hold was small, and smelled musty. Its walls were lined

with mostly bare shelving stacked here and there with sacks and pottery jars. Llewelyn helped Kung clear a space on the deck, kicking aside scattered ropes and empty sacks.

Kung lit a lantern, then cast around and found some thick woollen blankets. He arranged them into a bed, onto which the two sailors gently lowered Gelert.

Llewelyn stroked his old friend's stumpy left ear. The old dog's troubled, fitful sleep eased into a deep slumber. Llewelyn smiled at Kung, relieved this man had known what to do. But Kung ignored him – he was only interested in the dog.

Glancing up, Llewelyn saw the crew peering through the hatchway, their worried faces framing the darkening sky.

The captain called down to Kung. With Gelert now sorted, he was reasserting his authority. Chang gestured to the two sailors to return on deck, and indicated that Llewelyn must come up too.

Llewelyn stood, but stopped. A sudden gush of indignation exploded in him.

"Don't you dare tell me what to do! He's my dog, not yours! I shouldn't even be on this boat. And what are you going to do about getting me home?"

He felt a hand on his leg. It was Kung, now shushing him and gently pulling him back to sit next to Gelert. Kung addressed the captain in a firm voice, countermanding Chang's orders. Llewelyn was to stay by his dog's side. He felt the satisfaction of a little victory.

The captain crouched over the hatchway muttering at Kung, who ignored him as he went about hanging the lantern from a deck beam. It cast a soft, warm light, made cosier by the calming gurgle of the water coursing past the hull.

Kung sat beside Gelert, absently scratching his shoulder.

He then began scratching his arm, and next the back of his hand, which he inspected with a frown. Llewelyn saw confusion on his face as the itching and scratching intensified. From above, the captain started laughing and beckoning to crewmen to take a look.

Soon, they too were sniggering.

Kung, still scratching, was becoming annoyed. He reached

over to Gelert and gingerly lifted his good ear, and recoiled in disgust.

Puzzled, Llewelyn leaned over to see what was so repulsive. He feared that Kung had uncovered a horrific injury to Gelert's head, but all he saw was a handful of lice and some fleas and a few fat ticks.

Appalled and grumpy, Kung was now scratching vigorously. Captain Chang snorted with laughter, but then grew serious. He snapped his fingers and spoke to his crewmen, three of whom nodded and climbed down the stairs to Gelert's bedside.

Llewelyn and Kung squirmed to one side to make room for the odd threesome. The first was the giant sailor who'd pulled Gelert from the sea; his trousers were still wet. He was so tall he had to bend at the waist to stand in the cramped hold. The other two were comically short identical twins who chattered like squirrels, digging each other in the ribs with their elbows. Kung tutted at them to be quiet. Still jabbering, they sat cross-legged next to Llewelyn in a tight semi-circle.

The big sailor shoved his hand deep inside his shirt, rummaged around, and carefully withdrew something. Whatever it was, it needed to be held delicately.

The two tiny crewmen looked on, barely suppressing giggles. Llewelyn ignored them, focused instead on the sailor's hand as he slowly opened his fingers.

There, dwarfed in his palm, sat a tiny, round, entirely hairless dog. No bigger than a pear, it was perfectly pink and looked softly squishy. It gazed up at Llewelyn, shivering in the cold of the hold.

He was entranced. He looked closer. The minuscule dog's skin was so thin he could see the pulsing tracery of its veins. Its paws were no bigger than his little thumbnail and each toe was tipped with a scarlet claw the size of a rose thorn. Then he caught the animal's scent, a peculiarly sweet smell that reminded him of a baby.

"He's beautiful!" crooned Llewelyn.

The giant sailor nodded encouragingly and gently offered him the tiny dog. It yapped a little bark and wagged its stubby tail.

How do I hold something so small and delicate?, he thought as he reached out. The giant tipped it gently into his hand.

Llewelyn feared he'd drop or, even worse, crush it, but the strange creature was heavy and felt surprisingly strong and muscly.

The dog sniffed at his palm and licked off some dried sea salt. Then it sat down and shivered its skin, deliberately making itself quiver. The peculiar baby smell grew stronger.

A few seconds passed.

Llewelyn felt a feathery tickling sensation in his armpits, scalp and groin that quickly spread across his body. It was as if he was sprouting a new skin, which slowly began to move by itself. He saw a thin crust of tiny white blobs emerge at the cuff of his tunic. They rolled slowly down his forearm creating a second sleeve, creeping towards the tiny dog in his hand.

Llewelyn's new skin was an army of lice and fleas. Thousands of the wretched bloodsuckers. He felt them everywhere, moving all over his body. They trickled down from his hairline and squirmed up from his feet, climbing his chest and back, and over his shoulders.

He watched, fascinated but slightly sickened. The advance party of shedded insects curved around his wrist and hand like a glove. They wriggled and writhed onto his palm and around the tiny naked dog, which sat quietly, tongue lolling and tail wagging. As the lice enveloped its body and crept onto its head, the dog closed its eyes. Its nostrils clamped shut, and its ears smoothed flat against its skull. In less than a minute, it was caked thickly with lice.

Llewelyn, on the other hand, felt clean and fresh. For the first time in his thirteen years he knew what it was like to be vermin free. Wide-eyed, he looked to the others. The sailors had stopped laughing. Everyone was silent, staring at the scale of the infestation that had poured from him onto the little animal.

Then one of the dwarves jabbered excitedly and pointed at the seething miniature dog-shaped blob.

The thick layer of vermin seemed to boil from within. The lice were dying, falling like a shower of sifted flour. The pale husks piled up on his hand and spilled over onto the deck. The tiny dog shook itself happily, throwing off the last of the dead insects and looked up at him imploringly.

"Chi," said the giant sailor.

The tiny dog barked happily, before snuffling into the mound of dead insects, greedily lapping them up and crunching them down.

Slack-jawed, Llewelyn stared in wonder as it cleaned up his hand.

"Chi" he said, handing the tiny dog back to the giant. "That means 'eat', doesn't it?" He mimed putting food into his mouth and said it again. Everyone nodded approval.

Then Kung pulled out his own lice dog from inside his tunic. *God's truth!* thought Llewelyn, *everyone's got one of the little buggers!*

Kung mimed something tiny jumping from Gelert onto his clothes then scratched himself.

Of course! We brought our lice on board.

He watched as Kung's lice dog went to work, attracting then killing and eating the lice and fleas that had migrated onto him from Gelert during his examination.

Meanwhile, the two dwarf sailors took out their lice dogs and placed them beside Gelert's sleeping body. Each was hardly bigger than one of the wolfhound's feet. They shivered their skin and the baby smell filled the hold.

Then it was as if Gelert had turned himself into a louse shower. A thick drizzle of vermin poured from his tangled fur and tumbled onto the deck. They appeared in all sizes, from barely visible lice and fleas, through to inch-wide ticks and leeches. The shimmering, slimy exodus swarmed and hopped and slithered from Gelert over to the tiny dogs, a carpet of living filth that moulded around their bodies to form two indistinct dog-shaped shells. After a few moments, the flimsy, quivering carapaces twitched, died and collapsed into piles around their paws. The two dogs looked expectantly up at their masters and yipped.

"Chi," said the sailors, smiling and clapping their hands. With nubby tails wagging, their pets devoured the piles of dead vermin.

Llewelyn sat, mesmerised. Questions bubbled in his head and blurted out. "What are they called? Where did you find them? Do they eat anything else?"

The sailors smiled but didn't respond. Instead, they picked

up their pets and caressed them briefly, then returned them to the folds of their tunics before rising and climbing out of the hold.

The captain was squatting at the hatchway. He called down to Kung, and they chatted in a business-like fashion. Llewelyn tried to interrupt them, to ask what was happening, but they ignored him.

Kung checked Gelert over one more time and looked satisfied. The huge dog was breathing easily and sleeping untroubled. Kung packed up his bag of medicines and, with barely a glance at Llewelyn, made his way back on deck.

The Captain pulled the hatch cover over and it thudded shut, blocking out the dying light of the sunset. The dim glow of the lantern suddenly seemed thin. Now, the hold felt empty and the sound of the sea slopping outside was cold and lonely.

"What about me?" called Llewelyn plaintively. "When are you going to take me home?" As an afterthought he said, "I thought you were going to feed me!"

But all he heard in reply was the groan of the ship's rigging and the creaking of the hull as the sea pounding by outside. He slumped down next to Gelert.

An hour ago he'd been a Prince of Wales; now he was just cargo. He felt clubbed dull by the indifference of his new surroundings.

Gelert lay unconscious, lost from him. Llewelyn tried to find some comfort in his old friend's sleeping body, but his mind slowly closed down, chilled by all that had happened.

It was his first ever night alone.

Llewelyn woke with a start from an empty, dreamless sleep. A bright light had flashed across his eyes, but then it was dark again.

Where am I?

Wherever it was, it smelled woody, spicy, wet and salty. He felt dizzy, but lay still, frozen with a dread and fear, listening to the confusion of sounds around him: deep snoring, muted voices, distant hammering, sloshing and trickling. He felt himself tip gently onto his left side, then slowly he was rolled back the other way. He watched a thin white band of light drift lazily away from him. It paused for a second against a nearby wooden wall before floating back towards him. It passed over his face, hurting his eyes again, then drifted over Gelert's sleeping body.

Oh! My old friend!

He rolled over and stroked Gelert's shoulder. His chest juddered at Llewelyn's touch and his shallow breaths sounded wheezy. Llewelyn felt the patches of thick paste plastered over his friend's body and, as his eyes grew used to the dark, he saw glistening red through the smears of green. Gelert's wounds were still oozing blood and he was in a sorry state.

Llewelyn panicked as everything abruptly came back to him. He scrabbled around the small space on his knees, hemmed in, desperately banging against shelving and stout wooden walls. *Last night! They took us! I'm in the hold of the Chinese junk! I'm a prisoner! What am I going to do? Think! Think! Think!*

He forced himself to sit, and as he fondled Gelert's stubby ear, the wave of panic subsided. His eyes found the glowing white band of light wandering aimlessly around the hold. *No, not aimlessly.* It moved deliberately and smoothly from one side to the other. It was a shaft of light seeping through a thin gap in the hatchway lid, and the pitch and roll of the junk was moving it around the confines of the hold.

The sun must be almost overhead. I've been asleep a long time.

Then the hatch was thrown open and he was fully blinded by the blaze of light pouring in. Voices and seagulls' cries were suddenly loud, and someone was climbing down the steps into the hold. As his eyes became accustomed to the light, Llewelyn saw that it was Kung with his bag of potions. The medicine man squatted to examine Gelert.

"Is he alright? When are you going to take us home?" blurted Llewelyn.

Kung just looked at him blankly. But then, almost as an afterthought, he reached into his bag and handed him a large steaming bowl full of soft white grains and hunks of dark-red meat.

"Chi," he said, motioning his hands to his lips.

Ravenous, Llewelyn shovelled everything into his mouth. Whatever the white grains were, they tasted good. The meat, too, was delicious, tangy but sweet.

In thirty seconds it was all gone.

He burped, and a thought struck him. *He doesn't understand Welsh, but maybe…* he repeated his questions in English. Nothing. French. No. He tried Greek and Latin, but Kung just shrugged and shook his head. He gabbled something with that 'gou' word again and gently prodded one of Gelert's wounds.

Still sleeping, the old dog didn't flinch. Whatever his green ointment was, it had cut off the pain.

But it hadn't stopped him farting. Gelert's belly began to heave, and Llewelyn heard the tell-tale sounds of a proper stinker boiling up.

Instinctively, he shuffled backwards.

When it came, the lamplight dimmed for a few seconds. Kung gasped, then retched. When his eyes started to water, Llewelyn laughed and Kung crossly motioned him to go away.

Llewelyn stood up. The hold was small. There really wasn't anywhere to go.

"Can I go on deck?" he asked, pointing at himself and up at the hatchway. Kung was busy. He just shrugged and waved him off.

At least they're not going to keep me cooped up down here, thought Llewelyn, glad of the chance to get some fresh air and stretch his legs. He climbed up the ladder.

꧁꧂

The second his head reached deck height, a wash of cold sea spray slapped his face, stinging his eyes.

The hatchway was just a few feet from the stern rail. He

climbed on deck. Looking back at the junk's wake, there was no land, not even a hint of a distant mountain. He scanned the horizon. A watery grey sky blended imperceptibly into a shattered steel of the sea. The wind blew hard and steady, thrumming the taut rigging. Llewelyn watched the bows dip below the horizon and shoulder into the oncoming swell with a dull thud. The ship rolled slowly up the next wave and a heartbeat later, a fine mist of sea spray fluttered over him.

Two gulls flew past the slatted main sail, one chasing the other in a looping swoop. They glided over his head and off over the trailing wake, their bickering cries fading into the distance.

Forward, the junk looked almost empty. Here and there a few sailors were working in the rigging; others were seated, coiling ropes. Away to the left, two men were busy patching up the smashed hole in the railings and another couple were swabbing the deck.

Llewelyn remembered how few crewmen he'd seen last night – only a couple of dozen at most.

Where's the big fellow and the twins?

Further along, between the stern and the mainmast was the cockpit. Llewelyn recognised the back of the old helmsman, his white hair streaming in the stiff breeze. Beyond him was the captain, standing beneath the mainmast, his head craned upwards as he spoke to a sailor squatting on the yardarm. The lookout squinted north and called down. Whatever he said seemed to satisfy the captain who walked back to the cockpit and sat beside the old helmsman.

Llewelyn glowered at the captain, wanting to march right up and confront him, but what could he say? They didn't understand him, and the only Chinese he knew was a couple of names and the words for 'dog' and 'eat'.

He moved towards the bows.

The ship was bigger than most that had visited his father's castle, and he wondered why there were so few sailors on board. He heard laughter from below and smelled food.

Everyone else must be downstairs eating.

The carpenters at the railings and the two men scrubbing at a wide red patch on the deck were bent to their tasks with grim resolution. Llewelyn gulped. Their crew-mate had died horribly last night, and all that was left of him was a wet patch. One of the swabbers looked up at him. Llewelyn couldn't tell what he was thinking behind his green eyes, and turned away feeling somehow guilty.

Then he saw his chainmail tunic and breastplate tucked next to a hatchway. The armour lay in a pool of thick orange goo, already rusted. He picked it up. The chainmail was a bedraggled mess, crumbling and useless in his fingers. The breastplate was slimy, and one of its strap buckles had been torn off. It all felt puny and pathetic, toy armour for a little boy. *Fat lot of good you were last night, and you're no good now!*

He shoved the sloshy mess of chainmail into the breastplate and picked up the bundle. He carried the two pieces to the railings, carelessly dripping a tawny smear along the deck. Broken links of mail fell, scattering everywhere. Llewelyn angrily heaved the armour overboard. The breastplate sank immediately, scooping first one way then the other like a leaf falling from a tree. The chainmail tried to float for a brief moment, before plummeting out of sight in a hissing froth of orange bubbles. The two patches of rusty broken sea fell behind, blending into the junk's wake.

Llewelyn immediately felt guilty and sorry; his father had given him that armour on his tenth birthday, to go with his longbow and sword.

Where IS my bow?

He faced the captain who was still talking with the helmsman. Unable to stop himself, he cupped his hands to his mouth and yelled.

"Oye! You! Where's my bow, and my sword…?" He skimmed through all the forbidden words he could use; no-one here would clip him round the ear for swearing. *What's the worse thing I could call him? I know!* "… you green-eyed, turd-eating Chinese bas– !"

It was a bad idea.

The Captain looked up, saw the mess Llewelyn's rusty armour had made on the deck, and stormed over.

Scared, Llewelyn cut off his cursing mid-stream, but Chang was already there, grabbing him by his collar and forcing him to his knees. He roared, pointing at the rust stains, then shoved

Llewelyn's face into the slippery, gritty mess before pulling him up and yanking him over to the railings.

Oh my God! He's going to throw me overboard!

The captain pushed him further and further back over the railings until Llewelyn was hanging more out of the boat than in. He could feel the empty space between his back and the sea as it coursed below. The void seemed to pull at his shoulders as Chang screamed at him.

"Sorry!" squeaked Llewelyn, meaning it.

The captain stopped yelling but, as if wanting to make clear who was in charge, he dangled Llewelyn for a few more silent seconds before pulling him back on board. Llewelyn slumped gratefully to the deck, his heart pounding, arms and legs shaking.

The captain called to one of the crewmen working on the blood stains. He hurried over with a scrubbing brush and a bucket slopping pale pinkish water, its handle trailing a length of rope. The sailor offered the bucket to the captain, who rolled his eyes and gave the crewman a 'not me, HIM!' look.

Llewelyn took the bucket and brush. The captain pointed at the trail of rust stain, turned and stomped back to the cockpit.

Still trembling, Llewelyn got to work.

Great! he thought as his panic subsided. *Yesterday I was picking up arrows, today I'm scrubbing floors.*

He paused. But today it wasn't his father telling him what to do, and why it would be good for him to do it. No 'duty', no 'lesson to be learned', just a simple task.

The thought was strangely liberating, but it didn't make the job any less horrible. The water in the bucket was pale red from the blood of the dead sailor. As he dunked the brush into it, Llewelyn breathed through his mouth, taking care not to splash his face.

They could've at least given me clean water to work with, he muttered to himself as he set about scrubbing the deck.

Soon the bucket water was such a deep rusty red that using it was only making the deck dirtier. Llewelyn looked up and watched the crewmen cleaning the other stain. One of them got up and tipped his dirty water overboard, then, using the rope on his bucket's handle, brought up clean, fresh seawater.

Why didn't I do that before I started?

Llewelyn gulped, slightly ashamed; it was because he'd never even had to think about such simple things before. He understood geometry and philosophy, read and wrote and spoke in six languages, and could apply a field tourniquet, *but I've only just learned how to use a bucket.*

He copied the sailor and refilled his bucket, then carried on scrubbing. Soon he grew colder. His knees and elbows ached, his muscles started cramping and his hands were chaffed raw. Whenever he banged his chilled fingertips on the deck, the dull, bone-deep pain made him wince. But the mindlessness of the job gave him a chance to think and take stock of his situation, and his thoughts turned to home.

Come nightfall they'll have to head for a port. No-one crosses open sea by night. We're heading south, so we'll hit Dyfed, maybe Ireland, and then I'll tell them to let me off.

But then he remembered that the Chinese ship had already sailed through the night. *But sooner or later they'll have to make for port. Even if it's Brittany or Normandy, I can jump ship and I'll be safe. It's not far. I'll get home somehow.*

Better still, Llewelyn smiled to himself, back at the castle, once everyone realised he'd been taken, the King would have gone berserk and he'd be moving heaven and earth to get his son back. He didn't know quite how his father might do this, but he did know the fat Admiral would be having a hard time of it.

I don't need to do anything except wait.

Eighteen buckets and an hour later, his patch of deck was spotless. If anything, he'd made the rest of the deck look dirty. It felt good to have the job done.

Llewelyn heard a grunt from the cockpit and looked around. It was the captain who nodded at him. There was even a faint twitch of a smile. No thanks, no lecture, just the acknowledgement of a job done well. Llewelyn felt a sense of acceptance, as if a cease-fire had been declared between him and Captain Chang.

What's the point in fighting? he thought. *I'll soon be off this junk.*

Llewelyn took the bucket and brush back to the sailors who were still scrubbing at the blood stain. It had seeped deep into the deck's timbers. Maybe they'd never clean away the last of their dead friend.

The two men looked up at him wearily.

Your job's worse than mine was, Llewelyn thought.

He suddenly felt the need to tell them what had happened to their fallen crew-mate, how his body had slipped quietly into the sea on a slick of his own blood. But all he could do was smile sympathetically.

No, I can do more than that.

He got down onto his knees next to them and started scrubbing.

❧

An hour later, Llewelyn finally made it back to Gelert.

Kung was still with the old dog. He'd rigged up a skin of water connected to a thin, flexible tube that ran into Gelert's mouth.

That's clever, thought Llewelyn, wondering what the tube could be made of. It wasn't leather, too supple and thin. *Something Chinese.*

As he stepped down into the hold, Gelert woke up. Seeing Llewelyn, he whimpered weakly and even managed to wag his tail a couple of times. Llewelyn's eyes pricked with tears. The wolfhound noticed Kung and growled half-heartedly, but the medicine man ignored the feeble threat and fed him gruel from a bowl, letting the Great Dog lap up as much as he wanted.

He then rubbed some more green paste into Gelert's wounds, and the dog slowly drifted back into a deep sleep. Kung glanced up, caught Llewelyn watching him and held his stare. There was something in those green eyes, a fierceness and focus that reminded him of … *Who?*

A shiver ran between Llewelyn's shoulder blades.

The next morning, when Llewelyn opened his eyes and stretched, Gelert was already blearily awake. Despite being hooked up to Kung's feeding tube, he fixed Llewelyn with an unmistakable look that said: 'Need Food NOW'.

That's a good sign, thought Llewelyn and gave him a bowl of food.

It was gone in a gulp, followed shortly by a full-bodied, gruel-scented fart.

Llewelyn climbed up to open the hatchway to let in some fresh air and stood halfway up the ladder, leaning his elbows on the hatch.

A thin mist filtered the weak dawn light, and everywhere dripped with cold dew. He saw the ghost-like figure of the captain calling up to the man on watch at the masthead. The mist deadened the air, flattening his voice.

The lookout seemed lethargic and took his time to reply. This angered Chang, and to Llewelyn's surprise, an argument erupted between the two men. The lookout finally said enough to pacify the captain, and the row faded as quickly as it had flared.

Something about the ensuing silence made the hairs on Llewelyn's neck stand up – the atmosphere on the junk had changed, but it wasn't just the fog.

Then Kung appeared from his forward hatchway and stomped towards him. His apparent irritation wasn't helped when he stumbled on a rope. Llewelyn laughed, but stifled his sniggers when he saw Kung's twitching eyes and furious expression.

Kung climbed past him into the hold, but missed a rung and fell, landing awkwardly on a pile of sacks. Llewelyn jumped down and tried to help him up, but Kung was now steaming red with rage and pushed him away.

Beneath his bluster, Kung looked older and more withered. The wrinkles on his face seemed deeper, his skin more wax-like, and Llewelyn heard his knees crack as he crouched next to Gelert.

The old dog was just waking up and wagged his tail feebly,

which was a good sign, but Llewelyn was shocked when Kung roughly, almost spitefully, jerked the water tube from his mouth.

Gelert gagged and threw up some gruel on Kung.

Llewelyn laughed, making Kung even angrier. He swore at Llewelyn, and tossed the water skin at him, gesturing angrily that he should fill it. Resentful at being at the end of a slapping chain, Llewelyn stomped up on deck.

As he walked the length of the junk searching for a fresh water barrel, he realised that the crew, to a man, had sunk into a bleak weariness. They were trying to work, but the tasks that only yesterday had been routine now resembled hard labour. One sailor stood staring at the halyard in his hand as if he'd never seen one before; another lay flopped on his back in the middle of the deck, eyes screwed shut, his arms flailing weakly in the air as if trying to bat off flying insects.

Llewelyn found the giant sailor leaning against the mainmast gazing blankly out to sea. He reached up and waved the water skin in the huge man's face.

"Where ... do ... I ... get ... water?" he asked.

The giant didn't even blink.

Llewelyn turned and saw the captain flopped in the cockpit. He was muttering at the old helmsman, whose head was lolling from side-to-side with the roll of the boat. Chang's voice sounded like he was gargling treacle, as if he was trying to shout but was too tired to put in the effort.

At least he's half awake. He'll tell me where I can get some water.

Close-up, Captain Chang seemed loose, pale and flabby. Like Kung's, his face was laced with even more fine wrinkles, making him look well past middle aged. His half closed eyes were gummy and had lost their bright green sparkle.

Llewelyn showed him his water skin, and the captain stared at it for a few seconds before pointing him to a butt next to the cockpit.

As he filled up the skin, Llewelyn wondered what was going on. He'd had seen grown-ups acting like this before, but when? Then it hit him and he laughed to himself.

They've been on the ale all night! They've all got hangovers!

He returned to the hold to tend to Gelert. Kung was now

curled up in a sweaty ball, groaning at the bottom of the dog's bed. Old, weak and injured as he was, Gelert seemed more robust than the crumpled man. Kung looked so thin his skin appeared draped over his bones, his features sucked back onto a barely fleshed skull.

Llewelyn rolled his eyes. *Serves you right!*

Gelert turned his head back to sniff at Kung lying at his tail, and looked up at Llewelyn, whimpering with concern.

"No sympathy for them, mate. It's their own fault," he said, pouring water into his cupped hand. Gelert snuffled, wagged his tail and slurped thirstily.

Then the old dog's eyes turned back on themselves, showing bloody white, and he whimpered and shuddered in pain.

What's up, mate?

Gelert yowled weakly, trembled again, lifted his tail, then farted long and loud. But this time he followed through with a jet of thin brown diarrhoea. The reeking, steaming torrent spurted out over Kung, spraying deep and hard into the curled bowl of his chest, lap and thighs. Kung moaned, stirred and lifted his head to look up. Racked with more spasms, Gelert tried to alter his position and sprayed another filthy mess straight into Kung's face. Llewelyn did his best to pull the old dog away, but he was too heavy and his convulsions continued.

Kung was now covered from head to toe in steaming wolfhound shoppy water.

"Great!" groaned Llewelyn, and set about tentatively pulling off Kung's filthy clothes. The inner folds of his tunic suddenly writhed, and Llewelyn jumped, but it was only Kung's lice dog tunnelling its way out. The little animal tumbled slimily onto the deck, covered with filth and snuffling in disgust.

Gelert stared at it, bewitched, and sniffed its bum, knocking it over.

"Gerroff!" said Llewelyn, picking up the squirming lice dog. He doused it from his water skin until it was clean and pink.

Then he turned back to Kung, who lay moaning quietly, bubbles of diarrhoea popping from his mouth.

"Now for the big jobbie," Llewelyn sighed.

Llewelyn climbed back on deck with his bucket of slops and Kung's stinking rags.

The mist was clearing, the sun now shining through, but the deck was a desolate scene. The crew lay prostrate, slumped in odd corners and draped over hatches like scattered bundles of rags and bones.

Only the captain moved. Llewelyn watched him pry himself up from the cockpit, cross the deck and hobble down the ladder to his quarters, a dry, doddering husk.

Looking for more beer I'll bet, thought Llewelyn. He remembered Owain's theory about the best way to get rid of a hangover was to chase it off with more ale. He called it 'the hair of the dog that bit you'. Llewelyn looked around the wrecked crewmen. *Must have been a bloody big dog!*

As if on cue, there was the sound of a huge dog barking. Three barks so loud, they made him jump. He looked around. No, it wasn't Gelert. The noise had come from below, from the captain's cabin.

There's another dog on board. It sounds even bigger than Gelert!

But then the barking stopped and the stench of Kung's clothes invaded Llewelyn's nostrils, reminding him he had work to do. He threw the filthy slops overboard, brought up some clean seawater and began rinsing Kung's clothes. Eventually, the water in the bucket remained clear and there was only a hint of putrid smell.

Turning from the railings, Llewelyn stopped. While he'd been working, the crew had dragged themselves from where they'd fallen and were now congregating silently around the hatchway to the captain's cabin.

There was the giant sailor, towering over the others but shockingly stooped. The tiny twins clung to each other, shivering. Llewelyn counted up the rest of the crew. There were just twenty-three men.

Then he heard a groan. Kung was climbing up from Gelert's hold. Naked and still filthy, he fell, struggled to his feet and hobbled into place with the others.

No-one took any notice of him. Instead, they swayed with the pitch of the ship, shivering, gazing yearningly down into the hold, waiting.

Chang reappeared, looking even more withered, and heaved a large blubbery black bag over the coaming. It was a pigskin, stitched and waxed at the ends of the legs and stoppered at the neck. It wobbled, half full of liquid.

At the sight of it, the crewmen moaned weakly.

What a bunch of drunks!

The captain stood, lifted the skin and unstoppered it. As he did, the crew leaned towards him, desperate but patient, gazing unblinkingly as he carefully poured a few drops of the liquid into a thimble-sized cup, which he raised to his lips.

Llewelyn could almost hear Chang's neck joints creaking as he tilted back his head and sipped the precious fluid.

The crew groaned louder, visibly shivering with collective anticipation.

The captain began to unfold, straightening up and filling out like a dried sponge soaking up water. Within seconds, he stood tall and strong again, drawing deep breaths, his green eyes flashing brightly. His leathery face glowed and he shivered with profound pleasure.

He quickly began dispensing the liquid to the rest of the crew. One by one, each sailor drained his ration from the tiny cup and underwent the same miraculous transformation. As they shook themselves back to freshness, they smiled and stretched and strutted, slapping their chests gleefully. They were like bandy hares in March, gambolling in their renewed energy.

Kung was the last to drink. He stood dazed and shockingly skeletal in his slimy nakedness, cloaked in the stench of dog diarrhoea. Finally noticing him, the others went quiet and edged away.

The captain steeled himself, nearly retching as he helped Kung drink, and stepped away as he twitched and shivered back to life.

As he revived, Kung expelled a deep, grateful sigh. He hugged himself and rubbed his arms joyously, and was suddenly repulsed to find himself naked, foul and stinking.

"Here, I'll help!" yelled Llewelyn, pulling up another bucket of seawater. He ran over and sloshed the dregs of diarrhoea off Kung. "And here are your things," he added, holding out his damp clothes.

Meanwhile, the captain had carefully re-stoppered the skin. He'd watched Llewelyn help Kung, and gave him a long, measured look. Then he nodded at him, an almost imperceptible bow of respect.

The crew were more appreciative, smiling at Llewelyn and lining up to praise him. The twins gave him such a playful double slap on the back he was knocked down. The giant sailor set him back on his feet and scolded the twins, who just laughed, then jumped into the ship's rigging squirrel-like and disappeared behind a sail.

When everyone had finally dispersed, Llewelyn found himself alone with Kung. The old man bowed solemnly, then spoke awkwardly. Llewelyn realised he was being thanked.

Why all the fuss?, he thought. *It was only a bit of dog cack.*

But inside he felt good. Happy, even.

The realisation jolted him. He should be fighting with everyone, complaining that he'd been kidnapped and demanding he be freed. He should be burning with a fierce desire to escape. He shouldn't be cleaning his captors' decks and washing away their shit. But here he was, after just two days, beginning to feel almost at home and even appreciated.

Very odd.

🐉

As the next few days drifted towards their first week at sea, the junk continued to drive southward through the armour-grey waters.

Llewelyn began to notice the rhythms of the ship.

First thing each morning and throughout the day, the captain would check with the lookout, always with a view to stern.

Maybe he's looking to see if the rest of the Chinese fleet are catching up, thought Llewelyn. He found himself hoping he'd see the sail that would mean his father had come to take him home.

Meanwhile, life on board went on.

When it was time to eat, a small round man, the cook, strolled happily around the ship handing out warm parcels of food.

It was more of the moist white grains and spicy pieces of meat, but the fist-sized packets were wrapped in translucent sheets of what felt like very thin parchment. Llewelyn wondered what to do with it when he'd finished eating, and was surprised to see the crewmen rolling it up and scoffing it down. He nibbled on a corner experimentally; it dissolved in his mouth, tasting like the white grains. Greedily he tore the sheet into shreds and finished it all off.

Saves on washing up dishes I suppose.

The fat cook laughed at him as he did this, but in a kindly encouraging way. The little man was a crew favourite, not just because he brought everyone their food, but because he took the time to chat and share jokes.

Sailing the ship could hardly be called hard work. The wind was constant and the sea unchallenging. Aside from maintaining the rigging and swabbing the decks, there wasn't very much to do and the captain didn't seem to mind that his sailors were having an easy time of it. Mostly they spent most of the day just mooching around.

But everyone took turns at watch. Chang relieved the man at the masthead every half hour, and whoever was up there took their task very seriously.

The only sailor exempted from this was the old helmsman, who rarely left his cockpit. Regardless of the weather or the hour of day or night, he sat, glued to his bench. The only time Llewelyn saw him leave his tiller was in the early evening when he did slow stretching exercises. He was remarkably supple for his advanced years, easily able to put one ankle behind his head while standing tiptoe on the other foot. Llewelyn tried it and fell flat on his face.

Gelert remained unconscious, but his breathing was coming easier, and his twitching fever was gradually subsiding. Each morning, Kung descended into the hold, staying throughout the day, business-like, but fussing diligently over the old dog.

Sometimes the captain would stand over the hatchway, and he and Kung would talk. Before leaving, Chang would nod at Llewelyn.

When Kung was looking after Gelert, Llewelyn could hang around on deck. He didn't draw attention to himself, and even though the sailors now smiled at him, he still couldn't talk with anyone, and he felt almost invisible.

❧

One afternoon, standing at the aft rail watching the thin gurgling wake of the junk, Llewelyn realised he'd seen no seagulls for many days.

We must be far out to sea, he thought. But then they sailed into a flock of thrush-sized, snow-white birds with black heads and crimson beaks. They were terns, diving for sprats and turning the ocean foaming white. Disturbed by the junk, the flock exploded into the sky, wheeled around and drifted north like smoke on the water. Llewelyn wondered if the next land they'd see would be Wales. If it was, it would have been a long flight for them; his father's castle was many hundreds of miles behind by now.

The thought quietened Llewelyn. How quickly he'd grown used to being stuck on this ship. The idea of sailing through the night and never seeing land now felt natural to him. With a start, he also realised he hadn't thought about escape for a few days.

No-one would know it if I jumped overboard, he thought before immediately dismissing the idea. So far from land, he'd be shark food within minutes.

Lulled by the rhythm of the waves, his mind began to wander and he allowed a few more thoughts of escape to stroll around in his head. But until he reached a port, he knew they were stupid daydreams. Besides, his father would be looking for him, wouldn't he?

🐾

One day, Llewelyn saw the hatchway at the waist of the junk was open. It was the one the captain had used when he went to fetch the skin of hangover cure.

It was also the one that housed the huge dog.

I can't go down there! But his curiosity telling him that he must, he looked surreptitiously around the deck. Captain Chang was forward, talking to the giant sailor, when a sudden squall strained the sails and snapped a halyard. The mainsail flapped madly while the two men grabbed for the loose end of the rope. *Now's my chance.*

In a flash, Llewelyn was over the hatchway's coaming and down the ladder, standing in front of a closed door. His heart was pounding. *It's got to be the captain's cabin!* he thought with a thrill. *Only one way to find out!* He edged towards it, propelled by nervous curiosity. *I mustn't!* But he couldn't resist the compulsion to see what was beyond.

As he reached out to try the door, a low growling came from within.

It was the huge dog.

The growling grew louder – a malevolent, primeval sound that chilled Llewelyn's guts. He backed off slowly, turned quietly, then clambered up the ladder so fast that he launched himself out of the hatchway and landed running on the deck, his arms wind-milling and legs thoroughly out of control. He pitched up falling into the cockpit next to the old helmsman who saw his terrified expression and laughed, then suddenly woofed loudly at him.

Llewelyn flinched. *You mean old bugger!* But he knew the helmsman had seen what he'd been up to. He gave the old man his most imploring look. *Please, please, please don't tell the captain!*

Still laughing, the helmsman waved him off and Llewelyn scuttled back to Gelert and the safety of his hold. As he plonked himself down next to his friend his face was flushed, and his heart still pounded in his chest.

"You've got competition, mate!" he gasped. "There's a monster dog on board that'd have you for dinner!"

Kung was tending Gelert and regarded Llewelyn's agitation with mild suspicion. Llewelyn tried to act nonchalant, but inside he vowed never, ever, to go down that hatchway again.

❦

More days passed.

By now, Llewelyn had grown accustomed to life aboard the junk, but every morning he still looked to the horizon for signs his father was coming to rescue him.

He'd better get a move on though, he thought. The longer it took, the longer it would take to go home. He shrugged to himself. There was nothing he could do about it so he might as well enjoy the sailing.

It was a happy ship. Everyone knew their job and just got on with it, unlike on his father's ships where there'd have been fighting and flogging on a daily basis. These green-eyed Chinese sailors were bound by a common sense of purpose.

Captain Chang rarely smiled, but he was fair; discipline didn't come from his fists.

But one evening, as the sun began to set, Llewelyn noticed the crew becoming withdrawn, and watched as one by one they went below deck. Soon, only the captain and the old helmsman remained, slumped on either side of the tiller. They too looked listless and exhausted.

Here we go again, thought Llewelyn, *they're off on another drinking session.*

He headed for the safety of his hold. If the crew were going to send themselves into oblivion, he didn't want to be around. As he climbed down the ladder, Kung too was irascible and spiteful, pushing grumpily past Llewelyn on his way up.

Llewelyn and Gelert were left alone for the night.

🐉

The next morning, Kung didn't arrive at his normal time.

Suspecting the worst, Llewelyn went to discover what was going on.

The crew, once again, were all mortally hung-over and fit for nothing.

They were mostly asleep, some slumped about, others stooped and groaning like the walking dead. The equally shabby-looking captain climbed wearily on deck, holding his bloated black pigskin in one hand and his little cup in the other. The sailors stirred, got up and closed their shuffling circle around him.

Llewelyn rolled his eyes. *Idiots,* he thought as they revived.

He climbed back down into the hold and smiled.

Gelert was gamely trying to stand up straight, but flobbed around with the pitch and sway of the boat, like a newborn fawn, skittering awkwardly from one side of the hold to the other.

But he was up on his feet, and Llewelyn knew the worst was over. He fell in front of the old dog and held him tightly to his shoulder. Gelert was thin, like a leather bag filled with brittle branches, but his muscles were hard and alive.

Llewelyn was overcome by a surge of relief.

"Thank God you're back, boy!" he choked, sniffing back small tears between his laughs.

Kung appeared in the hatchway. The sight of Gelert on his feet made him yelp with joy and shout out. An answering cheer went up from the crew, and their bare feet drummed across the deck.

Gelert was stiff and shaky but eager to leave the hold, so Llewelyn led him to the bottom of the ladder and, together with Kung, helped him clamber up. The old dog was greeted by more happy cries from the crowd around the hatchway.

Llewelyn was taken aback by the intensity of their adoration of Gelert. Even the captain was cheering, and patted Kung on the back as the dog wobbled around, licking outstretched hands. He stood on his hind legs to give Llewelyn a slobbery lick and a chorus of "Aaaaahs!" erupted.

Chang shushed everyone. He intoned solemnly, raising his eyes to the sky. The men murmured a reply in unison.

Llewelyn couldn't believe it. *Now they're praying!*

The captain's voice grew louder as he spread his arms wide, smiling broadly. Llewelyn heard the word for dog repeated several times, and the crew cheered again and again with a fierce passion. He felt their spirit come alive, and when the captain barked out orders, his sailors flew to obey him. Within minutes, the junk surged harder into the oncoming waves, its rigging tighter, its sails catching more of the wind. Clouds of spray exploded from the scything bows, casting rainbows along the length of the boat, as if joy had infected the ship itself.

Gelert was better. Llewelyn was elated. This journey was taking them somewhere at last.

But it wasn't to Wales and, strangely, that didn't feel so bad.

Sunsets set, nights dreamed by and dawns quickly came and went.

By Llewelyn's reckoning, it had been ten nights and nine days since they'd seen land, and with each day the sun grew brighter. The sky was now an intense and unfamiliar cobalt. As they sailed ever southward, the air grew hotter and the following wind was like the hot blast from the forge in Owain's armoury.

Gelert quickly became a daily feature of everyone's life. None of the crew seemed to mind that he peed on every available surface, and his wolfhound-sized turds became a ship-wide subject of discussion. The largest of them were greeted with cries of admiration before being playfully flipped overboard.

No matter how carefully Llewelyn watched him, the old dog stole food at every chance – but then, he did have a lot of eating to catch up on.

When he wasn't eating, Gelert took to sprawling in whatever shade he could find, lying panting, farting, and generally getting underfoot.

Meanwhile, Llewelyn began to pick up the odd word of Chinese here and there: 'front', 'back', 'up', 'down', 'go', 'look'; simple building blocks of an increasingly less jarring way of speaking.

🐾

The sun was getting hotter. Llewelyn gradually shed his layers of coarse damp clothing and by the ninth day he was bare-chested and couldn't be bothered with his heavy boots. He bundled everything up and set it all to one side.

It was like closing another tiny door to his past. As each day grew warmer, his skin turned a shade darker, a rare occurrence back in cold, grey Wales.

Gelert was feeling the heat too. Even in the shade he was uncomfortably hot, his long tongue lolling like a steaming slab of liver.

With a pair of shears, Llewelyn began clipping his shaggy coat. It was tough going. The blades were blunt, Gelert was big, and his fur was wiry. Soon the deck was carpeted with coarsely chopped dog hair. The two dwarf sailors watched him as he worked. When a gust of wind wafted the pile into the air, they ran laughing through the grey cloud. One of them shaped a handful of fur and threw it at the helmsman like a snowball. The old man coughed and spluttered, cursing the two sailors. The rest of the crew joined in the fun and before long everyone was covered in grey blond fur.

The captain came up on deck, annoyed by the commotion. But when he saw what was going on, he almost smiled. Gelert rose and shook himself, releasing even more clippings and for a few seconds the junk shimmered in a hairy fog until a stiffer breeze carried it all away.

The men resumed their work, their spirits lifted by the brief diversion. Gelert, too, appeared fresher and happier.

His work complete, Llewelyn wiped the fur-crusted sweat from his face and back into his hair, which was lank and thick with dirt.

Why not? He took the shears and set about cutting his own hair, throwing the thick brown hanks overboard. The more he lost, the better he felt. The breeze cooled his scalp where he'd laid it bare, and it made his whole body shiver deliciously.

He wondered what he looked like, stripped to his waist, his skin tanned and his head shorn. *Not like a Prince of Wales!* Would his father even recognise him when he caught up?

Llewelyn watched the crew going through the lows and the highs of two more bingeing sessions. Or at least he saw the after-effects, never having seen them actually drinking or even drunk.

Each time, it happened overnight, but the next morning, there they were, shuffling into a queue to be revived by an equally dishevelled captain.

Llewelyn was surprised by how quickly he'd grown accustomed to their bleak cycle, but with Gelert back on form, he now had other things to think about.

His old friend continued to grow strong and the crew remained buoyed by his recovery. Kung glowed with self-importance – after all, he was the one who'd brought the wolfhound back from the brink – and the captain seemed happy for once.

I suppose they all want him well for the Emperor.

Whenever Gelert passed, the sailors would stop work and coo words of encouragement. Some, more daring, reached out to touch him, laughing nervously. More than once he saw a man take his lice dog from his tunic and let Gelert sniff and lick it. It was as if they wanted their little dogs to be blessed by the great wolfhound.

🐾

On the evening of the tenth day, the crew begin to go downhill again. One minute they were fine, the next they became bored, listless and clumsy.

The junk was pitching sharply in a choppy swell, and the prow suddenly hit a bigger wave with a jarring crash that shuddered through the boat. A moment later there was a cry and two light thumps. One of the twins had fallen from the rigging, but had landed on top of the giant sailor and bounced harmlessly onto the deck.

The giant, unmoved, stared out to sea. The crewmen nearby turned almost absently to see what had happened but did nothing.

Llewelyn rushed over and helped the dazed twin to his feet. The little man had a lump on his head the size of a pigeon egg and tottered crazily. He clawed at a trailing ratline and tried to climb up it, but only succeeded in twirling around in a dizzy circle before falling down again.

The giant sailor woke from his reverie and reached down to pull him up, but tripped over himself, falling heavily against the ship's railings where he promptly went to sleep.

Captain Chang had been watching. He frowned with lazy concern, and looked up to the rigging, sniffing the wind.

Night was falling. Overhead, the sky was a deep blue black, blending into bands of purple, mauve, and exquisite rose pink that melted into a molten red sea to the west. On the opposite quarter, a bleary full moon, huge and yellow, climbed out of the black horizon.

Still frowning, the captain cupped his hands to his mouth and slurred some commands to the crew. Wearily, they followed his orders and trimmed the sails. The bows dropped and the rush of the water quietened as the junk slowed.

He's worrying a storm might brew up in the night.

Llewelyn knew that out at sea the weather could change quickly, and if everyone was about to embark on another drinking session, the ship would need to be sailed more cautiously.

Thinking about it, he saw a pattern to their drunkenness. Three times in nine days; every three days.

All his life, Llewelyn had been surrounded by hard-drinking men. He remembered wild nights in the castle, before the siege. The King's great feasts would go on for weeks and could drain the surrounding countryside of beer and mead and wine.

It had been fun watching the men become loud-mouthed buffoons, seeing them throw up and bang into walls, but that had been in the confines of a castle, not on a ship bobbing in an empty ocean.

If the weather's going to turn bad, he decided, *I'll stay awake, just in case.*

🦢

By midnight, the junk was deathly quiet. Down in the hold, Llewelyn couldn't hear any rabble rousing; if everyone was getting drunk, they were being discreet about it. He decided to investigate, opened the hatchway and poked his head out.

The junk was sailing calmly over the swell of the rolling, inky sea, wafted by a warm, soft breeze. The sky blazed with infinite stars, great swathes of glittering pinpricks strewn across the cloudless night.

So much for storms.

The deck was bathed in the silver light of the full moon, but the silence was punctuated by deep snoring. The crew lay everywhere, some alone, some in groups, some slumped flat out on gratings. They'd fallen where they'd stood, not even managing to go below.

Piss-heads!

He climbed on deck for a better look. Gelert jumped up after him. He snuffled at the nearest sleeping forms, then trotted to a favourite corner and cocked his leg for a midnight pee. His splashing stream of urine was unnaturally loud in the silence of the boat.

"Shhhh!!!" hissed Llewelyn, not sure why he was trying to

keep quiet. As his eyes grew used to the moonlight a movement caught his eye. The captain and the old helmsman sat either side of the tiller, swaying with the roll of the junk. Llewelyn headed for them, stepping over bodies as he went.

But as he got closer, he saw they were both fast asleep, wedged either side of the tiller. As the junk rose on the ocean swell, the long handle tipped them over. No-one was steering the junk – it was steering them.

"Oye!" Llewelyn yelled at Chang. "Wake up. You've got work to do!"

Llewelyn poked him ineffectively. The captain snored on.

Gelert sniffed the night air, growled and loped to the ship's rails. He stood staring at something out at sea.

"What is it, boy?" said Llewelyn, a vague feeling of dread creeping over him. He joined Gelert at the railings just in time to see the surface of the sea beyond the ship begin to shimmer and change colour. He cried out as a flickering mass of flashing silver boiled up from the depths and exploded through the surface. A cloud of foot-long fish shot into the air and spread their fins into transparent spangled wings.

Within seconds, Llewelyn and Gelert were surrounded by a flock of glittering flying fish.

Laughing, Llewelyn leaned over the railings and reached out to catch one. Miraculously, he succeeded, gripping it behind its wings. The fish squirmed stiffly in his hand, cold and slimy, nothing like holding a bird.

Suddenly, a thick tube of slick grey muscle speared out of the churning water in front of him. It opened a mouth full of pointed white teeth and deftly snatched the fish from his grasp. Llewelyn gasped in shock. It looked as if as the dolphin was smiling at him as it splashed back into the sea.

Then there were dozens of dolphins leaping effortlessly from the sea, gorging on the airborne shoal of fish, which flew ever higher and more waywardly as they tried to escape.

More and more fell onto the junk like an impossible hailstorm of dozens, then hundreds of fish. They fell heavily, forcing Llewelyn to raise his arms above his head to shield his face.

Curiously, Gelert ignored the bedlam. Even when a fish slapped into his face, he continued staring silently into the night.

That's not good! thought Llewelyn. *What's out there that's more interesting than all these fish?* He squinted but could see nothing through the maelstrom of flying fish and leaping dolphins.

By now, the deck was covered in thousands of flapping silver bodies, slowly smothering the sleeping crew. Still more came thudding down. Hundreds of dolphins had joined in the hunt, driving more fish out of the sea and onto the boat. Llewelyn had to jump onto the railings next to Gelert or risk being swamped.

Oblivious, the old dog simply climbed higher onto the growing pile, still staring into the night.

What had started exciting quickly grew tedious, then repulsive. The thick layer of slimy writhing fish turned bloody red, mixed with the scales, entrails and broken flesh gashed open by the dolphins' snapping jaws. A heavy, fishy stench rose in the air.

Now, so many fish had landed in the growing mess that the comatose crew were hidden beneath the thick, foul-smelling blanket of silvery bodies. The captain and helmsmen were indistinct mounds sitting in the shallow depression of the fish-filled cockpit.

Still Gelert stood silently at the railings.

Then, just as suddenly as they had come, the vast shoal and the leaping squadrons of dolphins vanished. The wet percussion of falling fish and splashing dolphins faded away to nothing.

Llewelyn was exhausted. He heard Gelert whimper once.

"What's going on out there, you dumb dog?"

The sea once again became glassy black, the bright full moon's reflection oscillating languidly on the gentle swell. The junk glided silently on, trailing an oily slick of fish scales.

Gelert's whimper turned into a concerned growl. Llewelyn scanned the eastern horizon but saw nothing. Exasperated by his old friend's inexplicable behaviour, he was about to tell him to shut up when a shift in the blackness caught his eye.

A row of lights in the distance winked like fireflies, dipping in and out of view with the gentle pitch and roll of the ship.

"So there is something out there!" he whispered to Gelert, who looked back at him and woofed lightly, finally vindicated.

Llewelyn clambered over the dying fish and climbed up the rope ladder to the crosspiece of the mainsail. He stared through the inky darkness at the string of twinkling lights, which had grown in numbers and become brighter as the junk crept towards them.

They must be ships. Ships at anchor.

He scrambled down and stood on the railing, breathing hard, overtaken by a mixture of fear and exhilaration. Whose ships might they be? Traders? Friends? Enemies? If they were at anchor, land would surely be close by.

With no-one steering the junk, they could run aground.

The old dog was still growling, now more menacingly.

"Shut up, Gelert!" *Think. Think. Think!* Whoever these mystery lights belonged to, Llewelyn couldn't face them by himself; he must rouse the captain. He jumped down to the deck, slipped in the slimy fish and whacked his head on a bulkhead. Swearing in Welsh, Latin, Greek and French, he got up and squelched and stumbled his way to the cockpit where Chang sat beneath his mound of fish.

Frantically Llewelyn shoved the pile of stiff wet bodies aside. Spiny fins jagged his hands, and he gagged as burst swim bladders and guts sprayed him. Slowly he uncovered the captain's head and shoulders.

"Wake up!" Llewelyn yelled ear as he poked and shook Chang.

The captain moaned a couple of times, but wouldn't stir. Llewelyn glanced up. The lights were now visible from the deck and already they were much closer.

"Come on, come on!" he urged, daring to tap the man's face.

Nothing happened. His tentative taps became firm slaps. Still nothing. Suddenly Llewellyn was scared. He sat back, sweating.

Gelert was now growling intensely at the nearing lights.

"Will you please SHUT UP!"

He could now make out upright masts and crosspieces. The lights were definitely on ships, and they were now less than a mile away.

Llewelyn picked up one of the biggest flying fish by the tail. It was still clinging on to life and thrashed feebly in his grip. Taking aim, he swung it back, then walloped the captain hard across the face.

Chang spluttered awake. He croaked in Chinese, stumbling to stand, discombobulated. A cascade of fish slithered off him. He babbled, doubly confused by the slimy mess around him.

Llewelyn tried to shush him, but the captain continued shouting incoherently until he saw the lights in the distance and froze, silenced at last. Gelert now began to bark. The closer they came to the mysterious ships, the angrier he became. The captain swayed and put a finger to his lips.

"Shhhhh!"

But Gelert ignored him.

"SHSHUSH!" hissed Chang desperately. Still groggy and staggering, he reached deep into his tunic pocket and triumphantly pulled out his lice dog. He stared at the little animal, confused for a moment, then stuffed it back in his pocket, retrieving instead a small earthenware bottle.

He wants a drink at a time like this?

The captain fumbled unsuccessfully with the bottle's stopper.

"Give it here," growled Llewelyn, snatching the bottle and opening it. He thrust it back at Chang who took a single, small swig. Instantly, he was lucid and alert, his green eyes flashing.

He babbled something in Chinese, staring at the lights.

"I didn't know what to do!" said Llewelyn.

The captain rapidly took stock of the situation. By now, it was clear they were heading into a convoy of about two dozen boats, all dimly lit by glowing lamps at their topmasts, sterns and prows. Their shapes were indistinct, but their sails were furled.

By now Gelert's barking was uncontrollable. Llewelyn tried to calm him, but the old hound was having none of it.

Then a thin voice called out.

"I say! Yonder! What ship is that? Why are you sailing in the middle of the night?"

Gelert stopped barking, and Llewelyn froze.

"They're bloody English!" he whispered.

"Tamaul Shiu English!" hissed the captain.

Gelert started barking again.

As the junk drew closer, the convoy revealed itself as a full squadron of English men-of-war, menacingly large compared to the junk. Torches were being lit, and Llewelyn could see throngs of sleepy sailors and soldiers coming to the rails.

"I say again!" called the voice, "In the name of His Majesty King Edward, what ship is that? And, can't you silence your dog, old chap?"

Llewelyn felt his gorge rising. That aloof Englishness, so pompous, so arrogant, and so despised. Just the sound of it made his heart grow cold and his blood curdle. But he also felt fear. *They mustn't find me!* If the King of England were to capture the Prince of Wales, he'd have his father over a barrel. The ransom would be unimaginable.

Then Captain Chang cupped his hands to his mouth.

"Ahoy!" he cried, "Thank God you're here! We're just a fishing boat! English! We're lost!"

Llewelyn stared up at the captain, impressed by his quick thinking. *That's a good idea,* he thought, *they'll have been able to smell all these fish from miles away.* Then he went wide-eyed with surprise; the captain had spoken in perfect, unaccented English.

Stunned, he could hardly believe his ears.

He remembered to blink.

Meanwhile, the Englishman replied. He sounded suspicious.

"I'll say you're lost, old chap! What's an English fishing boat doing so far south?"

"We were caught in a storm," replied the captain, who turned to Llewelyn. "Can you speak English?" he whispered urgently, busily untying the ropes holding the tiller in place.

"Of course I bloody can," Llewelyn spluttered, "but YOU!

You speak English?"

"Strange," shouted the English voice. "I don't recall any bad weather recently, and you haven't explained why you're out and about in the dark."

Chang put Llewelyn's hands on the tiller and pointed at the line of English ships, which was now less than five hundred yards away.

"Head for that gap between the fifth and six ships," he whispered.

"What? I can't steer a ship!" snapped Llewelyn, thoroughly confused and slightly panicked. He fumbled with the tiller. It pushed against his hands and he had to force it over to keep his course straight.

But the captain had already gone forward to the hatchway above his cabin and was scooping aside the piles of fish so he could open it.

"Just keep that Englishman occupied. I'll be back in a moment!" he called back quietly before disappearing below.

Ahead, a patch of blackness showed the gap between two of the English ships. If they made it through, even if the English could up anchor and set sail straight away, they'd be lost in the night before their enemy could give chase.

There was a bustle of activity on the nearest ships.

"Your sails, old chap," continued the Englishman, "They're rather queer looking."

Llewelyn knew the slatted Chinese sails were like nothing this Englishman had ever seen.

"Ah yes!" he shouted back. "You see, we lost our sails in the storm and had to fix up new ones. This was the best we could do."

"I see," said the Englishman, dryly. "…You there, new chappie, you sound a touch 'Welsh' to me."

Bloody hell! Forgot about my accent!

"I tell you what, be a good sort, won't you," came the voice with forced politeness. "Haul in your sails and draw alongside and we can see how we help you out."

There was a brief loud barking from below. It was the dog in the captain's cabin.

"How many of those bloody animals do you have over there?"

whined the Englishman. "All this racket really is a tad annoying."

The other dog stopped, but Gelert continued his barrage; the closer they got to the English flotilla, the more frenzied he became.

They were a mere three hundred yards away by the time Captain Chang reappeared above the hatchway, manhandling a hefty red tube onto the deck. It was stout and pointed at one end, about five feet long and half that in width, with a six-foot stave protruding from the blunt end.

Gelert took one look at the squat fire arrow and went silent. Now the only sound was the gurgling of water past the junk's bows.

"Thank heavens for that," sighed the Englishman.

The English ships were now within two hundred yards. The captain lugged the fire arrow over to the cockpit, calling to the Englishman as he slipped and slid through the morass of fish.

"I say, old chap, have you ever seen a huojian?" As he spoke, he was fixing the stick of the red tube into a bracket on the railings.

Huojian thought Llewelyn. *So* that's *what they're called.*

"Sorry, old chap, can't say I have,' came the impatient reply, "Now, be a brick, won't you, and heave to."

The bright moonlight picked out details of the English men-of-war, now just a hundred yards away. Llewelyn concentrated furiously on keeping the junk on course, leaning his whole body onto the tiller, which fought back against him like a stubborn carthorse. The gap seemed to shrink the closer they got to it.

The captain adjusted the huojian, aiming it towards the voice.

"Can't do that I'm afraid, old chap," he replied, almost casually. "We're in a bit of a hurry. Got an important person on board – His Royal Highness the Prince of Wales."

Llewelyn nearly let go of the tiller.

"Why'd you tell him that?" he gasped.

At first, the Englishman sounded confused.

"Come again, old chap? What's all that about the Prince of Wales?" He quickly grew serious. "Haul in your sails at once."

Llewelyn could finally make out the face belonging to the voice. A lanky galoot with long fair hair, he stood at the railings of the nearest ship, busily buckling on his breastplate. A squire stood by with his helmet and sword. On either side, archers, at least fifty of them, jostled for position on the railings knocking up their arrows. Soldiers and archers lined the decks of the other English boats.

Llewelyn gulped. "Oh bugger!" *We're well within longbow range.*

Chang smiled. "They're bluffing. They won't fire on us now they know there's a Prince of bloody Wales on board." He struck a flint, and sparks leapt onto the fuse of the huojian.

"But they'll try to stop us now, for sure!" hissed Llewelyn, "I can't be captured by the English!"

The captain raised an eyebrow. "More to the point, we can't let them capture Gelert."

Llewelyn harrumphed, but Chang was smiling, "We'll be fine. Just hold your course, and when I give the word, do as I say."

The fuse ignited, sputtering and hissing loudly.

Terrified, Gelert skittered off for the hatchway to his hold, his tail between his legs.

"What's that fire thingy you have there?" called the fair Englishman.

Ignoring his question, the captain jumped into the cockpit beside Llewelyn and grabbed the tiller.

"The instant the huojian takes off, cover your ears, put your head between your knees and shut your eyes tight," he commanded quietly as a great gout of rushing flames erupted from the huojian. It began to roar and tremble. "Whatever you do, breathe normally. Don't close your mouth and DON'T hold your breath. Got it?"

"Got it," nodded Llewelyn, and at that moment the huojian launched.

"OOOOOOOOOOOOH!"

The throng of Englishmen standing at the railings watched it rise, gawping at the spectacle. Captain Chang wedged the tiller under his armpit, clasped his hands to his ears, and screwed his eyes closed. Llewelyn followed suit, crouching low and squeezing his eyes shut.

An instant later, the darkness fused into a blazing light, brighter than day. An almighty crack ripped the air apart, its thumping shockwave knocking Llewelyn face-first and winded into the mat of fish. The sound of Gelert's fearful howling was replaced by a piercing ringing in Llewelyn's ears. Echoes of the great bang assaulted him, and an awful light blared from above. Even with his eyes closed and his head stuck in a pile of entrails, his eyeballs ached with the intensity of the burning light. He sat up, hands now clamped to his firmly closed eyelids, but he could see his finger bones silhouetted against the red glare.

The light dimmed and the reverberations of the explosion faded. Through the ringing in his ears he heard the piteous wailing of a thousand voices keening in pain. From below deck came the muffled yapping of the lice dogs, Gelert's howls, and from inside the captain's quarters, the thunderous barks of the mysterious monster dog.

Cautiously, Llewelyn opened his eyes a slit.

The scalding blue light was slowly dropping from the sky, bathing the junk in its searing rays and casting flickering black shadows as it descended. The light was still too bright for his eyes to bear. He clapped his hand to his forehead like a visor, shielding the view.

Chang sat squinting at the tiller, his arms cloaking his head.

"Don't look at the fireball. It'll blind you until it hits the sea," he yelled as he guided the junk through the gap in the English fleet.

In a daze, Llewelyn gazed around the deck. The swathes of dead fish were now entirely mangled, every swim bladder ruptured and splattered about by the pulverizing explosion, the pulped bodies glistened silver in the awful flickering light. The stench of fish guts swamped his lungs and he felt a surge of nausea. Gagging, he stumbled through the gory slime to the junk's railings to throw up.

A few feet away the English fleet lay in chaos. Everywhere, men shrieked in agony, hands clamped to their eyes, blood coursing down their faces and streaming from their ears. A few lay still, steaming lumps of shredded flesh. The force of the cataclysmic fireball had burst their chests and blown their bloody lungs up through their throats.

Llewelyn recognised the remains of the fair-haired English officer. He must have been directly beneath the huojian when it went off, because he looked like he'd been crushed by a gigantic war hammer. His head was jammed down into his shoulders and his chest crunched into his midriff. His legs splayed at impossible angles, and all around him lay the glistening coils of his bowels, blasted from his rectum.

Llewelyn puked a long trail of vomit overboard, and he heaved and heaved until there was nothing left to bring up.

Shaking and wiping his mouth with the back of his hand, he chanced a glance at the English ships' rigging. The canvas of the boats closest to the explosion hung in shredded tatters. *They won't be going anywhere for a while.* Automatically, he checked the junk. Its sturdy sails had held fast, saved by the rigid fish-fin slats.

The junk came out the far side of the ruined flotilla as the descending fireball finally plunged into the sea with a roaring hiss of steam. The terrible aftermath of the huojian was snuffed from sight, replaced by an intense blackness.

Llewelyn panicked; he opened his eyes wide but could see nothing. It was as though his eyeballs had been pulled out, stamped into uselessness and squeezed back into their sockets.

"I can't see!" he cried, arms flailing.

"Wait," said Captain Chang calmly. "It's just night blindness."

Sure enough, Llewelyn found his sight returning and he looked back, guided by the fading cries of the stricken men. He began to see shapes forming in the darkness. The moonlight illuminated the shattered English fleet lying drably on the glistening black sea.

So much damage from a single five-foot by three tube.

Huojian. That's one scary weapon.

It was as if the captain had read his mind. "The Chinese call them 'The Angry Voice of a Thousand Suns'," he said grimly, his silhouette slowly revealing itself. "No wonder they've conquered half the world."

Silence.

Llewelyn scanned the horizon. In the distance, a slab of black sliced across the starry sky and the moonlit sea. He heard waves breaking, and glimpsed a flickering sliver of pale grey in the blackness.

"Land," announced Chang, putting the boat about. The junk's rigging creaked and the sail flapped as it heeled over.

"Here, take the tiller while I adjust the mainsail. Head straight for the moon."

Llewelyn wrestled the force of the rudder as the junk completed its turn. The moon made a white road to steer along as they sailed parallel to the dark shoreline. Returning to the cockpit, captain Chang took charge.

A thousand questions formed in Llewelyn's mind, but then Gelert came scrabbling to climb on deck. The old wolfhound looked sheepish as he squelched over to the cockpit where he sniffed the air and eyed the bracket from where the huojian had been fired.

Llewelyn took his huge shaggy head in his hands.

"You big coward!" he scolded mildly while he checked his old friend over. Gelert's eyes were clear and there was no blood in his ears, but he shook his head and whimpered.

"Don't worry about him," said the captain, "His ears will be ringing for a while but he was below; he missed the worst of it."

"What about the crew? They were on deck!"

"Yes, but they were lying under three feet of dead fish."

Just then, one of the tiny lice dogs squirmed up from beneath the fish, covered in bits of entrails. Llewelyn picked it up.

"Poor little man," he cooed, wiping its tiny muzzle as it sat shivering in his palm. "But you'll survive."

Gelert licked the lice dog and Captain Chang chuckled. "By the way, boy, how did you manage to get all these fish on board?"

Llewelyn was stung. Suddenly, ten days of anger, confusion and resentment poured out.

"I'm not a 'boy'. I'm Llewelyn!" he shouted, standing up. "I'm a Prince of bloody Wales! You kidnapped me! And you nearly killed Gelert! And I'm stuck on this bloody boat not understanding a bloody word anyone's saying, and all the while, you can speak bloody English!"

Gelert growled at the captain, tuning into Llewelyn's mood.

"How could I know you speak English?" retorted Chang. "All I've ever heard you speak is – what's it called? 'Weltch'?"

"Welsh! I'm from Wales," shot back Llewelyn, calming down a little as grudging curiosity took over, "And how come you know English?"

"What can I say?" shrugged the captain. "We sail, we trade, we pick up the languages of the people we trade with. Never traded with Way-Yells."

"Wales!"

"Sorry. Wales."

Llewelyn felt deflated and weary. Maybe it was the come-down after the horrors of the huojian. There was an odd silence. It was strange, knowing they could now understand each other but neither knowing what to say next. The blackness of the night seemed to suck conversation from the air. The junk sailed on for a few minutes and the last living fish flipped and flopped then died.

The captain spoke first. "You did a good job back there, Llewelyn Prince of bloody Wales. Without you, our mission would be over."

He hesitated, as if struggling to form his next sentence. "You know, we didn't mean to take you," he said, almost apologetically. "You were never part of our plans, but we couldn't wait. We had to get away."

Llewelyn wanted to be furious, but the Chang's sincerity tempered his anger.

"Couldn't he have waited just a few more days?" he muttered.

"Who?" said the captain, nonplussed.

"Your Emperor. He must be very impatient."

"Oh yes. No. No. It doesn't do to keep the Emperor of China waiting," he laughed, "But he wasn't to know, *we* weren't to know, that Gelert wouldn't come quietly. Not without you."

The captain stroked Gelert, then turned back to Llewelyn.

"It was wrong to take you. Llewelyn, Prince of bloody Wales, but I promise you that as soon as we reach the Holy Land, we'll find someone who can take you home."

Llewelyn reeled.

"We're going to the Holy Land?" he said reverentially.

"Not exactly 'to', more like passing through."

"B– but the Holy Land?" he blurted, "I get to see the birthplace of Our Lord, and where he died and was resurrected?"

"If you believe those tales, yes," shrugged the captain. "More realistically, your Crusader armies hold Jaffa, which is where we're headed, so there'll be plenty of ships you can …"

Llewelyn wasn't listening. The thought of seeing the Holy Land had transfixed him. Making a pilgrimage to Jerusalem was the life-long dream of all good Christians.

The Captain hadn't finished, "… you could be home in a couple of months."

Home, with a pilgrimage under my belt. That'll impress father!

Chang interrupted his reverie. "It's late, you need to get some rest, and you stink of fish. Clean Gelert and yourself and go to bed. We'll deal with this mess tomorrow."

Gelert pawed Llewelyn awake, keen for his morning piss.

It was late; from the angle of the shafts of light that filtered through the gratings above, he could tell it was mid-morning. Feeling rested and grateful for the sleep in, he threw open the hatch.

Although the stink of fish was heavy in the air, there were hardly any dead fish on deck. The crew, still insensible, lay clumped about. They appeared oddly shiny, like statues made of pale-blue shells thanks to the dried film of mucus and fish scales covering them.

Llewelyn extended his gaze beyond the deck. Last night they'd been close to a shore. Now, there wasn't much to see, just a smudge of brown, so flat and so dull it took a while for him to recognise it as land. But the passing sea was flecked with scraps of seaweed and a pair of seagulls squawked above.

Swish, swish! The captain was in the bows, stripped to the waist and dripping with sweat as he brushed a pile of fish paste through the leeward scuppers. In the cockpit, the tiller had been lashed into position with the sleeping old helmsman wedged firmly against it so that the junk held its course.

Llewelyn was impressed. Single-handedly, Chang had cleared nearly all the dead fish from the deck. Gelert sniffed at a pile of stinking entrails. Llewelyn could tell he was thinking of rolling in it.

"No you don't! GERROFF it!" he yelled. Gelert jumped guiltily.

"Good. You're up," called the captain. "Come and help me sluice off the last of this muck before it gets too hot." He seemed preoccupied and business-like, not in the mood to talk.

Llewelyn pointed at the sleeping crewmen. "Why don't you wake them? Get them to help?"

Chang glanced at the sun. "There's time yet. Let's just clean them up first, eh?"

Llewelyn took a broom to the sleeping figures. The hot sun had dried off all the slime, and before long the following wind had blown away the stink of fish in shimmering clouds of scales. Only then did the captain go down below to fetch his skin of mysterious fluid.

"So, what is that stuff you're always drinking?" asked Llewelyn.

Chang glowered at him. "We're not always drinking it. It is rationed, very carefully from a strictly controlled supply."

"What about your private little stash in your pocket?"

"That's for emergencies ..."

"Emergency hangover cure," scoffed Llewelyn. "I saw you when I woke you up; you were rolling drunk. You couldn't get a word out!"

The captain went forward to where Kung lay. He seemed mildly amused. "I can assure you, Llewelyn, that we're most definitely not drunks. This is our medicine."

He splashed fluid into his cup and lifted Kung's floppy head to wet his lips. Kung spluttered briefly and sucked down the rest of the cup, his eyes fluttering and his body twitching strangely. He woke slowly and seemed confused by the sight of all the crewmen lying around. He sprang to his feet and promptly fell down again. The drink was less effective this morning.

The captain helped Kung up, talking to him in Chinese. Concern clouded Kung's face and he snatched the skin of fluid from Chang. Unstoppering it, he sniffed and licked at the neck, frowned and grew quiet as he carefully re-stoppered the skin.

Llewelyn sensed that something was wrong. "What's the matter with your medicine?"

"It's not working the way it should."

"What do you mean? It just worked on Kung."

"Yes, but it should've taken effect much more quickly…"

Kung's eyes had grown wide as he'd realised the captain wasn't speaking Chinese. He interrupted their conversation, jabbing his forefinger at Llewelyn, who quickly worked out Kung's problem.

"Doesn't he understand English?"

The captain smiled, tight lipped. "No. He's young, and he's

never been away from home before."

Kung now held up the skin of fluid and shook it angrily at the captain, asking urgent questions. Chang replied, and Llewelyn heard his name mentioned, and saw a look of shock cross Kung's face. He snorted scornfully before going off on another tirade.

The captain just shrugged.

"What's up with him?" said Llewelyn, "What have I done?"

"It's not what you've done. It's what you might have to do. Come on, let's get the others back on their feet."

The captain jumped down into the cockpit next to the old helmsman and poured some of the liquid into his mouth. Kung squatted, watching closely. The helmsman reeled and blinked and his head flopped from side-to-side as if his neck was too weak to hold it up.

Kung blabbered, vexed by the old man's slow revival. He grabbed him by his hair and pulled back an eyelid to reveal blank white.

Meanwhile, Llewelyn was tugging at Captain Chang's sleeves.

"What do you mean? What am I going to have to do?"

"Not now. We're busy."

The old helmsman woke up suddenly, wide-eyed, looking to see who was speaking.

"Morning, captain!" he said, "Well, I've not heard you speaking in English in years!"

"Aye," said Chang, nodding at Llewelyn. "And I'm not the only one."

The old helmsman turned and beamed at Llewelyn. "What ho, young man! So, you speak the King's English?"

Llewelyn gasped. The old man was not only speaking in English, he had the plummy upper class accent of a high-born nobleman.

"Er, umm, er, ur …"

"Not very well, I see! Never mind. 'Morning, Kung!"

Kung huffed, still annoyed at his inability to understand anyone. The helmsman laughed. "Sorry! Forgot you're a stay-at-home …"

He began to talk in Chinese, but suddenly distracted by something, grabbed at the tiller and turned the junk toward the smudged horizon on the port bow.

"What ho! You never said we'd reached Spain!"

The captain straightened and eyed the distant haze. Cliff-like shapes came into focus. He grew serious.

"Yes, we're nearing The Great Gateway."

Llewelyn ran to the railings.

"Spain? What gate? There's a gate to get into Spain? I can't see any gates!"

But Chang had already gone. He and Kung were reviving the other sailors who tottered around uncertainly as they came too. The old helmsman watched them and laughed.

"Dozy buggers!" he laughed, and turned to Llewelyn. "So, what should I call you?"

"Er, um, Llewelyn."

"Air-rum Chloo-well-in. Pleased to meet you." He stuck out his hand.

"No, no, sorry. Llewelyn. Just Llewelyn."

"Chloo-well-in. Chlew-el-lyn. Llewelyn." repeated the old man, rolling the new sounds around his mouth and getting comfortable with them. Llewelyn was impressed. No Englishman had ever managed to say his name properly. They couldn't get their tongues around Welsh.

"Llewelyn," smiled the helmsman. "Very musical. Splendid. And you may call me Wudi."

"Wood-di?"

"That's right, Wudi. Now, tell me something, Llewelyn."

"Er, yes?"

"The Great Dog. Gelert. Does he understand English?"

Llewelyn had to think. "No. He's Welsh, you see."

"Right. Well, do you mind giving him a message for me? In Welsh?"

"Yes, of course."

"Could you tell him to take a piss somewhere else?"

Sure enough, Gelert had cocked his leg over the coaming of the cockpit.

"Sorry!" Llewelyn blurted as he tried, vainly, to push Gelert towards the railings. It was like trying to move a donkey. All his shoving achieved was to distribute wolfhound piss more liberally around the deck. He slipped in the wet and fell into the cockpit.

The old helmsman laughed and leaned forward to help him up. "Never mind. Worse things have happened at sea. Speaking of which...," his voice grew serious, "there's your Gateway."

He pointed to a range of mountains rising beyond the distant cliffs.

How can mountains be a gateway?

He was about to ask, but Wudi shouted for the captain.

"He'll want to take the fast route," whispered Wudi as Chang stalked towards them, snapping out orders on his way. "But I've sailed these waters before, and faster means trouble out here ..."

The crew heaved on ropes and the sails flapped and banged and grew taut. The junk responded smartly, its motion becoming more purposeful. Llewelyn could see everyone was preparing to reset the rigging for when the order came to go about.

Sure enough, the captain's call came and Wudi swung the tiller over. The junk turned smoothly to the east. Soon, it appeared to be sailing for a gap between two mountain ranges.

"I thought we were trying to find a gate," said Llewelyn.

"Not *a* gate young feller-me-lad," grunted Wudi, struggling to hold the tiller against the force of the sails, "*the* Gate. The Great Gateway to the Inner Sea."

Llewelyn stared at the unfolding landscape. By now he'd figured the gate must be a gap, and thought it would be just that, a narrow opening; but this gap was more than seven miles wide, framed on either side by towering mountain ranges facing each other across the expanse of white-whipped sea. If this was just the gateway, what lay beyond?

Chang barked out more orders, to which the helmsman replied. Their voices grew angry, and Llewelyn understood that the old sailor was questioning the captain's order. He pointed southward.

Their dispute was drawing glances from the rest of the crew.

"Not in front of the men," hissed Chang. "We'll talk in English."

Wudi switched language mid-breath. "We'll be safer in the middle, and you know it!"

"In the middle we'll be prey to two lots of the scum," retorted the captain. "This way is faster. We'll take them by surprise and the ones to the south won't even know we've even gone by. Now, head north by east to the northern gatepost!" he said, pointing to the nearest land.

"On your head be it," Wudi scowled, pushing the tiller over.

As the junk turned towards the alien landscape, a new odour enveloped them. They were leaving the fresh clean air of the open ocean and sailing into a dusty smelling muskiness. The seagulls had vanished. Llewelyn saw an eagle drifting high in the sky above.

Gelert sniffed the air and the hairs along his back bristled.

Who are the 'scum'? wondered Llewelyn.

~~~~

Two and a half thousand miles away, the girl watched the crew dogs jumping into the sea around the sampan.

She'd taken it out, beyond the harbour, telling herself she needed to exercise the dogs. If they got sloppy and forgetful they'd be no use when the time came to set sail for home, she reasoned with herself. But deep down she knew she was just fed up with the stifling heat and the sickly stench of the enclosed port. It was a relief, too, to be away from the unwelcome attention of the ruffians who infected the sleazy docks.

The crew dogs were in heaven, throwing themselves off the prow then swimming determinedly to the back of the sampan where they could clamber back on board and start all over again. Twenty of them, running and swimming in an endless black doggy loop.

Their excited barks and gurglings were a pleasant change from the racket of crows and vultures and the perpetual clattering of the plague carts and the moaning of mourners as corpses were tipped splashing into the cesspit harbour.

She kept a lazy eye out for sharks and looked back at the city.

From three miles out, it almost looked appealing; a maze of sand-coloured streets and bright-white buildings piling upwards from the harbour, culminating in the stern fortress that overlooked the city walls and the desert plains beyond.

It appeared peaceful too, but she knew that the city was heavily fortified, a garrison that had been captured only recently by the Christian Knights. 'Crusaders', they called themselves, battling with the local desert people over Dog knows what.

There'd been rumours that the Saracens were sending an army to retake the city, as if this pestilential dump of a backwater was worth battling over.

Men. Fighting. It reminded her why she'd stowed on board and the memory made her feel uncomfortable. Her conscience had told her that the mission was madness and that she had to stop it.

Now she was all that was left of the mission.

Now she knew the whole adventure was a hopeless, pathetic, lost gamble.

But what if the Great Dog really was out there? What if he wasn't a myth? What if the others had found him?

If they'd managed to escape with him, how would they handle it when they made the rendezvous and found out that she was all that was left from a crew of five?

Maybe it would bring them to their senses.

Unlikely.

Scowling, she whistled to the crew dogs to get them back on board. She knew how the others would react if the sampan wasn't waiting for them, so it was her job to make sure it was. It was time to set sail.

Time to get back to waiting.

PART III: THE INNER SEA

Chapter 15. Apes

In the distance, an enormous wedge of rock appeared beyond the headlands.

It was chalk white and impossibly steep, the summit of a massive triangular mountain rising from the water. A cloud, fully two miles long, trailed, tethered from its peak, soft and pale against the otherwise empty blue sky.

They were still several miles away, but already the slab of mountain appeared to loom above them.

"Jesus, Son of Mary!" said Llewelyn when he found his voice again.

Kung just stood, mouth open, transfixed by the sight.

Wudi turned to Llewelyn, frowning.

"The Great Rock! Gatepost to The Gateway to the Inner Sea! Never fails to send a shiver down your spine, always for the wrong reasons."

They watched, subdued, as the Great Rock grew bigger still.

Llewelyn could now see many caves of different sizes pock-marking the rock's face. As the junk sailed closer, he saw that the shadowy waters beneath the Great Rock were pricked by the masts of sunken boats that sprouted along the shoreline like a tangle of broken spears. A hush fell over the junk.

Llewelyn went to the bow, the better to see the swath of ominous wrecks. Kung followed.

The giant sailor was already there, hanging over the prow. He held a long pole and was letting it slide through his hand into the sea, checking the depth around the junk.

Gelert loped over and lifted his forepaws onto the railings.

"What is it, boy?' asked Llewelyn.

Squat, human-like figures were scampering round the jagged shoreline. They were brown and hairy, putting him mind of the ogres and trolls from the bards' tales. Their hooting cries echoed across the closing sea, a raucous screeching that sent uncomfortable goose-bumps marching up the back of his neck.

Gelert barked angrily in reply. His neck hairs stood stiffly and his amber eyes glowed. As if in answer, more of the hairy dwarves ran out from the caves that riddled the weather-beaten cliff. They streamed down to the boulder-strewn shoreline, some climbing the sunken masts and spars. Now, scores of them faced the junk, their strident yammering filling the air.

"Monkeys!" spat Wudi from his cockpit. "Rabid, flea-bitten, dirty, vicious little bas–"

"Monkeys?" said Llewelyn with surprise. *So that's what a monkey looks like*. They didn't look much like the pictures in Friar William's illuminated bestiary.

"Monkeys indeed!" replied Wudi. "Just the smell of them makes me want to take a bath. Yeurk!"

Even the normally sedate giant sailor was disturbed; he pulled up his sounding pole and brandished it at the apes, now less than twenty yards away, swearing at them loudly.

Hundreds more monkeys emerged from the caves until it was impossible to distinguish individuals. They were now a throng of brown fur and angry pink faces.

As the junk rounded the steepest face of the Great Rock, something made Llewelyn look up.

His gaze wandered up the cliff to the towering pinnacle where more figures were silhouetted against the low cloud. But they weren't monkeys; they were men, dwarfed by the wall of rock. They pointed animatedly at the junk, and their cries drifted down. Still barking, Gelert shifted his focus from the monkeys up to this new threat.

Llewelyn watched as a dozen men gathered around a great boulder standing at the highest point of the peak. It was the largest of several rocks, the smallest of which was at least as big as the junk. Squinting, he could see small trees growing on the top of the boulder. Now the men were manoeuvring long tree trunk poles under it, jamming them in *just like*, Llewelyn suddenly thought, *just like levers*.

He tugged at Kung's sleeve and pointed.

"Look up!"

Kung and the giant sailor squinted into the sky and gulped.

They saw the huge boulder shift and some smaller rocks began to tumble down the cliff face. The tiny figures above cheered and increased their heaving.

"Captain!" yelled Llewelyn, pointing upwards.

Chang squinted into the sky, but he just frowned. "I'm busy!" he growled back. Llewelyn realised the junk's mainsail was blocking the captain's view of what was unfolding above.

Then the smaller rocks splashed heavily into the sea at the base of the cliff. Chang could see these, and frowned in puzzlement.

Uho! They're not so small, thought Llewelyn. The scale of the mountain had only made them appear small. These weren't rocks; they were large boulders, some the size of a cow.

As Llewelyn looked back up the cliff, the dark men fell, sprawling onto the ground. Their tree trunk levers had done their job and the boulder began to tip over. The men cheered and scampered to the edge of the cliff to watch the huge rock fall.

Without thinking, Llewelyn ran to the cockpit and threw himself onto the tiller, knocking it out of Wudi's hands.

He struggled to force it over, but the junk was speeding under full sail and the pressure of the water on the rudder fought against his efforts. He was too small. He couldn't budge the tiller. Suddenly, the giant sailor was by his side, but even with his added strength the boat still wouldn't turn.

"What are you doing!" gawped the captain incredulously.

"Help us!" cried Llewelyn. Feeling their terror, Wudi took hold of the tiller and together they heaved and strained until the rudder bit and the ship quickly pivoted away from the rock face.

The junk tilted onto a sharp angle, and the captain fell and rolled sideways over the deck, pitching up against the railings. Half a dozen deckhands slid onto him in a tangle of limbs and a chorus of curses. Up in the rigging, the tiny twins yelped as the junk righted.

Chang freed himself and scrambled to his feet. Alarmed by a dull, rushing sound, he looked up and fell backwards at the bone-chilling sight of the titanic boulder hurtling down on them.

With a mighty crash like a thousand terrible claps of thunder, it smashed into the sea just feet behind the swinging stern.

The pale-grey slab was a blur of granite, so big that it took several seconds to disappear beneath the water. A moment passed as the sea sucked down behind it and stilled briefly before suddenly pulling itself inside out. Rumbling, then booming, a colossal column of water and white spray erupted skywards.

A bloated, expanding wall of sea roared outwards from the centre of the calamity. It pitched the junk up on its bow and tossed it away from the Great Rock's cliff face, surfing it forward, bows down. As he struggled to stand in the cockpit, Llewelyn watched Gelert roll down the deck to be trapped against the forward railings, pinned in place by a flailing Kung.

But the danger wasn't over. Seconds later, the wave on the other side of the enormous splash smashed into the cliff face. It rebounded, flinging upwards and backwards as a fifty-foot curling wall of water that broke over the stern of the junk, scouring the length of the deck.

Fortunately for Llewelyn, the giant sailor grabbed the back of his trousers and held him in the cockpit, so all he suffered was a drenching and a lungful of spray. The rest of the crew was tumbled forward by the surging water and smacked into the railings with Kung and Gelert.

Aloft, gasping sailors clung grimly to the rigging. The sails had been turned edge on to the deluge and were drenched but unscathed.

For a few agonising moments, the junk wallowed with the churning weight of water inundating the decks. But the torrent cascaded out through the scuppers and railings, and the vessel slowly lightened and righted. The sodden sails filled with wind, pushing them through the subsiding swell of water, away from the cliff and into safety.

Llewelyn blinked stinging seawater and saw that the deck was littered with scores of sodden shapes. They were the bodies of monkeys that the second wave had plucked from the shoreline of the Great Rock and flung onto the junk.

Many of the apes were broken and bleeding, and one or two lay still, grotesquely twisted corpses. Several were strewn among the tangle of crew in the bows, and sailors pushed the mangled monkeys away from them, squealing with terror.

Gelert, trapped with Kung beneath several crewmen, writhed angrily, his barks muffled.

Some of the monkeys stranded on the main deck began to squirm. They coughed up seawater, feeble and stunned by the shock of their ordeal. The one nearest to Llewelyn sat up and looked at him blankly.

Llewelyn was surprised at the size of it; though squat and barrel-chested, it was nearly as big as him. He almost laughed at the battered animal's dazed expression; it was ugly enough to be Owain's twin.

But then the monkey erupted into angry life and launched itself towards him in a lightning blur of fur and teeth.

Llewelyn flailed, tripped and slipped backwards, just managing to get his hands into the mangy fur around the ape's throat as it fell on top of him. Desperately, he held it off at arms' length.

The giant sailor grabbed at the ape's shoulders and tried to pull it off, but the beast was a mass of hard, wiry, twisting muscle, too strong for even him to budge. It bared its yellow fangs and lunged and snapped. Llewelyn felt its hot breath spraying his face as it scratched at his eyes, its back legs pummelling and tearing at his body. Despairing, Llewelyn's grip loosened as his arms weakened.

Now Gelert came to his rescue.

Full of hate, he scrabbled furiously up the canted deck and crashed sideways into the ape, clamping his jaws around the back of its neck and wrenching the monkey away from Llewelyn. The dog and ape fetched up heavily against the ship's railings, locked in a cartwheeling sprawl. Gelert landed on top, still gripping the ape's scruff. The monkey, pinned face down on the deck, squirmed frenziedly and tried to reach behind to scratch at him. But Gelert calmly stood up and, with a casual toss of his head, flung the animal overboard.

Llewelyn ran to the railings. The ape splashed by, hysterical with rage. He wasn't alone; the sea astern of the junk was thick with monkeys. Some floated face down, drowned, the rest were frantically doggy paddling back towards the shoreline.

A cacophony of screeches behind him alerted Llewelyn to another problem.

The rest of the surviving monkeys had recovered.

Singly, with their fangs and claws and brutish strength, they were bad enough; but as a demented horde, they careered around the deck, a troop of screeching, snarling beasts, hell-bent on random destruction.

The captain had finally disentangled himself and took control. He detailed a dozen men to the sails and the rest to arm themselves. They started jabbing the apes with boat-hooks and belaying pins, herding them towards the stern of the junk.

Llewelyn and Gelert joined in. The monkeys were most fearful of the huge wolfhound's snarling, snapping jaws. Some tried to escape by climbing into the rigging, but were beaten back down by the twins and the other top men. Before long, sixty or so were bunched up in a small space on the rear deck, hemmed in on three sides by railings and on the fourth by Llewelyn and the other sailors. Gelert stood growling at them, challenging them to fight.

Something approaching calm was briefly, restored. Llewelyn's heart was thumping with excitement and his hands gripped the boat-hook so tightly he couldn't open them. But the monkeys were growing bolder again.

"What shall we do with them?" he screamed at the captain.

"Not now!" came Chang's testy reply. "We've still got to get clear of what's round the corner!" he shouted, focused on the winds and waves that swirled around the Great Rock.

"We should have taken the middle channel!" growled Wudi.

Llewelyn was puzzled. "We've got the monkeys under control. What's up with him now?"

"Monkeys were never the problem." called Wudi.

"What is?"

"You'll see. Just keep those creatures away from me. I've got work to do."

The junk was reaching the furthest corner of the Great Rock. As they cleared the promontory and passed from its shadow into the full light of the sun, a scatter of crude white buildings came into view.

The settlement flowed higgledy-piggledy over the lower levels of the Great Rock, clustered around a harbour. A large white triangular sail was making its way out of the harbour, heading their way.

"What is it?" Llewelyn asked Wudi.

"A dhow. It's what they sail in these parts. But it's who's sailing it is the problem. They're pirates," said Wudi, his voice catching, "the filth of the ocean. Murderous, scavenging buggers who'll board us, torture us and feed us to the sharks if we're lucky."

"What if we're not lucky?" wondered Llewelyn.

"We'll be sold into slavery," replied Wudi, "and you'll spend the rest of your life starving in chains, working in the salt mines or rowing as a galley slave. Or worse."

Llewelyn shuddered to imagine what could be worse.

If the captain was worried by all this talk, he didn't show it.

"Don't you listen to him, Llewelyn, everything will be fine."

Llewelyn thought the dhow was a menacing-looking boat, low slung with rakish lines. It surged towards them, its deck swarming with figures.

Now concern clouded Chang's face as he scrutinised his own ship's rigging and sniffed the wind. Llewelyn sensed a subtle shift in the junk's sails. They no longer strained, and there was less creaking from the rigging. Having cleared the funnelling effect of the Great Gateway, the wind was dissipating in the openness of the Inner Sea.

The junk was slowing down, and the advantage lay with the pirates, now in the mouth of the strait and still in the teeth of the wind. They were catching up fast. Hundreds of men crowded the dhow's low deck. Spears and swords glittered in the sunlight, and dozens of archers were climbing the rigging in readiness for an all-out attack.

The Chinese crew grew silent, knowing the pirates would soon be upon them.

Sensing the men's disquiet, the monkeys at the stern became more aggressive and their gibbering intensified under Gelert's angry watch.

At Chang's order, six deckhands ran below, quickly reappearing with arms and armour. The crew hurried to don breastplates and helmets and stacked sheaves of arrows against the railings. Soon, captain Chang and Wudi were armoured up, and even Kung had a helmet and a sword.

Llewelyn was the only one without a weapon.

"I need my bow and sword," he called to the captain. Chang hesitated, looking back. The pursuing pirates were closing, but still a mile away.

"Very well," he said, "Come with me, but let's be quick."

Down on the lower deck, the captain reached into his tunic and pulled out two keys on a chain around his neck. As he unlocked his cabin door, the low growling erupted from inside.

"What sort of dog is it?" Llewelyn asked, nervously.

"You'll see," replied Chang. As he opened the doors to his quarters, the growling transformed into a threatening bark. Llewelyn clamped his hands to his ears.

"Anjing!" bellowed the captain. The noise stopped immediately.

As they stepped in, Llewelyn was surprised by how spartan Chang's quarters were, furnished with only a simple low bed and a thin grey mattress.

Sitting on the bed was a white dog with brown and black markings on its face. Its rear half was the size of a small terrier, but the dog's forequarters were immensely broad and its head was almost as wide as its chest, nearly a foot across. It was as if someone had grafted the front half of a bulldog onto the rear of a ratter.

The mismatched dog jumped up at the captain, quivering with joy and wagging its stubby tail furiously – a movement that, due to its odd proportions, threatened to knock the animal off balance.

"You mean this was making all that noise?" marvelled Llewelyn.

The captain ruffled the dog's ears, picked it up and put it on the floor, where it looked up at him adoringly, its chunky chest heaving.

"Little dog, big lungs! Shuo nihao!" he commanded.

The dog gave a single yelp so loud that it hurt Llewelyn's ears.

"He's my alarm dog," laughed the captain. "Now let's get your bow." He took the other key from his necklace and reached under the bed. There was the thunk of a lock opening and he raised the top of the bed, which was hinged along the back edge. It was the lid of a chest.

Inside were three bloated black water skins, wobbling and wriggling with the motion of the junk, like overgrown headless piglets.

So this is where he keeps the crew's medicine.

Chang moved the skins to one side, and there was Llewelyn's bow. Its string had been snapped, so it lay straight, nearly six-foot long, elegantly tapered at both ends, pale, simple and perfect. Next to it was his quiver. There were only seven white-fletched arrows in it, but their tips were heavy armour-piercing bodkins.

There was also his sword and scabbard. A boy's sword, but given to him by his father. He smiled, his eyes pricking with tears.

"Go on, then! Take them!" Chang gently chided.

"Thank you," Llewelyn said huskily. He laid everything on the cabin floor, opened the flap on the bottom of the quiver, and picked out a small, tightly tied, oiled leather pouch. Inside were three bowstrings looped at either end. Selecting one, he attached one end of it to the horn nock at the base of his longbow and wedged the foot of the bow into his instep, feeling the familiar taut springiness of the solid yew. Pushing, he bent it into its true, curved shape and fixed the other end of the quivering bowstring.

Llewelyn twanged the string: it vibrated in his hands, and he thrilled at the feel of it. His bow was now alive.

The captain watched, impressed. The longbow was nearly

as tall as Llewelyn, and its elegant curve whispered of simple brute power.

Wudi called from above. "Er, when you're ready down there!"

"Let's be at them then, Llewelyn, Prince of bloody Wales." Chang headed back up on deck and Llewelyn quickly strapped on his sword, gathered up his quiver and ran after him, buoyed by a rush of anticipation and fear.

❧

The crew had settled into their battle stations.

The pirate dhow was now less than five hundred yards away.

Wudi and the captain jinked and tacked the junk, but despite their efforts, whoever commanded the other ship was a match to their trickery. Soon, the gap had almost closed.

Llewelyn didn't care. He wished he still had his chainmail tunic, but with his bow in his hand he felt strong and ready to fight. His heart was hammering, and looking around his expectant crew-mates, he felt the infectious confidence of comradeship, like the time he'd joined in the fire fight in the castle. He was part of a team, but this time no-one was going to pull him away from danger.

Which was now barely thirty yards away.

The captain ordered one more course change. Wudi pushed the tiller over, and once again, the pirate ship instantly matched their manoeuvre, as if bound to the junk by invisible iron bars.

Both vessels were now heeling over extravagantly, their decks canted steeply to the starboard. Llewelyn saw that this gave the junk something of a defensive advantage; its deck was tipped away from the enemy, presenting them with nothing to shoot at but the sheer slab of their port side.

The monkeys, surprised by the sudden shift, slid as a single body to the starboard railings. This enraged them even more, and it was all that Kung and Gelert could do to stop them breaking free.

Llewelyn slung his bow over his back, using both hands to stay upright. He clambered up the deck and peered over from behind the safety of the port railings. From here, he was looking almost straight down onto the deck of the closing pirate ship.

It wasn't a pretty sight. An ugly bunch of louts crowded the bows, brandishing curved swords and yelling obscenities. Three had shimmied along their vessel's long bowsprit, keen to be the first to board the junk.

Llewelyn watched as an archer on the main deck drew his bow – it was double curved like the Chinese weapons. The pirate loosed and Llewelyn ducked instinctively, but the pirate was standing on a tilting, bucking deck, so his aim was wild and his arrow thudded harmlessly into the junk's hull.

It was much easier for Chang's sailors to shoot back and down – they could hardly miss. One stood up and took a pot shot. It found a target and a pirate fell overboard, screaming with an arrow in his eye. His writhing body sank in a smudge of pink in the foamy wake.

Incensed, the pirates let off another volley of ineffectual arrows. Llewelyn's crew-mates jeered and set about shooting back in earnest.

Llewelyn took a deep breath. This was it; the moment he'd dreamed about. He wished his father could see him.

To see that I can fight.

Crouching down behind the railings, he knocked up an arrow, and in one fluid motion stood and drew the bowstring, just like in the practice butts. In a heartbeat, he found his target, a weasely, olive-skinned man in a thin dirty shirt. Llewelyn let loose and saw his arrow hit the pirate, the white goose feathers suddenly showing like a badge on his chest. At such close range the force of the impact had sent the arrow clean through the pirate's body. As he tumbled back, the protruding arrowhead slashed the throat of the man behind him and the pair fell to the deck in blood-mingled agony.

Llewelyn was already seeking out his next target, pushed on by a raging excitement. He'd never been so close to an enemy before, and he found himself screaming out his anger in rhythm with his bowing action. In less than a minute, he'd used up all his arrows. He slumped safely behind the railings, his fingers bleeding and his chest heaving with the effort of using his bow for the first time in so long.

He caught the captain staring at him, clearly unsettled by the longbow's power and accuracy.

"I think I'll take that back off you when this is all over!" said Chang

For the moment, Llewelyn felt nothing but a calm elation.

He wondered when the shock of killing eight men would hit him.

Still the pirate ship closed, and its arrows hedgehogged the junk. It wouldn't be long before the stalemate ended; the junk would be forced into the wind and they would be boarded.

Llewelyn glanced desperately round the ship, searching for something that might help.

The monkeys were now making daring lunges at Gelert, but the old dog snarled and snapped, holding his ground. One ape, huge and red-faced, charged straight at him, all fur and claws, its rolled-back lips revealing barbarous fangs.

The pirates will get more than they bargained for when they board this junk, thought Llewelyn.

Then the idea struck him. He slid down the deck to the captain.

"Throw the monkeys at the pirates!" he shouted.

The captain looked at the apes, then back at Llewelyn, then over to the closing ship, as he weighed up the lunacy of the idea.

Chang's green eyes flashed. "Come with me."

Llewelyn unstrung his bow, wedging it safely under the railings, and followed the captain who had scuttled over to join Wudi.

"On my command, jink her to starboard, then get straight back on this course," the captain ordered the old helmsman. "I want their bows on our stern. Hold us there until I say when."

"But they'll catch us all the sooner!"

"Aye. When I give my second signal, put her hard about to port."

Wudi protested again. "But they'll be able to ram us!"

"Precisely – if I get my timing right!"

"But … but …" Wudi started to object. But the captain was already whirl-winding his way round the junk. The sailors stifled their surprise on hearing his orders but went to their stations, leaving their mates to defend the junk.

Chang now called Llewelyn to the stern where Gelert and Kung were struggling to keep the monkeys in place. By now, the apes had reached a pumped-up frenzy, jumping up and down and slapping the deck with their long grey hands.

Kung turned to them, a warning in his voice. As if on cue, a splat of foul, fibrous slime hit him in the face. It was monkey crap. He screamed and jabbed his spear viciously into the troop. The monkeys ratcheted up their vocal assault and Gelert raged back at them in full throat.

"That's it, make them good and mad," the captain laughed. "The madder the better!" He leapt up onto the starboard rails and wedged himself against a stanchion, looking down at the pirate ship.

The two vessels were now neck and neck, just two boat lengths apart. Forward in the cockpit, Wudi waited for the signal. Llewelyn watched as the gap closed up. A hopefully aimed arrow thwacked into the railings by his face, and another struck the captain on the chest but bounced harmlessly off his fish scale armour.

Chang ignored it, waiting, waiting, waiting.

Suddenly, he dropped his left hand and roared out a command.

Wudi grunted and heaved the heavy tiller over. The junk lurched to starboard, veering away from the pirates. They matched the turn, and their bows swung in behind the junk.

"Now Wudi! Hard to port!"

The old helmsman obeyed just as the captain dropped his right hand. On deck and aloft, the crew hauled at the sails, instantly spilling the wind and slowing the forward motion of the boat as it slewed round. As it came to a standstill, the junk's momentum tilted it sideways, presenting the angled deck as a ramp to the oncoming pirate ship.

The violent action threw Llewelyn, Gelert, Kung and the monkeys off their feet and they slid against the rails in a long heap. As he fell, wide-eyed and bewildered, Llewelyn saw the prow of the pirate ship looming towards them.

The dhow was still sailing at full speed as it ploughed into the stern of the junk. Its bows smashed through the railings and rode up over the tilted deck with a fearful grinding noise. The three pirates astride their bowsprit howled with glee as their ship lanced the air above the junk.

Llewelyn cowered as the black hull passed overhead. The noise of creaking, cracking timber and cascading water drowned out his world. The hull was so close he had to push away the long fronds of slimy seaweed that hung from it. He blinked the seawater from his eyes and a thick fouling of barnacles grazed his hand. A few tiny crabs scuttled down his arm.

To his left, Gelert growled menacingly at the pile of screaming monkeys just three feet away. Flailing in a twisting frenzy of panic, they edged away from the angry old dog.

By now, the pirate ship had ground to a halt and everyone held their breath in a hesitant moment of near silence before the noise recommenced. The dhow's hull lurched, then slid backwards as the two vessels separated, levered apart by the waves and recoiling after the initial impact.

Kung yelled in alarm, pointing up as the ship's prow fell onto them.

Llewelyn grabbed Gelert by his good ear and yanked him away from the monkeys. They squirmed sideways as the pirate boat's massive bowsprit crashed onto the deck where they'd just been lying.

The solid mast snapped upwards with a deafening crack. Lying on his back, Llewelyn watched as the three pirates riding it were flung into the air, then fell heavily onto the deck between him and Kung.

The nearest pirate stood up, dazed, and raised his curved sword, readying to hack down on Llewelyn. Gelert leapt to his young master's defence, but the captain jumped in front, his sword slashing. The pirate fell, dead in an instant. Within three heartbeats, his two companions had gone the same way.

Chang's green eyes gleamed fiercely as he turned to Llewelyn. "Well?" he laughed. "It was your idea! You've got one minute!"

Bewildered Llewelyn scrambled to his feet.

How can you throw an army of monkeys onto a boat? What a stupid idea!

But he wouldn't need to. The monkeys had seen their own escape route. Using the broken bowsprit as a bridge, they fled the junk, swarming along it onto the dhow in an unstoppable flood of teeth and claws. The pirates, who only a minute ago had been preparing to board, were thrown back in disarray. Llewelyn whooped, and jumped up onto the bowsprit to watch. The dhow had become a cauldron of monkey-fuelled confusion.

Meanwhile, those of the Chinese crew not working the sails continued their assault on the pirates, jeering as they shot their arrows.

Llewelyn still had work to do too; half a dozen apes remained loose on the junk, and he called for Gelert. "Come on! Let's get rid of 'em!"

They jumped down to the other side of the bowsprit, shooing and barking the last of the monkeys on their way. It was the devil's own job; the last of the apes were either stupidly stubborn or too scared to move. Confronted by a howling Gelert, a few were so terrified they leapt straight into the sea. Llewelyn shouted and jabbed the stragglers across the bowsprit to join the pandemonium on the pirate ship.

All except one. Llewelyn saw it scamper down the hatchway to the captain's quarters. It was the monkey that had confronted Gelert earlier.

Cocky little bugger! I'll get YOU later!

On the dhow, angry men fought off enraged monkeys, but swords, spears and bows weren't much help in the cluttered confines of the deck, and the mob of apes moved so fast and with so little purpose that the pirates could only lash out blindly at whatever was furry.

The Chinese archers continued to add to their misery. They shot indiscriminately into the throng of men and animals, caring only about how swiftly they could let loose their arrows.

Captain Chang gave new orders. His men hauled on the junk's sails, and as the slatted canvass clattered open to catch the wind again, the two vessels began to tear apart. The dhow's bowsprit groaned, and Llewelyn watched it slither back across the stern deck, ripping off yards of the junk's railings and tearing a great chunk out of the stern before falling heavily into the sea.

The ruin of mast, rigging and debris now tangled the pirate ship's bows, paralysing it in the water.

Llewelyn screamed in excitement, then grew quiet, his chest

heaving as he realised that all that had just happened had taken less time than it took to walk from one side of the castle to the other.

❦

The junk was now free and coming under sail.

Wudi held the tiller over and swore. The steering must have been damaged by the wrecking bowsprit because the junk seemed reluctant to turn. But turn it did, ever so slowly, and began to draw alongside the dhow.

Chinese archers lined the junk's deck, shooting down into the heaving mass of humans and monkeys. Llewelyn watched with calm detachment as one of the pirates rose from the throng.

He must be their leader, he thought, *he's bigger and less filthy than the others.* It was hard to say for sure, because the man was wrestling with an enormous ape that was chewing on his face with its six-inch fangs. The pirate stabbed furiously at the animal with an elegantly curved golden dagger that seemed far too delicate for the job. A second later, man and ape were lost in the melee.

It was time to leave.

More sails were hurriedly raised and the junk caught the wind, and Wudi steered them away from the wretched pirate dhow.

Llewelyn looked around; the sun was still overhead, a stark reminder that less than an hour ago they'd been sailing in a different sea, and already he'd witnessed the loss of several hundred lives, men and beasts. Some of which he'd been responsible for.

He began to tremble, teetering on the brink of shock.

"That was a good idea of yours," said Wudi, breaking into his trance. "You saved the ship, and we got rid of those monkeys …"

He stopped and listened carefully. "Is that Gelert I can hear below?"

Llewelyn shook his head to rid himself of thoughts of the eight men he'd slain. Yes, Gelert was growling from somewhere beneath their feet. It was a deep, throaty growl, not one he could immediately place.

At the stern, the captain was with some crewmen assessing the damage from the ramming. A jagged hole exposed the decks below and the surging sea beyond.

Mother of Jesus! That'll take some fixing. It was so big he could have ridden a carthorse through it.

"Don't worry, Llewelyn, we won't sink," said Chang, seeing his alarm. "It'll just delay us a couple of days …" He was trying to sound reassuring, but Llewelyn noticed that he couldn't help looking at the westward horizon as much as the damage to his ship.

Llewelyn heard Gelert's strange growling again. The deep snarls told him the old wolfhound was moving slowly through the ship. He was heading towards the captain's quarters.

He'd heard Gelert make these sounds before: when he'd smelled wolves. *He's stalking something down there!*

"What's wrong with Gelert?" asked Captain Chang.

Another much louder bark rung out from below. It was the huge honking alarm bark of the captain's tiny guard dog.

"And what's he doing in my cabin?" Chang added, now concerned.

"He's hunting!" yelled Llewelyn, running to the hatchway.

🐾

He was stepping onto the ladder when the alarm dog's booming barks were joined by Gelert's howling, and then a series of piercing shrieks. Suddenly, an appalling fight broke out. Llewelyn jumped into the hatchway, barely touching the ladder, and landed in a foot of water.

It was blindingly bright below. A shaft of spangling light reflected from outside, glaring through the great gash in the stern. Seawater sloshed through the splintered hole.

The little alarm dog stood outside the captain's cabin, chest high in the water, barking at the open doorway. He was frantic with rage, matching the clamour within. Inside the cabin it was dark, and Llewelyn had to blink to see through the door, but there was enough light to reveal what was going on: Gelert was locked in a brutal struggle with an ape.

Llewelyn gulped.

That's the one I missed earlier! But he's cornered now!

He drew his sword and stepped warily into the deafening din.

Gelert had the monkey's neck in his jaws, safe from its dagger-like canines, but it was using its paws to tear at him, ripping out great shanks of hair and kicking at him viciously with its strong hind legs. Together, they thrashed about the deck, a furious knot of fangs and writhing limbs. They thumped around the walls, crashed against the open lid of Captain Chang's bed chest, then tumbled into the chest itself. The lid fell heavily, smacking down on one of the ape's legs.

Llewelyn stabbed at the squirming leg, but the lid burst open again, throwing him back. He was struck in the face by a glutinous splash of thick fluid that seared his eyes and ran into his mouth. Gasping with surprise he swallowed some of it. His gullet prickled hotly, as if the lining of his throat was being scoured. He tried to spit his mouth clean; the fluid was almost tasteless, but his lips and tongue fizzed unpleasantly.

Half-blinded, Llewelyn staggered backwards and fell against the opposite bulkhead. The wetness was already soaking into his tunic, making his arms and body tingle. He tried to wipe his face off; the thick liquid oozed from his fingers, and he smelt a faint tang of mouldy barley and burnt hair. As he cleared his smarting eyes, Llewelyn saw the source of the wetness — the captain's precious skins of reviving drink had burst in the struggle. The spilled contents sloshed in the bottom third of the chest, like greasy thin mud.

The two animals continued their confined struggle, splashing clumsily in the fluid. By now, the small cabin was drenched by the chaotic splattering.

Gelert still had the ape by its throat, shaking it madly until the monkey found his eyes and clawed at them, forcing him to let go. The beast twisted around, grabbed the back of Gelert's head in his forepaws and jammed him face down into the churning fluid. The old wolfhound convulsed madly, but his paws couldn't find purchase in the slippery confines of the chest. He scrabbled and floundered, his snarling now a frantic gurgling.

Llewelyn leapt forward again, hacking his sword into the ape's shoulders. A sudden fire coursed through his body as he lunged; he felt his muscles becoming stronger, his blood rushing faster, his joints glowing from within. Hot elation drove his sword arm with a ferocious power. Thrilling with his new-found energy, Llewelyn slashed and hacked again and again, screaming his joy as he finally drew blood.

But the beast's muscles and thick wet fur were tough and unyielding and still the ape held Gelert's muzzle deep in the fluid, possessed by the same unnatural strength he himself was feeling.

The captain flew into the room, wrenched Llewelyn clear and laid into the ape with his sword, stabbing with all his strength. Blood sprayed with every thrust, but the monkey held on.

Llewelyn wiped his eyes in disbelief; it was growing bigger.

"Help me!" yelled the captain, his voice rising in panic. Llewelyn scrambled back to his feet and lunged with his sword, but the blade bounced off. The ape was not only growing bigger, but stronger too, as if possessed by some terrible demon. It continued to drown Gelert and rip at the old dog's skull.

Then Kung burst through the doorway. He grabbed at the ape between the others' sword thrusts, but it writhed and bucked too much. Its fur was so slick with the sticky fluid and blood that it was impossible to grasp.

Suddenly, the ape flew up and over them. It smashed against the ceiling and landed with a neck-snapping thud.

Everyone stepped back, startled, as Gelert erupted from the chest and threw himself onto the crippled animal, savaging its throat. The monkey twitched and twisted as gushes of crimson pulsed from its ruined neck, spreading in a steaming pool. With every weakened spurt, it drew closer to death, a look of puzzled anger fading in its eyes.

Gelert stood panting over the corpse, his jaws dripping red, his chest heaving, and his gore-soaked frame bristling with rage.

Llewelyn rubbed his eyes again. Was Gelert a foot taller at the shoulder and broader around the chest? He glanced at Kung and the captain, who were both equally dumbfounded.

The great wolfhound sniffed the corpse briefly, then shivered and shook himself, showering the cabin with fluid and blood. He turned slowly to look at them all. An orange gleam illuminated his eyes. He seemed to be smiling inwardly, thrilling in his formidable new body.

"The dog has swallowed the Essence!" whispered the captain.

The Essence! So that's what they call it!

"What will happen to him?" asked Llewelyn.

"I … I don't know!" came the captain's croaking reply. "We never give dogs the Essence!"

"What is this Essence? What does it do?" he pleaded, but Chang didn't reply. He and Kung were backing away from Gelert, fear in their eyes.

He turned to stare at his old friend who had grown bigger still, and now Llewelyn really began to worry.

Gelert seemed to be inflating; his frame creaked and bulged as his bones expanded and new muscles bunched in to fill the spaces. They distended and pulsed obscenely, rippling beneath his fur.

Kung clasped his head in his hands and moaned woefully.

Gelert whimpered to Llewelyn with a look of pained confusion.

Llewelyn stepped over the dead ape and squatted in its blood. "Don't worry, boy," he said to Gelert in Welsh, "I'll look after you." Tenderly, he took Gelert's head in his hands and looked into his eyes. "You'll be all right," he whispered, stroking him softly. He felt the bones of the old dog's head grinding underneath his shaggy coarse hair. Gently, he leaned forward and kissed his friend's gore-stained muzzle.

Gelert convulsed and vomited directly into his face.

Llewelyn pulled away, choking, but slipped in ape blood and fell sprawling on his back. He spat Gelert's puke from his mouth, but felt the tingling coursing through his body again, a hot, shivering sensation.

Gelert continued to spew on him and Llewelyn tried to squirm away, but kept sliding in the slick pool of blood. The wolfhound emptied his guts, belching bursts of thick fluid all over Llewelyn until he was dry retching.

"Finished?" asked Llewelyn crossly, the tingling sensation abating. He managed to get up, scraping puke from his face and arms, and stood, astonished. Underneath all the blood and slime, Gelert seemed unhurt. Llewelyn felt the back of his old friend's head and pulled back in surprise – his wounds had vanished. His fur was less grizzled, brighter and shinier. There were no patches of scabby skin, and the plummy growths that had bunched along his body were gone.

Gelert's body was returning to a more natural shape. He wagged his tail and barked happily, his back straighter and his eyes bright.

Kung approached warily, then knelt and examined him, gingerly at first but becoming more excited. The captain looked on, smiling but almost disbelieving his relief.

Llewelyn was scared. "What happened?" he whispered.

"I don't know," repeated Captain Chang impatiently. "The Essence … we never give it to dogs."

Llewelyn began to panic. "It turned him into a– a– devil monster! I got some in my mouth! What'll happen to me?"

Chang looked him up and down. "Calm down. You look fine to me …"

His eyes suddenly grew wide and he pushed past Llewelyn and reached into his bed chest. Groaning, he lifted out one of the black skins; it was a limp rag, slashed in several places, a last few drops of precious fluid oozing from it.

He held it out to Kung, speechless.

Kung froze, the colour draining from his face. He stumbled over to the chest and knelt beside it. "Bu! Bu! Bu!" he keened, rocking back and forth.

"What is it?" asked Llewelyn, looking in.

Two of the three skins had been punctured, and the third had popped its stopper. Kung wailed.

Llewelyn didn't understand. "There's plenty of your precious Essence in there. Just scoop it up and put it in a barrel or something."

"Too much contact with the air spoils it," said the captain grimly.

Kung continued to howl disconsolately.

The implications quickly dawned on Llewelyn. This 'Essence' was the cure for the sailors' three-day illness. If it didn't work, what would follow was unthinkable.

Captain Chang picked up the skin with no bung. He sloshed it around and peered into its neck. It was still a third full, and he searched around in the chest to find the stopper.

"I knew these skins weren't as good as bottles," he spat, twisting in the stopper angrily.

Llewelyn thought about the rest of the crew. "Will you tell the others?"

The captain paused to think. The skin hung wetly from his hand. The bulge of remaining fluid looked pathetic, insubstantial.

"Not yet. If things start going bad we'll have to, but until then it's best they don't know." He carefully placed the skin back into the sodden chest, closed the lid and locked it.

Kung was still sobbing.

The captain rolled his eyes impatiently.

"Anjing!" he barked. Kung went silent.

Anjing! thought Llewelyn. *Now I know how to say 'shut up' in Chinese.*

Chang shooed Kung from the cabin, turning to Llewelyn as he left. "You did well again. I'll not forget that. Meanwhile, I have a more immediate problem. Our ship is in need of repair."

Left alone, Llewelyn looked at Gelert, now bigger, brighter, stronger. Younger.

"Things turned out well for you!" he said, wiping him down.

The huge wolfhound barked lightly, pleased that his young master was happy. The fluid had done something wonderful to him. *Something miraculous*, thought Llewelyn as he hugged him.

But there was the dead ape, gashed, bloody and still steaming in its blackening pool. He'd watched it become monstrous, and death had frozen it as an obscenely misshapen beast. Deep inside, Llewelyn felt a dreadful awful thought forming. This fluid must be a dark magic. Did Gelert now have a monster lurking in him? He quickly crossed himself and mumbled a prayer.

He thought about the crewmen. What would happen to them once the fluid, this 'Essence', ran out? Would it be a horrible slow descent into a living nightmare? Would they die? Would he be the last person left on a boat in the middle of nowhere?

He shuddered. The Essence scared him.

Gelert yapped happily. His tail beat with new vigour and he bounded out of the cabin.

Llewelyn followed knowing he should be feeling happy or relieved, but all there was was a dread chill, creeping across his soul.

The stern took three nights and two long days to repair, and all the while the junk was a wallowing pig. It drifted sluggishly into the empty reaches of the sapphire-blue Inner Sea, barely making steerage.

Everyone had time to collectively draw breath. Their heroics during the fight brought them all together, and Llewelyn quickly discovered that several sailors spoke French. Chen, the ship's self-appointed cook, was immensely proud of his Spanish. Although Llewelyn's Italian was sketchy, he found he could chat easily with Zheng the giant, who spoke with a thick Neapolitan accent. The tiny twins were called Ao and Chao, and spoke Spanish, and another language that nobody else knew, called Yaghan.

No-one had any Welsh, which Llewelyn found depressing and vaguely insulting. The sailors sensed his disappointment and tried to reassure him, like the captain had, that it was simply because they'd never traded that far west. But Llewelyn knew they were just being polite because he heard Huidi the carpenter swearing in Irish Gaelic.

Although everyone was impressed that Llewelyn spoke the languages he did, they thought he was a bit 'European'. They were surprised he'd never picked up any Arab, Turkish, Circassian, Hindi or Viet, and about twenty other languages he'd never heard of. They all found his ignorance of Chinese completely baffling.

But at least he wasn't as bad as Kung, who stood out among the crew because he knew only Chinese. They gently mocked his ignorance but Kung seemed unconcerned, even scornful, of their jeers.

"He says, and I quote," explained the captain, 'that any language that isn't Chinese is no better than the cackling of crows.'"

"But he does have a point," said Wudi, sitting Llewelyn down in his cockpit one day. "If you added up all the people in the world who don't speak Chinese, they'd still be a pimple on the fraction of the ones that do. You can't go through life not understanding the world's most important language. So, lesson one ..."

Llewelyn began to learn Chinese.

※�

The days passed. Between his lessons with Wudi, Llewelyn noticed a fretfulness in the captain's mood. Chang stayed aft, standing over the carpenters, hurrying them to finish the repairs, and the rest of his time he spent anxiously scanning the western horizon, the direction from which they'd come. It was as if he was expecting trouble.

Llewelyn began to wonder again what threats lay behind them.

"What are you looking for back there?"

Uncharacteristically indecisive, Chang seemed to weigh up his answer.

"Oh, nothing. Just keeping an eye on the weather." He didn't sound very convincing and shifted the subject sideways, gesturing at his crew. "I'm more worried that we're coming up to the third day ..."

Llewelyn ran his eye over the ship. The sailors seemed fine, but Llewelyn knew what the third day meant, and that after the disaster with the Essence things were going to get worse.

He recalled something the captain had said the morning after they'd blasted the English fleet.

"Remember back when you'd cleaned up all the fish ...," he ventured.

Chang folded his arms. "Yes ...?"

"And it took ages for you to revive everyone ...?"

"Hmm ...?"

"You knew then that this Essence stuff was going off, didn't you?"

Chang glanced around to check that none of the crew was within earshot of their conversation. He lowered his voice. "I had an inkling it might be. I've told Kung to look at what's left of it, to see if he can do something with it. He's good with potions."

"Yes, but what if he can't? What if your Essence has all gone off? You said something about what *I* might have to do?"

The captain nodded.

Suddenly Llewelyn realised what that 'something' was.

"You think that if you're all laid out by this sickness of yours that I can take charge of the ship!"

The captain shrugged. "Why not?"

Llewelyn was so taken aback he snorted with laughter. "Me? I'm only thirteen! How could I take you, and your boat and all your men … to China?"

"Not China. The Holy Land."

"But I can't …," he stuttered.

The captain studied his face. "Llewelyn, Prince of bloody Wales, you've already done far more than you ever thought you could."

Llewelyn thought back over the events of the last day. It was true: he'd spotted the English fleet when Chang and the crew were all belly-up; then he'd helped destroy them; his actions had stopped the junk being sunk by that boulder; and it was his idea to use the monkeys as a diversion and save them from the pirates.

But for all that, he didn't know what to say. No-one had ever expressed such belief in him before. Not his father, nor Owain, and certainly not Friar William. To all of them, he was a boy, a lad, an adult in waiting. Not yet ready.

He shut his eyes and tried to close the gap between the person he'd always been told he was and the person Captain Chang saw in front of him. The person he knew he was. He saw a vague swirl of dark, scary responsibility, but here and there the uncertainty was pricked with shimmering sparks of confidence.

He opened his eyes and the captain saw the fire in his look.

"So, if the time comes, will you help us?"

"Um, er, I suppose so …" Llewelyn began.

The captain's face darkened and he waved dismissively to cut him off. His hand was trembling. "Um, er, you suppose so. I suppose we should be thankful for that." He squeezed the bridge of his nose and sat down, his voice becoming harsh. "If it gives you a more personal incentive, don't forget that if we don't get to Jaffa, you won't be able to get on a ship back to Wales."

His words and his tone stabbed Llewelyn. He'd made his mind up to help. The captain didn't need to resort to meanness and threats.

But then Llewelyn saw that Chang's shoulders had slumped. His face had dropped and the light had drained from his green eyes. It was the Essence that was making the captain bitter.

The third day had come, but it had come early.

🐉

Other than arriving sooner than expected, the slump in the cycle of the Essence seemed no worse than before. Maybe the crew's recovery was a wee bit slower, but Llewelyn couldn't really see much change.

The repairs to the boat were completed. Finally the junk could put its stern fully to the wind, and they were off again.

Although mightily relieved to be on their way, Llewelyn could see that the captain and Kung were worried about the crew. They watched them, searching for the slightest hint of any problems.

"You haven't told them?" Llewelyn whispered to the captain that evening.

"Not unless, or until, I have to," he replied. "But tell me, do I look any more wrinkled, am I moving more slowly, do I seem forgetful?"

Llewelyn assured him he was no worse than usual. But he worried about Chang's new habit of glancing over his shoulder at the western horizon.

"What is it back there?" he probed.

"Nothing. We're making good time."

Llewelyn was unconvinced. Captain Chang's confidence was collapsing.

On the third day, the crew sickened, and once again, it happened sooner than it should have. As usual, the captain pulled himself from his stupor and revived his crew. The wondrous Essence still worked its magic, but Llewelyn noticed him and Kung exchanging glances.

Thankfully, the fine weather held and there was little for anyone to do about the ship. The strong winds continued to scorch them eastwards, and although the captain enforced his vigil on the western horizon, none of the lookouts saw any other ships.

🐉

Llewelyn's lessons in Chinese quickly bore fruit. Wudi was a patient, inventive teacher, and Llewelyn's ear for languages meant the torrent of new words pouring into his head sloshed around and stuck in all the right places. He wondered if he could teach Gelert some of them, but the old dog was deaf to the Chinese words for 'sit' and 'stand' and 'stop', and just sat there looking at him with his head to one side.

Oddly, he soon picked up the word for 'dinner'.

Llewelyn decided to test his new vocabulary on a tougher audience.

"Come on," he called to Gelert, and they went looking for Kung.

He was in the captain's cabin. The alarm dog and Gelert greeted each other. *No language problems for them!*

Kung was scooping gobbets of coagulated Essence from the bottom of the chest and smearing it into pots. The gelatinous mush on his bony hands was streaked with skeins of red – monkey and wolfhound blood.

"Away with you, boy!" muttered Kung. "I'm busy."

"Happy afternoon!" beamed Llewelyn. "Blue sun hot sky windy boat go long way!"

Kung rolled his eyes. "Oh. You're finally learning to speak a proper language. Very good. Close the door when you leave."

Llewelyn chose to ignore Kung's snarkiness. "You very thank much. Wudi Chinese very learn me brilliant!"

"Wudi is as brilliant a teacher, as I thought Wudi would be. Tell him I give him one out of ten. No, make that out of a hundred."

Llewelyn pointed at Kung's pot. "Doing what Essence with?

"None of your business. Leave. Now."

Who do *you remind me of?* thought Llewelyn. He smiled broadly and slipped into Welsh. "Anything to get away from the sight of you, you bum-sniffing snot bag. Cheerio."

Llewelyn took Kung's cynicism as a challenge and urged Wudi to push him more during his Chinese lessons. He went back to Kung every day, and after just a week, the medicine man grudgingly admitted that he wasn't mangling Chinese nearly so badly. More surprisingly, he began to open up.

"You're doing well. For a Barbarian. I suppose."

"Thanks. Very gracious you are."

"Yes, I can see why the captain thinks he can have faith in you. But he's spent so many years with Barbarians his standards have dropped."

Llewelyn got the gist and ignored the barbs.

"Captain say look I the ship after crew all go sick," he said proudly.

"Chang's an incorrigible optimist," said Kung resignedly, "but he's right. You're the only person on the ship who isn't a slave to the Essence."

"Cheer up. Things not bad as. Essence still works think I."

Kung looked at him doubtfully. "Well, that's not what I think."

Llewelyn shrugged. "Everyone fine. Worry you don't."

※

However, a week later, changes began to happen.

A carelessness crept into the running of the ship. Forgetfulness affected everyone. Cheng the cook appeared on deck with a steaming pot of chicken soup, but had to hurry back when he realised he hadn't plucked the chicken. Zheng stood with his finger in his nose – he'd been picking it and had forgotten what to do next. Wudi, during one of his lessons, was unable to remember the Chinese word for the sea.

Even the captain was losing it, looking eastward as if he'd forgotten that his worries were to the stern.

Then, a day later, one of the crew died.

It was Jizi, one of the top men. He'd shimmied up the main mast to splice a frayed rope. Everyone on deck heard his scream and turned to watch as he fell, bouncing once on a hatchway, breaking open his skull in a spray of pink jellied brains and blood.

The crew encircled the body, wide eyed, as if they'd never before seen a dead man. Cheng the cook cried and Zheng the giant looked pale.

There'd been no reason for the fall. It was as if Jizi had simply forgotten he was thirty feet above the deck and had stepped back from his work, and that was that.

Worryingly, it happened just one day after the crew had been rejuvenated by their ration of the Essence.

Jizi's body was laid out on the foredeck. His lice dog sat by his head, howling with misery. Captain Chang gave the crew until nightfall to pay their respects, and they remained standing around the body, gripped in silent shock.

But after only half an hour under the brassy glare of the sun, the sickly smell of rotting flesh quickly became overpowering. The crew gradually moved aft, as far upwind as possible.

All except the dead man's lice dog, who kept miserable vigil at his feet, and Gelert, who found the nauseating stench irresistible. Llewelyn was disgusted to see him sidle forward and snuffle at the dead man's mangled brains. The lice dog growled, defending his master's corpse.

"Away!" yelled Llewelyn, but Gelert withdrew only a few feet.

Llewelyn stormed over, "Godammit, I swear I'll tie you up if go anywhere near him!" he fumed, and sneaked a quick look at the body.

His stomach leapt. He'd seen death many times, but this was different. Jizi's body was already half decomposed, but odder than this, his hair had grown white and wispy, his lips had pulled back to show long yellow teeth, and the joints of his clawed fingers were swollen and twisted with arthritis.

Jizi, who'd only been in his twenties, now looked as if he'd died a thousand years old.

❧❧

The stink of decay worsened as the hot sun cooked the corpse, and Captain Chang decided to send the dead man on his way. As the sun set, the crew gathered to say farewell and Jizi's body was lowered gently overboard. His lice dog howled, and Gelert and the captain's alarm dog joined in.

As Chang finished reciting prayers, his voice croaked with something more than the sadness of the moment.

The darkening orange sky silhouetted the assembled crew, and in that moment Llewelyn saw a pathetic group of doddering old men. They were greyer, more stooped, more wrinkled, and each of them knew something was wrong. They glanced questioningly at one another and saw themselves mirrored hollowly in their crew-mates' rheumy eyes.

A ripple of disquiet shivered through the congregation.

This shouldn't be happening. Not so soon.

"What's going on, captain?" asked Zheng quietly.

"Aye," chimed Wudi, "we should be fine for at least another day!"

Llewelyn saw Chang share a glance with Kung. They nodded at to each other, and Llewelyn knew the time had come.

"You've got to tell them," he urged.

"Tell us what?" said Wudi, speaking for the crew.

The captain took a deep breath and explained how Gelert had burst the skins of Essence during his fight with the ape.

Silence. Llewelyn watched the faces of the crew. As one, they turned to look at Gelert, who was stood forward sniffing the damp patch where the dead sailor had been lying.

"Great," spat Wudi. "We risk our lives to steal the dog and before we're even halfway back he signs our death warrant!"

The crew rumbled. Llewelyn could hear faint notes of panic in their murmurs. The captain raised his hands to placate them, but before he could speak, Kung pushed forward, glaring.

"Enough of this!" he said hotly, his voice rising. "The mission isn't over. We will find a way through. To fail is unthinkable. Do you want your women violated? Your children turned into slaves and your parents fed to the pigs? Your homes destroyed and your lands taken?"

Phew! Their Emperor's an unforgiving boss, thought Llewelyn.

A hush fell over the boat.

"Your duty is to the mission, not to yourselves," continued Kung high-handedly. "You're all expendable. Even if there's only enough of the Essence to keep just one man alive, Gelert MUST be taken home."

The sailors' disquiet turned hostile.

"Aye, and we know who that one man would be," someone jeered.

"You are nothing, d'you hear," spat Kung. "Your deaths will mean NOTHING!"

Idiot, thought Llewelyn, rolling his eyes at Kung. *You had them on your side, then you lost them again.*

The captain shoved Kung aside.

"Calm down everyone. We'll pull through if we work together. No-one's going to die…," he glared at Kung.

"Tell that to Jizi!" sniped Wudi, setting off more muttering.

"Enough!" The captain eyeballed each of his men in turn. Quiet returned. "That's better. Now. We've had time to think about things. Kung believes we can reduce everyone's dose of the Essence …"

The crew began to protest.

"Hear me out!" Chang barked. Sullen silence. "Yes, we'll be laid low, possibly for days at a time, but we're only two, maybe three weeks from the rendezvous. Am I right, Wudi?"

"Aye. I suppose so. If this wind holds," the helmsman cautioned.

The captain smiled broadly and spread his hands wide. "All we need to do is get to Jaffa. From there we're only a short ride from the rendezvous and all the untainted Essence we'll ever need. Simple. We just need to hold out, together, and everything will be fine."

Wudi wasn't done. "Who's going to set the sails? Who's going to feed us, and give us our Essence? Who's going to steer the boat?"

"And who's going to feed us?" bleated Cheng the cook.

Llewelyn felt his heart stop, then start beating again, now dangerously fast. Again, he knew what was coming.

The captain beckoned him over, and a ripple of disbelief shivered through the crew.

"You're kidding …" balked Wudi.

"I said hear me out. We've all seen that Llewelyn's a dependable, resourceful lad. In fact, if he wasn't here, Wudi, we'd have been feeding the fish five days ago, back there, underneath the Great Gate."

Wudi couldn't deny that, but he turned to Llewelyn.

"So," he said flatly. "Do *you* think you can take care of us …?"

Llewelyn flushed and shrugged and nodded weakly.

"I know he can, and so do you," interrupted the captain. "If we set the rigging and rope up the tiller, he won't have too much to do."

"And he'll make sure we get our Essence?" asked Cheng.

"Kung will show him how."

"… and he'll sail us, single-handed, all the way to the far side of the Inner Sea?" said Zheng.

"As I said, we're already halfway there."

"… With no landfalls, nothing to guide him …" chimed Ao and Chao.

"Wudi will teach Llewelyn all he needs to know, won't you, Wudi? You know he's a fast learner, and you're our finest navigator."

Llewelyn waited for the scorn to come. He wouldn't blame the crew for flatly rejecting the whole idea. Part of him wanted them to.

"Right!" pronounced the old helmsman brightly. "That sounds like a plan. Let's get started."

The crew were all nodding.

Oh Jesus, Mary and Joseph, and the donkey they rode into town on! What have I let myself in for?

The marvellous wind held, and the junk continued to fly on its way.

The swift progress lifted the crew's spirits and they remained optimistic, even though the intervals between taking the Essence were growing shorter.

Captain Chang used these closing windows of time to start drilling into Llewelyn all he'd need to know about the running of the ship.

He had much to learn and relentlessly quizzed everyone about what they were doing and why. The sailors were just as anxious to pass on their skills. Before long, Llewelyn knew enough to set the sails, splice a rope, and generally keep the ship on an even keel.

Kung took him to the captain's cabin where he explained the schedule and method of administering the Essence. He produced a measuring cup half the size of the one Chang had been using.

"One for each of us. No more, no less. And no matter what, you must wait the full twelve hours between when we fall asleep and giving us the Essence. Do you understand?"

"Twelve hours wait. Why?"

"Don't question me, boy. Although we will spend less and less time awake, we must sleep for those twelve hours. Do you understand?"

"Yes! Twelve hours wait. Why but?"

"Just do as I say. Now leave."

Llewelyn found it much easier working with Wudi, and he went to the helmsman eager to soak up the old man's wisdom.

"Maps and charts are no good out here," announced Wudi, arms spread to the empty horizon.

"How come we never see any other ships?" asked Llewelyn, wondering why they had the sea to themselves.

"Hah! Because they're coast-huggers, the lot of them. But I will free you from the earth. You will learn how to watch the wind and the way it skims across the sea and fills the sails. How to sense the caress of every wave on the rudder and to use your fingertips to push back against them through the tiller. To read the currents and smell the air. How, from a single scrap of drifting seaweed, you can tell how far you are from land and how deep the ocean is beneath. And above all, Llewelyn, you will learn …"

"What?"

"… that you need to make sure you pee regularly. Very bad for your bladder to try to hold it in."

Once he'd stopped laughing, Wudi looked around to make sure no-one was watching, then he took a round, fist-sized wooden box from an inner pocket. Inside was a glass sphere, within which a shimmering fish the size of his little finger floated freely in a clear fluid.

"Watch," said Wudi turning the sphere, shaking it side-to-side and inverting it. The fish tumbled in the agitated fluid but slowly 'swam' back onto the level. No matter which way Wudi turned the sphere, the fish kept facing in the same direction.

"My little friend here always says, 'Go north!' Of course, I don't necessarily always want to go north, but his obstinacy helps me see which way I *do* want to go," he whispered. "Now, look more closely …"

He handed the sphere to Llewelyn. Close up, he could see the details of the fish. Its scales were tiny individual jewels, and between its exquisitely crafted transparent fins were dozens of smaller fins, each one a different shade of the rainbow.

"See how each of the fins points in a different direction?"

Llewelyn nodded, mesmerised.

"Once I've shown you how to align the fish with the stars or the planets or the moon, you'll never be lost again."

Wudi put the sphere back in its box and snapped it shut.

It was the first time Llewelyn had seen him with this wonderful fish.

"How often do you use it?"

"Me … maybe once a week," Wudi mused. "You, maybe more often."

Llewelyn knew he would need to consult the fish every two minutes.

The old man was as a good a teacher of navigation as he was

of Chinese. In the perfect weather conditions, Llewelyn quickly absorbed the foundations of his wisdom. One morning, after he'd successfully shepherded the junk by himself throughout the night, Wudi pronounced that he had done a good job.

"You'll do," he said, and Llewelyn's heart fairly burst with pride.

Then Wudi showed him how to fix the tiller's course with ropes.

"Because it doesn't matter how well you can navigate if you're asleep!"

As the days wore on, the crew became clumsy, cantankerous and forgetful. When they finally succumbed to incoherence, Llewelyn patiently looked after them, feeding and giving them water where they lay. Gelert went with him as he did his rounds, and the sleeping sailor's lice dogs would clamber out to snuffle at the Great Dog, looking to him for reassurance.

The men suffered while they were unconscious, whimpering in pain, and juddering with shivers. Having to wait twelve hours to give them the Essence was a trial, but Llewelyn stuck to Kung's strict orders, puzzling about what was so good about this medicine that made it worth this sort of agony.

On waking, the captain drove his men directly to their posts, insisting that all the rigging be checked and reset, then double-checked.

Meanwhile, Kung questioned Llewelyn about everything that had happened while they were unconscious. He knew Kung was charting the crew's decline so he could more precisely manage the dwindling dregs of the Essence. He wondered if Kung would have cared so much about the crew's welfare if it hadn't been for the mission. *Probably not.*

Llewelyn's suspicions were confirmed two cycles later when Kung summoned him to the captain's quarters. He took care to make sure everyone was busy on deck, and pulled the doorway quietly shut before motioning Llewelyn to sit.

"Now, boy, I've had to accept that only you can save our mission," he scowled, "And thank Dog you haven't messed up so far ..."

Here comes the 'but', thought Llewelyn.

"But, very shortly, things are going to get a lot worse. We will succumb to our circumstances …" Kung picked up the last skin of Essence and shook it, "…but this will no longer revive us."

Llewelyn felt sick. The crew's agonies were horrifying, but knowing he'd soon be alone scared him more.

Kung carried on. "However, so long as you keep dosing us once every twelve hours, we will still be safe. Tell me you understand this."

Llewelyn nodded.

"Good. Now I've made this happen because …"

"Me excuse!" interrupted Llewelyn, "You maked happen this?"

Kung rolled his eyes, "Yes, I 'maked' it happen. The Essence you've been giving us has been diluted. By me."

"You give men less Essence, and you put water it down as well," sputtered Llewelyn, outraged. "You not see how much pain men feel?"

"Oh spare me, boy!" snapped Kung, "I suffer as much as anyone. Trust me, if we had carried on using the Essence as it was, we'd all be dead by now. This diluted Essence is strong enough to keep us alive as far as Jaffa. Do you understand?"

Llewelyn nodded grudgingly.

"Good. Now pay attention. I've held some of the undiluted fluid in reserve. Here, take these…" He handed Llewelyn a thick cloth bag. It clanked. Inside were two heavy black bottles, about a pint each.

"Proper bottles," said Kung. "This Essence is stable and won't lose any more of its potency. When we reach Jaffa, there's enough to revive us and see us through until we get fresh supplies. Do you understand?"

Llewelyn thought about it. Kung's methods were cruel, but his reasoning was coldly correct. He put the bottles on Chang's bed.

"Yes, I do. Do captain know you do this?"

"Of course not," scoffed Kung, "And neither should you tell him. Chang is a sentimental fool. He'd take the chance of keeping everyone on undiluted Essence rather than see his men in pain. This mission is too important to be dictated by his misguided sense of fair play."

Llewelyn bristled, not liking that Kung was drawing him into a lie against the captain.

"Oh, you're as bad as him!" said Kung, reading his doubtful expression. "Listen, boy, you might not care for what I'm doing, but would you rather you were left alone with a crew of corpses?"

Llewelyn shook his head. But he still didn't want to lie.

Kung smiled thinly and gestured to Gelert, who rose and woofed happily. His tail knocked one the black bottles off the bed. Kung only just caught it before it smashed on the floor.

"He's the reason for everything. The Great Dog must be brought home. None of us matters except in doing this. Now leave."

Llewelyn went back on deck, subdued. Being part of Kung's plan should have made him feel more confident, but subterfuge, half-truths and deceit didn't come easily to him.

The captain spotted him climbing through the hatchway and beckoned at him to join him at the stern railings.

Llewelyn gulped. *What if he suspects I'm in cahoots with Kung?*

But it wasn't that. Chang looked more haunted than suspicious. The sickness was already coming upon him, and he glanced nervously westward, back along the junk's lazy wake as Llewelyn leaned next to him.

"What is it back there that worries you?" Llewelyn couldn't help asking.

The captain faltered, the sickness draining his thoughts.

"You're a good lad, and I trust you with my life. With my ship. With our entire mission. So it hurts me what I'm about to ask you, because I can't tell you why."

"Is it that you're scared of my father?"

"What? Scared? Of your father?"

"Yes! Are you worried what he'll do to you if he catches you?"

The captain laughed weakly, "No, I'm not worried about your father, wherever he is!" He grew urgently serious again. "But I do want you to promise me that if you see anyone following us, you'll wake me."

"So who is it? What's so bad about them?"

"'Trust me, I can't tell you! The knowledge could tear you apart and you wouldn't know what to do! And then where would we all be?"

More bloody secrets! thought Llewelyn.

Chang was beginning to shake as he shrunk into the dry horrors of the cycle. He slipped between languages, losing control of his tongue.

"Promise me, Llewelyn! You know where I stash my emergency supply, here in my top pocket. Promise you'll wake me!"

"I promise," he sighed. "Now let's get you comfortable."

🐾

Less than a day passed before the crew relapsed into their misery, and twice more they went through the cycle of the Essence, their moments of bleary wakefulness quickly shrinking to just a few hours.

When it finally came, Wudi was the last to go, determined not to give in but finally forced to. Dawn was rising when he croakily called Llewelyn into the cockpit and handed him the tiller.

"I'm just going to have a bit of a lie down," croaked the old man, "Wake me if you need me."

But at the end of the twelve hours, just as Kung had predicted, no-one would waken, and Llewelyn took permanent control of the ship.

He called Gelert into the cockpit.

Behind them, the bloated orange disc of the sun sank through a cloudless, dusky-pink sky. The slatted sails and rigging creaked soothingly as a steady, warm wind blew, sliding the junk across the gurgling, amber sea.

It should have been a tranquil, beautiful evening except that, one by one, their friends began to twist in agony and shriek at unseen terrors.

"You didn't tell me this would happen!" he shouted at Kung.

Gelert howled the ancient wolfhound song for the dead, and slowly, the sailors' lice dogs came crawling from their masters' pockets to sit at his feet. Their high-pitched cries blended with Gelert's, and from below the booming yowl of the alarm dog rose to join them.

The wind freshened and set the taut rigging thrumming a

deep, mournful whistle.

Llewelyn shivered. He hoped Kung's plan would work and that none of the captain's fears would materialise in the west.

❦

Days passed. Llewelyn did his rounds with a drinks bucket and a pot of Cheng's broth. He dripped water and gruel into everyone's mouths, then made sure they were comfortable. As the blistering sun made its way across the sky, Gelert helped him drag the sailors into whatever shade there was.

Zheng's prostrate body was too big and heavy to move, so Llewelyn draped him with a spare piece of slatted sailcloth. When night fell and the temperature dropped, he covered everyone with blankets and fed them once again.

Then he returned to the cockpit, lashed the steering ropes to the tiller and tried to sleep.

For five days, every twelve hours, he doled out the Essence, and for a few brief hours, the men's awful moaning abated. But eventually, the groans would return, and Llewelyn took to stuffing his ears with cloth.

Things became more miserable when he realised the men all needed cleaning. Although they weren't eating and drinking much, what was going in one end was still coming out the other, and it wasn't pretty.

"And you," he complained to the sleeping captain as he fetched a bucket of seawater and some rags, "you didn't tell me *this* was part of the deal!"

Fortunately, the ship ran itself. With the wind so fine and steady, nothing changed. The sails and rigging seemed carved from wood, and when he wasn't looking after the men, Llewelyn was able to sit back in the cockpit carefully checking Wudi's fish for his position against the sun and stars.

Eventually, the crewman's agonies stopped. At first Llewelyn was relieved, then he grew anxious. They lay as still as statues and barely breathed. The temptation to break open Kung's black bottles was strong, but Llewelyn resisted, having to trust his instructions.

Things grew boring after that. There was only so much feeding and cleaning and navigating he could do, and he looked for something to fill the time.

He heaved Kung's comatose body into the cockpit and began talking to him in Welsh, just to annoy him. He recited the poems and sang the beautiful songs of his homeland, of the dragons and the giants and fairies that roamed the brooding mountains and green valleys of Gwynned.

Gelert listened, rapt at the familiar Welsh words. The lice dogs watched, yipping whenever the wolfhound's tail started wagging.

When Llewelyn grew tired of educating Kung, he pulled the captain in, leaning the two men together with their arms wrapped around each other as if they were the best of friends. Soon Wudi was there too, the three men sprawled as if having a party. Llewelyn tied cups in their hands and recreated scenes from nights in his father's castle, with the King and Owain retelling tales of adventure and Friar William sneering at them. Chang took the King's part, Wudi Owain's. Kung, inevitably, became the miserable, angry Friar William.

Just wait till I get back from the Holy Land and I tell you my stories, he laughed at them. *The Holy Land!*

Llewelyn took Wudi's fish from his pocket and checked it against the setting sun and the shadows on the deck. In his mind he saw the junk, as if on a map of winds and currents and stars, just as he'd been taught.

Not too far now, he consoled his lonely self.

🐚

On the twelfth hour of the eleventh morning, it was time to give the men their next dose. First on his rounds were Huidi the carpenter and Liu and Huang, two of the top men. Their withered, lined faces were pale and bluish, and their skin felt clammy, like a washed-up jellyfish.

Llewelyn felt the first glimmerings of dread. Even after he'd poured Essence into their mouths there was no change. He bent over Huidi and listened at his nose and mouth for signs of breathing but heard nothing. Gelert sniffed at Huidi and looked expectantly at Llewelyn as he pulled back one of the carpenter's eyelids, searching for life.

Suddenly, a gobbet of slimy white fluid with a kernel of solid green and black gunk splatted onto Huidi's eyeball. Nothing. No blink, no reaction.

Hold on! Llewelyn squinted into the sky. A solitary white bird wheeled high above. It squarked once, and was joined by three or four noisy friends.

"Seagulls!" yelped Llewelyn.

Gelert loped towards the junk's prow.

Llewelyn strained his eyes into the brightening sky. There wasn't much to see, just a veil of brown haze on the eastern horizon. But then he saw the sea was flecked with scraps of seaweed and he heard more squawking from above – a sizeable flock of gulls was following them.

He scrambled up the mainmast and perched on the crosspiece. Even before he saw the distant smudge of land, a dry dusty smell in the air told Llewelyn he had made it.

He had brought the ship halfway across the Inner Sea.

"The Holy Land!"

He slid back to the deck and ran below to get one of Kung's bottles of Essence. *But this time it's the real thing!*

He sat beside the captain in the cockpit, his hands trembling as he measured out the precious liquid. He tipped Chang's head back, opened his withered lips and poured in the Essence.

Chang sputtered to life, leaping to his feet, instantly alert, looking straight away to the west. "Is anyone following us?"

"No!" said Llewelyn, slightly taken aback. He was expecting some thanks or congratulations.

The captain was relieved. Only now did he look east.

"How close are we to landfall?"

"I dunno. Maybe you should wake Wudi," Llewelyn muttered.

"That old duffer? Who needs him?" said Chang.

Shocked, Llewelyn looked up and saw the captain was smiling.

"Well done, Llewelyn! I knew you could do it. Wudi will be proud of you. Come on, let's get everyone up and about."

They started with Wudi, and he sat up in the cockpit, stretching and yawning, then eyed the sun and sniffed the air.

"Good lad!" he beamed at Llewelyn, "Jaffa's just a day away! Am I not the best teacher in the kingdom? And are you not my finest student?"

Llewelyn blushed, but inside he bathed in the glow of praise.

Meanwhile, Chang had revived Kung.

"I'm thirsty!" he complained as he woke up, stretching stiffly.

"What am I doing in the cockpit? And why's this cup tied to my hand?"

"Shut up and help me with the rest of the men," laughed the captain climbing out of the cockpit.

Then Llewelyn remembered the three still crewmen.

"There's something wrong with them. Do them first."

The captain sprinted to the three men, Kung hurrying after him.

Chang tapped the carpenter's cheek. He'd given the sleeping sailor his Essence, but nothing had happened. Not even a hiccup.

"Come on, Huidi mate, rise and shine, you've got work to do," whispered. His gentle taps turned to slaps.

Kung knelt beside him and gave Huidi a cursory examination.

"He's dead." He got up and pointed to the others. "Those two as well by the look of it. Don't waste any Essence on them."

Eyes wide with concern, the captain ignored him. He dripped some of the fluid into Liu's and then and Huang's mouths. Nothing.

"I don't understand! What's happened?"

Llewelyn joined them. "They were fine last night ..."

"Don't worry about it, boy," Kung said. "We're better off without them."

"Better off?" snapped Chang, standing up. "Huidi was a friend and the best carpenter I've ever worked with. Liu and Huang were our best top men. In what way are we better off?"

"For Dog's sake," retorted Kung. "Think of the mission. We're nearly at Jaffa, but we still need to cross the desert. We don't need sailors any more, but we do still need the Essence."

Llewelyn thought Chang might punch Kung but the captain forced himself to calm. "I hope you're happy being right," he glared. "Come on, Llewelyn, let's see to the others."

The crew revived, exalted and chatty, but were immediately silenced by the sight of their three dead friends. The shock was immense. One death had been bad enough, but three rocked them to their souls.

Cheng the cook sobbed uncontrollably. Ao and Chao tried to console him, but he just howled.

"I'm sorry, it's just that ...THREE! So many! So much dying!"

Llewelyn was surprised. Three was half an hour's tally on a quiet day back in the siege. *Haven't you seen death before?*

Just then, the man at the masthead called out, "Land ho!"

The crew was surprisingly unimpressed.

Llewelyn guessed that their dead crew-mates were occupying their thoughts, but even he was disappointed with his first proper look at the Holy Land.

He'd been hoping to see something worth going on a crusade for – golden spires, heavenly choirs of angels or maybe a mighty burning cross in the sky. But there was nothing but beige and brown rocks and not even proper trees, just twisted scabby collections of dry branches and drooping twigs.

The crew livened up at the lookout's next announcement – there were ships, plenty of ships. The captain sprang up onto the railings, scanning the horizon, and Llewelyn joined him.

The closer the junk drew to the land, the more vessels they saw; tens, then hundreds, of all shapes and sizes sailing along the coastline. They were mainly dhows, though Llewelyn recognised more familiar shapes – trading vessels and warships from the north. Then he caught a rancid whiff wafting up from the deck. It was the three dead bodies.

Chang grimaced too. "We'd better get them sorted," he muttered. "I'll say a few words for the men."

❦

Huidi, Liu and Huang's bodies were already in a bad state. Llewelyn was surprised, again, by how aged they appeared. These weren't the fresh corpses of seamen in their prime, but the dried husks of wizened, impossibly old men.

The captain offered up a prayer as Zheng picked the bodies up and gently dropped them, one by one, into the sea. Ao and Chao were stoically miserable; Liu and Huang had been their two closest crew-mates. Llewelyn saw them pick up their friends' orphaned lice dogs and put them in their pockets. Wudi took Huidi's. He was touched by their tender concern for the tiny animals. It was a good way to keep alive the memory of the dead.

The captain cleared his throat.

"More good men gone. Kung says they must have been needed more of the Essence than the rest of us. If we'd known,

I know we'd all have gladly given them some of our share."

Everyone muttered agreement but Llewelyn caught Kung rolling his eyes.

Chang continued "But let's not forget that none of us thought we'd all make it through. We knew how dangerous this mission would be, and still will be. Our friends died for a reason."

He called to Gelert. The Great Dog came bounding over, lifted his paws onto the captain's shoulders, and slobbered his face. The crew crowded around the wolfhound, patting and stroking him.

Gelert relished the attention, his tail swishing extravagantly.

Llewelyn was glad his old friend was happy in their company, but his chest tightened. With the Holy Land so close, it wouldn't be long before they'd finally be going their separate ways; Gelert to his Emperor, him back home to Wales.

"Captain!" screamed the lookout, his voice full of panic.

"What is it?" yelled the captain.

"Ahead! Chinese war junks!"

🐾🐾

Llewelyn watched as the face of every crew member drained of colour. Cheng fainted to the deck and another sailor vomited.

No-one uttered a sound. They just stared at the captain who stood stock still, gawping up at the lookout. Llewelyn had never witnessed such collective shock and a full minute passed before Chang broke the gobsmacked silence.

"You're certain?" he yelled back up to the lookout.

"On my life!" came the trembling reply.

The captain was once more a picture of decisive action. "How many?"

"Three mediums, one fast!"

"At least it's not the whole fleet!" Chang muttered grimly.

"How can they have got ahead of us?" gasped Kung.

"What going on?" said Llewelyn, flummoxed. "He say they Chinese!"

The captain put his hands on his shoulders.

"Llew! Get Gelert out of sight. Don't let him up on deck unless I tell you!" he commanded, then turned his attention to the crew. "Full sail!" he bellowed. "Wudi, hard to port! If we're in luck, they won't have noticed us among all these other ships!"

He continued volleying out orders. The crew responded, running hither and thither, and soon the junk was heeling into its new tack.

"What going on?" Llewelyn asked Kung, "Why run from Chinese …?"

"Not now, boy!" he replied, trying to keep his voice even. "Just get the dog below deck!"

He pushed Llewelyn roughly to one side and ran after the captain.

"Come on, Gelert," said Llewelyn, baffled, and they dropped out of the chaos that had engulfed the deck.

❧❦

Llewelyn was back where he'd started, shut away in the dark hold, wondering what was going on.

Several hours passed. He racked his brains trying to work out why they were fleeing from the Chinese navy. The question brought up matters that, until now, had flitted in the back of his consciousness. He tried to piece together the dozens of puzzling evasions he'd heard from Captain Chang and his crew, but found only threads of stories that simply didn't connect.

The more he thought about it, the less sense everything made.

He knew he must confront Chang.

"Stay here!" he ordered Gelert and climbed on deck.

The junk was kiltered at a recklessly steep angle, its taut rigging singing a piercing chorus of whistles and the sails bulging alarmingly. By now, they were out of sight of land, but Llewelyn sensed they were on a course taking them to the southwest of Jaffa.

Although the darkening sky was clear, the atmosphere on board felt storm-like and brooding. The crew were transfixed at their stations, gazing fearfully backwards at the horizon.

Then Llewelyn saw the slatted sail of another junk, tiny in the distance, but glowing bright orange against the sun.

His breath caught. *We really are being chased!*

The captain was in deep conversation with Kung and Wudi.

Kung looked up at his approach. "Is the Great Dog safe?" he asked, coldly.

Llewelyn ignored him and addressed the captain in English. "Something very wrong is going on here. Tell me what's happening."

"Not now!"

Llewelyn flipped into Chinese.

"Just. Tell. Me. What. Is. Going. ON!"

"Tell him for Dog's sake," said Wudi. "He's earned the right to know. You can't keep the truth from him forever."

Kung hissed his disapproval, but a murmur of assent rippled around the crew. They were on Llewelyn's side. Chang glared at Kung, then at Llewelyn, then at Wudi as he weighed up his answer.

Eventually he sighed. "Llewelyn. You've saved our mission five times now. It's time you know what you've been saving.

"We aren't Chinese. We've stolen Gelert from the Emperor."

Llewelyn stared at him.

The two simple statements had turned his brain into a mush. Questions tumbled from his mouth.

"Stolen? But, the deal you made with my father? He gave you his oath. He gave you Gelert. You didn't have to steal him."

"No, the Chinese made a deal with your father. They got Gelert, and then we took him away from them." Chang pointed at the distant sail. "But now they've found us, and we mustn't let them catch us."

"But ... who are you?" stuttered Llewelyn. "Why do you want Gelert?"

"We haven't got time for this!" barked Kung.

The captain spread his hands in apology. "I'm sorry Llewelyn, he's right." He turned to Zheng. "Take him below. Put him with Gelert and lock them up safe. Remember, the dog is everything!"

"But what if it's my father out there!" cried Llewelyn, but the decision had been made. He tried to resist Zheng, who was forced to carry him squirming downstairs.

"Let me go!"

"Sorry, Llew! Orders. Mind your head on the hatchway."

"Ow!"

Gelert met them, growling with concern. Llewelyn stopped struggling; there was nothing to be gained in fighting Zheng. The giant, despondent at having to treat his little friend this way, gently but firmly ushered them into one of the cook's storage lockers. He gave Llewelyn a lamp and some blankets, and with many apologies, bolted the door shut and went back up top.

It was hard to track the passage of time.

Bitter and brooding, Llewelyn knew the junk was still close hauled to the wind, heeling steeply over on the port tack.

More hours passed.

It must be midnight by now, he thought, but still nothing much had happened except his backside had grown numb from the constant thudding of the bow hitting waves, the shock transmitting through the fabric of the ship. The captain was squeezing the utmost speed from his fleeing vessel.

A strange quiet had descended on the junk. Now and then, Llewelyn heard the muffled drumming of the sailors' bare feet moving around the deck as ropes were hauled in and sails trimmed, but Chang was talking his orders and the men were whispering their replies.

Gelert became fretful, then fearful, then fractious.

It seemed an eternity before there was a change in the ship's course, but when it came, it was a violent turn to port that threw Llewelyn and Gelert to the other side of the storage locker.

The lamp was extinguished, and bags of rice and pots and pans came tumbling down on them. The dark was total and the crash of falling objects only added to the confusion. Gelert, already at the end of his tether, started barking. Nothing Llewelyn could do would shut him up, so he sat dazed in the impenetrable gloom as the ship righted itself. It had turned in a slow curve and was now heading back along its original course.

Gelert carried on barking.

Suddenly there were voices at the door. It was the captain and Kung. They were whispering, but Llewelyn couldn't hear a word over Gelert's din.

"Llew! Get the damned dog to shut up!" shouted Chang.

"Let us out!" yelled Llewelyn.

"You must keep the Great Dog quiet!" ordered Kung, whispering hoarsely.

"Why should I help you?" screamed Llewelyn.

He heard more furiously whispered exchanges from beyond the door, then a strange clattering noise, as if earthenware pots were being dragged up to the door. Gelert threw himself at the door, howling and baying like a hell-hound and scrabbling dementedly at the timbers.

"Please get him to shut up!"

But now Llewelyn was screaming too, adding to the din.

"You stole us! You lied to us! You used us!"

"I'm sorry, Llewelyn," said the captain.

"Oh get out of the way!" said Kung fiercely, and suddenly there was a bubbling hiss. In the dark, Llewelyn could hear nothing. Then he smelled a sweet, heavy odour filling the storeroom.

It was almost like honeysuckle.

~~~~

A hundred and forty miles away, it was dark.

The girl and the crew dogs dragged the dead ass into place. It had to look just right. It had to look as if the beast had tripped over the harbour side and broken its neck falling onto the sampan's deck.

Moving the flyblown carcass wasn't easy. It was already two weeks dead and, bloated with gas, it rolled awkwardly and was hard to grip. Its slimy hide came away from the greasy blue-white meat beneath, and hundreds of tiny fleeing crabs scurried over her hands.

It didn't help that the deck was covered in a tangle of jagged debris; snapped masts, broken decking and shards of rusting metal that poked and prodded at the ass as they heaved it around. She didn't want anything to puncture the inflated body — the stench would be unbearable.

She realised she should have put the ass in place before she'd begun trashing the sampan. Oh well. Too late now.

To the north, the city glowed against a dimly red sky. The glimmering light came from camp-fires of the Saracen army that had thundered out of the desert just four days ago, immediately laying siege to the city's walls.

At first, she'd felt safe enough tucked away in a corner of the harbour, far from the coming fight. What did she care if the Saracens and Christians were finally facing off? Besides, there was only one war she was interested in: the war she had come all this way to stop.

But when the city's inhabitants started streaming down to the harbour and loading up their clumsy sailing boats, she knew her precious sampan would soon become a coveted means of escape.

Although she'd had to work at night, it wasn't hard to disguise the boat. There was more than enough discarded rubbish mashed up in the corners of the harbour to be collected and strewn about the deck. Old sails and shredded nets added to the general feel of decrepitude, and the dead ass, she congratulated herself, was a particularly brilliant and deliberately repulsive addition. Even the most desperate fugitive would look elsewhere.

The hardest part had been lowering the masts, which were hinged at the base because the sampan had been built to pass beneath bridges. But the masts' massive securing pins and locking bolts were jammed in place, and it took all the crew dogs' efforts, pulling hard on jury-rigged ropes while she heaved on the biggest crowbar she could find, to lower the lanky but immensely heavy teak columns safely to the deck.

Anyone looking at the sampan now wouldn't see a sampan. They'd be hard pressed to see any sort of vessel at all. She went below and locked herself and the crew dogs in the hold.

All just in time. As dawn rose, the girl heard screams. She peeked through a hawser hole and saw a fight breaking out just a few hundred yards away. A Christian Crusader knight was trying to get a woman and three young children on board a dhow, but the fisherman who owned it protested that his boat was already full.

She bit her lip when the knight drew his sword and ran the old man through, kicking his body into the sea.

So, this was war. It was just as she'd imagined it would be: a brutal stupid waste. But she'd change that.

Everywhere, dozens of boats were pulling out of the harbour, a panic of sails heading for the open sea. The crowds of people abandoned at the sea wall shook their fists at long-gone vessels, milling around the harbour-side for hours, pleading to be rescued. But no-one came close to the sampan. All stayed upwind of its stinking cargo.

As the sun set once more, the masses turned and walked sullenly back into the city and their fate. The girl relaxed. All she had to do now was sit tight and stay out of sight.

A thin, pink ooze dripped through the deck planking above. The dead ass was leaking. She moved to the other end of the hold.

Surely she wouldn't have to wait much longer now.

PART IV: THE DESERT

Chapter 20. Navigator

A second later, Llewelyn woke up inside a brightly lit oven.

Bewildered, he sat up. Searing orange sunlight forced his eyes shut, but not before branding the after-image of scorched sand and rocks into his eyelids. The air smelled dry and dusty, like old sackcloth.

Gelert, frantic with happiness, was bouncing around him like a month-old puppy. He whimpered and slobbered his face.

Llewelyn slowly opened his eyes again, adjusting to the light. He was sitting on a crude stretcher, cobbled together from an old blanket and poles. One of the handles was his longbow. *Who's the idiot who did that?*

He looked around, still woozy.

"Where are we?" he mumbled, his brain frying in the stifling heat. Gelert slurped the back of his neck – the drying slobber felt briefly cool. Llewelyn now saw that they were in a simple campsite, beneath a thorny bush that had been draped with slatted sailcloth. It failed to shade them from the light of the reddening sunset.

It can't be evening! It was night-time a few moments ago!

He blinked painfully and saw blurry human shapes thirty yards beyond the camp. It was the captain and Ao, Chao and Zheng, standing on a bulbous boulder the size of a haystack.

Where'd that come from? Llewelyn thought dimly. He blinked again and saw Kung walking back towards the camp.

He yelped as he tried to stand. The sand was hot and seared the bare soles of his feet. The scenery spun as he fell.

"Finally," said Kung. "Be careful, boy, it will take some time for the effects of the drug to fully wear off. Here, have some water."

Llewelyn's tongue felt fat and dry like a woolly sock. He took the proffered skin and glugged down the lukewarm water. It tasted delicious. Already his head was clearing, and with it his eyesight.

He noticed the captain's alarm dog. It was guarding Kung's

bag of medicines and a pile of supplies, panting in the heat, its huge tongue lolling from its wide mouth. Dozens of the lice dogs snuffled around it in the shade, their pale skin almost camouflaged against the sand.

"What are you lot doing here?" he called to them. *And where are your masters?*

The little dogs yapped at Llewelyn's voice, and the alarm dog barked loudly, alerting Chang.

"Careful with our water, Llewelyn!" he yelled. "Our moisture traps are small and it's a big desert out there."

Desert? He scrabbled up to his knees and took in the panorama.

The camp stood in a dirty bronze-brown wasteland that dipped down to the west, stretching back into the setting sun and lengthening shadows. In the distance was a glimmer of sea. The captain and the others stood on their boulder gazing in the opposite direction into a dusky horizon.

How'd I get here? Llewelyn tried again to stand up, but the blistering sand made it impossible.

"Put these on," said Kung, handing him his boots.

You found my bundle of clothes!

His boots felt heavy and stiff with salt. When he pulled them on, they pinched his toes, but it was less painful than the baking earth. Kung supported him as he hobbled to join the others, Gelert following, trailing a noisy pink carpet of yapping lice dogs. The rocky earth was cooking the leather soles of Llewelyn's boots; he wondered how the little dogs could bear the heat.

He struggled to climb the boulder. It scorched his hands and he was too weak to pull himself up. Zheng reached down, lifting him in one easy motion.

Llewelyn's head swam. The rock was perched on the edge of a dizzying precipice. Below stretched a bleak plain shadowed by the cliff. A dust devil skittered across the expanse and the setting sun splashed the peaks of impossibly distant mountains with fiery red light.

Llewelyn recovered his equilibrium, but continued to goggle. Somehow he'd left the junk, and the sea he'd become so familiar with had drained away, leaving this brooding fractured landscape.

The captain pointed out a rough track running down the cliff. It traced its way in a series of tight loops, disappearing into the shadows below.

"It'll be hard going but we'll make it."

Llewelyn looked around the tiny group – five men and a handful of dogs.

"We?" he croaked. "Where are others?"

Zheng, Ao and Chao looked to Chang, who folded his arms and gazed into the immense emptiness. In the distance a bird screeched.

It wasn't a seagull.

Something really bad has happened!

"Tell me! What happen to ship?"

Kung began to answer. His voice was stern and cold.

"It doesn't ma–"

"No, it doesn't matter, does it?" The captain glared at Kung, his green eyes flashing angrily "So long as the Great Dog is safe."

He turned to Llewelyn.

"The ship's gone. Forever." His voice was husky with emotion.

How can a ship 'go'. How can it go 'forever'?

"How we get here? You lock us in storeroom."

"Ha!" said the captain. "We needed to sneak past the Chinese in the dark, but you and Gelert just wouldn't shut up, would you?! Kung had to drug you."

"What you mean 'drug'?"

"The vapour I use to induce sleep," said Kung. "Don't worry, Gelert wasn't harmed."

"How long were we sleep?" Llewelyn had no idea, but guessed that it must have been several hours if the ship had reached land.

Oh! And then they've carried us halfway up a mountain.

"Gelert slept for six or seven hours. You were out a little longer – three days."

"Three days!"

Kung shrugged. "Yes. Gelert was wedged against the door when he passed out. We couldn't open it. You'd fallen underneath him, and the vapour sinks. You breathed in more of the drug than he did."

Chang took up the story.

"We evaded the Chinese but we had to land in the middle of nowhere. So much for all our plans to buy supplies and horses in Jaffa! We trekked inland, to here, waiting for you to wake up while we dodged the snakes and the scorpions." He shuddered with revulsion. "Millions of scorpions."

"What are 'scorpions'?" asked Llewelyn warily.

"Just insects," said Kung. "Small, deadly insects."

"How deadly?"

Kung shrugged. "Deadly enough to kill Wudi."

"Wudi dead?" Llewelyn's throat constricted.

The captain hung his head and Ao, Zheng and Chao looked away.

"Yes," continued Kung. "It got him in the small of his back, right in the spine. The scorpion has a most ingenious sting, a small balloon of poison on the end of its tail and a sharp hollow spike, which it uses to stab into its victim. A most efficient mechanism for the delivery of a toxin."

He seemed morbidly fascinated, as if Wudi's death was nothing but a useful introduction to a subject worthy of future study.

Llewelyn looked to the captain while Kung rambled on.

"Was it quick?" asked Llewelyn.

Chang's expression drifted from sadness into anger.

"He took a day to die. A whole day. He was waiting for you to wake up. He wanted to say goodbye to you. The pain was turning him inside out and there was nothing I could do for him. But he never cried out. My mentor and oldest friend is dead and buried in a scrape in the ground a thousand miles from home." His voice dried up.

"But it's not a problem," added Kung brightly.

What? Wudi's dead! That's not a problem?

"Before he died, he told us which way to go," Kung explained. He waved vaguely to the south. "We have to head into those mountains."

Llewelyn was still scrabbling through his shock.

"But, but … that terrible!"

"I concur; they weren't the most precise directions. But the good news is that Wudi asked that we give you this." Kung took something from his pocket. It was a small, round wooden box.

It was Wudi's fish.

The captain found his voice. "His last words were to tell you how to get to our next waypoint. That you should 'show his little friend's greenest fin to the setting sun, and follow its opposite till he faces the bey-ji-sing.' Does that mean anything to you?"

Llewelyn nodded.

"Thank Dog for that! I've no idea how to use his contraption, but once we reach the waypoint, I'll know which way to go. Here, take it."

The old helmsman's fish felt insubstantial in Llewelyn's palm. Tears ran down his face. *Is this really all that's left of you, Wudi?*

"I don't see what's to whinge about," said Kung. "We have a new navigator. You. And now the mission can go on."

Llewelyn felt blank. "But where everyone else?" he sniffed.

"Llewelyn, they all dead," mumbled Zheng.

"Scorpions got them all?" shrieked Llewelyn, jumping. *Jesus, Son of God, help me. They must be everywhere!*

His reaction startled Chang into dark laughter.

"Scorpions? Ha! No. Not scorpions. They died like sailors should, at sea. They took the junk back out to open water, to lead the Chinese away. To fight them if needs be." He looked to the horizon. "There were huojian, explosions ..."

Gelert was chasing the lice dogs, snuffling at them and tumbling them in the dust. One ran over Llewelyn's foot. He bent down and picked it up. "Why they leave their lice dogs with you, unless ... they knew they going to die!"

Chang nodded.

Llewelyn felt drained. "They die to save us?"

"No," said Kung indignantly. "They gave their lives to make sure the Great Dog will be safely delivered."

The captain's faced darkened with anger.

"Now, boy," continued Kung, oblivious to the callousness of his words. "Wudi told you what you must do, so do it."

"Why I agree to be your navigator?" hissed Llewelyn, "You steal me, you lie to me ..."

Kung eyed him coldly. "Oh do be sensible. You're in the middle of a desert. We have all the supplies. Without you, we are lost, but without us, so are you. And nothing is more important than the …"

"For Dog's sake, shut up about the mission!" snapped the captain, taking Llewelyn's hand. "Please. It's only a few more days and then we'll be in Aqaba and we can see you on your way home."

"I owe you nothing!" said Llewelyn in English, pulling away. It was all coming back to him now. "My father made his bargain with the Chinese. They were the ones who fought the English army for us. Gelert belongs to the Emperor, not you, whoever you are."

"Take us to Aqaba and I'll tell you everything."

Chang's promise came out of the blue. Llewelyn gulped.

"You'll tell me everything?"

"What are you telling him?" said Kung, suspicious of their intimacy.

Ignoring him, the captain continued in English. "Help us, Llewelyn, and I'll tell you why you mustn't let the Great Dog go to the Emperor."

There was something in his voice that troubled Llewelyn – an implicit threat to Gelert. He looked into Chang's emerald eyes, saw sincerity, and wavered.

"Why should I trust you? You said you'd take me to the Holy Land."

Chang laughed hollowly and spread his arms at the grim landscape. "The Holy Land?" his voice dead in the dusk. "You're already there."

Llewelyn looked around at His Lord God's Promised Land.

"It's not worth the trip," he said, nearly laughing.

"I'll thank you to not speak your gibberish in my presence," interrupted Kung, "The sun is setting. Tell us which way to go, boy."

Chang looked at Kung with contempt. That was enough for Llewelyn. He opened Wudi's box.

"I'll tell the captain," he said in English, smiling at Kung all the while. "But you can go stick your head up a donkey's shithole."

He held Wudi's sphere up to the sun. It glowed, warming in his hands, and inside the jewelled fish slowly swam to face north.

He squinted at it and found the greenest fin, then adjusted his position so the fin aimed directly into the centre of the sinking orange disk. The blue fin on the opposite side of the fish pointed just east of south.

Far across the empty plain stood mountains. Their lower slopes were lost in the shadows of the deepening twilight but their peaks glowed orange pink in the sunset. The tiny blue fin lined up with a jagged notch in the middle of the distant range. Llewelyn rechecked the fish, just as Wudi had taught him to. Yes, the notch was where they must go.

"There," he pointed.

"You're sure, boy?" asked Kung.

"No," he said flatly in Chinese, returning the fish to its box and putting it in his pocket. "No, I'm not sure, but I trust Wudi, you two-faced worthless piece of bum-wipe," he added in English.

Kung glared, correctly guessing Llewelyn's insulting tone.

The captain laughed out loud. "My thoughts exactly Llew," he said, pushing past him. "Come on, let's get packing. It's getting dark and we need to get moving."

Llewelyn waited, watching them scurry back to the camp. Fifty feet away from the encampment of bamboo poles and slatted sailcloth a broiling swarm of flies buzzed around an isolated bundle.

Even at this distance, its sickening stench made his nostrils smart.

Back in the camp, Kung had collected his moisture traps and was topping up everyone's water skins.

Meanwhile, Ao and Chao were taking bags from their bundles.

"Catch!" said Ao, tossing them to Llewelyn. "You can carry them now."

Inside the bags were his clothes and sword and arrows and a water skin. Chao showed him how to tie everything up into a single bundle using the blanket from the stretcher. Llewelyn's belt became a shoulder strap.

Mother of Christ, that's heavy! he grunted, as he picked up the pack.

The captain called to his alarm dog and Kung shepherded the masterless lice dogs into a straw basket, which he strapped to the top of his pack. The others hefted their bags and poles onto their shoulders and Captain Chang carefully checked their loads, pulling straps tighter.

Then he looked around. "Who's taking the Great Dog's food?"

No-one replied.

The captain went over to the fly-blown package in the distance and returned, carrying it at arm's length. Gelert followed him there and back, his eyes fastened on the rank bag, which trailed a long tail of buzzing flies in its wake. Llewelyn's heart sank as Chang tied it to the back of his pack.

"Looks like it's your turn," said the captain, wiping his hands.

The stinking meat made him gag, but Gelert looked at it hungrily. Llewelyn knew he'd scoff the lot given a chance, and kicked the wolfhound away.

"Now, now," said Chang. "Don't do anything to harm the Great Dog." He adjusted Llewelyn's pack "There you go."

"Thanks," he said.

"Thank me in ten hours' time," replied Chang as he walked to the front of the group. He looked back, satisfied.

"Right, everyone, try and keep up."

❧

They made their awkward single-file decent into the plain below.

Llewelyn knew why he was at the rear of the column. The haze of vile flies around his pack wouldn't budge. Half the swarm was trying to get into the stinking meat, while the rest seemed determined to lick his eyeballs dry. He dared not breathe through his mouth for fear of inhaling a lungful of them.

As they scrambled down the track, the sun finally set, drowning them in a dispiriting blackness. But soon, as the moon gradually rose in the opposite quarter, the dreary scenery was bathed in an eerie cold light and Llewelyn's spirit's lifted.

He called ahead to Zheng. "This not easier at daytime?"

"Too hot," the huge man grunted. "We wouldn't get more than half a mile. Mind you," he laughed, "you'll be amazed at how cold it will get! If we weren't on the move, we'd freeze in our boots!"

Llewelyn could already feel the heat leaching from the rocks on either side. As they cooled, he heard some of them cracking. To his relief, the swarm of flies vanished as the temperature dropped.

After two hours of trudging, the steep slope began to ease. Soon they were on level land and the captain ordered a stop.

Just in time! Llewelyn's shoulders were beginning to rub raw. He sat next to Zheng and took out his water bottle.

"Who carry me from junk?" asked Llewelyn, wondering how he'd got to the last campsite if he'd been asleep.

"The captain mostly," shrugged Zheng. "He feels bad that he's had to lie to you so much. Him and Kung."

"Kung! Kung carry me?"

"Of course! Gelert won't budge an inch without you, and after Wudi died, you became even more vital to his precious mission."

That figures, thought Llewelyn, bitterly.

"In fact, I think Wudi made sure you got his fish because he knew Kung would have left you ..."

Zheng didn't finish his sentence, but it gave Llewelyn some grudging satisfaction that his usefulness now went beyond being merely Gelert's little friend.

When the captain called the next break, it couldn't have come quicker. Llewelyn chewed on some tasty strips of meat. He was still starving, and guiltily he found himself reaching for more.

"Go on," said Chang, "we've no shortage of meat, but be careful with your water; what you carry is all you have."

The desert was mostly quiet save for nocturnal bird calls and the ever-present scuttling sounds of insects. Then they heard other noises. Loud throaty roars punched the still night air, followed by deep hacking grunts. The sounds seemed to be coming from behind them.

"What is it?" Llewelyn whispered nervously to Ao and Chao. "Shizi."

It was an unfamiliar Chinese word. Ao saw his confusion.

"Shizi. Huge cats, nearly as big as Zheng; sandy coloured, claws everywhere, shaggy hair around the head and lots of big teeth. You know – Shizi."

"Oh! Lions!" said Llewelyn. He'd heard terrible stories about these ravenous fanged beasts. "Shizi."

"You've got it, lions. They followed us up from the coast. Persistent creatures. More like hunting dogs than cats!"

"Are they dangerous?" said Llewelyn.

"Not as dangerous as this," said Chao touching his bow. "There were four of them, now there's only three."

"You kill one?" asked Llewelyn, impressed.

"What do you think we've been feeding the Great Dog?"

"Gelert eating lion meat?" He nearly laughed. *A dog eating a cat.*

"Why not? Meat's meat. But I don't think the lions are too happy with the arrangement."

Llewelyn shivered at the thought of carrying the butchered remains of a lion.

The guttural roars were drawing closer.

A different sort of shiver shook him.

Dawn was a long time coming, and everyone cheered weakly when the final halt was called. They found a slab of rocks beside some tangled sharp-thorned bushes that promised some midday shade. Groaning with pleasure, they eased their packs off their sore shoulders.

"We make a stockade from the bushes," explained Zheng. "The thorns keep the lions away while we sleep."

The flies had returned with the sun, and the warming lion meat stank. Llewelyn quickly humped the rancid bag upwind. There was no way in Christ's Kingdom he was going to put up with that torment for a second more than he had to. A hundred yards seemed sensible enough.

Licking his chops, Gelert watched him stash it in the shade of a low rock.

"No!" Llewelyn scolded. "Wait till we set up camp."

❦

Llewelyn had seen beetles and spiders back home in Wales, and even adders and the odd grass snake, but nothing prepared him for what he saw when he returned to the camp.

The captain and his men were smacking the rocks with their swords. Under every boulder and in every crevice lurked scorpions, spiders, snakes, and other unidentified, but no less deadly, creatures. Out they came, brown and yellow, scuttling, repulsive, and ready, said Kung, to bite or sting him to death.

"Crush the insects, but just chop the heads off the snakes!" Chao yelled to Llewelyn, stamping on a swarm of scorpions that poured out of a cranny.

"Why chop off heads?" he asked, joining in the stamping.

"You wouldn't want to eat a snake's head, would you?"

"You eat snakes?" squirmed Llewelyn.

"It's what the strips of meat we've been eating are!" he laughed. "And don't waste the blood – very nutritious! See, that's how to do it …"

Llewelyn watched squeamishly as Ao expertly dealt with a ten-foot-long snake. It rose, hissing, from beneath an upturned rock. Its head appeared to have been flattened, so it looked like it was wearing a hood. It swayed as if hypnotised by the little sailor's distracting left hand.

Then, with a swift stroke, Ao sliced off the serpent's head. Its body fell heavily, writhing and twisting, spurting dark-red blood into the sand. Ao snatched it up and greedily sucked on the severed neck. The snake's body coiled around his wrist and forearm as he swallowed. Ao looked at Llewelyn and laughed, his mouth and teeth were crimson.

"Mmmm! Cobra blood! Here, try some! It'll make you strong!"

"Uh, no thanks," retched Llewelyn.

Within half an hour, the camp had been cleared. The men chopped up thorn bushes and arranged them across the front of the rocks, draping them with sailcloth to create a shady oasis. Already the sun was baking the land.

Llewelyn was impressed. The simple construction would keep everyone out of the sun, and any cooling breeze could blow through the thorn bushes, which were indeed a formidable barrier.

Kung had started a fire and set a few inches of water to boil in a tiny pan. Llewelyn felt ravenous for some rice, but remembered he still had to feed Gelert, who sat patiently outside the stockade, gazing longingly at the distant bag of lion meat. The swirling haze of black specks and droning hum beckoned. Llewelyn groaned. He couldn't put off the task any longer.

Chang tapped him on the shoulder as he left. "Take your bow."

"Why?" asked Llewelyn, suddenly wary.

"It's not just flies that are attracted by meat."

Llewelyn gauged the distance between the camp and Gelert's food. The hundred yards suddenly looked like a thousand.

Ao and Chao laughed at his nervousness.

Llewelyn ignored their mocking and picked up his bow and quiver. The heft of the Chinese arrows was weedy compared to a heavy Welsh broadhead, but they were better than nothing.

As he neared the smoke-like column of flies, he was hit by a wall of stench that made his eyes water. There was nothing for it; he took a deep breath, closed his eyes, and thrashed his way through the thick buzzing swirl.

It was like walking through a fuzzy storm of tiny pellets of dry shit and crusty vomit. He opened the bag by touch, groping inside to grab a thick chunk of the slimy, fibrous meat. Even as he pulled it out, a cloud of bloated flies landed on his fist and forearm, their bodies forming a close-fitting, vibrating sleeve.

He re-fastened the bag and scurried backwards away from it.

Gagging and gulping, Llewelyn threw the slab of meat wildly, as far as he could, then finally dared to open his eyes, letting out his breath in a shuddering gasp. The swarm of flies, still connected to his bloody hand, coalesced and stretched, following the meat like a thick black rope as it somersaulted through the sky. By the time it thudded to the ground, ten feet away, it was so infested with insects it had quadrupled in size, and the mass of flies was still growing.

Gelert gave a great bark of joy and leapt after his breakfast, happily snapping at the swelling ball of flies as he waded into it.

"God! You really would eat anything!" spat Llewelyn, looking at his hand in disgust. The glistening mass of flies had turned his hand into a squirming club.

Revolted, he slapped at his hand, then rubbed it into the sand. All that did was turn the living flies into a thick smear of dead flies, which only attracted new hordes. He scraped the mess off with his sword.

Eventually he was relatively clean and fled back to the camp. Gelert, who'd finished off his meat in three bites, loped along behind him, licking his fly-blown chops and enjoying the bonus of insects for dessert.

Llewelyn fell gasping to the ground, his skin still prickling with the ghosts of a million flies. The pack of pink lice dogs came running over to him and began chomping and scrunching on the remaining flies on his arm. He'd never been so grateful to have them around.

The captain and sailors sniggered.

"No sign of the lions then?"

"I think I like lions more ..."

Unable to master his heaving stomach, Llewelyn puked. His vomit was flecked with crawling black bodies. Gelert promptly began to lick it up.

"Welcome to the desert!" said Zheng, giving him some snake soup.

Llewelyn fell in with the rhythms of their trek, just as he'd adapted to life on board the junk. It didn't take him long to know that he preferred life at sea.

Miserably dull, bone-chilling nights of trudging were followed by stiflingly hot days lying beneath a makeshift sunshade and trying to sleep off the ordeal. All the while he was being harried by a menagerie of repulsive insects and reptiles.

On the third day, the debilitating part of the cycle of the Essence flared up.

It was evening, and Kung had just finished reviving the men. Llewelyn watched him carefully put away the bottle of medicine.

Kung had adjusted the timing of its rationing so that everyone could carry on journeying through the night. That he controlled everyone's well-being made Llewelyn uneasy. He knew the medicine man would resort to anything if his mission was threatened.

"What if you run out of Essence in desert?" he asked.

"There's plenty enough to get Gelert to Aqaba," replied Kung testily. He wrapped the bottle in a thick, soft blanket and placed it in a sturdy wooden box beside the other bottle, then closed the lid. "Ten days' worth at least."

"Ten days enough for everyone?"

Kung glared at him. "If you do your job right, there is. Just make sure we're going in the right direction. Boy."

As the nights passed, their goal grew ever closer.

Before they set out, Llewelyn rechecked his fish. The moon had begun to wane, but the mountain range was still clear in the distance. The tiny notch in the mountains was now a great gash.

Llewelyn wondered when Chang would tell him why they'd run from the Chinese ships, but now they were on the move, the moment never seemed right. Too busy walking or too fast asleep. He suspected Chang was biding his time, waiting for the right moment when the ever suspicious Kung wasn't around.

Meanwhile, their loads were slowly being lightened as they ate their food supplies. The captain joked that once the lion meat ran out, they'd just kill another.

The three lions were still following, unseen, but Llewelyn heard their guttural roaring most nights. When on the move, everyone bunched close, and no-one went anywhere alone, not even to pee.

🐾

Five days in, the food supplies were gone and snacking on snakes no longer satisfied. There'd been no sound of the lions as they struck camp, and the captain declared it was hunting season.

"But be careful out there. Swords as well as bows.

"Come on, Llewelyn," said Zheng. "Let's get some grub."

He was thrilled at the prospect of using his longbow again. Soon, Gelert was prowling in a wide circle, snuffling at the ground with the simple joy of being a dog. After so much time on the cramped decks of the junk, loafing around, pissing and sleeping, out here on the flat plains he was free to run and chase and kill.

Suddenly his ear pricked up and he was off, disappearing over a low ridge.

"The Great Dog is FAST!" gasped Zheng.

Faster than he ever was! thought Llewelyn. All this strength. All this energy to burn. *Ever since his bath in the Essence.*

They heard a clamour of hissing and growling. A stocky beige cat with ludicrously tufted ears came sprinting over the hill with Gelert in hot pursuit. With his long loping strides, the wolfhound appeared to be running in slow motion in contrast with the cat's blurred, stubby legged movement.

The lynx turned, spitting. Llewelyn laughed, then winced as the cat slashed Gelert sharply across the muzzle. The dog leapt into the air and raced whimpering to Llewelyn, his tail between his legs as the lynx strolled haughtily off into the night.

"That'll teach you," chuckled Llewelyn, but the gashes in his old friend's face were deep. One had just missed his left eye.

"That looks serious," said Zheng.

They hurried back to camp where Kung anxiously examined Gelert's muzzle. "I'll have to put something on these," he announced.

Chang and the sailors watched nervously. Llewelyn was bemused.

"What? There nothing wrong with him!" he said. "Since he fall in Essence he been fine. Look, he already stop bleeding."

"Maybe so," said Kung, reaching into his bag of medicines. "But cats' scratches are dangerous. Their claws have a thin groove that ..."

Lost in his diagnosis, Kung was just thinking aloud. He rubbed his green paste into the Great Dog's cuts, then sat back, stroking his chin. "Hmm, that's what might have happened when he fought that damned ape. The Essence must have got into his blood through his wounds ..."

"Is that what make him five years younger?" said Llewelyn.

Kung whirled at him, glaring with a ferocity he'd never seen. "What gave you that idea?" he shouted.

"Since he swallow the Essence he different. Younger."

"Get the thought out of your head!" screamed Kung.

Llewelyn recoiled at this unexpected attack and looked at the captain for support, but Chang shook his head at him.

"Do as he says, boy," he frowned. "No good will come of it."

But, of course, the captain's warnings had quite the opposite effect.

Llewelyn said nothing, but already his brain was racing with fantastic thoughts.

The night's march carried on in sullen silence.

Llewelyn watched Gelert springing lightly over boulders. *Kung's wrong.* How could he deny that the Essence had made the old wolfhound younger? *He must be trying to hide something about it.*

Maybe, Llewelyn thought suddenly, *maybe it keeps them young.* "No, that's stupid," he said aloud in Welsh to Gelert. "Wudi was as old as the hills, and he guzzled it down like the rest of them."

Kung called back to him. "Quiet back there!"

Llewelyn turned the facts over and over in his head. Everything pointed to the Essence being something to do with ageing, but nothing made any sense. Eventually he stopped his musing. There was a long way to go.

Plenty of time to work things out.

Now the journey took them into a new part of the desert. The scrubby thorn bushes slowly disappeared; there were fewer rocks underfoot and more sand.

As dawn broke, they stepped from the rock desert onto an expanse of smoothly undulating dunes that stretched away to the horizon on either side. Ditching their heavy packs, they climbed the nearest dune.

An eternity of sand lay ahead. The distant mountains now seemed a long way off.

"The moisture traps won't give us much out there," said Kung

Shade would be the priority now so they scraped a shallow trench and jammed the bamboo poles into the sand. The battened sailcloth was draped over the growing frame.

Then, out of the corner of his eye, Llewelyn noticed Kung with his sword chasing after a snake. It sped across the dunes at a remarkable pace, leaving sinuous C-shapes in the sand. Kung finally caught and decapitated it, but Llewelyn was puzzled to see him ignore the body. Instead he picked up the bloody head and carefully snapped off its long fangs. He put them in a bottle and moved off in search of another snake.

"Why he collect teeth?" he whispered to Ao.

"Search me. If he wants snake poison for his potions he's

going to be disappointed. Their poison is in sacs at the back of their throat, not their fangs."

Llewelyn shrugged. Kung could do whatever he wanted so long as he kept his distance. Besides, it was time to feed Gelert.

Just one smallish chunk of lion meat remained in the bottom of the bag, and the dawn air was still cool so there were few flies. He threw the meat to the wolfhound, who swallowed it whole.

"Well, that's the last of that!" he yelled, coming back into the camp.

Chang wiped sand from his hands.

"We'll have to get some more meat for the Great Dog before we tackle those dunes," he shouted, a little too loudly. Then he whispered to Llewelyn in English, "Let's get away from that man!"

Kung was still scampering around the dunes, now collecting scorpions and slicing off their tails.

"Gladly!" said Llewelyn. "I'll go get our bows!"

Gelert heard him and bounced around, knowing the hunt was on.

"There'll be game there," announced the captain confidently, pointing to a low rocky outcrop to the north, about a mile away.

"Come on, let's pick up the pace."

They jogged towards the rocks, Gelert lolloping ahead. *Is this a good time to fish for some answers?*, wondered Llewelyn.

"You know what I said last night …?"

"If it's about the Essence, forget it! I've already told you too much."

"But, I was just wondering …"

"You know, boy, that in China, all young people are brought up to obey their elders without question."

Llewelyn thought about this for a second or two.

"Well, as you're not Chinese, that shouldn't be an issue for you."

Chang laughed. "You're precocious, aren't you, Llewelyn Prince of bloody Wales. But I won't tell you anything about the Essence, so don't bother asking."

He sensed it was time to change tack. The subject of "The Essence' might be a closed door, but Chang seemed open to talking.

"No, no, no. What I was wondering was, if you're not Chinese, who are you?"

The captain stopped jogging. He folded his arms and regarded Llewelyn thoughtfully. The wind had shifted to the east and was picking up in force, blowing rivulets of sand around his feet.

"I did promise I'd explain. It will help you understand us, once you know why we are on this mission."

He walked on, marshalling his thoughts. "You remember when I asked you why the Welsh were fighting the English?"

Llewelyn ran to catch up. "Yes. Because we want to stay Welsh."

"Well, you and me, we're much alike. I am from the Kingdom of Jiang," explained Chang. "We're a small country on the edge of a much larger, more powerful neighbour. We have a Queen, and we have our dogs, and just like you Welsh, we want to keep it that way. The big difference is that Wales only has the English after you, whereas we have the Empire of China."

"The Chinese have invaded you?"

"Not yet they haven't. But they will."

"Why? What do you Jiang have that they don't?"

Chang scowled bitterly. "That's not the point I want to make. As far as the Chinese Emperor knows, Jiang is just another kingdom for his set. You see, the Emperor is a collector. Just as he wants the Great Dog for his menagerie, he collects countries. In recent years he's swallowed up many of the smaller countries that surround China. We're not so foolish to think that we won't be next."

Llewelyn stopped in his tracks. "Hold on! He wants Gelert for a menagerie?" he gawped. "He sent a fleet and an army around the world so that he can take my dog and put him in a cage?"

"A very nice gilded cage. But a cage nonetheless."

Llewelyn's blood boiled. His father hadn't agreed to *that*.

The captain saw his anger.

"You don't like it that the Emperor wants your dog just on a whim? Imagine how we feel about losing our whole country! But he'll have both unless we stop him. Once the Emperor decides he wants something, he gets it, either by buying it or by making war. He just snaps his fingers and it will be done."

Llewelyn reeled at the idea that all this fuss over Gelert was little more than a self-indulgent trip to a flea-market, but now Chang had set a ball of questions rolling in his mind.

"How did you find out he wanted Gelert?"

"We have spies. And once we knew the Emperor was preparing his expedition, they helped us infiltrate the Imperial fleet."

"All that way so you could steal Gelert from him?"

"Yes! The Great Dog is the key to our plans for survival."

Llewelyn knew he was close to the crux of the matter.

"Because … having … Gelert … means … you … can …?" he prompted tentatively.

The captain stopped. "It's hard to explain ..."

"Try me," said Llewelyn calmly, but inside he was squirming with curiosity.

Chang pointed at Gelert, who had chosen that very moment to take a dump. "Believe it or not, that is the greatest dog ever born. With him by our side we can defy the Chinese." Gelert was now scratching sand at his steaming turd in a half-hearted attempt to cover it up.

"But how?"

The captain smiled. "Ah well, Llewelyn, that's where we arrive in 'I can't tell you' territory."

They'd reached the rocky outcrop. It was cut by gullies and trails.

Chang unslung his bow and lowered his voice. "We'd best stop talking now."

Llewelyn nodded. He beckoned Gelert over, hushing him to be quiet. As they walked on in silence, the captain's revelations cartwheeled in his head and a rage welled up from deep inside him. The Emperor's power and arrogant self-indulgence made him feel insignificant and angry. He scratched his old dog's head. Gelert closed his eyes in bliss. Llewelyn made up his mind.

"There's no way I'm letting you end up in that maniac's menagerie!" he whispered.

Just then, Chang hissed and signalled a way to the top of the escarpment. They heard noises coming from the other side and Gelert went into hunting pose, ear pricked, his eyes steely bright.

Chapter 25. Claws

Climbing silently was difficult; the sharp rocks were hellishly hot and crumbled noisily under their fingers. Fortunately, the wind was growing stronger. It blew dust into their eyes, but drowned the racket they were making. The captain reached the crest of the ridge and peeked over it, then slowly lowered his head.

"Yes!" he mouthed excitedly, and held up two fingers.

Llewelyn took a look. On the other side of the scarp there was a short drop into a gully. His eyes widened. Below, not twenty yards away, was a pair of wonderful animals. They looked like deer, but not like any deer he'd ever seen.

They stood tall; the height of a man, snowy white with a blaze of tawny red along their necks and throats. But it was the horns that amazed him. They were beautiful, long and ribbed, and curved elegantly back and over the animals' shoulders, almost reaching to their beefy hind-quarters. One tilted its head back and carefully scratched its rump with its left horn.

Llewelyn unslung his bow and reached for an arrow as he considered which deer to go for. He gestured to Chang. *Let's take the one on the left.*

Together, they drew back their bows.

Trembling at Llewelyn's side, Gelert had forgotten about hares and rabbits. This is what he'd been bred for: bringing down large animals.

The deer were so close they couldn't miss, but he felt the stiffening breeze on the left side of his face and adjusted his aim.

His arrow thwacked deep into the deer's chest. It fell to its knees, then crumpled to the ground, a startled look in its already-dead eyes.

The captain shot at the other animal. It must have moved at the last second, or maybe a fluke in the freshening wind threw his arrow off. It hit the deer high in the neck and it sprang forward, careering out of sight around a corner in the gully.

"Dammit!" yelled Chang. He scrambled over the lip of the scarp and slid down the scree slope.

"Why didn't you go for the one on the left?" Llewelyn shouted

186

after him, exasperated. Now they'd have to go running after a wounded animal. At least it wouldn't get far, not with a wolfhound on its trail.

"Go get him, boy!" he urged, but the great hound was already on his way, leaping to the gully floor in one bound and overtaking the captain with his next. In a moment, he was around the corner and after his prey.

Llewelyn slung his bow and made his way down to his kill. He knelt, drew his sword and went about butchering the carcass. A few hundred yards away, Gelert's hunting growl was followed by the high-pitched bleat of the other deer.

Then growls of a different type pierced the air.

Louder, deeper, and terrifying.

Lions!

He heard the captain yell a fear-struck challenge, and there were sounds of a snarling struggle. Without thinking, Llewelyn was on his feet, sheathing his sword and running as he unslung his bow and knocked up an arrow.

The captain's yells turned into screams.

🐾

So that's what a lion looks like! was Llewelyn's first coherent thought as he skidded round the blind corner into a dead-end gully.

He'd almost tripped over the dun-coloured, shaggy-maned beast.

The lion's breath rasped and bubbled. It was bleeding out, an arrow in its chest. Llewelyn ran past it. Ahead stood two more lions, their backs to him, roaring furiously into the narrow, closed end of the gully.

Beyond them, just twenty yards away, was Chang. He'd fallen, and was wedged up against the rocks, lying against the corpse of his dead deer. He was trying to knock up another arrow, but his left shoulder was pouring blood from three parallel slashes.

Standing between the captain and the two enormous lions was Gelert. Although barely half the lions' size, he bristled with fury, barking and growling savagely, holding them at bay.

The two cats seemed bamboozled by the wolfhound, but not afraid. Their long tufted tails lashed the air, and they seemed ready to pounce.

Llewelyn was already aiming his bow.

His first arrow hit the nearest lion in its backbone, exactly nine inches above the hips. The beast's back legs buckled uselessly, its spine severed. It yowled in startled pain and twisted its forequarters to swipe at the arrow.

The second lion turned its head and immediately spied Llewelyn. It shifted around, preparing to jump. Seeing his chance, Gelert leapt onto its back and sank his teeth into its left ear, almost tearing it off.

The lion reared up, and that was all Llewelyn needed. His arrow thumped into the huge cat's chest, closely followed by another.

The lion fell, dead. The wolfhound hopped down from its back and sniffed it.

Llewelyn was cautious as he walked past the first lion, which was still very much alive. The crippled animal was full of fury and tried to haul itself back into the fight, roaring and spitting at him. Llewelyn knocked up his fourth arrow and calmly, at point-blank range, sent it straight into the great cat's heart.

The captain had lost a lot of blood. It steamed darkly as it soaked into the hot sand. Already the flies were swarming.

"I was saving the Great Dog, but he ended up saving me!" croaked Chang.

"He does that," said Llewelyn. He unstrung the captain's bow and bound the string above the gashes in his upper arm. The tourniquet slowed the bleeding, just as Owain had told him it would, but he needed something to staunch the bigger deeper shoulder wounds. Unsheathing his sword, he sprinted to the nearest lion and hacked off fistfuls of its mane.

Returning to kneel beside Chang, he waved away the storm of flies from his wounds, then pressed the fur tightly onto the bloody mess, ignoring the man's agonised screams. The mass of fibre quickly matted with blood and Chang gasped as Llewelyn stuffed more handfuls of mane until the gore stopped seeping through.

"Stop your whining," he ordered, "Here, hold the hair in place with your good hand and keep it pressed down hard."

Llewelyn stood to take off his shirt, then heaved the captain into a sitting position against the fallen deer, tying the shirt arms tightly round his chest and shoulder.

Chang sighed. His face was impossibly pale, and his lips were blue. He still found the strength to chuckle as he looked slowly from one dead lion to the next.

"I see you needed two arrows to kill the second one," he grimaced.

"Ah well," replied Llewelyn, as he adjusted the captain's makeshift dressings. "It's these toy arrows of yours. If I'd had some proper Welsh broadheads, I'd have only needed one for the both of them."

Chang winced with pain. "You, both of you. You saved my life. Twice. In three minutes." He gritted his teeth. His breathing was becoming short and sharp, but he reached up with his good arm and grabbed him by the shoulder. "Llewelyn, Prince of bloody Wales, you're a fine young man. Gelert really is the bravest most loyal dog in the world! I'm glad you're on our …"

He gasped once, then slumped unconscious.

Llewelyn stood, absently brushing flies from his blood-soaked hands. His heart was pounding, and his lungs were heaving, but he felt remarkably calm, almost serene. He looked around the gully.

Slowly, the reality of what he'd done crashed into his mind and he had to sit down again. He hadn't just killed two terrible creatures and saved the life of a man – he'd done it by himself. *Well, maybe with a bit of help from you.* He looked over at Gelert, who was lazily licking congealed blood from around the captain's shoulder and arms.

"Get off, you disgusting creature!" he yelled, throwing a rock.

"What the– ?" came a startled voice from above.

Kung and the others were standing at the lip of the gully, dumbfounded by the bloody tableau below them. They had all the supplies with them; packs, poles, sailcloth, the lot.

He skittered down the scree slope with his medicine bag and knelt by the captain and peeled back the makeshift bandages. He raised an eyebrow at the compress of lion's mane and glanced at Llewelyn, impressed.

"Ingenious," he muttered. He reached into his bag and pulled out some dried poppy heads. When he squeezed them they oozed a thick, ivory coloured paste.

"What's that?" asked Llewelyn, woozy but fascinated.

"Pain killer. My strongest." He opened the captain's mouth and smeared some on his tongue. Chang smiled, then went limp like a doll.

"What happened here?" asked Zheng.

Llewelyn looked at the dead lions and all the blood.

Isn't it obvious? He was about to say so when a different thought struck him. "How you know we in trouble? How you get here so quick?"

Kung pointed up at Ao, Chao and Zheng who were still on the ridge. They looked fidgety, worried.

"Ask them, but hurry!" he hissed. "I'll tend to the captain."

Llewelyn saw fear in his face and knew something was wrong, something much worse than a wounded captain and three dead lions.

Llewelyn climbed up to the others.

"What is it?" he panted. All he saw was that the wind had grown stronger, bending plumes of sand across the barren landscape.

"We're being followed," said Chao and Ao together.

"Watch," interrupted Zheng. "Beyond that ridge ..."

Gelert howled. Llewelyn squinted. On the horizon, a prick of light trailing a smoky tail slowly climbed into the sky.

"A huojian!" he gasped, as it puffed into a tiny blue flower surrounded by white sparks. The silent explosion vanished and the steep curve of the smoke trail was quickly whipped away by the wind.

"Wait … Now, there, over to the north," growled Ao.

Another smoke trail crept into the sky. It was red when it exploded. Then, further away in the northeast, another red huojian burst.

"They Chinese, aren't they?" said Llewelyn.

"Can't be anyone else," said Chao. "They've sent up four blues since you left us, and the reds go up in reply. Three separate parties, and they're using the huojian to home in on us."

Three dull, almost inaudible thuds rippled the air. The dying sounds of the explosions had finally reached them.

Llewelyn's heart thumped. "How far away are they?"

"Fifty? Sixty miles at most," said Zheng.

Two night's trek.

"If they have horses ..." Ao left the grim thought unfinished.

Bugger! I hadn't thought of that!

A sudden gust nearly blew Llewelyn over. Gelert grumbled, his wiry fur standing almost horizontally from his bulky frame. Zheng had to grab at his wildly flapping bundle of sailcloth.

Llewelyn turned into the wind. It was blowing at gale strength.

Squinting, he saw a range of towering dirty-brown mountains in the middle distance. But the pass they were heading for was many miles away. He realised that what he was looking at wasn't mountains. It was a rolling wall of clouds.

"What is it?" he shouted into the wind, thoroughly perplexed.

"Sand storm!" Zheng bellowed. "Forget about the Chinese,

we must find cover. Quickly!" He snatched up his sailcloth and poles. The twins were already hop-skipping down the scree slope with their loads.

"Why quickly?"

"Look again!" yelled Zheng, jumping after them.

In the moments he'd turned away, the towering dust storm had grown larger. It was now a mile high, and hurtling towards them at an impossible speed. Gelert knew the approaching storm was dangerous. He barked at it, fearless but foolish.

"Get moving, mate!" hollered Llewelyn. He picked up the remaining bundles of supplies and jumped.

Down in the gully, Zheng and the twins had already braced the larger bamboo poles around the still unconscious captain and the fallen deer. The sturdy framework was just big enough for everyone to sit inside. Ao and Chao sheeted home the slatted sailcloth and wrapped its edges around the bamboo poles, then started stitching the seams together with thick twine.

The wind was now picking up loose bundles of supplies and tumbling them around the gully. Llewelyn ran to gather them, yipping as belts of scorching sand lashed across his bare torso. The air was filled with a deep rumbling sound and the wind was growing hotter the faster it moved, making it harder to hear or see anything. Llewelyn was forced to screw his eyes almost shut or be blinded.

The hut was nearly completed as he brought the last of the supplies in. Outside, Kung was helping Zheng pile rocks against the lower edges of the sail.

"Thank Dog you found this little nook!" he screamed over the howling din. "The worst of it should pass over us. Where's the Great Dog?"

Llewelyn peered inside the shelter; "Where you think?"

Kung looked. Gelert was draped contentedly across the carcass of the dead deer, chewing on a hindquarter.

"We take body outside?" Llewelyn yelled at Kung, cupping his voice to make himself heard.

"No!" he bellowed in reply. "It's food to hand!"

"It enough meat for two weeks!"

"Some sandstorms have lasted a month!"

The sailors finished the shelter ten minutes before the storm hit.

Everyone bundled inside, just in time to start plugging the gaps and stitching up any holes in the cackling sailcloth. Working within the tight confines of the hut was miserable. The heat was suffocating and a fine dust seeped through the seams. The floating grit worked its way into Llewelyn's armpits and elbow joints, chafing them raw. Rubbing his eyes only made them sting more.

Finally they were secure, sewn in tightly with no door or windows, nothing but flapping, banging canvas. It was impossible to speak. The shrieking of the battering wind reduced them to crude hand signals.

This was only the beginning.

When the face of the storm finally smashed over them, Llewelyn felt like he'd been slapped around the ears. The noise redoubled, as if all the dead of the world were shrieking straight into his soul. The passing pressure waves bowed the slats of the sailcloth inwards and it felt as was as if someone was trying to suck his lungs out through his eyeballs. He watched in horror as Kung's nose suddenly haemorrhaged a bright gout of blood. The stream instantly mixed with the misting dust and caked into a red mud stalactite.

He knew things were getting really bad when Gelert stopped chewing on the deer and, shivering, crawled over to be with him.

Then things got worse.

The hut grew darker. A rent suddenly appeared between two of the battens in the sailcloth. The force of the wind blew a jet of sand straight across the shelter like a rod of stone, breaking up against the opposite wall in a spattering fan. Zheng threw his back against the hole, shutting off the torrent. Ao busied himself behind the giant man's back and repaired the hole with his twine and needle.

For hours, the storm continued to bellow and shake them in their shelter. The pounding noise drilled into their minds and threatened to turn their brains into dust.

Their water skins were still three-quarters full, but Kung signed to everyone to only take sips. Llewelyn kept his mouthful in his cheeks for as long as he could, only swallowing a drop at a time, a teasing agony for his parched throat.

The captain woke briefly, choking, his nostrils clogged with dust. Kung cleaned his nose and wound his head with gauze bandages so he could breath properly. Soon they'd all wrapped their heads in cloth.

A darker darkness fell, and still there was no sign of the storm abating. Unknown hours passed and it grew faintly lighter again. A new day?

🐾

Kung butchered the deer from the head down. Its flesh had begun to dry and he had to work hard to slice off the fibrous neck meat. Everyone had to chew interminably until the flesh was remotely swallowable. Even Gelert found the meat tough going.

Kung fed the smaller dogs by regurgitating into his hand, then offering the vomit to the miserable animals.

As he gnawed at his strip of gamey meat, Llewelyn noticed that the others weren't hungry. They were heading into the third day of the cycle of the Essence.

Still the tempest blew. He re-wound his head with bandages and eventually fell asleep with only his worst dreams for company.

When he woke, the rest of the crew were insensible. The cycle of the Essence had descended upon them. Llewelyn didn't know how long he'd slept. Had the twelve hours passed so that he could safely revive them? In the hazy gloom of the tent there was no way of knowing. Taking the risk, he dug out one of the black bottles from Kung's pack. He felt the fluid sloshing in the bottle, and felt jealous that the others would get some extra moisture. He resisted the temptation to take a sip, his dry throat screaming to taste it.

He revived Kung, who gestured a groggy thanks, took the bottle and treated the captain, tipping back his head and letting him swallow a few drops. The Essence had an immediate effect; Chang sparked into life and opened his eyes. He was bewildered by the cacophony of their cramped quarters, gave an unheard shriek and passed out again.

Still the terrible sandstorm raged.

The days dragged into more days.

The sand piling up around them threatened to cave in the walls of the tent, and they had to push the structure upwards and keep readjusting it to prevent disaster.

At first, Llewelyn had despaired of ever knowing silence and stillness again and thought he might go mad. Now he accepted he would, and all that kept him from finally tipping into insanity was working to keep repairing the walls and ceiling of their rudimentary shelter, and to hold it above the suffocating sand.

Then, as if in posthumous revenge, the dead deer's stomach began to bloat with putrefying gases. Its guts exploded through its mouth and anus, spattering everyone with stinking green-and-black bile and slime. Unwinding their head bandaging, they writhed and wriggled, trying to scrape off the filthy sludge.

Zheng went into a fit. Llewelyn watched his mouth turn into an opening and closing rictus. The giant's eyes streamed and he twitched and shuddered and rolled, as if in agony.

Then Llewelyn understood. He heard Zheng's laughter. He wasn't having a fit, he was laughing at the disgusting mess and their terrible circumstances.

But if he could hear the laughter, it could only mean one thing – the wind had begun to drop. The light in the shelter grew brighter until the glare began to hurt his eyes. Even the air felt cooler.

"Everyone quiet!" he screamed, and because everyone heard him, they began to smile.

Almost as quickly as it had arrived, the sandstorm was gone.

The roaring wind slowed, and the pummelling flapping of the shelter's walls diminished. Now everyone was laughing. Gelert and the other dogs bounced around excitedly.

"Thank Dog!" shouted Kung as the wind petered out. He used his knife to slash through the seams of the lee wall.

They spilled out into the gully, sprawling onto perfectly smooth sand. An expanse of blue arced above them. In the west, the searing sun was beginning to set, heralding a warm, tranquil evening.

The lice dogs tumbled everywhere, running round in tiny little circles and yapping with excited relief. The captain's alarm dog scampered up the nearest pile of sand and bayed with delight. Llewelyn's ears were filled with dust and battered senseless, but even muted, the dogs' barking was welcome.

Nothing was the same; the gully was now much shallower, filled with swathes of sand. All that was left of the jagged pinnacles of rock that had surrounded them were isolated stumps sticking out of the sand. The dead lions were gone, buried under fifteen feet of sand.

Llewelyn climbed the nearest rock outcrop to see more, disorientated. It was as if they'd been blown into a new world.

Their goal, the notch in the distant mountain range, was still there but the great sea of dunes that had barred their way had completely disappeared.

The land was scoured bare to a flat, bleached surface. But for the desert heat, he'd have thought he was looking at a snow plain. *Where's all the sand gone?*

Then he remembered the red and blue huojian. *Are we still being followed?* He looked westward, blinked, then laughed loudly.

"What is it?" asked Kung from below.

"Come look! You no worry about Chinese now!"

The great storm had lifted the entire desert, carrying the unimaginable volume of sand over their heads and dumping it behind them.

The wind had left it carved into colossal curving scoops and falls, a series of steep escarpments that hadn't yet had time to soften and fold back into ordinary dunes.

Kung joined him. It was his turn to gasp.

"Nothing can follow us through that!" laughed Llewelyn.

"Just as well ..." said Kung surveying the landscape. An edge of apprehension had crept into his voice.

"What the matter?" asked Llewelyn.

"It's the Essence. We had enough, but the storm has held us up."

Llewelyn was lightheaded with optimism after the confinement of the last few horrible days. He pointed at the flat, blanched landscape. "So? Now we no have to cross sand dunes! We walk fast. How far Aqaba after then?"

Kung looked thoughtfully at the expanse of white plain.

"It's hard to say. Three or four days? Chang might know."

He finally brightened. "Or, if he dies, we'll have his share of the Essence."

He turned to go back to the campsite. "Hurry now. We must keep moving. We'll face our problems when they arrive and not before."

Ao, Chao and Zheng had dismantled the shelter in just a few minutes. Then they butchered the last of the dead deer, quickly piling up a week's worth of meat.

Meanwhile, Kung and Llewelyn and Gelert went ahead to examine the newly exposed, flat white ground ahead.

Close up, the expanse glistened in the setting sun. Llewelyn ran his fingertips over it. The texture was hard and slightly warm. It reminded him of sharkskin; slick to the touch in one direction, but harsh and abrasive when rubbed the other way. His fingertips stung, as if slashed by a thousand tiny knives. He tasted his fingers and spat. *It' salt.*

"We must be especially careful with our water now," said Kung.

When they returned to the camp, the captain was asleep on a blanket. Kung removed the matted cake of lion mane and examined him, sniffing his wounds.

"They're clean. They're healing well," he pronounced.

Zheng brought over two poles. "Step aside, I'll make a stretcher."

But Kung had an idea. He instructed the giant to add the deer's two long curved horns to the base of the stretcher so that they would act as runners.

"I've heard about this from our travellers who've been beyond the eastern ocean," he explained as Zheng worked. "The barbarians there don't know about wheels and use their tent poles to make contraptions for dragging things …"

Llewelyn quickly saw what he was talking about. The sharp edges of the horns would slide along the smooth salt flat, like a snow sled. It would be a much easier way to transport Chang.

"…and they use their dogs to pull the loads," said Kung, looking at the Great Dog.

"Him? Pull something?" scoffed Llewelyn.

"Of course," said Kung. "We Jiang have several types of dog breeds just for pulling carts and trolleys."

"Good luck telling Gelert that," said Llewelyn.

Zheng tightened up the final piece of rope and stood up.

"That'll do."

He'd fashioned a simple harness from leather straps, attaching it to the stub ends of the deer horns. The stretcher balanced lightly on the horn runners – the whole thing looked surprisingly elegant and springy. The captain lay comfortably between the poles, secured in place by two straps across his chest.

Llewelyn called Gelert over, curious to see how he'd react to being made into a beast of burden. The old wolfhound eyed the sled with suspicion, and Llewelyn had to push and pull him into place. Once harnessed, however, he looked purposeful, and seemed eager.

As Gelert stepped forward, the sled skittered lightly over the sand.

This might just work!

Ao and Chao finished bundling up the supplies and they all shouldered their heavy loads.

The sun set swiftly, the horizon transitioning from pink dusk to violet twilight. The air itself seemed to glow with intense reds and oranges and purples.

Llewelyn took out his fish, checked their direction again, and led them off toward the salt flat.

As the band reached the freshly scoured plain, a gibbous moon rose, flooding the pale ground with a cold bluish light.

The salt wasn't quite as flat as it had seemed in the daylight. The low angle of the moonlight revealed countless tiny craters, and the jagged crust of each indentation cast a long shadow, painting the sheet-white plain with countless, blade-straight black lines.

Gelert stepped tentatively onto the surface, and yelped. The sharp crystals were too much even for his hard-padded feet. Hastily, Llewelyn hacked up some strips of deer hide and tied them around his paws. Then they were off.

After their hideous confinement, walking on the salt flats was liberating. The ground was firm beneath their feet, yet yielded slightly, like a dusting of snow. As the temperature dropped, their breath began to cloud, adding to the sensation that they were tramping through a winter landscape.

Gelert trotted, his long tongue flapping happily, great clouds of sweaty steam rising from his thick pelt. Pulling the captain along on his deer horn sled was wonderfully easy. It hissed over the hard salty surface as if weightless.

As the night drew to an end, they looked back and were astounded by how far they had travelled. The dawn transformed the blue night into a soft pink glow. When they were finally able to see each other properly, they laughed, for they were all caked in a light film of salt; their eyes, nostrils and lips pink smears on their alabaster faces. Gelert looked particularly strange; the salt crystals made his straggly fur look like thistledown.

Llewelyn asked Kung if maybe they should press on into the day. He balanced the amount of remaining Essence against the time lost.

"No, we'll stop. The third day is already on us – I can feel it in my blood."

He was right. Llewelyn had noticed the onset of dullness in his companions, so they set about making camp.

At least they didn't need to chase away the creepy crawlies. There was no life on this desolate expanse. With no thorn bushes or rocks either, the sailors had to drape the battened sailcloth over a simple bamboo frame for shade, leaving the sides open to keep them cool. Everyone bedded down, glad for some rest.

Soon, they were asleep, but Llewelyn tossed and turned. For a while, it was bearable in the shade, but as the sun climbed higher in the sky, its searing heat and blinding light hit the salt flats and scattered sideways. The open-sided shelter soon became like the interior of an oven. The light magnified the heat, but worse, it battered his eyes and gave Llewelyn a throbbing headache.

By now, the Jiang were slumped deep in their cycle. He pitied them; the torture of Essence withdrawal must surely make this dreadful heat even worse.

Wearily, he got up and went around the sides of the tent, hanging up bolts of canvas. The new drapes hung limply in the dead air. It was still hot, but the extra shade eased the pounding in his skull.

Drained, he flopped beside Gelert, who panted heavily near

a gap in the walls of the shelter. Sweat pricked Llewelyn's skin but evaporated instantly, failing to cool him. He felt withered, as if the salt flats were sucking his will to live from every pore.

He tried to will himself to sleep, praying that Kung had called it right. If the Essence ran out while they were in this wasteland, he had no hope of bringing any of them out alive. Llewelyn realised he was bitter with the Jiang for being so dependent on the Essence. Whatever good it did them, this helpless paralysis was too much of a price to pay.

And why's it such a secret?

Someone moaned. It was the captain. He was sweating, flushed with fever.

"Pigskins no good … Should have used bottles …" he cried out deliriously.

He's thinking about the Essence.

An idea struck him. He checked that Kung and the others were sleeping, then crawled over to lie next to Captain Chang.

"Why do you need to take the Essence?" he whispered in his ear.

The captain shivered, "No. Secret. Jiang's greatest secret. No."

"What is Jiang's greatest secret?"

"No! No! No!"

Llewelyn sat back. "It must be some secret if he won't even talk about it when he's half out of his head," he said to Gelert, and tried another tack. "Why do you need the Great Dog?" he whispered.

"Save. Jiang. Save Jiang's greatest … secret."

"Which is …?"

"Never grow old. Emperor must never know."

Llewelyn gasped. *Never grow old?* Disconnected threads and thoughts untangled in his mind and knitted into a coherent idea. *The Essence does stop you growing old? I was right!*

But what about the dead sailors who'd turned ancient in moments? *That wasn't natural!* But it made sense of Chang's ramblings.

He had to know more.

"How does the Essence stop you from growing old?" he whispered again, but the captain had fallen still.

Llewelyn sat up and glanced at Kung and the others to make sure no-one had seen or heard anything. A wave of guilt flowed through him. He must never reveal that he had this kernel of knowledge and the captain must never know that he'd been tricked into giving it away.

He crawled back to lie with Gelert. He tried again to sleep, but the secret of the Essence boiled in his mind. If it stopped the Jiang from growing old, how long did they live? How old had Wudi been? He looked ancient, so how much older was he really? Could the Essence cure you of sickness? *Do Jiang children take the Essence?*

He couldn't help wondering, too, how long had the Jiang kept the Essence secret. Hundreds? Thousands of years?

And why keep the secret?

He remembered the stories; the tales of Bendigeidfran and his Cauldron of the Dead; of the great Welsh King Arthur and the quest for the Holy Grail – *wasn't that supposed to grant eternal youth?* What about the Church? The eternity of paradise was a cornerstone of the priests' promises to all good Christians.

With a start, Llewelyn realised that whoever conquered death was powerful beyond measure. No wonder the Jiang wanted to safeguard their secret.

Then, gradually, the dread consequences of knowledge and the miserable guilt of knowing the Jiang's secret seeped into his soul.

Chang had warned him against asking questions.

That it was best if he didn't know.

Now he knew why.

He felt as if he'd swallowed a lump of gold.

If anyone suspected he held the secret of eternity, they'd rip it from him.

🐉

Twelve hours passed, a new night arrived, bringing with it blessed cool.

Llewelyn took the bottle of Essence form Kung's bag.

He shook it and there wasn't much left.

He measured some out and revived Kung, who went to attend to the others.

Llewelyn observed their awakenings closely, looking keenly

for signs of immortality. He tried to appear nonchalant, but failed.

Kung noticed his odd expression. "What's the matter?" he asked, dripping a measure of the Essence into the sleeping captain's mouth.

"Nothing!" he stammered. "I just wonder how long he stay sleep?"

"A few days. And it's best that he stays under," added Kung, "the more he sleeps, the more energy his body has for healing."

Rejuvenated, the sailors ate their breakfast and sipped their mouthfuls of water. The pack of dogs waited patiently for their ration, wagging their tails and whimpering in expectation.

Then the men packed up in silence and with a sense of urgency; the sooner they were all off this lifeless crust of salt, the better, and there wasn't time to talk.

Good. If I don't say anything, they can't know I know.

Trekking on the flat increased their travelling speed immeasurably, but for three nights and two days there was still only salt ahead. It hung in the air and etched their throats, making their urge to drink a torture.

Day by day their water skins lightened, a mouthful at a time.

As the hours passed, Llewelyn's guilt became less troublesome. Time was doing its trick of smoothing out a nagging problem. He learned to distract himself instead with fantasies about jumping into a cool deep lake or sucking on a juicy pear.

The notch in the mountains drew closer. Knowing they must surely find water in the lowlands spurred them on but, inexorably, Kung and the others began to slow down as the third day of their cycle loomed.

Dawn bleached the horizon on the third morning, and the band of weary travellers cheered croakily when they saw they were near the end of the salt flats.

As the sun climbed, the blinding salt was slowly replaced by sand and pebbles and increasingly bigger stones.

Finally, they trudged gratefully onto solid brown ground and halted. Kung groaned with the effort of simply standing still. Ao and Chao could only remain upright by leaning against Zheng. The land rose ahead of them to a low escarpment of flat rocks, but even the slight rise in gradient from the salt flat was too daunting. Everyone flopped to the ground, too tired to even shed their packs. The alarm dog and the lice dogs jumped down from Kung's pannier, and Gelert wrestled himself out of his harness, dropping the captain heavily to the ground.

The jolt made Chang groan softly, and he moved his arms and legs for the first time in days.

The dogs began yapping and yipping. Gelert's ear pricked up. He briefly sniffed the air before lolloping away up the side of the escarpment, followed by the other dogs.

"Oye!" croaked Llewelyn. "Get back here!"

The wolfhound reached the top of the hill and looked back briefly.

"What is it?" shouted Llewelyn, but Gelert ran off down the other side. Resigned, he eased off his pack and hobbled after him.

From the top of the hill, all he could see was dogs' bums. Every one of them was head down, tails wagging furiously.

The dogs had found a pool of water.

"Everybody! Water! There's water down here!"

Kung and the sailors were electrified by his shout. Although they were falling into Essence lethargy, they hauled themselves up to the crest of the ridge and staggered down the other side, abandoning their bundles as they went. Pushing the dogs' bums aside, they joined Llewelyn, collapsing face first into the puddle, which they promptly drank dry.

Miraculously, it began to fill again.

It was a spring, an insignificant puddle of water in the desert, but a precious, life-saving wonder nevertheless.

Groaning but happy, the men lay back, too weak and bloated to move. The last surge of effort had sped up the their decline. The lice dogs and the alarm dog sniffed around them, yelping plaintively. They knew something was very wrong and so did Llewelyn.

He ran back to the scattered supplies, rifling through them until he found Kung's bag. Inside was the last of the Essence. Llewelyn shook the black bottle; it was nearly empty and his hand came away wet. There was a crack in the glass. The bottle had broken when Kung had dropped his bag.

Llewelyn trotted back to the oasis with a heavy feeling of dread.

Kung and the sailors were now comatose, oblivious to his presence.

He dripped a few drops into Kung's mouth. He stirred and groaned; a pink glow slowly infusing his pallid skin and then he was alert and sitting up.

He took one despairing look at the bottle in Llewelyn's hand and groaned again. "I heard it break when I was running. Is that the last of it?"

"Tiny bit for others ..."

Kung stood up and stumbled. "It can't end like this!" he said, his voice thick with emotion. "We must ..." He fell to his knees.

"What if I mix it with water, like on the boat?" said Llewelyn helping him up.

"Yes, yes," mumbled Kung, his knees again buckling beneath

him. He sat, looking oddly bemused for a few moments before keeling over. "One part water, two parts Esssssss ..." he hissed, then passed out.

Llewelyn felt a familiar rush of loneliness and anxiety as he looked at the fallen men around him. What could he possibly do to save them? What was he doing here? Gelert sat beside him, seeking reassurance.

"Holy Father, Jesus Christ and the Holy Spirit, Mother Mary, Saint Petroc and all the rest of you out there," Llewelyn yelled at the desert, "What do I do?"

"First you come and untie me!" came a distant voice.

Llewelyn leapt five feet into the air, tripped on Kung and tumbled back into the spring. Spluttering, he looked around.

It was the captain, still strapped into the sled on the other side of the hill. He didn't seem very happy about it.

"And hurry up! I'm being eaten alive!"

Llewelyn sprinted back over the escarpment and found Chang writhing in a swarm of ants. He lay squirming and swearing as Llewelyn unstrapped him. With their huge pincers, the vicious ants began biting him too, spraying an acrid stink onto his skin.

Finally freed from the sled, the captain jumped up, batting off the biting ant battalions. "Little buggers! Ouch! Ouch! Ouch!"

Together, they made their way back to the others, Llewelyn supporting him. "How are you feeling? Apart from the ants?" he asked, brushing off the last of the ants.

"I need a drink!" croaked Chang, as he walked stiffly up the slope.

"How's your shoulder? Better?"

"Hardly,' grumbled the captain, his breath coming in gasps. "It feels like that damned lion's still chewing on it, and on top of that a dozen porcupines have moved into my pants, and my throat is full of monkey fur!"

Despite his bluster, Llewelyn could see that he was in the end-grip of the three-day cycle; his skin was withered and grey, and he shook like an old man. They reached the puddle and Llewelyn tried to help him kneel.

"I can do it myself!" spluttered the captain. He leaned forward to scoop water into his mouth, then submerged his entire head in the pool. Llewelyn watched him drink, wondering when he'd come up for air.

"Slow down!" he cautioned.

But Chang sucked up a couple more pints before he was finished.

Finally he knelt back, belched deeply, and wiped his sleeve across his mouth. Llewelyn started to relax, but then was overcome by panic.

"Oh! There's no more Essence!"

Captain Chang said "Oh, no?" Getting to his feet, he pulled out his emergency bottle from his tunic and winked at Llewelyn as he took a quick swig. His cheeks glistened pink and his eyes glittered green as he looked around at his sleeping comrades, piecing things together.

He squinted into his bottle and smiled. "Just enough for one more dose each. We should be fine till you get back."

"Why, where am I going?" squeaked Llewelyn, startled.

"Aqaba, of course, to rendezvous with our boat, pick up some fresh Essence, and get back here before we're all vulture fodder. Mission accomplished. Well, the first part of it, at least."

Llewelyn baulked at the barrage of instructions. "But Wudi's directions were only to the mountains. Where do I go from there?"

Chang sighed, picked up a stick and started sketching in the dirt.

"We're here, on this side of the mountains," he explained, drawing in the mountains and the route through them. "The waypoint's at the other end of the pass. If you head south, you'll hit a road here, where you'll see a river to your right and the sea straight ahead. The road curves left, straight on to Aqaba."

"How do you know all of this?"

"I scouted it two years ago."

"Two years ago? What were you doing out here two years ago?"

"As I said, scouting. All that matters is that if you get moving, you'll be there and back in three days. Less if you don't stop to admire the view."

Llewelyn shook his head. "There's only enough Essence for one more hit!"

"Exactly; three days. Just in time."

"But what if the Chinese are on our trail. What if they catch up?"

"They might if you stay here yabbering! Oh come on, Llewelyn!" said Chang, taking him by the shoulders, "It's simple: if you get moving, the Chinese won't be a problem."

Still he hesitated. It was all too much.

"Llewelyn, you know what's at stake for us. You know how important the Great Dog is to Jiang."

Something snapped in Llewelyn. "Yes, but I don't know what for!" he blurted. "Why do you want him?"

"Why must you know?" The captain seemed confused. "You're on our side now aren't you? Isn't that enough?"

"It's hard to be on someone's side if you don't understand the game they're playing!" he shouted. He surprised himself with his outburst and gulped. "Sorry," he mumbled. "It's just that you keep asking me to do all these things for you but I don't know why. You've told me nothing."

The captain glanced at Kung's prostrate body and sighed.

"Tell you what Llewelyn," he said, very quietly. "Go to Aqaba, bring our people back here, and as my parting gift to you I'll tell you everything; why we want Gelert, what we plan to do with him, and how we'll return him to you when we've finished with him. I might even tell you the secret of the Essence. Will that get you moving?"

"Yes, it will," said Llewelyn huskily, his throat closing with emotion.

Chang smiled, relieved. "Good lad. We've come so far and risked so much to get hold of Gelert. If Kung there knew I was letting the Great Dog out of my sight, he'd die of apoplexy. So you know how much it means to me that I can trust you in this …"

Llewelyn nodded, his heart growing hot with joy. It was the feeling he'd had when he'd been fighting the fire in the castle so many months ago. The same thrill when he'd saved the junk from the falling rock and when he'd brought it across the inner sea by himself.

"Well then?" said the captain impatiently, "Why are you still here? You've got three days, not three weeks!"

Llewelyn stuttered, still scared, but Chang shoo-ed him on. "Move. Before it gets too damned hot!"

It took no time to pack enough rations for him and Gelert, then all he had to do was strap on his sword and pick up his bow and arrows. The captain silently waved him towards the mountains.

Not much of a send-off, thought Llewelyn grumpily.

He took a bearing from his fish, pocketed it and they set off at a trot towards the sunrise.

~~~~

Forty miles away, the girl went to check her moisture traps.

She only had a few minutes before the rising sun would blast any dew away. Then it wouldn't be long before the harbour-side loafers would spot her.

One of the crew dogs scampered after her. She waved it back down below. Too late, mate. If you want to take a dump you should have done it in the night. Everyone knew the rules; the only time anyone was allowed on deck was in the dead of night.

Best not to let anyone know they were here.

The moisture traps were empty except for a film of the insufferable fine red dust that a howling wind that had blown into the city a week ago. Her throat constricted. What saliva she could muster was thick in the back of her mouth, and swallowing gave no relief.

She went below, secured the hatch behind her, and lit an oil lamp. The dusty, dark hold filled with its warm glow. Horizontal shafts of dawn light needled the grit-laden air, and as her eyes grew accustomed to the dark she saw crew dogs rolling around mock-fighting and playing.

She called to one of them, and was answered with a familiar yip. The crew dog ran over. It was Zazu, wagging his thick tail and licking his muzzle. He knew what she wanted and was happy to help. He was always good for a drink.

The girl picked up her glass jar and offered the rim to Zazu. He took it in his teeth and began chewing happily, slobbering his tongue and chops around the thick glass. Soon, the jar began to fill with drool.

Crew dogs had been bred to drink seawater. They could never go thirsty – certainly not at sea – so if fresh water ran low, they became a lifeline. The girl knew this. Everyone did. She took the half-full jar from Zazu and he barked up at her, eyes bright.

The first time she'd drunk dog spit, she'd gagged, but she'd soon learned to quite like it. Perhaps it was a bit too warm, and maybe too thick to be properly refreshing, but it had a musky tang and was surprisingly unsalty.

She reached into a sack and pulled out a handful of dried meat, giving some to Zazu. Then she extinguished the oil lamp. When the sun rose properly, the sampan's hold would heat up, and there was no point in adding to the fug.

She sat back in her throne of coconut hair and relaxed, sipping from her jar and chewing on her pork.

She waited.

PART V: FEIYAN

Chapter 29. Crusader

The day grew hotter.

The land rose steadily upwards, slowing Llewelyn's trot to a dusty slog. After five hours, the sun was so bright he could hardly see his next step. Gelert seemed impervious to the heat and circled the way ahead, snuffling the surroundings for interesting smells.

As they slowly drew closer to their goal, the pass revealed itself as a black gash, as if a giant had taken a battle axe to the mountains. It was just wide enough for a pair of horses, and its deep shadows sucked the light from the sun. By now it was insufferably hot, and time to rest.

Despite the promise of coolness, the shadowed gorge looked menacing. Llewelyn found an overhang surrounded by thorn bushes, and he and Gelert crawled into its shadow and were asleep in seconds.

❦

In his dreams, Llewelyn heard Gelert growling.

The growls became deep and threatening, then exploded into barks so loud they shook him awake. Iron-shod hooves trampled the dust just inches from his face, and he looked up into the belly of a magnificent warhorse, its chestnut coat flecked with bloody foam. The huge stallion reared and backed away from the big dog's defiance, and in a heartbeat Llewelyn grabbed his bow and rolled away from the pounding hooves.

A knight, in full-helmeted armour, sat astride the horse, struggling weakly to stay in the saddle. The front of his white tabard was tent-poled by a bloody spearhead poking through the centre of an embroidered cross – a Crusader cross.

The horse wheeled, nearly dismounting the knight, and Llewelyn saw the stub of the broken spear shaft embedded in the man's back. Two arrows were buried, feathers deep between his shoulder blades, the wounds flinging out sprays of blood as the knight laboured to stay on his horse.

"Get back, you damned hound!" the Crusader yelled in English, his plummy voice thick with pain.

Llewelyn now saw the three stylised lions on the man's shield and stood back, happy to watch Gelert terrorize the Englishman's warhorse. It bucked once more, finally throwing the knight, who fell to the rocky ground in a clatter of chainmail, broken flesh and blood. The horse bolted, the wolfhound snapping at its fetlocks.

The knight groaned in agony, held in a sitting position by the tripod of spear and arrows in his back. Fresh blood welled up around the spearhead in his chest and pink foam frothed from beneath his helmet. As flies settled on his pin-cushioned body, he just sat there gasping, lost in a personal hell.

Llewelyn knew he'd be dead within minutes. Compassion welled in him; English or not, no-one should suffer such agony. He reached for an arrow.

The dying knight caught the motion and raised his visor to look at Llewelyn; his face was a mask of blood. He flinched when he saw the longbow.

"Don't worry," soothed Llewelyn, "you'll soon be in heaven."

A look of hope broke through the knight's agony. "I say! You're English!"

"You wish!" Llewelyn snorted.

The knight didn't register his Welsh accent. "Good oh! Now, be a good Christian and take my message to Jerusalem?"

Curious, he lowered his bow. "What message?"

"Aqaba ... siege ... Saracens. Got to tell Jerusalem. Must send a relief force. Or. Show's. Over ..."

"Aqaba is under siege?"

" 'Fraid so. Came out of the desert. Half our chaps wiped out ..."

"When did this happen?" Llewelyn asked urgently.

The knight frowned, trying to remember. "Couple of days ago? Had to kill a few locals to get the wife and kids off on a boat before things got too hairy. Things really started brewing up last night. We took the secret passage out of the city to get reinforcements ... but this morning we were ambushed by the Saracens! Now, be a good chap and get the word to Jerusalem!"

But Llewelyn was only interested in one piece of information.

"What secret passage?"

The knight was turning pale, his life draining him from his wounds.

"What? Secret? PASSAGE?" hissed Llewelyn, shaking him.

"Of course! Silly me! You'll need the secret passage to get you back into the city. There, in my saddlebag, a map …," he spluttered through bubbles of blood and bits of lung. A look of panic flitted across his face. "You will go to J– J– Jerusalem, won't you? Swear to me as an Englishman that you'll … rally … the … men!"

Llewelyn pulled his hand away. "I swear as an Englishman," he replied, watching the light dying in the knight's eyes.

When it was gone, he stepped back and hollered to Gelert.

"Oye! Stop frightening that horse and bring him here!"

❧

It felt good to ride again. After the slow sea voyage and the tedious trek across the desert, the speed was exhilarating. Gelert bounded alongside, equally happy to be stretching his legs. Having the horse would quarter the time it would take to reach Aqaba, but Llewelyn had to get there before the city was ransacked.

After an hour, they reached the killing ground of the Saracen ambush.

The English knight had been lucky to escape; his companions had been stripped of their armour then hacked into unrecognisable chunks of meat.

Sniffing at the dead English troops, the wolfhound suddenly yipped loudly and sprang into the air. He gnawed at his front paw and began scratching himself furiously. The skin on Llewelyn's ankles began to crawl. He scratched his leg and felt blood. The itching quickly moved up his body, and he noticed fleas on his forearm. It had been months since he'd seen any vermin, but now the cold Englishmen were giving up their parasites, and the hungry insects were flooding to warm hosts.

"Dammit!" he spat in disgust. "I should have brought a lice dog!"

He kicked away from the dreadful scene, scratching painfully.

❧

As they wore on, night fell, and the moon rose over the dusty plain. They came upon a wide road running along the side of a steep valley. The river was where the captain said it would be, winding its silvery course along the valley floor.

Beyond, far on the horizon, lay an expanse of water.

Llewelyn took a few moments to gaze at the wonder of it. He'd crossed a sea, and a desert, and now faced another sea.

Presently, the road swung away from the river to the left.

Llewelyn remembered Chang's map. From now on, he'd ride with the sea to his right. He looked around, scratching absently, fixing in his mind the landmarks that would show him the way back. It was another trick Owain had shown him when moving through unknown territory.

Always keep looking back so you know which way you've come from.

He spotted an ominous red glow against the night sky. It could only mean one thing: Aqaba was on fire. Scowling with foreboding, Llewelyn urged the horse on.

An hour later, he crested one last hill and all thought of scratching stopped.

There was the port, less than five miles distant.

The burning city sat huddled around its moonlit harbour, its outer fortifications surrounded by a crescent of flickering orange lights. Thousands of torches and hundreds of campfires illuminated the surging masses of the Saracen army. Llewelyn found it unnerving seeing a siege from the outside in.

The attackers' force was vast, and the town looked hopelessly vulnerable, like a sandcastle facing an on-rushing tide of fire.

The Saracens loosed unending streams of flaming arrows and missiles over the doomed city's outer walls, and fires raged through the maze of inner streets. The air was thick with falling ash and the smell of burning.

The fortified citadel at Aqaba's centre was still intact, and Llewelyn was relieved to see that the port area below was out of range of the siege engines. Everywhere else, the fighting was intensifying and he knew the walls wouldn't stand for long. A glimmer of dawn tickled the eastern horizon. He needed the cover of darkness. He had to hurry.

He studied the Crusader's map and located the landmarks that would lead him to the tunnel entrance – a single straggly pine tree between two low hills.

With the map stuffed into his tunic, he urged the horse on, and picked his way through the low brush. The clip-clop of horses and jangling armour of Saracen patrols rung out in the dark, but Llewelyn and Gelert reached the pine tree safely.

Just in time: the first rays of the sun now lanced the horizon.

The entrance to the passageway had been carefully hidden. Pushing through a dense thicket of thorn bushes, Llewelyn found the tunnel, a six-foot-wide hole in the darkness. He tried leading the horse into the passageway, but it shied away and dropped a load of dung. *It's remembering the tunnel. It's terrified of going back in.*

Gelert began rolling in the steaming pile of manure.

"NO!" hissed Llewelyn. "Get over here!"

He tethered the stallion to the thorn bush and pulled branches around it, then stepped warily into the tunnel.

Gelert sauntered nonchalantly ahead.

Good. If he isn't worried, it can't be too bad in there.

Nevertheless, Llewelyn strung an arrow onto his bow before heading in.

❧

The tunnel was quiet and echoless, a thick layer of sand muffling their footfalls. The darkness was profound, so black that when Llewelyn squeezed his eyes shut it seemed lighter.

He walked with his bow held horizontally in front of him, its tips acting as feelers.

In the blackness, time vanished. He could have been walking for hours or minutes. Suddenly Gelert ran ahead, the sound of his loping gait fading instantly. The thought of being abandoned in the dark set Llewelyn's heart pounding as he followed blindly.

"Don't leave me alone! Get back here!"

Hearing grunting and squirming ahead, he started to run, and promptly tripped over Gelert, landing heavily in something mushy and earthy-smelling. *Goddammit! Horse muck!* It was moist, barely two days old. The old dog writhed next to him, happily lolling in the dung.

"Thanks a bunch!" scolded Llewelyn, and then a thought struck him; the dead knight and his companions had come this way. Maybe their horses had crapped themselves being led into the dark, and he was now lying in it.

If we're getting close to the end of the tunnel ... he hissed at Gelert to be still.

But the wolfhound was already motionless.

🐾

There were indistinct sounds ahead.

Llewelyn tiptoed forward, all his senses bristling with anticipation. The noises grew louder and more distinct; muffled shouting and screaming, banging and lots of running. The sound of men fighting.

Llewelyn gulped. *Don't tell me the Saracens have taken the city already!*

He hurried on with a new sense of urgency, and groped his way around a succession of twists and turns. Soon the floor of the tunnel began to rise and Llewelyn saw a rectangular frame of dull light in the roof, the outline of a large trap door. They'd reached the tunnel's end.

He smelled smoke and heard creaking above. Iron hinges squealed, followed by wood slamming against stone – a door being opened. The loud crashing and shouting sounds bloomed briefly, then muted as the door was shut again. Llewelyn looked up at the trap door, listening to the nervous clip-clopping of horses and men walking over it.

The light framing the trap door flickered.

Whoever it is, they're carrying torches.

Then he heard voices. Two men were talking softly, but urgently, just loud enough to be heard above the cacophony outside.

"Do hurry! There's really not much time!"

More Englishmen! Llewelyn bristled. Gelert growled.

The other voice sounded petulant. "If we'd left earlier, as I suggested ..."

"Don't blame me! You insisted we still had plenty of time for dinner."

"Well, it's not my fault you don't know when to stop shovelling down the cake! Just open the damned trap door and we can be off."

A loud clanking followed, and the trap door shivered a cascade of dust and began to open downwards. Llewelyn threw himself over into the deep shadows, calling Gelert to him. The hefty door lowered, forming a ramp up to a softly lit chamber.

The bickering voices carried on.

"Are you sure you closed the outside door? We don't want the Great Unwashed following us."

"Yes, I'm sure. Did you bring the water?"

"I brought my water. Did you bring yours?"

"I assumed you'd have thought of me for once. Silly me!"

Two magnificently armoured English Lords led their horses down the ramp. Their ornate helmets, plumed with outrageously flouncy feathers, shimmered in the flickering light of their torches. Their chainmail tunics, burnished and oiled, shone brightly. The red cross of their Crusader piety glowed gloriously against pure white tabards and the three-lions crest of England, embroidered in metallic thread, glittered on their breasts. The stallions were equally splendid; fully armoured in plates of blue steel, and draped in billowing scarlet caparisons, they snorted nervously and stomped their hooves skittishly. One whinnied in Gelert's direction, edging away from his dark corner.

"Stop stinking so much!" hissed Llewelyn, but the knights were now headed into the tunnel. Their torches lit a yellow ring of brickwork around them that was quickly swallowed by the gloom until all that was left of them was their fading argument.

"Well it's too late now. You'll just have to give me some of yours."

"Typical! Why is it always me who has to ... Oh! Well! That just about takes the biscuit!"

"What now?"

"Your horse has just shat all over the place! Typical!"

Llewelyn and Gelert ran up the ramp into a courtyard.

The sky was black with smoke and showers of sparks and embers flecked the billowing pall. The clanging of battle echoed around, mingling with the shouts of Englishmen as they answered the roar of the besieging Saracens. A flight of fire arrows fluttered above, and the thwumping sounds of heavy rocks smashing into masonry told of the awful damage being inflicted by the siege engines. The noise of running men and galloping horses was everywhere.

Good! No-one will be watching us in all this.

Llewelyn undid the bolts of the door to the street and eased it open. Beyond was a deserted alleyway. He looked at his map, but it lacked the detail to get them to the port. Beckoning Gelert to stay close, he ran towards the mayhem of the citadel's central square.

At the far side of the square stood a single massive gateway. Through it poured throngs of soldiers, defenders retreating from the outer city. The outer walls of Aqaba had been breached and the Crusader infantrymen were rushing to take their final stand. Llewelyn would have to go against the flow to exit the citadel before the gate and portcullis were closed.

He threw himself into the chaos. If he fell, he'd be trampled by the stampede, but Gelert ran ahead, magically parting the torrent of soldiers.

Soon they were at the barbican. Llewelyn poked his head around the corner, and peered down into the main street of Aqaba.

The soldiers from the outer-most city walls had the furthest to run, and staggered up the steep slope into the citadel with the exhausted, haunted look of the hunted.

Llewelyn heard a new commotion. A fierce rear-guard action was tackling the first waves of encroaching Saracens. A man backed into sight from an alleyway. He was an English bowman, loosing off arrow after arrow at unseen enemies. But his fellow soldiers surging up the hill crashed into him, knocking him off his feet.

Then the clanking of a massive ratchet started and the portcullis began to drop.

"Keep dem friggin' gates open!" yelled the bowman, kneeling. "Dere's still loads ovvus out 'ere!"

He crawled towards the gate, bareheaded, pale and dazed from a deep cut to his scalp. Other men, blinded by fear, stepped on him in their rush to sanctuary. Groggy, the bowman got to his feet.

A mounted English knight came clattering up the street, ploughing his horse through the fleeing men. The clanking portcullis was now halfway down. The knight brandished his sword, bellowing at everyone to make way, but the bowman was blocking his path. The knight's horse halted and reared.

"Stand aside, you stupid oaf!" roared the knight.

The bowman raised his hand to his eyes to see who it was.

"You wha'?" he croaked.

"Idiot!" cursed the knight and hacked his sword down, partially severing the soldier's arm above the elbow. A great spray of blood arced from the neat cut, splashing the knight's white tabard.

"Look what you've done now, you ungrateful ox!"

The knight spurred his mount forward, trampling the bowman to the ground. The wounded archer pleaded for mercy, but the knight forced his horse on. Llewelyn watched its stomping hooves crush the man's arm. The last of the skin and tendons attaching it to his body snapped, and the bloody limb was kicked into the dusty melee of running feet.

Without thinking, Llewelyn stepped into the gateway, strung an arrow to his bow and loosed it at the knight towering above him. Such was its force, it pierced his skull, shooting straight up through the crown of his helmet. Llewelyn then grabbed the archer by his tabard, and Gelert helped drag him to the front of the gatehouse.

The dead knight tumbled heavily to the cobblestones, blood spouting from his helmet's eye slits. The portcullis dropped its last ratchets, skewering the knight to the roadway. His horse stood sniffing at his corpse.

Stranded English soldiers reached through the portcullis, begging to be let in. The iron gate rose a few feet, dropping the body of the dead knight, and the grateful men scuttled and squirmed beneath the portcullis, weeping with gratitude.

Just feet away, Llewelyn quickly undid the crippled bowman's belt and tied it around the spurting stump of his arm to staunch the flow of blood. Choking back his pain, the Englishman looked at his tightly bound arm, then at Llewelyn.

He forced a grim smile. "Cheers dere, mate!" he croaked, "I see you know 'owter use a longbow too. Very pro-fesh-null!"

His accent was nothing like the cultured tones of an English nob.

"Lewkarrit!" He flapped his stump. "How am I goin' t'scratch me arse now?"

Llewelyn couldn't help grinning. Gelert sniffed the man's mangled stump, licking his chops appreciatively.

The bowman noticed the wolfhound for the first time. "Christ! Dassa big dog yev got der! I bet he's a birrovvan 'andful!"

Llewelyn laughed as he shooed the dog away. "A very big handful," he said, slipping into English. He liked this Englishman, and an idea popped into his head. "Here, take this." He handed his map to the bowman and pointed back into the citadel. "See that alleyway over on the other side of the square?"

"Yes, I see. Worrovit?"

"There's an open doorway into a courtyard, and inside there's the entrance to a secret tunnel. It'll get you out of the city."

"A secret tunnel?"

"Yes. Your knights have been using it to escape. You should too."

"Turd-sucking toe rags!" growled the soldier, as he rose awkwardly to his feet. "I knew summerdem were skiving off summwheres!"

He took the map, then looked at Llewelyn. "Dat's a Welsh accent, innit?

Llewelyn nodded. The man looked embarrassed.

"Yew've got no reason to hclp us English, so whydjer gimme dis?"

"I don't need it anymore."

It wasn't much of a reason, he knew. Maybe, he realised deep down, it wasn't the English he was fighting. Just whoever led them.

Then the order was given to lower the portcullis again. Most of the English soldiers had scraped through.

"Tanks, mate. I owe yer," said the soldier, absently dabbing at his bloody stump with the map. "Now, less gerrinside the citadel …"

"No, we've got business out there."

"Do yer now?"

Llewelyn nodded. The bowman shrugged.

"Worrever. Burriz der anytin' I can doofer yew?"

Llewelyn didn't know what to say. Then he saw the bowman's quiver of broadhead arrows. There were only eight, but his eyes lit up.

The Englishman laughed. "Take 'em! Dey're no good to me now!"

Llewelyn stuffed the weighty arrows into his quiver next to the weedy Chinese ones. Then the massive barred gate shuddered and began to clank down again.

"Anytin' else?" urged the archer.

"Just one thing – which way is it to the port?"

Minutes later, Llewelyn was cantering the dead knight's horse through the doomed deserted streets of Aqaba with Gelert running alongside. The bowman's directions took them down, away from the citadel, and the clattering of the horse's iron-shod hooves echoed around the empty houses. They reached the port area quickly.

Llewelyn was dismayed. There was no Jiang ship.

There were no ships.

Other than a tiny rowing boat, there was nothing that could be described as even seaworthy – just a mess of half-submerged wreckage over to the right with the remains of a dead donkey lying across it. He whirled his horse about, his eyes pricking with tears and a rising sense of panic closing his throat.

Back across the harbour, the glassy sea reflected the climax of the siege of Aqaba. The upper reaches of the city burned from end to end. Great curtains of flames engulfed the skyline, throwing up columns of smutty orange smoke that blotted the dawn sky. It wouldn't be long before the rest of the Saracens flooded in to take control of what was left of the city including this stinking, miserable, empty harbour.

Then, above the tumult of destruction, Llewelyn heard Gelert barking. *What's he up to now?*

He expected to find the dog with his head stuck in a barrel of rotting fish heads. Instead, he was stood by the harbourside. He seemed excited by something down in the water, but there was nothing there, just the rancid donkey on the tangled wreckage.

Looking again, Llewelyn saw the mess was about twenty-five feet long, a bedraggled ruin of broken planking covered in coils of frayed rope, splintered masts and bolts of mildewed sail cloth. The half-sunk barge looked like it had been used as a dump. The putrid donkey straddling the wreck's prow reeked.

"Oye! Gelert," he shouted and turned his horse. "Come on, we've got to get out of here quickly!"

The wolfhound watched him trot away, but stood still.

"Come! HERE!" fumed Llewelyn, annoyed by his old friend's wilfulness.

But Gelert simply sat down and looked back at him, whimpering.

All at once, Llewelyn heard some scrabbling from the mess below. A smashed-up hatchway in the centre of the derelict barge's deck was thrown open and a young girl's face suddenly appeared in the broken frame. She stared up at the wolfhound, a look of wonderment in her sparklingly blue, almond-shaped eyes.

She was beautiful.

Gelert barked and stood up, his tail thwacking from side-to-side.

And then the girl spoke: "Gelert? Is that you?"

"Who are you?" squeaked Llewelyn in surprise. He realised too late that he was speaking Welsh.

"Idiot round-eye," she muttered in Chinese, and turned back to Gelert. "You really are something else,' she said softly. In one lithe movement she climbed up through the hatchway and up onto the harbour wall. "You're even bigger than we were told! And here you are, all the way from Way-yells."

Way-yells?, puzzled Llewelyn.

She means Wales! She knows I'm from Wales!

The girl walked around the wolfhound, then dipped down onto her knees. The Great Dog towered over her, but she showed no fear and simply lifted her palm for him to sniff. He slobbered her whole hand, almost swallowing it and her eyes widened with pleasure. Gelert wagged his tail harder and looked over at Llewelyn as if to say, 'Now will you listen to me?'

Then a lice dog's head emerged from one of the girl's top pockets. It yapped shrilly at Gelert, warning him to keep his distance.

She's Jiang, thought Llewelyn. She looked two or three years older than him. It was hard to tell. She was so beautiful. She wore a loose blue tunic, gathered at the waist with a thick black belt, and white calf-length canvass trousers that were far too big for her and had seen better days. She was also barefoot. *Why does that look so good?*

"Who you?" he piped, flipping from Welsh into Chinese. His tongue was numb like he'd swallowed a barrelful of snow.

She stared up at him, one eyebrow arched, her curiosity piqued by his fluency. But before she could reply, she noticed the scenes of citywide destruction over his shoulder. Tearing his gaze from her face, Llewelyn looked around. A section of the citadel's walls was crumbling and hordes of Saracen warriors were swarming over the rubble. The last of the Crusaders were doing their best to defend it, but the citadel would soon be taken and then the fighting would spill down to the port.

The girl broke the spell. "We haven't got long. Where are the others?"

"What others?"

She gawped back. "Chang? Wudi? Kung? The others."

Llewelyn gawped again. "Captain Chang?"

"Oh, for Dog's sake, yes! Chang, captain of the ship that got you to Jaffa!"

"Er, er ..." stammered Llewelyn. He hoped she couldn't see his blushes. His mind flip-flopped in different directions. Despite her blazing temper, he felt oddly giddy in her company.

"Where ... are ... the ... OTHERS?" she shouted, bristling with impatience.

Llewelyn gathered himself. He was glad to be sitting on his horse, ten feet away from her vicious tongue.

He pointed vaguely. "They over there, in the desert, that way."

"Why aren't they here?"

"It complicated!" flustered Llewelyn.

The girl's face darkened.

"Why did they send you?" She was clearly thinking he was a poor choice of messenger.

"They run out of Essence." He offered, hating his clumsy Chinese.

The girl stood up, confused but still furious.

"When? How far away are they? What sort of state are they in?"

Llewelyn tried to reassure her.

"Everything all right. The captain have emergency supply."

Then he remembered the pursuing Chinese.

"Er ... but Emperor soldiers following us."

This didn't seem to worry her. Quite the opposite.

"Good. Maybe I can still turn this expedition to good. Is there anything else you can tell me that'll cheer me up?"

There was only one thing he could offer her.

"Yes. I can take you to them."

She shook her hands above her head in mute frustration, but his honest reply forced her anger to subside. She breathed deeply.

Llewelyn tried to take control of the situation. "We won't be able to go back through the city, but if we go around the walls ..."

"No. We'll sail there."

Now he knew she was mad. "What? Sail over desert?"

"Oh for Dog's sake," she groaned, rolling her eyes. "Of course not, idiot! You said they are north of here?"

"Maybe north, northwest." He thought about getting Wudi's fish out. Maybe that would impress her, but she was off again.

"Fine. We'll sail up the coast. Take the river as far north as we can."

Llewelyn thought about it. "Yes. The river. It go north ..."

Sniffing the wind, she looked out to sea and then back to the citadel. He could almost hear her mind working things out.

"Let's get going. We can do it if we get our fingers out of our bumholes."

She jumped down onto the decrepit barge and pulled on a rope.

Confused, Llewelyn made no move.

The girl flashed her blue eyes up at him. "Get down onto the boat, and bring your horse!" she snapped.

Llewelyn looked at the wreck she was standing on. "What boat?"

"This one," she grunted, straining at the rope.

"But where your crew?"

She glared at him briefly. "Here's my crew."

She gave a loud pirriping whistle that hurt his head. Gelert's ears pricked up, and he barked, puzzled.

A dozen stocky, black, short-haired dogs ran up through the open hatchway. They were identical, each about the size of a small sheep. They resembled very large corgis, but with broader, shorter muzzles and more heavily boned heads. The dogs trotted into line behind the girl, and took hold of the loose end of the rope she'd been pulling in their strong, wide jaws.

On her next whistle, they all began tugging backwards.

Llewelyn's jaw dropped slackly as this astonishing, bewitching girl and her crew of dogs hauled up a mast from the surrounding wreckage. As it rose to the perpendicular, it slid perfectly into a neat hole in the deck, falling into place with a loud thump.

"We'll put up the front mast once we're out of the harbour," said the girl. Llewelyn wondered if she was talking to him or the dogs.

Having tied off the rope and locked the mast in place with a thick greased iron bolt, she scowled at Llewelyn.

"Oye! Finger! Bumhole! Out!" she yelled, pointing from the horse to the deck.

In a daze, he dismounted. He took hold of his horse's reins and coaxed it onto the boat. Gelert jumped down, eager to make friends with the black dogs. He sniffed at a couple of bums, but they were too busy working and ignored him.

The dogs had split into two teams, hauling on different ropes that pulled a sail up the main mast. It concertinaed open, clean bamboo slats against deep red cloth. The dog teams yanked their ropes into cleats and pulled them fast.

Meanwhile, the girl walked the length of the barge, kicking the last of the rotting planks and coils of frayed rope overboard. What had been a floating pile of rubbish had become a sleek, low-slung, ship.

"Why you want horse?" asked Llewelyn, feeling a bit useless.

"You'd rather we walk across the desert?" she replied curtly. "We can only sail so far up river, then we'll ride the rest of the way. Here, give me a hand."

She pulled aside more debris to expose a low cockpit and a long black lacquered tiller handle. Together they slotted it into place and she pushed the handle hard over. The rudder responded; the stern moved gently in the opposite direction.

"Right. Now get rid of that!" she ordered, indicating the dead donkey draped across the boat's bow. Gelert had his head stuck deep in its ruptured guts.

"And wash your hands afterwards."

❦

The sail caught the slight breeze and the boat drifted away from the harbour. Llewelyn sensed this was a beautifully balanced, fast vessel.

"Why you change boat – make look crap?"

"The minute the Saracens appeared from the desert, the Christians started commandeering anything that floated."

A roar erupted from the citadel. It was the sound of a thousand men cheering and another thousand screaming. A large green banner with a white crescent rose above the fortress tallest tower.

"It all finished up there," said Llewelyn quietly, hoping the one-armed English bowman had escaped the carnage.

"There's another futile waste of life over and done with. What a pity it won't be the last. Come on, let's be off," she said curtly, and whistled another set of commands. Her dogs pulled on the mainsail sheets, hauling it into the wind, and the boat quickly picked up speed, surging towards the end of the mole and the open sea beyond.

Llewelyn felt the deck vibrating through the soles of his feet and the whisper of a tangy sea breeze on his face. He was on a boat captained by a beautiful girl and crewed by a pack of dogs. It felt good.

She patted Gelert to sit by her side, but ordered Llewelyn to keep out of her way, banishing him to the stern rail.

"What your name?" he asked the back of her head, vaguely jealous of the dog.

"Feiyan. Now please be quiet; there are sand bars out there. I've got to concentrate.

'Feiyan,' sighed Llewelyn.

He winced as she gave another series of ear-splitting whistles.

From the forward hatchway, a decidedly strange-looking, tan-coloured dog clambered delicately on deck. Gelert was suspicious of the newcomer and growled quietly as it trotted towards Feiyan.

Only a foot shorter than Gelert at the shoulder, but fine-boned and fragile-looking, the dog had long drapes of fur that hung between its long front and rear legs, brushing the floor as it moved. Gelert sniffed at its behind, nearly tipping the animal over. In response, it whipped round and snapped at the old wolfhound.

He's a toughie! thought Llewelyn. *Just as well. If he was any skinnier, he'd blow away.*

Cooing softly, Feiyan picked up a small leather harness, which she fastened around the delicate dog's chest. With a start, Llewelyn saw that what he'd thought was long fur were actually flaps of thin skin covered in fine down. Feiyan threaded the straps through holes in the skin that had been reinforced with stitching.

"That horrible!" said Llewelyn squeamishly.

Feiyan ignored him, drew the harness tight, and stood. "Here, take the tiller and hold this course while I launch Sashin."

The strange dog yipped with excitement.

"Launch?" stuttered Llewelyn.

Feiyan walked to the main mast, Sashin bouncing and yapping by her side. She hooked the back of its harness onto a rope and began pulling it up the mainmast. The dangling dog's yapping grew more excited the higher it went and it skittered its back legs against the thick wooden mast.

"Wait!" said Feiyan.

Sashin calmed, holding himself steady against the mast, the wind ruffling the folds of skin between his legs. He sniffed the breeze, feeling it gust around his body, then gave a joyful yap.

"Off you go then!" laughed Feiyan.

Sashin launched himself away from the mast, out into the air.

Llewelyn gasped and Gelert yowled as the dog opened its legs wide. The flaps of skin between them stretched flat and caught the breeze, and Feiyan paid out more line as the dog sailed up into the sky. Yapping happily it adjusted its legs and steered itself from left to right.

Llewelyn squinted into the bright sky.

"It's a kite!" he squeaked in Welsh. There was no other way of describing it.

Feiyan trilled words of encouragement to the floating dog and peeled out more rope, allowing it to fly itself even higher. When she was happy with its altitude, she tied down the rope and came back to the cockpit.

"Flying dog? What he do?" asked Llewelyn.

"He's our eyes in the sky, and he's better than any local pilot. Watch." She whistled to the kite dog again. It glided itself into a position above the centre line of the Jiang vessel, craning its long neck around so that it could look backwards to the prow of the ship. It barked once, then slowly glided to port. Feiyan put the tiller over, re-centering the boat beneath the dog.

Llewelyn looked over the starboard railings. Close to the surface, a sandbank slid by just ten feet away.

"They're everywhere at low tide," remarked Feiyan. "They'd be a nightmare without Sashin."

Llewelyn looked back at Aqaba. Smudges of black smoke hung over the citadel and odd licks of red showed where fires still burned, but distance and daylight had robbed the scene of menace.

Above, the dog yapped again and glided a few points to starboard. Feiyan readjusted her course, and once more they avoided running aground.

For another half an hour they zig-zagged their way further out to sea until they were safe in deep water. Feiyan set a new course, running north along the barren coastline and whistled fresh commands to her black dog crew. They trimmed the mainsail and the boat settled into a pleasant rhythm, riding smoothly through the slight waves.

Llewelyn watched the kite dog drift around the sky. "When you bring him down?"

"He'll come down when he's hungry. Watch out!" She moved to one side.

Llewelyn looked up. Sashin was pissing and the stream of urine fell in a delicate golden arch and spattered onto his face.

He wiped it off and changed the subject.

"It fast ship. Nice and low in the water." He tried to sound knowledgeable. "What class junk is it?"

"It's not a junk!" snapped Feiyan. "Junks are Chinese! It's a Jiang sampan, the best sailing boat in the world, strong enough for the biggest seas. Sam … pan. You think you can remember that?"

"Alright! Alright! SAMPAN! I get it!" scowled Llewelyn in Welsh. He wondered why someone so beautiful should be so unapproachable.

Bugger this. I'll go feed the horse.

The day wore on in brooding silence. The midday sun sent most of the black dogs below deck, and Gelert lay snoozing in the shade of the mainsail. Llewelyn flopped in the shadows of the rear railings and fell into a deep slumber.

He woke to find a couple of the black dogs playing with Gelert. The great hound stood patiently over them as they ran between his legs, barking and chasing each other's tails in a perpetual figure of eight.

Llewelyn sleepily scratched himself, and then continued scratching until he'd scratched himself raw.

"Hey!" he called to Feiyan. "Can I use your lice dog?"

He could see her figuring out why he wanted it. Her reply was tinged with mild disgust.

"I suppose so. Here. Come and get him."

She handed him her little pink dog and he sighed with blessed relief as the swarms of vermin fell from him, died and were lapped up. The lice dog scrunched happily at the pile of corpses around him and burped when it was finished.

"This one's full," said Llewelyn. "We need do Gelert too. He covered in lice."

"There are five spare lice dogs below deck," Feiyan said, then went quiet, preoccupied by dark thoughts.

Llewelyn thought about that. "Oh. There was more of you on ju–sampan?"

Feiyan glared at him but her eyes were wet. "Yes. But now there's just me." She sniffed. "And I don't want to talk about it."

Neither did he. Not if it made her angry. Or sad. He changed the subject.

"Black dogs work boat?"

She looked at him disdainfully. "No. They make fairies' underwear. They're crew dogs. Of course they're here to work the boat. At least until we pick up the others. It'll be good to see Wudi again … What's the matter with you?"

Llewelyn sat up. Suddenly he felt sick to his stomach.

"Wudi dead. Most of others dead. There only five Jiang left."

Feiyan stayed quiet as he told her, first about how the shortage of the Essence had chopped four of the crewmen down, and then how the rest had sacrificed themselves to keep the Great Dog from the Emperor.

She cried when he recounted how Wudi had died.

"I told everyone there'd be a price to pay, but no-one thinks they'll be the one who get it in the neck," she said, trying to ignore the tears flooding down her face. "No-one thinks of the consequences."

She sniffed back her tears and laughed a hollow laugh. "On the upside, going home won't be so much of a squeeze. I mean, look at the size of this sampan! It was bad enough with just six of us. Can you imagine another twenty-five men on board?"

Feiyan was right. The sampan was small compared to the junk.

"Things get smelly," joked Llewelyn, hoping not to tip her further into despair.

"I'm glad the twins and the big man made it," she said. "But why did Wudi have to die? He taught me everything I know about sailing."

"Me too." He took out the old helmsman's fish. "He give me this."

Her wet eyes grew wide. "Wudi gave you his fish?"

She studied him for a while. "Maybe you're not so bad after all," she muttered.

"I wish Wudi still here use it his self."

"Well he's not. And he won't be the last to die!" spat Feiyan angrily. "The Emperor will never give up. He'll chase us to the ends of the earth to get what he wants, and spend a lifetime doing it. What am I talking about? It'll be *our* lives that will be spent."

Llewelyn thought about the relentless pursuit; the middle sea, the fight against his fellow sailors, the awful desert, the terrible sandstorm, and then the nightmare of the salt flats. All just ruts in the road to the Emperor's men.

"They very determined."

Feiyan's eyes glared. "And we're foolish enough to think we can beat them!" She glared at him. "Do you think we can beat them?"

Llewelyn was about to say something foolish about how he'd do anything to help her, but she shushed him.

"Hold up …" she piped, rising and staring at the coastline, "There's the river mouth."

She pushed the tiller over and whistled up at the kite dog, pointing towards the distant break in the surf where the river poured into the sea. Then she sent the crew dogs skittering around the boat, pulling on ropes and resetting the mainsail.

Twenty minutes later, they were in smooth water. The sea was calm and the full flood of the incoming tide surfed them up river on a series of pulsing waves.

Llewelyn couldn't see much beyond the riverbank, just loose

gravel, weedy birch trees and tangles of bleached white tree limbs. But soon, swathes of tall, dry yellow reeds covered the flood plain.

He shimmied up the main mast for a better look. The blanket of reeds was gouged by channels, each a strand of the main waterway that had split and split again as it wandered towards the sea.

Now there was no sign of the incoming tide. They were sailing against the smooth flow of the river, pushed by a soft land breeze.

"We out of sea now," he called to Feiyan, and was surprised to see her run to the railings with a bucket and dredge up some river water, which she began drinking.

No, not drinking, gulping, guzzling.

She poured great drafts of it down her throat, swallowing heavily. Eventually she finished, and belched loudly, wiping the back of her sleeve across her mouth before belching again.

Thirsty, I guess.

🐦

Sashin guided them from above, keeping them to the deepest part of the channel, avoiding the braided shallows and making sure they made good progress for another hour.

Eventually, as dusk fell, the boat's flat bottom began to drag on the gravelly riverbed. Feiyan grounded the ship and tied up. As she lowered the kite dog back to the deck, Llewelyn jumped the horse down onto dry land. He left it grazing, and squirmed up through the head high reeds to higher ground.

He had to turn the scenery round in his head before he recognised one or two landmarks.

"I think know where we are!" he called back to Feiyan.

"Tell me when you actually know where we are."

Higher still, to his right, the slope of the valley was cut by a flatness that could only be man-made. Then he knew where he was. It was the trail he'd followed to Aqaba and he was standing below where he'd first spotted the river. Taking out his fish, Llewelyn double-checked his bearings and went back to the sampan.

He tried to sound casual as he told Feiyan his news.

"Yes. Me right." He pointed at the mountains to the north.

"See gap in rocks?"

"Well done," she remarked flatly. "Let's get moving then."

Llewelyn got the impression that she'd wanted to find fault in him, but had to bite her tongue. This thought cheered him up no end.

Despite Llewelyn's assurance that it would only take two days at most, Feiyan insisted on supplies for four. She also loaded three fat skins of Essence. They hauled everything off the sampan and began to load up the horse. Then she became curiously indecisive.

"Should we bring weapons?" she scowled.

"Er, yes!" said Llewelyn, surprised she'd even had to ask the question. "What if there are Crusaders, or Saracens, or robbers, or lions ...?"

She went back to the sampan and returned with a Chinese bow and a handful of arrows. Llewelyn was already slinging his longbow over his back.

"Why d'you lug that plank around?" asked Feiyan.

"It not a plank! It my bow. My longbow!" he said in Welsh with pride.

"Doesn't look much like a bow. Looks more like a tree trunk."

She handed him her double-curved bow.

"*That's* a bow," she said, her voice challenging. But the way she handled it told Llewelyn that she wasn't familiar with the weapon.

He hefted it. It felt light, and the skimpy layers of bone and wood seemed too thin. He pulled on the string; there was an initial resistance as the staves arced back, but then the strain magically relaxed. At its furthest pull, he was hardly aware of any tension.

He shrugged, and thought about what Owain would make of it.

"Good for girls."

Feiyan was outraged. "Oh, and that log of yours is better?"

"You try pull it," he retorted, offering her his longbow. She couldn't hide her surprise at how heavy it was and took hold of the bowstring and began to draw.

Nothing happened. The longbow quivered in her hand, but no matter how hard she strained, she couldn't pull it back. Her face reddened and sweat beaded her brow. Eventually, she flung the longbow down and massaged her sore hands.

"Useless! It was going to cut my fingers off!"

Llewelyn laughed. "Not if you know what you doing. Here, I show you," he said standing behind her. "Put your hands on mine."

A delicious tingle shot up his arm as her fingers closed over his.

He explained the bowman's grip. "You see, you pull your bowstring with thumb and finger, but you use first three fingers with longbow. Hurts until your skin hardens up. Now, you try."

Feiyan followed his lead and then Llewelyn slotted his fingers between hers so that they held the bowstring together.

"Now, feel …"

Llewelyn pulled back in the single fluid draw of the practised archer and she went with him. The action brought their cheeks together. The smell of her hair was intoxicating. He was doing most of the pulling, and he held the bowstring at full draw before slowly letting her take up the strain. Feiyan squeaked, determined not to let go, and he saw blood welling from her fingers. He took hold of the bowstring again and let the bow relax.

"See. Not hard."

Feiyan sucked at her bleeding fingers and eyed him with respect.

Her eyes widened. "How did you do that?"

"Ten years' practice."

"Ten years practising for war. Figures. But at least it's made you strong. And your hands must be made of hippopotamus skin."

Llewelyn had no idea what a hippopotamus was. He shrugged and slung the bow nonchalantly over his back.

"Can all of you Welsh do that? Do you all have these longbows?"

"Bows are all we have against bloody English. We make sure we good with them."

Feiyan looked thoughtful. "Yes. You can only use what you have, I suppose."

❧

"Crew dogs be all right?" asked Llewelyn.

The Jiang dogs gathered on the railings of the beached sampan.

"I'd worry more for anyone who tried getting on board while we're gone," said Feiyan grimly. "Crew dogs are trained to rip throats out first and chew on your gizzards later."

Llewelyn sprang up into the saddle, then pulled her up to sit in front of him. She leaned forward so he could pull the reins over her head.

Twilight turned to night and the moon rose over the hills. It was cool and windless, a perfect night for moving fast. Llewelyn hustled the horse into an easy walk and soon they were passing waist high through the sea of glowing white reeds that parted on either side leaving a trampled black wake.

Feiyan stayed silent, not signalling the slightest desire to talk. He gazed at the back of her head. Her long black hair bounced with the cadence of the horse and sometimes it flew back in his face. It should have been irritating, but this was Feiyan's hair. It smelled delicious, almost like flowers, but darker and spicier. His chest tightened in a new and pleasant way.

The horse stumbled on a stone, lurching to one side. Instinctively, Llewelyn grabbed her around the waist.

"Watch it, sonny," she growled at him without turning.

He let go of her, reluctantly.

A thought struck him; she'd never once asked his name or even questioned what he was doing so far from Wales. At least she seemed to know about Wales.

Way-yells.

Gelert ran ahead, snuffling, alert for any danger; his sharp ears and eyes would keep them safe.

They cleared the sea of reeds, riding through tussocks and loose rocks as the gradient of the valley's side increased.

Thank God we brought the horse.

The upper level of the valley was a nightmare of loose footholds. The horse stumbled repeatedly on crumbly earth, and when they reached a ridge of low cliffs and jumbled boulders, they dismounted to let it find its way through the craggy terrain.

It was a relief to finally reach the level trail, and when they did memories of the climb were erased by the sight of the valley falling away steeply below.

The sampan was a tiny speck, almost lost in the lacy braided river that shone like mercury against the blue-grey landscape. A drifting night breeze shivered across the expanse of reeds and a soft hissing filled the air.

Llewelyn wondered how he could hear it from so far away, but then he realised it was just Gelert pissing noisily against a broken boulder.

Feiyan stared at the wolfhound, shrouded in his cloud of steam. Llewelyn thought he detected a look of mild disgust on her face, and he laughed to himself. Maybe she was beginning to see that the Great Dog was just a great big dog.

❧

On the flat, they made much better time, but Feiyan remained silent.

With only the back of her head to go on, he wondered what she might be thinking about. Was it her dead crew-mates? Was it Gelert? Could she even be thinking about him? He shook his head at such a foolish, stupid, idiotic thought.

They plodded on, and Llewelyn found himself nodding off. He woke with a start when Gelert gave a low growl and ran off. Llewelyn called him back, not really expecting a response.

"He's not very well trained, is he?" said Feiyan.

Llewelyn sniggered. "No! And you want him to save your kingdom!"

Feiyan tried to sound outraged by his flippancy, but he heard the mockery in her voice. "The kingdom of Jiang stands alone against the oppressive merciless despot, and it is the duty of all Jiang to resist by all means possible; to make whatever sacrifices are demanded of us, regardless of personal liberty or even our lives. The Great Dog is everything!"

"You sound like Kung," laughed Llewelyn.

She became thin-lipped and serious. "Ah yes, Kung. If any of us ever forget it, you can be sure he and his like will be there to remind us that we're dispensable."

"He not worry a lot of people die for mission. You think it will work?"

Feiyan stiffened and her voice took on a steelier tone.

"Oh, we'll get Gelert to Jiang, and I've no doubt the 'Great Dog' will be everything that everyone wants him to be, but things won't work out the way anyone imagines."

He was about to ask her how the Jiang would use the 'Great Dog', but suddenly she gagged.

"Eeeew! What is that awful smell?"

A sweet stench filled the air; the sickly smell of rotting meat. The horse skittered and snorted. As they rounded the corner they found Gelert standing on the pile of rotting Crusader corpses, his fur black to the knees. After days in the hot desert sun, the remains had turned darkly greasy. Unseen animals had chewed the body parts to a soupy mess. A crust of flies and maggots, made slow by the chilled night air, moved thickly on the human carrion.

Gelert sniffed at his mound of meat and licked his chops and looked at Llewelyn guiltily, ear drooping and his tail wagging slowly.

"Oh, get off, will you!" he sighed in Welsh. "How many times have I told you? No eating the English!"

The dog cocked his head and thought about obeying his young master, but decided he was hungry and bent his head to eat.

"Gelert!" screamed Feiyan, appalled. "Get away from there!"

The old wolfhound flinched at her sharp words and thought better of carrying on. Sheepishly, he climbed down the macabre pile, his tail between his legs.

"Me impressed!" said Llewelyn. "He never do what I ask when food around!"

"He's revolting!"

"He a dog!" said Llewelyn, digging in his heels to hurry them on.

❧

A few hours later, they had reached the far end of the dimly lit gorge. Llewelyn could see milky dawn light a hundred yards ahead.

Gelert barked and ran ahead again.

This time, he knew what to expect. "Get back here!"

"What's going on?" yelped Feiyan.

"You see."

They emerged from the gap in the rocks into bright sunlight. There sat the corpse of the dead English knight.

He was facing away from them and was still propped up, pinned to the ground by the arrows and the spear stump. Something about the remains made the warhorse skittish.

Gelert stood growling at the corpse, his back ridge of fur bristling. The chainmail clad body seemed fatter, and it was moving. Llewelyn's heart lurched. How could the Englishman still be alive with such terrible wounds?

Suddenly, the body tipped off the supporting spear stump and rolled to the ground. The helmet turned towards them, visor open, and Llewelyn felt Feiyan flinch. There was no face inside, just a skull.

Gelert growled, then leapt toward the body, snapping at the empty helmet. A pack of squealing rats swarmed out through the neck and sleeves of the knight's chainmail, glistening red with slick, thick blood from head to tail. In an instant frenzy, the dog managed to gobble up a few of the slower creatures before Llewelyn shouted him off.

"And they sing songs about the glory of war," said Feiyan, swallowing her urge to vomit. "Get me away from here!"

Morning slowly pushed away the dawn, warming the bleak landscape. The strengthening sunlight blasted the distant smear of the salt flats into life.

Gelert was beside himself with excitement; he ran along the trail, sniffing at the air and barking happily before racing to the edge of a ridge overlooking the desert basin.

"What's he found now?" asked Feiyan, her voice tinged with disgust at what the wolfhound might be thinking of eating next.

"He smell captain Chang and the others!" said Llewelyn. He got down and joined Gelert on the ridge.

"They close now. Yes, there the spring." He ruffled the fur on Gelert's head. "Is it the captain?" he whispered in Welsh, winding up the old dog into an even greater frenzy. "Yes? Yes? Is it the captain?"

The wolfhound was now jumping frantically up and down.

"He know where they are!" he called to Feiyan. "We let him

go to them?"

"Might as well," she shrugged, not sounding all that excited about seeing everyone again. "Here, sling one of these round his neck," she said as an afterthought, and handed him a skin of Essence.

Good idea. Who knew what state Chang and the others would be in by now, but minutes might count and Gelert would reach them faster if he ran ahead. He tied the bulging skin to the wolfhound's back, and then he was off, trailing an expanding cloud of dust.

And when we get there, the captain will tell me why the Jiang want Gelert.

The thought had popped into Llewelyn's head unbidden, which gave him an extra thrill. He'd fulfilled his task. He smiled broadly, his hands on his hips. Feiyan, however, seemed nervous.

"Ah well. Better get moving. Can't keep father waiting," she said.

Llewelyn, who'd been about to vault back up onto the horse, froze.

"Father?" he choked.

She looked down at him blankly.

"The captain. He's my father. Well? What are you waiting for? Come on. And shut your mouth."

They cantered after Gelert; Llewelyn silent.

The revelation that Feiyan was Chang's daughter had filled his brain with a cold fog. The last miles disappeared, and it seemed like only minutes before they crested the ridge to the oasis.

The Jiang sailors were up and recovered, lavishing Gelert with affection.

The captain looked up as Feiyan slid down from the horse. When he saw her he staggered backwards and nearly fell over.

She walked slowly towards him. But he ran to her, arms outstretched, his face flickering between joy and surprise.

"What? How? It's good to … But! How! Ow!" His mangled shoulder made him wince as he pulled Feiyan to his chest, but he squeezed tighter, pressing his lips to the top of her head. "Look at you! My little Princess!"

She smiled weakly and, seeing the captain's blood-caked wound, used it as an excuse to pull away.

"You're hurt. Better not strain it, eh?"

"I'm fine …" Chang was looking around. "But what are you doing here? Did the plan change after we left? Where are the others? Waiting in Aqaba?"

She pulled further away. "No. They're all gone. Dead."

The captain blanched. "Dead? All of them?"

"Yes. I said, didn't I?"

"But … How?"

"They got sick. It was messy. I don't really want to talk about it."

"But … how?" Concern made Chang wide-eyed.

Kung approached them, staring at Feiyan. Though far from happy to see him, she seemed relieved by the interruption his arrival provided.

"Kung, you survived. Who'd have thought?"

His eyes narrowed but, to Llewelyn's surprise, he bowed deeply. Ignoring this act of respect, Feiyan squirmed past him.

"Ao! Chao! The big man!" she beamed.

The three sailors ran to her, hooting with joy. She seemed

happier to share their hugs than she had her father's. Zheng threw her bodily into the air, and she giggled and fell back into his arms as if she'd done it a thousand times.

The dozens of lice dogs gambolled around, and the alarm dog boomed out loud yaps. Gelert bounced into the reunion, yapping like a puppy.

Captain Chang paced around the cavorting group, just far enough away to be part of the celebration without joining it. He smiled, but seemed sad.

Llewelyn was melancholy too. He wasn't part of Feiyan's grand reunion. Why should he be? He'd known her for, how long? Barely a day? But that didn't stop him feeling left out. Ignored. Miserable, he heaved himself from the horse. It was tired and sweaty, in need of food and water.

That's something I can do right, he moped.

"Hey, Llewelyn. What are you doing?" called the captain, smiling and beckoning him over. "Come here! Tell me all about the journey!"

Llewelyn flared, angry. "Someone's got to do some work around here!" he snapped, leading the horse towards the spring. Chang was taken aback, and was about to reply when Gelert let out a doleful howl.

A loud bang in the sky made everyone look up. The dying light of a single green huojian was falling back upon a drifting plume of smoke.

Llewelyn ran across the oasis to the far side of the bowl, Gelert at his heels. He crawled up the hill and peeped over the top. The glaring white salt flat opened up in front of him.

He squinted into the sky, following the drifting smoke plume to its source.

About a mile away stood a horseman, his silhouette quivering in the salty heat haze. Silent and impassive, he seemed to be staring straight back at Llewelyn. He was unmistakably a Chinese soldier. His horse snorted and pawed the salt crust.

The others joined him a moment later.

"So that's what they look like," said Feiyan. "Not very threatening."

"A scout," replied the captain. "Looks like a northerner from beyond the old walls. Best trackers in the empire, and their most brutal killers." He scanned the horizon, muttering to himself. "But where's the rest of the buggers?"

"Look at the hoof prints!" whispered Chao.

The side of the hill was covered in fresh tracks. The twins interpreted their meaning.

"He was watching us, waiting," said Ao. "See, that's where he ate some nuts. But he's only been here for a day and a night."

Chao pointed. "Look, there, that must be when Gelert came back …" The freshest trail of hoof prints led directly to the horseman.

Then two more huojian flashed in the sky above the salt flats far away. The tiny pops of their explosions followed a few seconds later.

"Now we know where the main group is," said Chang. "How far?"

"Forty miles? Maybe more," said Ao.

"Thank Dog! But it's only a day's ride behind us, maybe less! Let's get moving."

"No!" said Feiyan. "Let's wait. Let's talk to them!"

Kung gasped. Even Llewelyn was shocked by the suggestion. The sailors looked at each other, embarrassed, and the captain ground his palms into his eyes and shook his head before glaring at her.

"Not this again!"

"Has anyone even considered just talking?" Feiyan pleaded.

Chang sighed. "I'm surprised they let you join the mission if you're still spouting this nonsense of yours."

She threw up her hands and pointed at the scout. "Well, why not just go out there and kill him? Start as we mean to finish!"

"He's too far away. And there's no time, little one," replied the captain.

"I can have a go," offered Llewelyn, unslinging his longbow.

Feiyan glowered at him. "I didn't mean it! Dog above! You men! Killing; that's your answer to everything."

The captain got up wearily. "That may be true. But it may have escaped your attention that that scout over there is also a man, and so are all his friends who are coming to join him. Come on everyone, we're in a race now. If we're caught before we get to Aqaba, we lose and they've won. Let's get going, everyone."

They squirmed down the slope and hurried back to the campsite.

Zheng scooped the pack of lice dogs into a saddle-bag and the captain placed his alarm dog on the horse's rump. Kung lashed the skins of Essence, together with his bag of potions, onto the saddle. It went unsaid that no-one would be riding the horse. Their escape would only be as fast as the slowest could walk.

The midday heat was already scorching, so they drank as much as they could from the spring and filled their water skins to the brim.

"Y'know, " said Ao mischievously, "the Chinese will be stopping here too ..."

"Ooh! Ooh!" Let's piss in the spring!" giggled Chao.

"No," said Llewelyn, "let's get Gelert to piss in it!"

Feiyan rolled her eyes crossly.

"I've got a better idea!" shouted Kung. He hurried to his bag of tricks and came back tearing open a waxed cloth packet. "Stand back everyone," he said grimly, emptying a bright blue powder into the spring. It frothed briefly.

"What's that?" asked Llewelyn, intrigued.

"Poison," replied Kung. "It boils the lining of the throat. If you don't drown in your own blood, the pain will kill you. This spring will be deadly for a year."

"You can't do that!" said Feiyan. "What about travellers who need water?"

"Yes!" said Llewelyn, "What if someone had poisoned it before *we'd* found it?"

Kung just shrugged and walked back to the horse.

Llewelyn stared after him. The water in the spring had stopped bubbling and was clearing. Feiyan pulled him away by his elbow.

"As you said," she scowled at Kung's back, "he's very determined."

As they made their way towards the boat, Gelert was full of energy, trotting ahead then doubling back, then running off after rustling sounds in the scrub.

Llewelyn just felt numb.

This was the third time he'd travelled this way in three days, but the relentless rise of the landscape wasn't made easier by familiarity. The stifling heat of the afternoon sapped his energy and made his sore hamstrings ache. He didn't feel much like chatting.

Feiyan and her father walked ahead of him.

Her father. The captain. Llewelyn was still struggling to process this new information. They talked, and he couldn't help listening to their conversation. Her replies to the Chang's questions were curt, sometimes hostile, and mostly non-committal.

Feiyan told him that she'd been "fine" waiting by herself all that time, and "no" she "didn't want to talk about what had happened to the rest of her crew", and "yeah, it was sad that so many of our friends have died, but can we stop talking about it now?" and "yeah, no really!" she was "fine!"

To Llewelyn, it sounded as if she couldn't be bothered to talk to her father, as if she thought there was no point. Her dull answers seemed designed to beat her father into silence, making his questions more trouble than they were worth. If so, it worked on Llewelyn. He tuned out of the conversation, finding her sullenness perplexing. If he'd just been reunited with his father, he'd want to tell him all about everything that had happened.

But then he wondered if maybe he wouldn't. So much had happened. He'd changed so much. Would his father even recognise him? These sudden thoughts of Wales made him feel vaguely guilty.

He fell to the rear of the band, wallowing in his confusion. But the others were much more alert to the danger behind, and every hundred yards, they glanced anxiously back to see if they were being followed.

※

The higher they climbed, the better was their view of the route they'd just taken. But the shimmering heat haze of the afternoon blurred the details and it wasn't until evening began to fall that anyone spotted anything.

"There!" cried Feiyan.

They stopped, chilled by a burst of apprehension.

Far below was a drift of dust made minuscule by the dreary landscape. They stared, hoping it might be nothing, just a dust devil or a shadow. A flash of metallic light reflecting off some armour or a spear tip confirmed the uncomfortable truth.

"That amount of dust, I'd say a hundred, maybe a hundred and twenty of them," grunted the captain. "They're making good time."

※

Night fell as they reached the mountains. Ahead, the gorge was an unwelcoming black gash in the still sunlit mountains. They rested, alert for their pursuers in the shadowed plain below.

"There's about fifty of them now," said Ao.

Kung's poison hadn't killed all the Chinese, and darkness hadn't stopped the survivors. Torches were being lit one by one, and the column of pinprick lights snaked towards them.

"Surely we'll lose them in the dark?" said Kung apprehensively.

"Not with those scouts," said Chang, chewing his bottom lip.

"Not with this moon," remarked Zheng, chin in hand.

"I told you it was hopeless," said Feiyan, folding her arms.

Llewelyn was annoyed at their pessimism. "I've come this way already; we'll soon be into broken country. If we cover our tracks, they'll never find us."

His words hung in the stillness of the night. The horse snorted wearily. He could almost hear the men mentally discounting his advice. Kung began whispering to Chang, and they eased to one side, into the darkness. Llewelyn heard their conversation quickly become a serious spat. He glanced quizzically at Feiyan, but she just shrugged, still in a huff.

A sudden high-pitched screeching in the scrub nearby startled them all, and Gelert loped out from behind a thorn bush with the bloody carcass of a rabbit in his mouth.

"He's why!" shouted Kung, pointing at the wolfhound.

The captain sighed, then gathered himself.

"Well, if Llewelyn's right, we won't have to do what you're suggesting," he retorted, ruffling Llewelyn's hair as he scowled at Kung. "Come on, everyone, pick up the pace. Llew, take the lead."

Llewelyn straightened up and walked to the front of the troop, glad that someone was finally listening to him. He glanced back and saw Kung talking earnestly with Zheng, Ao and Chao. Their expressions were grim.

"Hurry!" called Llewelyn, "Chinese not standing still!"

After four hours of hard marching, they arrived at the gorge.

The deflated corpse of the English knight lay waiting, still squirming from within.

Ao, Chao and Zheng drew their bows and fanned out into the rocks, scouting the terrain surrounding the passageway. Kung muttered something to Zheng, who nodded a silent reply.

"No worry, no danger here," said Llewelyn. "Only problem is him!"

Gelert had wandered over to sniff at the ghastly remains.

"No!" yelled Feiyan and threw a stone at him. "Bad wolfhound!"

Llewelyn helped her drag him away from the faceless body.

"What happened here?" asked the captain, gagging. "I don't know what's worse, the stench or the rats."

"It gets worse," muttered Feiyan, pointing down the track.

"Why, what's ahead?" asked Kung.

"You see soon," replied Llewelyn, toeing Gelert down the trail. He looked back. Ao and Chao and Zheng were lingering near the dead knight.

Don't hang around too long, he thought, but plodded on.

🐝

They emerged from the claustrophobic gloom of the gorge into open moonlit country. Soon, the macabre collection of Crusader body parts came into view.

Llewelyn knew to hold his breath well before they reached the grisly pile. The smell of death hung in the air.

Kung stumbled and stopped, dry heaving at the sight.

Llewelyn heard the captain muttering: "Christians and Saracens! Haven't they got better things to do in the name of their gods?"

"The stupidest thing," remarked Kung, "is that they're fighting over a god they both stole from the Hebrews!"

"Idiots!"

Llewelyn bristled at the jibe. What right did these heathens have to criticise the Holy Crusade? He turned to tell them as much, but stopped dead in his tracks.

"Where are Zheng and Chao and Ao?"

Chang and Kung were silent, and in a blinding moment of clarity Llewelyn knew what had happened.

"You send them stop the Emperor men!" he hissed. How could he not have noticed that they'd stayed behind?

"No, I didn't," replied the captain quietly.

"Where are they then?" said Feiyan hotly.

"Back at the gorge, little one … "

"We didn't send them," interrupted Kung. "I *suggested* that it was their duty …"

"… it was a perfect place for an ambush," continued Chang.

"But no have to!" yelled Llewelyn, stamping his feet. "I telled you we can escape!"

Feiyan also exploded. "Three men against fifty? Men you've known and lived with and worked with for hundreds of years …?"

Hold on! thought Llewelyn, *What? Hundreds of years. She said it out loud!*

Kung interrupted, taking the high ground once again. "It wasn't your father's decision. They went gladly. It was their duty …"

Feiyan ignored him. "Did you even try to stop them?"

Chang's face twisted at her question. Tears welled in his eyes. He shot Feiyan a glance of such pained reproach that she briefly fell silent. Taking the horse's reins, he headed off wordlessly down the trail.

But Feiyan hadn't finished and chased after him. "Don't you see? This is how it will be, and how it will end. Maybe we'll kill a few, but they'll still keep coming. We can't beat them. The only way to stop …"

"Enough!" bellowed Chang and raised his hand, balling it into a fist.

Feiyan stepped back, staring at her father in shock. He looked at his hand and lowered it.

"Enough," he said, quietly and carried on walking.

"You could have stopped them," said Feiyan quietly after him. "You could have stopped them." She noticed Llewelyn staring at her and pulled herself together, knuckling back her tears. She glared at Kung, then followed her father.

Llewelyn seethed at Kung's determination and walked past him, refusing eye contact.

But inside he was remembering *'Men you've known and lived with and worked with for hundreds of years'*.

Feiyan had blabbed the secret of the Jiang.

Chapter 37. Diversion

The journey continued in a silence laden with bitterness and recrimination.

An hour went by, then two. Llewelyn rolled 'hundreds of years' around his head. Feiyan's slip felt oddly liberating. Now she'd said it, he could forget his guilty feelings about stealing the information from the captain. But it only provided a momentary relief before his mind clouded with dark, apprehensive thoughts. Before long the Chinese soldiers would reach the gorge where his three friends waited in ambush.

Another hour passed. In his mind, Llewelyn saw the Emperor's men advance up the hillside, their horses stepping over the very rocks he'd walked around.

It won't be long, just about ... now.

Then the still night air wafted with half-heard shouts, fleeting screams and snatches of horses squealing in pain. Distance reduced the clash of steel battering steel to pathetic clinks and clunks, but Llewelyn knew what would be happening. He remembered one of Friar William's history lessons where three hundred Spartans had held back an entire empire, and knew the captain was right; Ao and Zheng and Chao's ambush would wreak havoc with their pursuers.

But how long would they hold the gorge? *An hour? Maybe two?* Even a few extra minutes could make a difference to their escape.

The sounds of battle petered away as they hurried on, and Llewelyn suddenly remembered the captain's promise to tell him about the Jiang's plans for the Great Dog.

But somehow that no longer seemed important.

🐾

The cold gloom of night gave way to day.

They finally reached the part of the trail where the road to Aqaba curved off to the left.

The river lay below. Its looping main channel glowed in the pale dawn light, spreading its many fingers outwards to the distant sea. Best of all, less than three miles away lay the sampan. It was tiny against the wide river and looked lost in the rippling swathe of yellow reeds.

The captain hugged Feiyan. "My old boat! Just where you said she'd be!" She shrugged him away but he persisted in his cheeriness. "Wonderful! And it looks like the tide is on the rise. We'll be on board before the sea breezes come in!"

"We're going to make it!" announced Kung.

"Yes, we will!" Chang hugged Feiyan again. "Well done, little one!"

What did she *do?* Llewelyn felt a twinge of jealousy that compelled him to interrupt.

"Hey, you lot! We still being chased."

"Nonsense. We're almost there. Look how close my little one brought her boat to us!" laughed the captain.

"Not close enough. Look! The sun rising. We easier to be seen."

"We'll be in the shadow of the valley; harder for the Chinese to spot us!" said Chang.

But Llewelyn's disquiet was growing. "You say their scouts good trackers?"

"Best in the world."

"They see our tracks. And they see the sampan."

"He might be right," said Kung, nervously. "We must get going."

Llewelyn was thinking fast now, working out times and distances, figuring out relative speeds. "No!" he shouted. "They on horseback. If they catch up they run us down like … Gelert run down a deer."

An outrageous idea popped into his head. "Look. Chinese chase Gelert, not us. They follow his tracks, not bother with sampan. We send him off while we go down hill …"

"You're mad!" said Kung, but Feiyan was nodding approvingly.

"… Gelert will turn back and catch up with us and we get away," finished Llewelyn.

The captain was still considering his proposal when, suddenly, a green rocket shot into the air behind them. There was barely any gap between the flash and the clap of the explosion. Gelert howled.

Llewelyn yanked a small bush from the ground and started sweeping up their tracks. "Need make it hard them follow us."

Feiyan joined him. "Well, come on!" she hissed at her father and Kung. "Or did Ao and Chao and Zheng go to their deaths for nothing?"

There was a brief silence.

"Very well," said Chang.

🐾

The horse stood in the roadway, snorting and tossing his head.

They'd stripped him of his saddle, harness and supplies and thrown them into a crevasse. The great charger looked nervously magnificent, as if losing the trappings of war made him feel vulnerable.

Llewelyn wondered if he was doing the right thing. He'd killed this horse's master, galloped him through a burning city, forced him aboard a strange ship, and used him as a lowly pack animal. Never once had the animal complained, but Llewelyn still had one final indignity to heap on him. He felt a guilty lump in his throat, not proud of what he was about to do.

He picked up a fist-sized rock and threw it as hard as he could at the animal's rump. It gave a startled whinny and pelted off down the roadway.

"Gelert!" he yelled. The wolfhound's ears pricked up. "Fetch!"

Instantly, the hunting hound ran after the fast disappearing horse. Their two sets of tracks were deep and fresh in the dirt of the road.

"This had better work," said Chang grimly.

"He won't catch the horse, will he?" asked Feiyan, now having doubts.

"He try, but he get bored and come back. Always."

"I hope you're right," said Kung, wringing his hands.

"I know Gelert," replied Llewelyn confidently. "Come, hurry."

They swept their tracks clean and scrambled over the edge of the road into the valley, stepping on bare rock so as to leave no trace of their passing. It was a steep climb down, and their bows and swords caught repeatedly on rocks and bushes. The blubbery skins of Essence made the task even harder for the captain. Every scraping step sent a torrent of rocks tumbling noisily into the shadows.

Although they had to press on, it was impossible to avoid looking back, dreading every second that might bring about

254

their discovery.

After what seemed like an age to cover a quarter of a mile, they reached a ribbon of huge boulders strewn across the steepest part of the hillside. Clambering over the gigantic rocks, they rested, just in time to hear a clattering of hooves from the trail above.

A shout pulled the unseen group of horsemen to a halt in a jangle of armour and harnesses. Llewelyn squirmed back behind the nearest boulder, trying to disappear into the rock. He knew it would be hard for the Chinese to see any detail in the valley; the shadows were deep and the dawn sky was too bright. But he also knew the slightest movement would immediately catch any onlooker's eye. It was like being chased by the English after a raid. *Keep still or stay still forever,* he heard Owain whispering in his ear.

He found that he'd stopped breathing, and it was only with a deliberate effort that he could start again.

They heard riders dismounting, then the ridgeline was broken by movement. Five heads appeared, bobbing up and down. There was some whispered arguing. The heads pulled back, and a few seconds later, Llewelyn heard soldiers remounting their horses and the entire troop thundered off down the track.

Silence returned as the thudding of hundreds of hooves faded.

"They fell for it!" hissed Feiyan excitedly. "Come on!"

"Wait!" cautioned Llewelyn.

A few minutes passed, and a single silhouetted head slowly reappeared over the skyline. The Chinese had left someone behind to make sure they hadn't been duped. Llewelyn knew they'd do this – it's what he'd have done.

Feiyan squirmed impatiently beside him, and he held his hand up, silently ordering her to keep still. The captain hissed at her to be quiet.

The moment dragged on, and the lone watcher remained impassively in place. *How long's he going to wait?* It was an impossible situation; if they broke cover too soon, the sentry could call the others back. If they stayed too long, Gelert would lead his pursuers back to them. Meanwhile, the sun was rising; before long, they'd be visible and the game would be up.

Bugger this! Llewelyn knocked up an arrow to his longbow and stood.

"Oye, you!" he yelled to the figure above. The watcher's head craned up, and then he was dead, shot through the left eye.

"You killed him!" Feiyan gasped.

Llewelyn was already slinging his bow.

"Yes. Now we can get going."

Beyond the boulders, the gradient was gentler and the ground easier to negotiate. The sampan lay tantalisingly close, less than a mile away.

They increased their pace.

"How did you know there was only one sentry up there?" panted the captain, wincing from the pain in his shoulder.

"I didn't."

"Let's hope you're right about the Great Dog too."

Llewelyn smiled and put his fingers to his mouth. His piercing whistle echoed around the valley.

"Don't you worry about Gelert."

🐾

When they reached lower ground, the wall of tall reeds hid the sampan from view. Lighter on their feet, Feiyan and Llewelyn began to pull away from the two older men.

"You two go ahead. Get the boat ready," Chang panted after them. The flabby skins of Essence bounced maddeningly, throwing him off his rhythm.

They were glad to obey, leaping over rocks and low bushes. It quickly became a race. Llewelyn was pulling away when Feiyan called to him.

"You didn't even blink."

"What?"

"That horseman. You killed him without a thought."

"He'd have killed me. I not have time to think."

That shut her up. They carried on running through the reeds; he was still pulling ahead. Then she called again.

"You're a brilliant archer, you know; that was some shot!"

Surprised and distracted by the admiration in her voice, Llewelyn tripped over a reed tussock and fell clumsily into the dirt.

Feiyan laughed, effortlessly jumping over him before

disappearing over a low hill and into the reeds.

Swearing under his breath, he picked himself up and pushed through the reeds. They were dry and brittle, snapping aside easily and crackling underfoot, but thick enough to slow him down. Then the tall grass gave way to gravel, sand and pebbles, before the river and the sampan appeared before him.

The crew dogs were leaping into the shallow water, splashing towards Feiyan when the captain and Kung pushed through the reeds and lumbered past him.

"Thank Dog!" wheezed Kung, pulling off his backpack and spilling all the lice dogs and the crew dog onto the ground where they joined the others in an excited canine reunion.

"We made it!" gasped the captain. "But where's Gelert?"

"Here he come now!" interrupted Llewelyn, laughing but relieved.

Three or so miles to the south, a small cloud of dust appeared over the crest of the valley and hurtled down the hillside, a streak of grey at its head. Llewelyn whistled again, and the streak of grey turned towards them. Chang, Kung and Feiyan cried with joy.

There was no sign of any horsemen.

The Great Dog streaked towards them, flying over the boulders and scree. Soon he was on the easy part of the lower slopes, then he was lost in the reeds, and then he burst through the wall of grass right in front of them. Unable to stop, he barrelled into Llewelyn, throwing him into the shallows.

"Oi!" he cried as he tried to get up, but the other dogs swarmed all over them both, pressing Llewelyn back into the river.

"Let's move it," said the captain, clambering on board the sampan, "The tide's turning, the river will be with us, and the wind's fair."

Feiyan whistled for the crew dogs to hoist the ship's main sail. There was a creaking of pulleys and the flapping sailcloth stretched open and caught the wind. The sampan jerked with a groan of timbers as it began to move away from the bank.

"Look!" shouted Llewelyn, as he pointed up to the crest of the valley.

Three miles away, a new dust cloud appeared on the horizon, glowing bright against the sun. The Emperor's horsemen surged over the skyline, pouring down the hillside in a glittering cascade of armour that only slowed when they reached the broken line of rocks and boulders of the upper reaches. They separated into strings of riders, picking their way carefully but remorselessly down into the valley.

The captain steered the sampan into the deepest part of the river.

The current was flowing strong and hard and, with the wind behind them, the vessel picked up pace. But it would never be faster than a galloping horse.

Llewelyn anxiously scanned the landscape for the Chinese. They'd changed course and cut across the valley to intercept the sampan somewhere up ahead.

Now Chang had spotted another danger. The river was beginning to split into its maze of channels. If they didn't choose the correct course they'd end up grounded in a shallower backwater.

"Which kite dog do we have?" he called to Feiyan.

"Sashin".

"Send him up. He might even add a little to our sail area."

Llewelyn was relieved when Sashin soared gracefully into the sky. Now they had his eyes to steer by.

Feiyan whistled to the crew dogs and they began rigging another sail from the forward mast. Llewelyn ran to help. The two sails spread out on either side of the sampan like the outstretched wings of a bat. The boat picked up more speed.

Gelert's ears pricked at a distant roaring sound.

"Breakers!" shouted the captain, with a flicker of a smile. In half an hour they'd be at sea, beyond reach of any horseman.

But the danger was far from over. The Chinese had cleared the line of boulders and were now galloping along the gentler slopes of the lower valley, directly for a point on the river ahead. Soon they were lost from sight, behind the reed beds.

"Their horses will be tired," ventured Kung.

"They'll be slowed by the reed beds," suggested Chang, hopefully.

"They're the Emperor's men. They won't give up," scowled Feiyan.

Llewelyn thought he could still hear the thundering of their horses' hooves. He forced the thought from his mind; there was nothing to be done but pray they'd reach the sea before they could be caught. If not ... he spotted his longbow and the quiver of broadhead arrows.

At least I can go down fighting.

Then he had an idea. "Get fire going," he yelled.

"Aren't you hot enough?" said Feiyan.

Llewelyn had pulled off his tunic and was tearing it into strips. He quickly bound them to the head of an arrow. "Reeds out there are dry. They'll burn like a witch," he added in Welsh.

"Oh! A smokescreen, of course!" enthused Feiyan. "There's some pitch in that bucket over there. I've a steel and flint down below ..."

The wind was blowing from behind the sampan.

"But won't the smoke blind us?" asked Kung, twisting his fingers.

Chang, excited, looked up at the kite dog. "No, we'll be moving ahead of the wind so we'll be ahead of the smoke."

Back on deck, Feiyan scraped sparks into a tinderbox. Llewelyn stood waiting for her at the rails with his longbow and treated arrows. The flappy rags meant the arrow would fly like a pig, but with its heavy double-bladed broadhead he knew it would fly a long way.

"There!" announced Feiyan. Her tinder had caught and she tipped it into the bucket of thick pitch, making it burst into flames.

Llewelyn knocked up the arrow, dipped it in and withdrew its burning tip. Sooty droplets of fire splattered onto the deck as he drew the arrow behind his ear. At maximum elevation, and with the bowstring cutting into his fingers, he let fly. The arrow streaked high into the sky with an unfamiliar fluttering sound. It wobbled, trailing a spiral of black smoke before falling out of sight.

Feiyan handed him a fresh arrow. He lit it up and shot it, followed by another and another, purposefully bracketing a wide stretch of the reeds behind them. Soon, all his English broadheads were gone. He thought about using Chinese arrows but dismissed the idea. *Too light.*

They waited, the sampan drifting downriver. Two or three minutes passed. Nothing. But then a thin tendril of white smoke appeared above the reeds. It twisted and writhed into a thick yellowish skein. Soon it was joined by another. A roaring, crackling sound reached their ears as the dry, dusty reeds exploded into flames, sending up fresh plumes of smoke and glowing cinders. Shortly, the palls of smoke fused into one.

"Go up and see what's happening," Chang shouted to Llewelyn.

From thirty feet, the view from the masthead was stupendous. Llewelyn's fire was already a thousand yards across and growing. Its voracious appetite spewed a wall of flames fifty yards high and the smoke grew higher still. The wind blew it diagonally away from the sampan, gobbling acres of reeds and cutting across the route of the horsemen. The twisting heat haze distorted them into a jumble of macabre figures.

"Where are the soldiers?" yelled the captain.

"The smoke's pushing them back up the side of the valley," he called down.

The Chinese were now falling behind the sampan. The ground they'd been forced to take was rocky, uneven, and criss-crossed with gullies that could only be negotiated at walking pace.

Llewelyn descended, bursting with the success of his idea. "It worked!"

"Excellent," said the captain. "But we're stupid to think they'll give up … Everyone to the poles!"

Feiyan and Kung pulled out long bamboo poles from under the sampan's railings. Leaning over the prow of the boat, they thrust them deep into the water until they made contact with the riverbed. They pushed down and began walking slowly backwards, straining to shove the boat along. When they reached the stern, they lifted their dripping poles, ran to the front of the boat, and started over again.

Llewelyn had seen salmon fishers on the Glaslyn poling their flimsy boats to their nets like this. P*unting, that's what they called it*. It looked easy, fun even. He ran to get his own pole and join them.

"Good work," said Chang, as they got into the rhythm of the job.

Soon the sampan's decks were slick with water. Gelert followed Llewelyn movements, barking like a puppy, and skittering and sliding along the messy deck.

"Get out of the way!" scolded Llewelyn.

"Leave him alone," laughed Feiyan. "You're trying to help, aren't you, Gelert."

Thinking Feiyan was calling him, the wolfhound ran to her, but he skidded on the greasy deck and slid into her, tripping her just as she was leaning overboard with her pole. It caught in the mud and yanked her overboard. Llewelyn rushed back along the boat to grab at Feiyan, but collided with Kung, tumbling them both over the stern rail and into the river. Gelert instantly leapt in after Llewelyn.

Instinctively, the captain threw the tiller over – it was a mistake. The strain on the rigging was abrupt and with a mighty twang, the jury-rigged second sail's boom ripped away from its lashing and the entire rig crashed overboard in a tangle of timber, ropes and cloth. The mainsail held, but with the forward rigging now dragging in the river, the sampan refused to steer properly.

In less time than it took for an arrow to fall, the escape was undone.

High above, the kite dog yapped forlornly, trying to adjust his wing flaps to the sudden changes in the wind around it. The crew dogs ran around barking in confusion, waiting for their next orders.

Meanwhile, Feiyan, Kung, Gelert and Llewelyn were picked up by the current and carried past the crippled sampan.

"I'll catch up with you!" Chang shouted after them.

Feiyan was livid. "Stupid dog! Why couldn't you keep him out of the way!" she cursed at Llewelyn.

"Oh. So it's *my* fault?"

"Damned children! Shut up and get to the shore!" spluttered Kung.

They paddled to the steep riverbank where they grabbed at roots and branches, and helped drag each other up onto dry land. Llewelyn looked back. The sampan was fifty yards away, drifting towards them with the current.

The captain stood at the tiller, trying to steer against the drag of the tangled rigging and straining to swing the boat close the riverbank.

"Get ready to jump!" he grimaced through the pain in his shoulder.

"Here I go," called Feiyan, timing her run carefully. She accelerated into a sprint and leapt gracefully over the gap, landing in the middle of the deck ahead of the main mast. The sampan rocked.

"Your turn," she urged Llewelyn.

As he trotted to match his speed with that of the boat, he was determined to hide his nerves from Feiyan. Gelert loped alongside him, not understanding what was happening. Llewelyn aimed for the front of the sampan, took a deep breath, sped up, and jumped. He landed, cracking his shin on the railings, and the sampan lurched again.

Back on the riverbank, confused and indecisive, Gelert yelped. Llewelyn hobbled over to the railing and called encouragingly.

"It's all right, boy. Come on, come to me! Jump!"

Bewildered, the wolfhound looked up and down from the river to the boat. Llewelyn grew worried, and turned to Feiyan. "Maybe we should run a plank out to …?"

A second later, he lay sprawling and winded under Gelert's soggy mass. The sampan shifted again.

"That's the last time I worry about you, you smelly lunk!" Llewelyn wheezed, trying to pushing the Great Dog off.

Now it was Kung's turn. He jogged alongside the boat, anxious and reluctant.

"What are you waiting for?" snapped Feiyan.

"Give me a moment. I've just got to think about this!"

"What's there to think about?"

"It's very complicated − I have to work out the vectors of two independent bodies and the variables of their convergent velocities!"

"Yeah! Just like Gelert had to!" called Feiyan angrily. "Just jump!"

Kung started his run. Feiyan and Llewelyn reached out to help.

As he propelled himself off the riverbank, Kung's foot slipped and he yelped with fear, twisting as he caught the railings. The sampan lurched violently and they scrambled to grab his arms, tilting the deck further. Kung hung from the railings, chest deep in the river, his extra drag swinging the boat towards the bank.

"Pull him in!" bellowed the captain, wrestling with the tiller.

Terrified, Kung looked back at the nearing riverbank, and scrambled his feet against the slippery planks of the boat's hull.

"Don't let me go!" he pleaded.

They hauled at him, but he was wet and heavy. Gelert grabbed hold of Kung's drenched tunic in his strong jaws and together they managed to haul his shoulders over the railings.

But it was too late.

The sampan thudded up against the riverbank, catching Kung by the thighs. He squealed as he was crushed, then spun by the scraping collision.

Feiyan and Llewelyn had hold of his arms, but his body was being rolled between the moving hull and the unyielding banks like a grass stem being rubbed between two fingers. They had no choice but to hobble along the deck, passing him between them as he spun, hearing the bones in his knees, ankles and feet snap. Kung stared helplessly into Llewelyn's eyes. Then, unable to endure the agony, he passed out.

A sudden blast of smoky wind and a too late eddy in the river's current swung the sampan away from the riverbank, allowing them to finally haul Kung on board.

Llewelyn tore the poor man's trousers open. His legs resembled those of a broken puppet – twisted and black with bruising, and already swelling. The knees and ankles had been so pulverised that his feet were facing in opposite directions.

"Never mind him! Come and help!" roared the captain.

The sampan was now wholly out of control. The clouds of choking yellow smoke had caught up, engulfing the sampan.

"Quickly, get the wreckage off while I steer!" coughed Chang.

Taking axes, Llewelyn and Feiyan hacked at the cordage, their eyes streaming. The sampan wobbled, but immediately settled when they heaved the wreckage overboard. Feiyan whistled the crew dogs into action and they pulled the mainsail back into position.

The ship responded and the captain gasped a sigh of relief. "That's more like it! Llewelyn, get back up the mast and see what's going on."

He could hear the roar of breaking surf intensify as he broke clear of the smoke and climbed above the muffling effects of the reed banks.

Sashin drifted past him just a few feet away, yapping and drawing his attention to the river mouth, now just five hundred yards away.

Things had changed from the few days ago when he'd arrived with Feiyan. Then, the transition between sea and river had been calm, but now the main channel of the river thrust through monstrous white breakers in a surge of whirlpools and undercurrents.

Llewelyn looked around. To his left, he could see beyond the smokescreen. The burning reed beds were sparser toward the beaches either side of the river mouth. Soon the fire would run out of fuel and already the smokescreen was thinning.

The Chinese horsemen were two miles away, still on the hills. Even as he watched, the column began to angle down the slope toward the beaches. They would close the gap in only six minutes at full gallop.

In his mind's eye, Llewelyn pictured the three-way race between the sampan, the fire and the horsemen. He calculated that the sampan was ahead of the pack.

"What's happening?" yelled the captain.

"We're very close to the sea. I think we're going to make it."

"How's Shasin?"

"He's nervous about the waves. It's looking pretty rough out there."

"Dog dammit! Come down."

Llewelyn slid back to the deck. On either side, the reed beds were emerging through the thinning smoke.

Meanwhile, the sampan began to twitch and buck. The sea represented safety, but by now the roar of the approaching breakers was deafening. Gelert whimpered, looking to Llewelyn for reassurance.

Suddenly, the smoke cleared and the pounding surf was revealed.

Instinctively, Llewelyn and Feiyan grabbed hold of the mainmast.

Where they met, the river wrestled with the sea in a struggle for dominance. The emerald river coiled and twisted through the pounding surf, throwing aside swirling ridges of spume. The blue sea sucked the river down into deep troughs that coalesced into dark maelstroms.

Llewelyn heard thundering hoof beats and looked over just as the reeds on the left bank suddenly erupted into flame, throwing back the horsemen one more time.

"We're safe!" screamed Feiyan. She grabbed Llewelyn round the waist and hugged him tight.

"No we're not!' growled the captain. "Hold on!"

❧

The sampan's bows smashed into the first line of breakers, sending up a mast-high curtain of spray. Llewelyn felt the impact shudder through the boat and Feiyan squeezed him tighter. The sampan bucked backwards and began to turn.

The captain whistled commands to Sashin, and as the kite dog adjusted his flight, Chang threw the tiller over. The sampan ploughed this way and that through the churning waters, pounding into troughs and rising giddily above the crests, jinking left to right as Sashin led them past unseen terrors.

Then, abruptly, the wild ride was over. The river had lost the battle. The sampan was beyond the surf, riding the swell of the triumphant sea, already fifty yards from the shore. Llewelyn looked back and saw the Emperor's soldiers through the towering wall of flames, their outlines quivering through the distorting veil of heat.

"We made it," said Feiyan, still hugging him tightly. They were soaked through, but the salt water was clean and cool, and he could feel the warmth of her body against his just before she pulled away.

Chang beamed. "Good job, you two. Now you can attend to Kung."

"Just a moment ..." said Llewelyn.

Gelert was at the railings, watching the horsemen, his tail wagging.

"What is it mate?" he asked, squinting through the flames.

One of the soldiers had dismounted and was walking up to the edge of the fire. It was impossible to see his features through the swirling acrid smoke and shimmering heat, but he raised what looked like a longbow.

Llewelyn edged back to the captain, keeping the figure in

sight as the man put an arrow to his bow.

"Get down!" he yelled, throwing himself to the deck.

Unaware of the danger, Chang hesitated and turned. The arrow hit him square on his good shoulder, throwing him backwards from the cockpit. Landing, he grunted in agony and looked down.

It was an ash-shafted, goose-feathered arrow.

Llewelyn gawped. It looked like an English arrow. *Can't be!*

"Let's out of here!" yelled Feiyan, already crouching at the tiller.

Keeping low, Llewelyn scurried over to Chang, who was straining with pain and grunting with anger. Llewelyn tore his shirt away and was relived to see that although his shoulder was sheeted red, the captain's wound wasn't pulsing blood.

"You're lucky, you won't bleed to death," he said, trying to sound reassuring.

"Thank Dog it wasn't my bad shoulder!" laughed Chang weakly, now white with shock. Then it was his turn to pass out.

The arrow had snapped Chang's collarbone and pierced his shoulder blade. Llewelyn gently turned him on his side and saw the flesh-carving broadhead sticking half a yard from his back. It was definitely an English arrow.

He sneaked a glance over the railings. The mysterious bowman had returned to the main body of Chinese, now invisible beyond the fire.

By now the sampan had clawed further out to sea, out of range.

Llewelyn stood and looked around the boat. Despite the recent calamity, everything seemed mostly intact. But it would be months before Chang's new wound healed, and poor Kung would never walk again.

Overcome with dizziness, Llewelyn sat down, knowing he'd fall over otherwise. He felt exhausted, bewildered and hopeless. Here he was again, pulling away from a hostile shore and into the open sea.

"Hey!" yelled Feiyan, snapping him back to reality. "Get Kung's bag of medicine and some bandages! And bring Sashin down while you're at it."

Chapter 39. Confirmation

Gelert quickly established himself as the top dog on the sampan.

The thirty or so lice dogs were particularly devoted to him, and followed him wherever he went, gazing at him adoringly and fighting for the honour of sleeping on top of him at night.

It had been seven long, hot days and nights since they'd escaped the Emperor's men. Now their relief at knowing they were no longer being chased had been replaced by sapping boredom.

Llewelyn had constructed a shade sail over the cockpit, and this small area of the sampan became the coolest, freshest place to be – and consequently the most cramped.

The captain rested his maimed shoulders on a sack that Feiyan had stuffed with threads of unpicked rope and dog hairs.

Llewelyn had also made a daybed for Kung, who lay beside Chang. Kung had woken on the second day, and despite his agony, had managed to mix up some pain-killing medicine from his brown poppies. Once it had started to work he'd shown Llewelyn and Feiyan how to set his mangled legs with bamboo splints.

Now the drug made him uncharacteristically mellow, and he drifted in a happy haze, distracted and prone to babbling.

"So why it called the 'Red Sea'?" Llewelyn asked Kung.

"Ah yes, the Red Sea," he trilled. " I do believe the Kingdom of the Pharaohs was known as 'The Red Land', hence the 'Red Sea'."

He lolled to one side, whacking the captain, who snorted with pain.

Chang had refused any of Kung's poppy juice medicine, claiming it took the edge off his thinking. It meant that he had to endure constant pain in both shoulders, which manifested itself in a very short temper.

"Idiot!" he snapped. "You know nothing 'cept what you've read in books. It's the 'Red Sea' because of the sunsets!"

Llewelyn sighed. Even though there was now plenty of the Essence, they'd soon discovered that it was still only effective for three days. Kung had declared that they no longer needed to wait twelve hours to dose themselves, a statement that had provoked the first of many petty rows between him and Chang. Bedridden, the two men had continued to argue like old priests, and now they were again in need of the Essence, they were becoming even more fractious.

"You're both wrong," interrupted Feiyan from the prow where she'd been brushing Gelert down. "It's called the Red Sea because it's red."

She was lost in the glare of the midday sun, and the sea ahead was so bright, it was painful to look at. Llewelyn tied the tiller up and walked to the front of the sampan. He was curious to see what she was talking about, but mostly he just wanted an excuse to be with her. Despite her prickliness, he was irresistibly drawn to her.

When he saw what she'd found, his mouth dropped open. The sea that had previously been a deep blue was now a flat pool of blood.

"What is it?" he asked nervously.

"Panda snot, idiot." said Feiyan, rolling her eyes. Her hostility faltered when she saw his hurt expression. She didn't know it was mostly because he had no idea what a panda was, but she did know she'd somehow crossed the line.

"How should I know?" She leaned over the bow, scooped up a handful of sea and sniffed it.

"It doesn't smell of much, but it looks like millions of tiny red insects."

Llewelyn peered at the pool of red water glittering in her delicately cupped palm. It wasn't blood; more like tiny crimson flecks, suspended in the water like sawdust.

Feiyan offered up her wet, red-speckled hand to Gelert.

"Go on, lick it off."

But the wolfhound just looked at her blankly. Llewelyn knew she might as well have asked him to eat a turnip. Feiyan frothed her hand in the bow wave, wiping it clean against the rough timbers of the hull.

He glanced at her profile. He found her almost too beautiful to look at, especially when she wasn't shouting at him. Feiyan had rolled back the sleeves of her blue tunic and her toned, pale arms glowed in the sunlight. He sat down next to her, but she scowled and shuffled aside so there'd be no chance of them touching each other.

She continued staring out to sea.

"Listen to that pair of idiots," she scoffed at the captain and Kung.

"They old," shrugged Llewelyn. "They must know more than us."

Feiyan turned on him, eyes blazing. "Father? Maybe. But Kung? Pha! He's a machine with all the feelings of a pulley block. Besides, if those two are so clever, how come Wudi and all the others are dead? But no – they've made their plans and now they only see what they want to see. All these deaths are just the start."

Llewelyn had learned it was best to avoid Feiyan's pet subject for a rant. He looked at the two injured men who were now snoring gently.

"They gone to sleep," he said, glad to be able to change the subject.

"I'll go prepare their Essence," said Feiyan, rising.

Llewelyn got up to go with her.

"Do you have to follow me everywhere?" she sighed as she lifted the mid-deck hatchway.

Yes, he thought, but said "I thought you might need help."

"Believe it or not, I don't need your help to fetch a water skin," she replied curtly and jumped into the hold.

Llewelyn held his tongue, wondering why he so readily forgave her aloofness, but climbed down after her anyway.

Below decks it was swelteringly hot and poorly lit. Every available inch was packed with enough supplies to last several dozen men and a crew of dogs well over a year. What space remained was filled with snoring canines. Llewelyn had to tread carefully in the dark so as not to step on a sleeping crew dog. Making his way aft, he found Feiyan opening the heavy chest where the skins of Essence were stored.

A thought that had long been in the back of his mind popped out unbidden. "How old you?"

She turned to him. "Too old for you, laddie!"

Undeterred, he tried again. "How old is that?"

Feiyan rolled her eyes at him. "If you must know, I'm sixteen."

Relieved, Llewelyn smiled. He'd been secretly worried that she might be two hundred and thirty-six or something.

Feiyan glared at him suspiciously.

"You think I'm really old don't you!"

"No! Sixteen. That's what I thought." The lie warbled his voice.

She grew more suspicious. Then her expression changed and she gasped. "What do you know about the Essence?" she demanded, her eyes flashing as she poked him in the chest.

Llewelyn blushed hotly. 'Uh! Not much."

"Not much? No-one outside of Jiang can know anything about the Essence! Who told you? Wudi, Zheng? Kung?"

He shook his head vigorously, floundering for a response. He knew how easily she could catch him in a lie.

"No, not Kung. You telled me!"

"What?" Feiyan was shocked. "I never told you anything!"

"Yes. You did. You say that your father have been with his men for hundreds of years, and I worked it out from …"

"Shut up! I never …" She gulped, realising the truth in his words.

Feiyan was suddenly silent. She frowned and chewed her lip. Her obvious distress contrasted sharply with the wave of relief now flowing over Llewelyn, washing away his guilt at having tricked Chang into revealing the Jiang secret.

She put down the bag of Essence and grabbed him by the shoulders.

"You mustn't tell ANYONE that I told you," she implored.

"I will not!" he replied, shocked at the desperation in her voice.

The colour had drained from her face and tears pricked her eyes.

"You mustn't. No-one outside Jiang can know that we can live forever! If anyone ever found out you'd got it from me …"

Llewelyn was instantly deflated. Having a hold on Feiyan gave him little satisfaction. On the contrary, knowing he could make her unhappy only made him miserable.

"I promise I will not tell anyone."

Sniffing back her tears, she looked into his eyes and smiled. "No, I don't think you will." But then she frowned a warning. "You'd better not, or else."

An awkward silence fell between them.

Feiyan was puzzled. "You're pretty smart to have worked out the secret of the Essence just from what I said."

"Well, there were other things I see before then," Llewelyn admitted. He told her about the unnatural ageing of the dead sailors' bodies.

"Yes, that happens if somebody dies deprived of the Essence."

Feiyan now seemed willing to talk, as if knowing he'd already deduced the secret of the Essence gave her permission to open up to him.

"The older someone is if they die, the quicker they revert back to how they would have looked without it," she added.

Llewelyn pictured the Jiang dead and remembered the old helmsman's impossibly wrinkled face.

"Wudi! How old was he?"

Feiyan had to think for a minute before replying; "I think he was around twelve hundred years old. Even he wasn't sure. Apparently you lose track of the years after the first few centuries."

Llewelyn reeled as he counted back through so much history.

"But that means he was alive at the same time as Our Lord Jesus!"

"If you say so. He never said anything about anyone called Arlawdjeezus to me."

"That why he knew so much about the Inner Sea!"

"He was old enough to know about every ocean of the world."

Llewelyn's mind was racing. "So Essence make you immortal?"

"Of course not! Or Wudi would still be here. No. People do get older, it's just that it takes them a lot longer."

"I not see you drink any Essence."

Feiyan laughed sharply and picked up the black skin.

"Well, you haven't worked out everything about the Essence, have you?" she said, coming close. She stared at him. "Look. The eyes are the giveaway." Llewelyn gazed back, hypnotised by her ice-blue eyes.

"Blue. Not green. If you meet a green-eyed Jiang, you can bet they're up to their eyeballs in Essence. Literally."

Her voice was harsh now. "Besides, I'm too young. All Jiang are forbidden to take it until they're adults." She was now struggling to conceal her anger. "And it's a doubly forbidden for me. Women have to wait until they've done their duty and had their babies."

"Why?" asked Llewelyn. It didn't seem fair.

Feiyan scowled, her hands reflexively twisting the neck of the skin of Essence. "This stuff is really bad if you're pregnant."

"How? Does it hurt the baby?"

"Yes. And the mother. Especially the mother." Her face was dark now.

"What happens if you drink it before you grow up?"

She glared at him. "I just told you, it's not allowed!"

Llewelyn persisted, "I swallow some Essence when Gelert fight with monkey. And I get mouthful of it when he puke on me."

Feiyan came close again, concern on her face as she reached out and touched his cheek. His skin tingled at the caress of her fingers.

"Oh no!" she whispered. "You didn't swallow any of it did you? Oh dear! That explains everything! That must be what's turned you into …"

"What?" urged Llewelyn, his mouth falling open into a worried 'O'. For a heartbeat, he thought he saw sympathy, even affection, in her expression.

"Turned you into … an idiot, idiot!" she said, shutting his mouth with a fingertip. "Dog knows, you can't have been born this stupid."

But seeing the hurt in his eyes, she softened.

"Well, maybe you're not an idiot. But you should only worry about things you can do something about. And right now, we have to go give those two old duffers up there their medicine."

A week later, they sailed into the Arabian Sea.

The rolling swell of the deeper waters was steeper, and the small boat required more attentive seamanship. With more work to do, there were marginally fewer arguments.

For a while Feiyan was almost friendly with Llewelyn, but she soon reverted to coldness. His hopes that their shared secret might bring them together withered, but he consoled himself with the thought that her hostility was usually directed more at her father and Kung.

It was the dead hour of the night, and Llewelyn's turn on watch while everyone else slept.

Suddenly the horizon shivered with a flickering light that flashed into a searing brightness. The after-image of towering clouds burned into his retinas. Gelert woke with a start, scrambled over everyone, and ran to the prow, followed by his retinue of yipping lice dogs. Feiyan sat up, rubbing her eyes and trying to shush the howling crew dogs and the barking alarm dog.

"Bloody animals," winced the captain, yawning. "What's it now?"

"Watch!" yelled Llewelyn, just as a whumping wall of sound swept past the sampan, making its sails tremble. It was a deep noise, so low it was barely audible, but it echoed in his chest. The lice dogs scurried back into the safety of the cockpit, quivering with fear.

"Thunder, by Dog!" muttered Chang.

Then the lightning burst again, and the bank of distant clouds became a series of monstrous forms and cavernous holes.

Kung began rambling about storms, called typhoons, that tore through these parts at this time of the year.

"And what do you know about typhoons!" scoffed the captain.

"You can learn a lot from a book," piped Kung happily.

"You could read every book in the world and you'll still know nothing about how bad a typhoon really is," muttered Chang. "And, Dog willing, you never will."

"And Dog willing, you two will stop squabbling over nothing," muttered Feiyan, lying down and pulling a blanket over her head.

The storm banged and crashed and flickered for the rest of the night, gradually fading as dawn approached.

⭑⭑

The next morning, the sampan lurched through heavier waves.

Hot winds picked and scrabbled at the sea, scratching it up into ugly, angry waves. Soon, they were all soaked by drifting skeins of yellowish drizzle. The crew dogs grew restless and whimpered. Even Gelert seemed intimidated.

"This is nothing," reassured the captain. "Just the storm's last twitches."

As if to contradict him, the wind coalesced into a screaming blast that made the mainsail convulse and the rigging shriek like a herd of pigs being gelded. A slash of brittle rain rattled across the deck.

It was the storm's parting gesture.

The weather seemed to die around them. The wind faltered into the merest whisper of a soft breeze. The air grew thick, and the oppressive humidity seemed to flatten the sea, making it steam and melting the horizon into the yellow-blue sky.

Chang asked Feiyan and Llewelyn to rig makeshift masts and sails, anything to catch the fluky zephyrs, then he sent Sashin up. The kite dog revelled in the light airs, flitting up and down, and steering the boat to wherever it could gain advantage.

The sampan slid through the still water, leaving behind it the ghost of a shallow, perfectly symmetrical triangular wake.

So on they travelled, making progress despite the fickle winds.

⭑⭑

A new dawn found the sampan shrouded in mist.

All sounds were muted. Dew dripped from the rigging into Feiyan's moisture traps. Gelert shook off his damp blanket of wet lice dogs and went off on his pissing rounds.

Llewelyn checked the captain's battered shoulders.

"I not believe it," he said. "I thinked you never use that arm again."

"He's strong and fit, like me!" burbled Kung, whose legs were straightening as his bones gradually knitted together. The

275

terrible bruising, that just a few weeks ago was purple-black and sulphurous yellow, was now a marbled blue and crimson.

Both men's injuries were healing far more quickly than Llewelyn ever thought possible. He wanted to say something about the Essence and how it must be helping them recover, but bit his tongue. He knew better than to bring up this taboo subject, or anything else to do with Jiang secrets, especially now that he was protecting Feiyan.

His thoughts were interrupted by a whiff of a sickly sweet odour. Feiyan called him forward. She sounded nervous.

Gelert was with her, standing at the railings, drooling.

"What is it?" he started, then fell silent.

The low dawn mist was dispersing. Fleeting glimpses of something ahead teased them. The last foggy tendrils slid by as the sampan sailed towards a chaotic spectacle.

The flat, oily sea was messy with an ugly swirl of broken wreckage floating sluggishly in the dead calm.

It was as if a careless sea monster had scooped up a fleet of ships, smashed them all together in its claws, then tossed them back onto the sea. The heaps of splintered wreckage were so scattered it was hard to see which broken part of a boat could have fitted onto any other. The tangle of masts and planking was so wide it barred their way.

Feiyan sent the kite dog up, and the captain turned the sampan, drifting it along the face of the floating barricade until Sashin barked down, guiding the boat towards a slight gap in the jumble.

At its mouth, the passage was only just wider than the sampan.

"Llewelyn, come and give me a hand," called Chang. "Feiyan, get a pole out, you might need to fend us off this mess."

The sampan drifted through the cluttered wreckage, carefully avoiding half-submerged hulls and spear-like shattered masts.

"They look like dhows, or what's left of them," mused Kung. "They must have been caught in that big storm. My word! Look at that!"

He pointed at the surface of the sea. Sinuous shapes slid by below, their sharp fins slicing up through the calm water. Gelert and the crew dogs leaned over the railings, growling at them.

"They're sharks! Don't lean out too far!" shouted Llewelyn

to Gelert in Welsh. "You don't want to be that lot's breakfast!"

The sampan broke through the swath of broken ships and into a circular lake of clear water a mile across, its banks formed by the floating debris.

There were now so many sharks that the surface seethed with fins, all swimming toward a mysterious white cloud that seemed fastened to the centre of the lake.

At first, Llewelyn guessed it must be a ball of fog. But as the sampan drew closer, he saw it was a great flock of seabirds swooping around a nucleus gathered about a hundred yards across.

His arms began to ache from pushing the tiller hard over, just to keep the sampan on course. They were cutting across the stiff current of a slowly turning whirlpool.

The captain saw what was happening. "It's the remains of the centre of the storm," he muttered, and leaned his weight onto the tiller, helping Llewelyn keep the boat straight. "The lightest parts of the wreckage have been spun into the middle ..."

The sampan drifted towards the flock of wheeling and plunging gulls. Their raucous cries prickled Llewelyn's ears, and the cacophony intensified as Gelert and the crew dogs added a chorus of anxious barking. Above, Sashin yapped excitedly.

"Do you think we must bring him down?" shouted Llewelyn.

"What's a couple of seagulls going to do to him?" said Feiyan.

By now, the way ahead churned with the dark shapes of countless sharks. As they reached the periphery of the white cloud, their slick black bodies broke the surface, sending up flurries of gulls.

Then, the following wind shifted slightly and their nostrils were assaulted by the foul stench of rotting meat.

Now they could see the huge flock of birds and the great shoal of sharks was swarming around the bodies of a thousand drowned sailors.

Corpses floated jerkily at the edges of the grisly banquet, mauled by the thrashing sharks. Seabirds strutted across the jiggling remains. They pecked at the bluish bloated carrion and squabbily defended their patch of the precarious island of food from the cartwheeling birds above. Llewelyn recognised gannets, terns, skuas and shearwaters, and even thought he saw an albatross or two. All were bloody headed and fat with food. His stomach turned, but he gripped the tiller firmly and held course across the revolving sea.

The noise of the birds became unbearable as the sampan pierced the outer edges of the cloud. Then it was as if they'd been thrown into a blizzard of fluttering thorns. The gulls, maddened by the furious competition to eat, smacked blindly into the deck and thudded into the sails. Gelert and the crew dogs went berserk, snapping at the birds and catching them in mid-dive.

Below, the hull shook with larger impacts as the sharks ground up against the sampan, oblivious to it as they tore into the human flesh.

As the boat moved further into the sea of corpses, the battering from above and below intensified. The sampan was lifted bodily from the sea by a huge shark, and dropped back down with an unsettling splash. Llewelyn, Feiyan and Chang curled into balls, their heads tucked protectively into their arms, but Kung had no other option but to lie prone as gulls barrelled into his exposed legs.

Slowly the gale of beating wings and sharp beaks began to thin. The screeching din and deck thumping gradually diminished as the sampan eased through the disgusting feast towards the far side of the encircling mass of debris.

Relieved, but gagging, the sampan's human crew uncurled and looked around.

The deck was red and white with bloody bodies and spattered bird shit. Gelert and the crew dogs, still in their own frenzy of killing, tore into the broken seabirds that littered the boat.

Llewelyn heard plaintive barking from above.

"Sashin!" cried Feiyan.

The poor kite dog fluttered to the deck. He was bruised and battered, and the delicate webbing of skin between his legs was pierced in several places, the ugly rents rimmed with blood. Feiyan quickly unfastened his harness and carried him to Kung, who was already reaching into his medicine bag.

Suddenly, the captain saw something ahead.

"What now?" he asked, squinting into the rising sun.

The movement caught Llewelyn's eye; something was swimming quickly towards the sampan from the nearing line of wrecks. He went forward for a better look, and his first thought was that it must be a small shark. But it leapt from the water to run across the back of a passing shark before splashing back into the sea.

Then he heard the animal bark. *It's a dog!*

Both Kung and Feiyan looked up from their work with Sashin. Gelert and the captain hurried to join Llewelyn.

The new dog's body was about four feet long and its muscular tail was at least as long again. It swam directly towards them with a smooth sinuous motion, using its tail to propel itself exactly like ...

It's an otter! thought Llewelyn. *A big, bright-red otter.*

It had reached the sampan and yapped excitedly as Llewelyn reached through the railings to grab its scruff and pull it onto the deck. Water poured off the animal as it shook itself dry, ignoring Gelert's attempts to sniff its bum.

It sat up on its hind legs, straight-backed with its short paws held out in front. Like an otter, it had long whiskers, tiny ears and webbed feet; and yet it was unmistakably a dog.

Settling, the swimming dog gave six precise barks, then turned its head back in the direction from where it had swum. It then carefully and deliberately repeated the sequence.

Feiyan stumbled over to the railings. "He's telling us to head west for about six hundred yards. Good dog!"

Knowing he'd been understood, the dog yelped once then threw himself overboard and swam off in the direction he'd been pointing.

"But what's an otter dog doing out here?" said the captain, his face a picture of excited confusion.

"Bloody hell!" gawped Llewelyn in Welsh. "Not another Jiang dog."

Llewelyn turned the boat, carefully keeping the otter dog's scarlet-coloured head in sight.

It led them to a patch of wreckage undistinguishable from the rest, except that it floated slightly higher in the water. Scrambling up onto it, the dog barking happily back at the sampan.

As they drew closer, Llewelyn saw the wreck of a partially submerged boat, its stern floating clear of the sea at a steep angle. With a gulp, he recognised the lines of the hull. It was another sampan.

Another Jiang sampan.

The Captain, Feiyan and Kung were shocked at the sight. How could one of their own have floundered?

"It must have been rammed by another ship," offered Chang.

"Its cargo probably shifted," suggested Kung.

"Maybe they had some kid from Way-yells steering it," said Feiyan.

"You get sails in or we crash into it," said Llewelyn, deftly turning the sampan alongside the derelict vessel.

The lazy swell made deep sucking and plopping noises as it sloshed around the creaking wreckage. Everyone went silent – something about the hulk evoked a feeling of dread. Even Gelert stopped chasing birds and padded to the ship's side.

Then they heard a muted whimper from inside the half-sunk sampan.

"There a dog in there!" cried Llewelyn.

"A wild dog. Maybe a jackal or a small wolf. Definitely African."

"You know that from one noise?" said Llewelyn in disbelief.

The whimper from inside the wrecked sampan rose to a soft, mournful howl. The Great Dog's hackles rose, and he answered with a low baying yowl, which set off the rest of the ship's dogs into a chorus of yipping and yapping. Llewelyn was about to hush his old friend when a new, terrible sound suddenly erupted from deeper inside the sampan.

It was the cries of banshees mixed with the braying of demented donkeys – nerve-jangling, hacking, honking, grating barks that collapsed into a stutter of yips. These were followed by a series of crashes and splashes. Something, or rather, some things, were going horrifyingly mad inside the wreck.

"There's two of them, and I don't like the sound of either!" said Kung.

Chang turned to Feiyan and Llewelyn. "Well, what are you waiting for?" he said. "Tie alongside. Find out what's going on in there."

They looked at each other.

"I get my longbow," said Llewelyn, regretting there were only Chinese arrows left.

❧

It was an easy step across onto the upward sloping deck of the other sampan, but the instant Feiyan and Llewelyn were aboard the unsettling racket below increased. Whatever was inside was either very anxious to get out or determined not to let anyone in.

Bristling for a fight, Gelert jumped across too, and started to slide down the steep deck. He recovered his footing against the side railings, which he used as a ladder to scramble back up to them.

Llewelyn and Feiyan followed his example, scaling the tilted railings, then edging across the deck into the cockpit where the otter dog sat patiently waiting. Feiyan reached up to pet it, and it licked her hand. Gelert growled jealously.

Meanwhile, Llewelyn checked the fastenings to the hatch.

"It is bolted!" he shouted down to the captain.

Chang paced the deck, twisting his upper body and wincing in frustration at not being able to use his shoulders.

"Try the middle one!" he called back.

That's easy for you to say, thought Llewelyn. Feiyan joined him as he slid down the centre of the deck onto the hatchway.

Gelert followed, but couldn't gain purchase on the timber and slipped onto Llewelyn with a thump.

The noise provoked more insane snarling from within, and when Gelert growled in reply, the commotion inside grew louder still. The hairs on the back of Llewelyn's head stiffened with fear.

The hatchway had been locked from the outside. Gingerly,

Feiyan pushed back the heavy iron bolts. Llewelyn knocked up an arrow, wishing it was a double bladed broadhead. His fingers trembled as he pulled back his bow.

With a grunt, Feiyan slammed the hatchway back on its hinges.

A tawny dog-shaped beast sprang from the exposed hole, skittering and tumbling down the deck and splashing into the sea. Llewelyn followed its fall with his bow, but held his arrow. The animal was magnificent. Gelert didn't bark, but fidgeted with excitement, torn between following it and staying with Llewelyn

"It's the wolf!" yelled Kung. "It's not what's making all the noise!"

That was obvious to everyone. With the hatch open, the awful barking and banging was deafening and now it was accompanied by the rattle of chains. *Whatever they are, they're tied up. Thank God.*

Meanwhile, feeble and thin, the wolf was floundering in the water. The otter dog launched itself off the boat, diving gracefully after it. It swam over to the wretched animal, grabbed it by the scruff of the neck and, with powerful strokes of its tail, pulled it to the side of the boat.

Unable to lift it on board, the captain called up to Feiyan for help.

She wasted no time, sliding down the wreck to the sampan and dragging the choking wolf across to Kung in his daybed. Her father looked on anxiously as Kung pushed and shoved some life back into the half-drowned dog. It spluttered and lay panting, exhausted.

"I'll give it something to make it relax," said Kung. "Not wise to have a wild wolf running around, eh?"

Feiyan made her way back to Llewelyn. The otter dog had returned to the sunken sampan and sat behind them, perched once more on the topmost railings.

The frightful din from the hold below shook the half-sunk boat.

"They trying to break free," said Llewelyn.

"What do we do?" whispered Feiyan.

"Stop them, I suppose ..."

They peered into the hatchway. It was too dark to see anything.

"Yes. If you just drop into the hold …" suggested Feiyan.

"You want me to just drop into there?"

"I rescued the wolf. It's your turn!"

"Bugger that!" said Llewelyn in Welsh. "I've got a better idea."

Together, they wedged themselves above the hatchway.

Gelert sat awkwardly beside them, refusing to budge, as if he alone could protect them from whatever lay below.

It hadn't taken Kung long to prepare the device that would deliver the sleeping vapour. It came in two separate stoppered glass jars, each a foot in diameter. The first was filled with blue liquid, connected by a bamboo pipe to the second jar that contained a white powder.

"This will make things down there sleep?" Llewelyn shouted down to Kung.

"It knocked you out, didn't it?"

"How long it keep them asleep?"

"As long as we need," replied Kung, "Relax!"

"And when I go in hold, it won't make me sleep?"

"The vapour disappears after a few minutes, but the creatures will remain asleep. Don't worry!"

The captain paced impatiently. "Less talk, more action please!"

Llewelyn shrugged. He couldn't put it off any longer. He tilted the two linked jars, pouring the liquid onto the powder. It began to bubble violently, quickly filling the jar with a dense white vapour. Kung hadn't mentioned how much vibration the bubbling would produce, how hot the second jar would become, or how long he should wait before unstopping it. He winced, half expecting everything to explode.

"Now!" shouted Kung from his bed.

Llewelyn and Feiyan each took a deep breath before he pulled out the stopper and began to pour. The vapour oozed out as a thick tail of mist that slipped down into the hold. A minute passed, and the powder in the jar continued to bubble fiercely as the miasma slowly filled the dark void below. Kung had judged the proportions of his potion to perfection; the level of the vapour reached the lip of the open hatchway just as the frothing subsided. Slowly, the din from inside the sampan subsided, replaced by rough snores. Llewelyn and Feiyan finally exhaled in huge gasps of relief.

The air hung thick with the scent of honeysuckle, and then Gelert stuck his head into the open hold.

"No! You stupid oaf!" Llewelyn and Feiyan tried to stop him, but before they could pull him back, the wolfhound succumbed to the potent vapours and collapsed against the bulkhead.

Kung and Chang roared with laughter.

"That'll teach you!" Llewelyn admonished his sleeping friend. "Kung, how long before we can go inside?"

"A while. Come down and we'll take a proper look at the wolf."

They crowded around the animal. Kung's potions had made it sleepy and Llewelyn dared to stroke its head. "He much smaller than wolves in Wales were," he said. "And skinnier, with longer ears. He red. Look more like a big, er, fox" He didn't know the Chinese word for 'fox'.

"It's definitely a wolf, from the mountain kingdom of the Habasha," said Kung. "And it's not a he, it's a female."

The captain rolled his eyes. "That we could do without."

"What you mean?' asked Llewelyn.

"All the dogs on Jiang ships are male. Bring a bitch on board and you bring trouble."

Feiyan looked crossly at her father. Llewelyn blushed.

Kung was unconcerned. "If she comes on heat I can give her potions so our dogs will hardly notice her. Right now, it's more important that we feed her up." He delved back into his bag for more medicines, lost in his art.

"But why she on board?" said Llewelyn. "And why things still in there chained up?"

"Well, that's no mystery," answered Feiyan. "They'll have been caught by one of our collectors."

"What you mean 'collectors'?" asked Llewelyn.

"What do you mean 'what do you mean?' We're Jiang; we collect dogs."

Llewelyn scowled and turned to Chang for an explanation. "What she mean … collect? Jiang collect dogs?"

The captain was bemused. "You have a problem with that?"

"Yes! I do!" he shouted in English, his Chinese not up to the furious questions welling in him. "All along you've been telling me how terrible the Emperor is for collecting Gelert for his menagerie!"

"It's not the same!" grunted the captain, stomping away from him. "We only collect wild dogs. We don't take them from anyone."

Fuming, Llewelyn chased after him. "You took Gelert from the Emperor! Stole him in the night!"

"That's different. We need the Great Dog to save us from the Emperor ..."

"So you'd have stolen him from me if you'd had to?"

"The other difference," continued the captain in a whisper, "is that we'll give Gelert back once we're done with him."

"Why are you whispering?" said Llewelyn, lowering his voice.

The captain nodded back at Kung, and Llewelyn noticed that Feiyan was watching them suspiciously. She was no doubt wondering what their conversation was about.

"What do you mean, 'done with him'? And what are you going to 'do' with him." His voice rose. "You promised you'd tell me!"

"What's going on?" asked Kung, looking up from his ministrations.

"Nothing!" Chang shouted in Chinese.

"Good!" interrupted Feiyan, keen to stop the whispering, "because we still have the small matter of what we're going to do with whatever's down in that hold."

"Well, that's easy," said Kung. "We shall bring them with us."

"What?" Llewelyn was incredulous, forgetting his quarrel with Chang. "You take those ... things to Jiang? Why?"

"Our collectors scour the world for new dogs. If they've captured these, it will be for good reasons. It is providence that brought us here so that we can continue their mission. It is our duty."

Feiyan rolled her eyes. Chang groaned.

🐾

Llewelyn sat on the edge of the hatchway, a rope tied around his waist. He was about to be lowered into a dark, half-sunk wreck containing two beasts from hell.

He checked again that there was plenty of oil in his lantern and that its wick was burning brightly. He fingered the edge of his sword before sheathing it. Despite being razor sharp, it felt puny and inadequate as a defence against the unknown threat below. He'd had to leave his longbow behind; it would be useless in the confines of the hold, and he couldn't have carried it and his lantern.

Feiyan stood next to him, checking that the pulleys were running smoothly and testing the tension of the ropes. Satisfied, she gave him the nod. He wished he had Gelert by his side, but the stupid dog was still passed out. At least that meant the creatures below would also be unconscious.

Swallowing his fear, Llewelyn signalled to the captain down on the deck. Chang whistled to the team of crew dogs who took up the slack on his rope and pulled. Lifted up off the deck, Llewelyn dangled over the black maw of the hatchway.

Then, slowly, they lowered him into the honeysuckle darkness.

The hold was a shambles of shifted cargo, up-ended and piled randomly against bulkheads.

The storm had done terrible damage; crates and barrels were smashed open, sacks ripped apart, and everywhere were shards of shattered pottery.

Llewelyn turned slowly at the end of his rope. The flickering yellow light of his lantern conjured dancing shadows that made it hard to fix on anything. He steadied his legs on a toppled wooden crate.

"I climbing down the cargo now!" he shouted up to Feiyan, "Don't let rope go loose. I scream, you pull!"

"I won't. And I will," she called back.

The light was steadier now, and his eyes were growing used to the gloom. Whatever he was looking for was at least ten feet below him, at sea level, lost in the maze of broken supplies.

The air was filled with a revolting musky stench that reminded him of burning soap mixed with dead badger and cat droppings. He could distinguish two different muffled snores, deep and loud enough to tell him that his quarry was substantial. He drew his sword.

Cautiously, he clambered down the jumble, blade in one hand, lantern in the other. The nauseating soapy-shitty odour was now stronger, and the snoring grew louder.

A snuffling grunt interrupted the snores and Llewelyn froze. Were the creatures waking up? No, the snoring continued.

But he now knew that it came from just beyond the next bulkhead.

He lowered himself onto it and reached around with his lantern. The wan light flickered alarmingly; his hand was trembling violently.

He peered around the corner, and then he saw them.

🐾

Two dun-coloured, black-blotched beasts lay collapsed against the far bulkhead on half-submerged sacks.

They resembled dogs, nearly as big as Gelert, but with bulkier shoulders and shorter, stumpy hind legs.

Their long foreheads seemed mismatched to their stocky heads and their chewed ears lay too far back on their skulls. The wiry fur on their faces and necks was crusty red and matted. To his relief, Llewelyn saw heavy iron collars around the animals' necks, chaining them to what would have been the hold's roof.

The stench was now almost unbearable. Shit was piled everywhere, caking the sacks and nearby walls. Gagging, he played the lantern around and saw that all the filth was strewn within a semi-circle described by the length of the beasts' chains.

He swung the lamp to the right, and through the lurching shadows, Llewelyn was shocked to see what was left of a man, pinned in place by a huge crate. It must have fallen against him during the storm, trapping him within biting range of the animals. His head was untouched, and gazed directly at Llewelyn with a look of abject terror on his gaunt face.

Suddenly Llewelyn understood why the two beast's heads were red; they'd been buried neck deep inside the corpse, devouring the man from the inside out. The creatures must have started eating him by ripping open the nearest side of his chest and belly, favouring the soft internal organs, and leaving only the scooped-out shell of his ribcage and pelvis.

Then they'd moved onto the man's limbs. His right shoulder, arm and leg had been stripped of flesh, and the chewed and splintered bones gleamed white in the lantern light. If Llewelyn and the others hadn't arrived, his shoulders and buttocks would surely have been next on the grisly menu.

Steeling himself, Llewelyn looked back at the corpse's eyes. Wide and staring, they were filmed over, a milky green hue. He shivered with the awful thought that maybe the poor man had still been alive when this hideous feast had begun.

He felt his mouth grow cold, and a thin film of sweat beaded his forehead. Then he puked violently.

"Everything alright down there?" shouted Feiyan.

It took the rest of the morning for Llewelyn to prepare to pull the beasts out of the foetid hold – a miserably tedious job made longer because he had to do it by himself. Feiyan had insisted that only she could muster the crew dogs and take care of the ropes and pulleys.

With the utmost self-control he managed to force himself to cross the invisible line that separated safety from flesh-tearing terror. Kung had assured him the beasts couldn't possibly wake up, but then he hadn't seen the damage they had done to the man in the hold.

Unhooking the heavy chains from their collars wasn't all that difficult. What proved harder was fastening the makeshift chest harnesses that Kung had insisted he use so as not to hurt the animals.

Llewelyn started with the smaller of the two.

Up close, it really was revolting. He felt his skin crawling and wondered if any Jiang lice dog would have been let near it. Probably not. Most likely it was infested with God-knows-what African filth. He dragged the animal up into a seated position so that he could fasten the harness around it. Then, gagging, he let it flop back to the floor.

The bigger of the two was much heavier and more difficult to haul up. Llewelyn tried to ignore the mangled human corpse in the corner as he shifted around, looking for a better angle, but then he slipped on the wet wood of the hold and his legs shot out from under him.

As he landed, something scraped his right leg: he'd jabbed himself on the splintered end of the dead man's chewed femur.

He jumped up, squirming with revulsion and spun round, immediately losing his footing again. Staggering backwards, Llewelyn's right foot landed squarely on the smaller creature's head, twisting its mouth open. He felt the sole of his boot give way and a sharp pain told him immediately what had happened. *Great!* He'd been stabbed by a dead man and bitten by a sleeping dog.

Llewelyn pulled off his boot to examine the tiny gash in the soft flesh of his instep.

The beast's tooth had only just broken the skin, but the wound felt sore and hot, and the scratch on his ankle was surprisingly painful.

Grumpily, he limped back to work.

By the time he'd harnessed up the second animal, there was a dull throbbing in his leg. He let the monster crash to the floor, not caring if it had been hurt.

Finally, he was able to give Feiyan the word for the crew dogs to start heaving. The two beasts were slowly dragged up through the jumble of cargo. Llewelyn climbed up after them and steered them past obstacles into the sunlight.

The filthy animals now hung from the main yard arm of the sampan, and Feiyan whistled the orders that swung them over the deck.

Then Gelert woke.

※

The great wolfhound was still woozy from the effects of the sleeping vapour, but he sniffed the air in disgust and glanced up. At the sight of the two creatures floating above him, something snapped inside him. Insane with fury, he leapt at the dangling animals, trying to drag them down.

The ruckus alerted the alarm dog, then the lice dogs who swarmed up from below decks to add their shrill yapping to the clamour. When the teams of crew dogs saw what they'd been hauling on board, they too went berserk, let go of the rope and started barking. In a flash, Feiyan caught the end of the rope and managed to cleat it off. Her quick thinking stopped the beasts crashing into the pack of baying dogs beneath.

From the hatchway's bulkhead, Llewelyn watched the display of hatred by Gelert and the Jiang dogs. Only the otter dog hadn't joined in. It sat perched behind him on the stern railings of the derelict sampan, silently watching the angry mob below. It hadn't budged from that position of safety since they'd started the operation to bring out the beasts, but now it growled softly, its eyes fixed on them.

"You don't like them either, do you?" Llewelyn said to the otter dog. *What have you seen those ugly devils do?*

A wave of dizziness washed over him. His leg was sore and

it had been a long day, so he slid wearily down the deck to join the others.

The captain yelled at the dogs to be quiet and stomped around, kicking Gelert and the crew dogs aside.

"Why they so mad?" shouted Llewelyn above the noise. All the barking was making his head hurt.

"I don't know!" Kung hollered from his daybed. "Get them back into the rear hold; they can't stay out here in this mood."

This was easier said than done; Gelert and the pack of Jiang dogs were determined to bring down the hateful animals. It took all of Llewelyn's authority over the wolfhound and a barrage of whistling from Feiyan to force them all below. Even after the hatchway slammed shut, their mad barking continued.

The effort of rounding them up had drained Llewelyn, and his leg was stiff with pain. He leaned on the railings.

"What's the matter?" asked Feiyan. "You look dreadful!"

"I tired. It hot down in hold. One of the buggers bited my foot."

"What? But they were asleep! How?"

"Hard to explain," he replied, wiping a film of cold sweat from his forehead. He reached for the pulley ropes. "We get on with it."

Feiyan frowned, concerned. They swung the two filthy animals around and down onto the deck, landing them gently in front of Kung.

There they lay, safely chained and asleep, but dangerous nonetheless.

"They look like dogs," said the captain as Kung cast his expert eye over them. "Not very pretty dogs, I'll give you …"

"They're called hyenas," interrupted Kung with distaste, "And they are most definitely not dogs." He carried on his examination, prodding the smaller animal's ribs and swollen belly and listening to its chest.

How he managed to not throw up was a mystery to Llewelyn. The hyenas didn't smell any better for being out in the open.

In daylight, they were like primitive versions of dogs, chewed and battered, as though they'd lived their lives fighting and losing. Even from a couple of feet away, Llewelyn could see they were mangy and infested with lice and ticks. Meanwhile the pain in his leg had migrated across his groin, and his stomach was cramping. He wondered if it was the bright daylight that was making his head ache so much.

Feiyan regarded the hideous creatures with undisguised revulsion. "Throw them overboard!" she announced suddenly.

Kung sucked in a shocked breath and Chang turned to her, startled.

"Kill dogs?"

"You heard Kung. They're not dogs."

"They look like dogs! We can't kill dogs!"

"Why do all our real dogs hate them so?" growled Feiyan. "Get rid of them now!"

The captain was still incredulous. "Should I drown the wolf too?"

Feiyan hesitated. In all the commotion, everyone had forgotten about the beautiful red wolf, which lay unconscious on the other side of Kung's daybed. Llewelyn wished he could lie down too. An aching sapped his quivering muscles.

"No, of course not. Listen to me," she pleaded with her father, "these two … hyenas, they're evil! Whoever found them chained them up for Dog's sake! What Jiang collector would do that to a dog?"

The captain tipped back the bigger one's head with his foot. Its huge mouth gaped open. "That's why! Look at those jaws. Look at the muscles! They were chained up because they're vicious fighting animals."

Kung had finished examining the biggest hyena. He propped himself up on one elbow, a strange gleam in his eye.

"Yes, I've never seen anything so brutal. It's as if they were created simply to kill and eat. Oh, and they're both pregnant," he added.

It was Feiyan's turn to look shocked. "Pregnant?"

She went quiet, the revelation conflicting her disgust for the hyenas.

Llewelyn reached for the railing again. A scalding flush coursed through his body, radiating up from the wounds on his leg. He'd have vomited if he hadn't already done so three times that day.

"Yes," Kung continued, "and they're not far from giving birth."

Chang's mind was racing. "With puppies, wouldn't that mean we'd have a breeding stock?"

"If the mothers aren't sisters, then yes, of course," replied Kung with a gleam in his deep-green eyes. "Once we get them home ..."

"You'd breed *more* of them?" interrupted Feiyan, wide-eyed.

"Look at them!" argued the captain, crouching down to look more closely. "It might take months to breed dogs this powerful."

"Possibly years," said Kung, stroking his chin. "Even with Gelert."

Breeding with Gelert? Llewelyn had been feeling increasingly vacant, but that woke him up.

"... Time we might not have," continued Kung, growing more excited. "With these two and their pups, our starting position would be so much stronger."

"I tell you," said the captain, "whoever the unlucky man was who collected these hyenas, he's found our army in the making!"

"What do you mean, army?" asked Llewelyn, now truly bewildered. A jolt of pain seared his body and he began to tremble. Cold sweat was gathering in his eyebrows and dripping into his eyes.

Everyone turned his way. Chang and Kung looked elated but Feiyan seemed horrified and desperately confused.

At that moment, Llewelyn saw in their faces all of the secrets of the Jiang mission falling into place.

They want Gelert to father an army of giant dogs! They're going to fight the Emperor with dogs!

Just as his mind made these connections, expanding rings of red fog clouded his vision, which narrowed to pinpricks of scorching white light. His brain was vaporising, and his throat and mouth filled with thick, frothy slime as his chest began to shudder uncontrollably.

Llewelyn fell to the deck and everything turned black.

Llewelyn woke to yipping and whimpering, followed by a loud bark and the wet slobbering of a wolfhound tongue on his face.

He struggled to open his eyes seeing only darkness and a shaft of light. His nostrils caught the familiar whiff of honeysuckle above the dank, salty odour of the hold. A heavy blanket was draped over his lower body and legs, and he felt a warm weight on his chest.

As his eyelids slowly ungummed, he recognised Feiyan, her face in shadow, and her hair haloed by the shaft of light from the gratings above. As she leaned into the light he saw she was hollow-eyed and tired. The weight on his chest shifted. It was the alarm dog, and it gave another loud honking bark as Gelert slobbered his face again.

Llewelyn tried to sit up. Only his arms seemed to be working. His neck muscles were oddly numb and his head was too heavy to move.

"Wha'hap'n?" he mumbled, his tongue too thick to talk properly.

"Chinese, please! I still don't understand Welsh," Feiyan chided gently. She mopped his forehead with a deliciously cool cloth that smelled of mint.

He reached round and grabbed the hair at the back of his head. It was longer than remembered, but it gave him plenty to get hold of. He dragged his head up to look around.

A long, warm, slippery object was hooked onto the side of his mouth and he began to gag. Panicked, he plucked at it with his free hand, pulling out a thin tube from deep inside his guts. It flopped onto the bed, greasy with mucus and splattering a thin yellow fluid.

They've been feeding me through a tube! A crusty sore at the corner of his mouth suggested it had been there for some time.

"I guess you're not hungry anymore," said Feiyan.

"I'm starving!" he replied as he held his hand arm up to the light, alarmed at how knobbly his wrist and elbow joints appeared.

Feiyan took him gently by the shoulders and, as she lifted his upper body, the alarm dog tumbled from his chest with another loud honk. Llewelyn noticed the dozens of the tiny lice dogs lying on his blanket and felt their hot bodies through the thin material. They mewled at him, pleased to see him awake.

Llewelyn saw how his ribs protruded and his stomach sank away into a deep hollow. Lying in Feiyan's arms, he felt as fragile as a baby bird, but his skin tingled at her touch.

She plumped some pillows behind him so he could sit up more comfortably. Gelert, still whimpering ecstatically, snuffled at him, his huge tail thwacking against the bed.

"How long I asleep?" he asked blearily.

"About two months. Here, drink some of this."

Two months!

She held a cup of thin, warm broth to his lips. Silenced by hunger, he slurped greedily.

"You keep me asleep for two months!" he eventually spluttered.

Feiyan wiped his mouth. "We had to. You've been very ill. Kung knocked you out with his potions so your body could fight back."

Llewelyn jiggled his memories back into order. Visions of encircling shipwrecks and the horrible stinking hyenas flooded his mind. He recalled the convulsing, fevered pain of his illness. But above all, he remembered the revelation that Gelert was somehow to be at the heart of a Jiang dog army.

"Gelert's your hope and your plan, isn't he?" he asked Feiyan. "He's your weapon against the Emperor."

"That was the idea," she said, growing serious, "but while you were asleep, my father and Kung have hatched an even more dangerous plan. Now they ..."

A voice interrupted from the hatchway above.

"Ah Llew, you're better!" It was the captain. "I thought I heard my alarm dog going off." He climbed down.

"Look at you, all skin and bones! Let's get you topside; you look like you need of a bit of sunlight!" He nudged the lice dogs aside and bent to lift him up. "Here, I'll take you on deck."

Chang's shoulders had mostly healed, and he barely winced as he carried Llewelyn easily up the steep stairs.

The captain laughed. "I've seen more meat on a sparrow's

lip! A girl could lift you!"

Feiyan was following closely behind. "I didn't notice you lifting him to wipe his arse at all during the last two months," she bristled.

The captain ignored her as he lowered Llewelyn onto the daybed in the cockpit. "Welcome back to the waking world," he smiled.

He sighed and lolled back. His watery eyes adjusted from the gloom below, his blunted senses gathering a full picture of his surroundings.

The sampan was humping through an uneven heavy sea, smacking uneasily into the troughs and twisting awkwardly up the following waves. A late afternoon sun flitted between dirty black and purple clouds. The wind blew hot and fitfully, but it was wonderful to breathe fresh ocean air.

There was a yipping bark from above. Sashin, the kite dog, soared against the scudding clouds and swooped down to look at him more closely. A score of crew dogs swarmed around Llewelyn, some jumping up onto his bed to lick him. Then he heard a wet thump, and saw the dripping red otter dog with a still wriggling, freshly caught snapper in its mouth. It trotted over and dropped the startled fish in his lap. Meanwhile, the lice dogs had all scampered up from the hold and tumbled around him, bathing him in their warm pinkness.

The innocent joy of so many animals infused strength and energy back into Llewelyn's withered body, so much so that he burst out laughing.

"Kung! Come see!" The captain called. "Yet another cure for you to notch up!"

Llewelyn heard a squeaking noise and then an odd shape emerged from beyond the mainsail. It was Kung, sitting on a two-wheeled bamboo carriage, pulled by the beautiful Habasha wolf. Kung's legs stuck out between the two delicate shafts of the carriage's spindly wheels.

"Who needs two legs," said Kung, tapping his still twisted limbs, "when you can have four?"

Llewelyn marvelled at the elegant fusion of man, machine and animal. The wolf stood patiently in his carriage's harness.

"She's wonderful, isn't she?" chuckled Kung, noting

Llewelyn's admiration. He threw the wolf a tidbit. "And such a quick learner!"

Llewelyn looked around, beaming at the throng of irrepressible dogs and overwhelmed by the insane wonder of their variety. Gelert's cheerful bark lifted his spirits even more and he laughed again.

Kung nearly smiled, but leaned over to feel Llewelyn's pulse.

"I saved you a dozen times," he said. "How do you feel now?"

Llewelyn lay back, drained. He twitched his fingers and toes, and flexed his arms and legs, and felt his muscles responding. His neck was working again. Strength and energy was creeping back into his body.

"Weak. Hungry. Woozy. But mostly good."

He thought about how long he'd been asleep. *Two months! That's a lot of sailing time.* He turned to the captain, suddenly excited. "Where are we now?"

"See those birds?" Chang pointed at a bedraggled flock of birds struggling against the wind. "In a week's time they'll be nesting on the cliffs of Jiang!"

Llewelyn jerked upright. "We're there already?"

"Almost, almost," smiled the captain. "But first we've got to get past this storm. It's shaping up to be a big one."

The weather was worsening. There'd be work to do. Llewelyn swung his legs over the side of his bed and tried to stand, but his leg and foot throbbed. *Bloody hyena bite!* Suddenly he remembered.

"Where are the two hyenas?"

"Oh there's nine of them now," said Kung. "Two litters of pups, born five and two weeks ago. The ugliest, stroppiest little whelps you've ever seen!"

Llewelyn looked around the deck. "Where are they?"

"Oh. Still in the forward hold," said Kung, evasively.

Llewelyn glanced at the hatchway. It was bolted shut and wreathed in stout chains. "You've kept them locked them up?"

Then he saw the fury on Feiyan's face; she was ready to spit.

"So, everything's fine," said the captain quickly. He sounded bright, but Llewelyn had seen his momentary look of disquiet.

Feiyan's frown deepened and she folded her arms angrily.

"Why are they locked up?" he persisted.

"Because they're evil," Feiyan exploded, her scowl turning into an expression of unbridled hatred.

Llewelyn looked to Kung, but he wouldn't meet his eye. Chang glared at Feiyan.

Llewelyn's foot and ankle still throbbed unpleasantly and the pain jogged a darker memory. "What's wrong with them?"

The captain began to speak. "It can wait, you're still weak."

"Just tell him!" shouted Feiyan, stamping her foot. "Tell him why they have to be locked up!"

Chang just glared at her impassively.

The throng of Jiang dogs had grown quiet, sensing the shift in the mood aboard the sampan. Gelert looked quizzically at Llewelyn as a blast of wind lashed cold spray across the deck.

"Tell him about the disease!" screamed Feiyan as Chang turned away. She followed him, determined to have her say, grabbing his hand and spinning him round. "Diseased with something unspeakable, something vile!" she raged.

The captain twisted out of her grip. Feiyan shrieked with exasperation and turned to Llewelyn.

"What do you think made you so ill?" she asked abruptly.

"The hyenas."

"Well done. Now, why do you think these two didn't throw the beasts overboard the moment they knew they were diseased?"

Llewelyn stared into Feiyan's eyes. She glared back at him, silently, desperately willing him to understand.

But he was baffled and looked to the captain and Kung for an explanation. They gave none, but suddenly he knew.

"You want this disease?" he blurted, shuddering at the memory of the sickness that had so quickly spread throughout his body, "Why?"

Chang spread his hands. "We're small, the empire is so big ..."

Kung interrupted, cold resolution steeling his eyes.

"Because with this disease, we will destroy the empire."

Llewelyn recalled the plagues that had laid waste to entire villages within a week, not a living soul left to bury the bodies. Friar William had told him that vast numbers had died across Europe, of death spread by miasmas drifting on the winds.

"But pestilences travel through the air," he said. "You'd be in just as much danger as the Chinese!"

"No! That's the beauty of it," said Kung eagerly. "We've been with the hyenas for months, but only you became ill. Only you were bitten!" He leaned forward, excited, and continued his explanation. "The conclusion being that the disease is transmitted via their saliva into their victims' blood. It's very interesting. I intend to do experiments …"

"So you see Llewelyn," concluded the captain triumphantly. "We control the beasts, so we control the disease!"

"You think you can control those *monsters?*" spat Feiyan.

Llewelyn's mind was whirling. "So, you going to send two hyenas and their puppies to bite whole empire to death?"

Chang rolled his eyes, but before he could go on, Feiyan interrupted.

"No. They're going to send a million hyenas."

"Yeah. Right," said Llewelyn trying to work out how much a million was, then remembering. "How can nine hyenas be a million?" he snorted.

"Be silent!" shouted Kung.

Feiyan ignored him and sat next to Llewelyn and leaned into him. "Just imagine it; a few months from now, an army of a million filthy, disgusting, diseased creatures will march forward from Jiang." She looked to her father and Kung, her voice dripping with sarcasm. "And they will be entirely obedient to us, and they'll kill the nasty Emperor and all his silly soldiers, and everyone will live happily ever after."

"A few months? That just stupid!" snorted Llewelyn.

"Enough!" yelled the captain, making all the dogs jump. "This isn't a matter for children! I'm in charge here. I'm the one who makes the decisions, and I'm the one who has all the responsibilities. Not you!"

"Hear, hear!" chimed Kung.

"Shut up, Kung!" glared Chang. "Right! Everyone clear on where they stand?"

Feiyan glowered, but remained silent. Llewelyn was speechless.

Gelert thumped his tail on the deck, glad at the end of the shouting. The rest of the dogs relaxed too.

"Good! Get Sashin down. I don't like the look of the weather. This storm's not going away and Feiyan and I have a lot of work to do."

It was a storm that gathered slowly, then quickly built in strength.

"Not long now!" shouted Chang as he tied down the mainsail's halyard. "Time for everyone to go below! You too, Feiyan."

They disconnected Kung from his delicate chariot, and the Habasha she-wolf shook her shoulders and trotted a couple of laps of the deck while they lowered him into the hold.

Feiyan helped Llewelyn down the steps and made him comfortable, then she gathered all the dogs and joined them.

It was cramped in the hold, with barely enough space to move, even with the sampan lurching on the mounting seas. The misery deepened as the storm growled and heaved into being.

Llewelyn heard the captain out on deck. He was manhandling something heavy over to the forward hatchway. Chains rattled loose.

"Meat for the hyenas," explained Feiyan, shivering with disgust. "They prefer the stuff that's gone off, the more rotten the better. We just tip it onto the hold, bones and all. Vile creatures."

There was a muffled hooting, yipping and snarling as the hyenas and their pups battled for the scraps. They were separated from Llewelyn and the others by no more than a flimsy bulkhead, and their din set off the dogs in the hold. Every one stood stiff-legged, barking furiously, their hackles raised and their bodies shaking with fury. Before long, the she wolf joined them in a plaintive howl.

All Llewelyn could do was stick his fingers in his ears and inch as far as he could from the bulkhead.

❧

During the first night, the wind shifted until it was square on to the bow. The captain was forced to shorten sail and lie to.

"It's blowing a bugger!" he bellowed down into the living quarters. "I'm roping myself into the cockpit now. Has everyone eaten?"

"Yes!" yelled Llewelyn, who'd been stuffing himself since he'd woken.

"No!" shouted Feiyan. "There's still another fifteen courses left in the banquet and the servants are about to bring us the grilled peacock."

"Good!" replied Chang. "Because it's not a storm; it's a typhoon."

"What's the difference between a storm and a typhoon?" asked Llewelyn.

"See this?" Kung picked up a lice dog, "This is a storm. See that?" he pointed at Gelert. "That's a typhoon. Now settle yourselves in. Things might get a bit rough for a while."

※

The typhoon arrived.

It smashed into the tiny sampan, almost up-ending it.

The boat skidded down a mountainous wave, then drove up the face of the next, hanging on its peak before tipping into a new oblivion.

That was just the start. They were soon lost in a bruising, unrelenting terror. The planks of the ship's hull twisted and strained, and seams would momentarily break apart, spraying up freezing jets of seawater.

They sat huddled and cramped, sucking on strips of dried meat and sharing from Llewelyn's pot of cold gruel.

Unable to go on deck, and barely able to move, he endured the misery of having to piss his pants. Later on, he felt a warm, spreading sensation on his side and knew that either Feiyan or Kung had also been obliged to do the same. The dogs simply pissed and crapped at will, and before long, the hold had become a salty cesspit. Soaked in a wash of unspeakable filth and seawater, the miserable group was gradually compressed into a single steaming body of limbs and paws that heaved from side-to-side, forward and back, the smaller dogs balancing precariously on top to avoid being crushed.

Llewelyn resigned himself to the squalor and Kung seemed equally accepting but, beside herself with disgust, Feiyan sat whimpering as she tried to flick off sticky turds and wipe away the stinking water. While her futile fussing exasperated Llewelyn, he was heartbroken by her misery.

※

Time had lost its meaning.

"How long you think it's been?" said Llewelyn.

"Two days?" offered Kung.

"More like three," spat Feiyan. "Three days of hell!"

Then, just when they all thought they would surely go mad from the relentless horror of it all, the terrible roaring wind abruptly fell away.

Although the sampan continued to pitch unpleasantly in a choppy swell, Llewelyn felt that the worse was over. The hatchway was flung open and a sickly light flooded the dank hold.

"By the Dogs, you lot stink!" winced the captain. "Come up and wash yourselves off. We're in the eye of the storm so we haven't got much time."

Feiyan was already up on deck. Shitty and matted, the she wolf and the Jiang dogs high-tailed it out of the hold after her.

"What he mean, the eye of the storm?" Llewelyn asked Kung, propping himself up on his filthy mattress. "Is it not ended?"

"Not yet. You see, a typhoon is like a huge ring. The wind spins around the centre, which remains calm. We've passed through one side of the ring, but we will hit the other side. More precisely, it will hit us."

Llewelyn felt like he'd been punched in the chest. They'd have to go through all that again? "But it won't be as bad, will it?" he pleaded.

"Oh, worse!" said Kung. "But the wind will be coming from the opposite direction."

"What are you two waiting for?" shouted the captain.

He lowered a rope to Kung, who began pulling himself hand over hand up into the daylight. Two months without legs had made his upper body surprisingly strong.

Miserable and weak, Llewelyn heaved himself up to a sitting position.

"Why don't you see if you can manage it by yourself," smiled Chang. "You've got to do it sooner or later."

Yeah, thanks.

As Llewelyn stumbled on deck, a random sheet of spray lifted from the surface of the sea and flung itself across the churning waves. It slapped him full in the face, but it felt wonderfully fresh. He went to the leeside railings and lowered a pail into the sea and poured it over his head. The cool water revived him and washed off some of the filth. He sloshed the next couple of buckets over Gelert, then looked around.

It was stiflingly hot. The sea was a milky yellow, and bathed in a pale, eerie light stabbed by sporadic bolts of lightning.

Llewelyn glanced up and Kung's description of the typhoon came to life. Overhead was a perfect dot of bright-blue sky, but all around was darkness. Several miles off, a twisted curtain of inky clouds churned in a menacing wall that rotated around the edge of the calm. The movement appeared slow from where he stood, but he knew it must be passing over the sea at a phenomenal speed. The sampan seemed to be sailing across the shattered pale patch of sea, but Llewelyn now knew that they were hardly moving at all; it was the seething carousel of stupendous weather that was moving, passing over them, unthinking and inexorable. Concussive thunderclaps boomed. Their shockwaves rolled across the trembling wavelets as arcs of ghostly spray that wafted past the bucking boat.

Feiyan's harping voice cut through his reverie. She was arguing with her father. Again.

Mother of God! Does she ever stop picking fights?

He heard snippets of their conversation – most of them Feiyan's words. "You can't control nature!" "How many have to die?" "No, of course I wouldn't rather the Emperor just walked in!"

Llewelyn wished they'd both shut up, and busied himself by sluicing down the rest of the dirty dogs. They splashed happily beneath the cascades of clean seawater, and scampered after the peculiar strands of whipping spray that lashed across the deck.

But then his eye was drawn again to the curtain of cataclysmic weather circling slowly towards them.

He'd glimpsed something in the maelstrom.

🐾

The cliff of clouds fused into the sea, a vague, false horizon of driving rain and crashing waves, but Llewelyn could see that the other side of the storm was now only a few miles away.

He squinted into the advancing veil. There it was again; something harder, blacker and sharper was emerging from the face of the typhoon.

The angular shape slowly resolved into a line of bulky objects – ten, then twenty, a hundred, with more behind.

"Shut up, you two! Look!" he shouted, pointing.

They turned and froze at the sight.

Now, spread across the curving horizon were hundreds of junks.

Imperial Chinese war junks.

A thousand naked masts quivered against the on-rushing storm.

From the van of the fleet, a single green rocket flew up and exploded silently against the charcoal clouds.

Gelert howled, his coat bristling.

A second passed, then, as one, the forest of empty masts and spars transformed the horizon into a rippling red ribbon as each junk unfurled its great slatted sails.

The sails filled, and the shimmering crimson line became a solid band as the immense fleet of ships turned to face the tiny sampan.

"About ship! Get the mainsail up!" said the captain calmly as he leapt into the cockpit and hauled on the tiller. Feiyan whistled the crew dogs to their allotted ropes. The sampan's mainsail dropped, caught the wind, and the rudder bit, slewing the agile boat around. The deck angled steeply as it turned, sending Llewelyn and Gelert staggering to the stern rail.

Still in the calm eye of the storm, the sampan slowly began to make headway. But three miles away and driven by the winds at the edge of the typhoon, the Chinese fleet was faster.

"How they know we be here?" blurted Llewelyn.

Chang thought for a moment and shook his head.

"They can't possibly know it's us."

"They must have sent news to China from Wales," said Kung.

"How? By land?" snorted Chang. "It's impossible." But doubt clouded his face. "Still, if we can see them, they can see him," he said, glancing at Gelert.

"I take him below!" said Llewelyn.

But it was too late. Annoyed by the rocket, the wolfhound

ran to the stern and began barking at the ships. The other dogs joined in with their chorus of yaps, barks and howls. That was enough to set off the hyenas and all their puppies, and their jarring hoots burst from the forward hold.

Llewelyn tried to drag Gelert back, but the huge dog had worked himself into a raging frenzy and wouldn't budge.

"Christ! They'll know it's you now!" gasped Llewelyn.

As if in confirmation, another rocket flew up from the nearest junk. It curved wildly away in the wind, bursting briefly into two diverging balls of spinning light, one blue, one red.

"Isn't that the signal the Admiral used to announce we'd found the Great Dog?" said Kung, his voice trembling.

"But it's impossible," gasped the captain.

A dozen small, sleek junks slipped ahead of the fleet of larger, slower ships. Their decks were crowded.

Gelert barked his guts up, ready to tear the entire fleet to shreds. Llewelyn laughed at his unabashed hatred of the Chinese.

"Do you think they know what they are getting?" he laughed.

"They haven't got him yet." Chang was defiant. "In fact, keep him on deck – if they're after Gelert, they'll not risk using their bowmen. Feiyan, keep the crew dogs up, but send the little ones below so they don't get trampled."

"What are you thinking?" she asked breathlessly.

"Simple. When they catch up, we'll turn and slip through them and lose them in the safety of the storm."

"Safety! In a typhoon?" gasped Feiyan. "Irony!"

"We'll be like a rat dodging a herd of buffaloes."

❧

By now, the prows of nearest junks were stiff with excited figures. Even at two miles, Llewelyn could see their crews pointing at Gelert. Voices snapped across the closing gap.

The Chinese fleet was colossal; their ships were so large and so numerous, and they were crewed by thousands. Silence fell upon the sampan. Even Gelert went quiet, puzzled by everyone's trepidation.

The leading, smaller and nimbler junks had outstripped the rest of the immense fleet. Their bows punched through the waves, throwing up spumes of spray that flew sideways in the driving gale.

"They're still gaining on us," observed Llewelyn, nervously.

"It'll be close, but the winds will hit us soon enough," affirmed Chang as he retook the tiller. "Then we'll see who sails faster!"

The first gusts stabbed into the sampan, building in force and thrusting them forward. But the on-rushing wind was closer still to the Chinese fleet, pushing it harder. The nearest junks were now only a mile away.

The captain looked around, his green eyes flashing. He was measuring the growing strength of the wind and the converging courses of the sampan and the Chinese, and turned to Llewelyn and Feiyan.

"You two! Go get bows and arrows!"

Llewelyn instantly felt the thrill of battle flood his body. Chang saw the fire in his eyes and grinned.

"You're right, they won't shoot on us, not with Gelert on deck. But who says we can't pick off a couple of them as we pass! As easy as killing pirates, eh?"

Feiyan stood open mouthed. She didn't seem afraid, simply stunned by her father's warlike words. For once she was speechless.

"Don't rush," said the captain patiently. "Take your time. We've got ages before we make the turn."

"Come on!" Llewelyn laughed, his exhaustion forgotten in fighting madness. He grabbed Feiyan's hand and dragged her down to the hold. Gelert followed, knowing the hunt was on once more.

❧❧

Llewelyn's longbow felt solid and reassuring. He grabbed a bundle of arrows and went to return on deck, but Feiyan still seemed preoccupied and uncommitted to the search for weapons.

"What's the matter now?" he asked.

She scowled at him, but then looked empty. "We were always going to end up fighting, weren't we?"

"It's better than giving in," he offered, handing her a bow.

"But we can't beat the Chinese! This dog army, it's just stupid men and their stupid ideas. If we just gave up and talked, would we really be worse off?"

Llewelyn shrugged. "Where I come from, people who give in are either strung up or sold into slavery. Either way, they spend the rest of their lives wishing they hadn't. Given in, I mean."

He handed her a bag of arrows. She stared at the ugly arrowheads.

"Don't you see? These will kill someone!"

"They better bloody had!" laughed Llewelyn, but suddenly he understood Feiyan's problem.

"You've never been into battle, have you?"

She frowned at him, trying to look strong, but her defiance withered. She shook her head as tears filled her eyes.

"Not like this," she said, pricking a finger on an arrowhead, "Not close up. What's it like?"

Llewelyn thought about the eight pirates he'd killed.

"Horrible. But wonderful. And if you win, like my father says, it's better than the alternative."

"Better than peace?" she pleaded.

"Of course not. Better than being invaded. Better than losing your country. Better than dying."

"But if we just talked to the Emperor …"

Not this again! But he didn't want to upset her. "Well, maybe he's not as bad as the English ..."

Feiyan was trembling now, and her eyes looked dead. "Oh, he's worse," she said. "If only a tenth of the stories are true, he's far worse."

"If he's that bad how can you even think you can talk to him!"

"So, if we fight we're killed, and if we give up we're killed?" she choked, gripped by a desperate sadness.

"Well my father always says, so long as you're not dead, you've still got hope," said Llewelyn. He knew it sounded a bit feeble, and he tried to be more positive. "But if you know you're not going to make it, make sure you take a couple of the buggers with you."

Feiyan sighed. "Your father would get on well with mine. A cliché for every occasion. But you're right, my fine Way-yells friend," she said, her voice becoming steely, "I would rather die on my own terms." She picked up her father's bow and arrows. "Come on. Let's go." Her fierce certainty was back.

"That's my girl!"

"I am not your girl."

"Aye, but you are my friend."

"Who says so?"

"You did. Just then!"

"That was a figure of speech."

🐾

Back on deck the strengthening wind made the rigging shriek. Kung sat in the cockpit, wrestling with the long tiller, just managing to keep the sampan on its oblique course. The captain and crew dogs hauled at the foresail, squeezing out a few extra knots.

"Good, you're just in time!" He chuckled and pointed at the blurred edge of the typhoon. "Watch!"

The storm had reached the farthest Chinese ships, which were desperately taking in their sails. Many had left it too late and were obliterated in seconds, dismasted and rolled over by the frightful winds. Mountains of water climbed over the stricken vessels, enveloping them into oblivion.

"There!" he laughed. "Half their navy already gone! I told you not to worry!"

But the fastest Chinese junk was now less than two hundred yards away, with a dozen more fanned out on either side of its wake. Gelert jumped up at the railings and began barking again.

A voice shouted across to them, thinned by the distance and plucked at by the wailing wind, but clear enough.

"By the power of the Emperor, I command you: Lower your sails at once! Surrender the Great Dog immediately!"

"Bugger off! He's ours now!" bellowed Chang in reply.

Llewelyn knelt in the lee of the railings carefully unwrapping his bag of bowstrings.

Then he had an idea; one so simple, so pure, it would give them more time to escape.

"You're sure they won't shoot at us with Gelert on deck?" he yelled into the captain's ear, struggling to be heard above the growing storm.

"What, and risk killing their Emperor's toy? Of course not!"

"What if we threaten to kill him ourselves?"

Feiyan heard him and gasped.

309

"Wouldn't that make them stop chasing us?" he explained.

The captain stayed silent, ignoring the wind and the stinging spray.

"It just might!" he conceded. "And just how would you threaten to kill Gelert?"

Llewelyn's mind was racing ahead. "We tie him up and dangle him overboard from the yardarm. We tell them we'll drop him in the sea if they don't pull up."

The captain raised an eyebrow, thought for a moment, then nodded slowly. The plan was feasible. He looked to Feiyan and Kung. She shrugged and Kung shook his head in horror, but Chang had made his decision.

"Right. If we're going to do it, we must do it now! Feiyan, you handle the rigging, Kung, take the tiller and make the turn. I'll fetch a rope, and Llewelyn, you help me tie Gelert up."

The wolfhound was still barking at the nearing Chinese.

Llewelyn gulped. He now saw the flaw in his scheme.

He's never going to let me tie him up, let alone be swung over the side of the sampan. Oh well, here goes.

Smiling sweetly, he called to his wolfhound in his most soothing voice.

Wary of his tone, Gelert turned. He looked beyond Llewelyn to the captain and became more suspicious. Chang had thrown his rope over the leeward end of the main yardarm and was walking towards him, knotting the end of the rope to create a loop. The dog ignored Llewelyn's cajoling and growled at the captain. The closer he came with his rope, the more threatening his growl became. His teeth bared in a menacing snarl, and his raised hackles added to his already intimidating size. Unnerved, Chang hesitated.

"He won't do it," said Llewelyn with a gulp, "not without me."

"You mean …?"

"Tie us together. Hurry!"

An angry shout erupted from the Chinese junk, which was now less than fifty yards away. "Pull up at once!"

A group of officers looked on anxiously. Their Emperor's prized possession was clearly in danger at the hands of madmen. Puce with rage, their leader waved his sword at them.

"Don't you dare touch the Great Dog!"

Ignoring him, Llewelyn walked forward and calmly ordered Gelert to put his front paws up on his shoulder. His old friend happily complied and Chang sprang forward and began looping his rope around the pair. Gelert looked uncertain, but accepted his fate. The coarse rope pricked Llewelyn's bare torso.

"It'll have to be tight," whispered the Chang into his ear as he bound them together.

"Better be!' he grunted, "I don't swim too well!"

The rope pinched nastily as it tugged into his skin.

Meanwhile, the junks were determinedly pressing their pursuit. Boarding parties were mustering at the railings.

The captain tested the strain of the rope. It was wet with spray, and as it pulled taut, it whipped out a V-shaped sheet of water. The knots held and the bonds grew tighter. Llewelyn felt himself lifting slightly.

The nearest junk was almost upon them.

"Untie the dog! Lower your sails! Hove too this instant!" screamed the opposing officer.

Llewelyn gulped and nodded to the captain.

"Heave!" he grunted, and pulled Llewelyn and Gelert clear of the deck, dragging them skyward where the wind caught them and spun them wildly over the sea. Their bindings dug tighter until the wolfhound howled. Llewelyn gasped with the constricting pressure of the ropes and mustered all his self-control so as not to scream.

"Are you alright?" shouted the captain.

"Just get on with it!" he wheezed. As he spun, he caught a fleeting glance of the sailors on the Chinese junk. "Hurry! They're going to throw boarding ropes!"

Chang turned to face his pursuers. "Ease off or I'll drown the dog!"

The Chinese officer was horrified. The possibility of being responsible for losing the Great Dog had an immediate effect.

"You wouldn't dare!" he yelled.

"Really," replied the captain. It wasn't a question.

He paused, then let go of the rope.

Llewelyn and Gelert plummeted into the sea with a great splash. They were dragged along the side of the swiftly sailing sampan, lost in a churning world of bubbles and scouring currents. Llewelyn could feel Gelert squirming helplessly against him. They were too tightly bound together to do anything but twist and writhe and suck in mouthfuls of seawater.

You weren't supposed to actually drop me! he thought, panicking.

But suddenly, they were being yanked from the water in a series of short upward jerks.

They'd only been drowning for a few seconds, but to Llewelyn it felt like an eternity. As they cleared the sea, the wind spun them again, spraying water everywhere. His eyes cleared and, as he got his bearings, the confusing twirling slowed. The sampan swung into view, and the anxious faces of Feiyan and Kung stared up at him.

"Sorry 'bout that!" Chang shouted sheepishly. "Had to show 'em we meant it!" The captain's palms were streaming with blood. He'd shredded the skin when he'd released the rope and caught it again.

As Llewelyn rotated, he saw what he'd envisaged when he'd conceived his idea. The Chinese had stopped dead in the water, their sails lowered. There they floundering in the heaving waters, their decks crowded with confused sailors and soldiers.

The sampan, however, was still under full sail and the captain knew exactly what it was going to do next.

"Now Kung!" he screamed. "Make the turn, then head for the biggest gap!"

Kung threw over the tiller, and Feiyan and her crew dogs pulled at the rigging that would put the sails about.

The ship canted over, dipping the mainmast towards the waves. To Llewelyn's alarm, he and Gelert were lowered back into the choppy waters and next moment, he was up to his waist in the cold sea being dredged along and sinking fast. Gelert struggled, pulling their bonds ever tighter and squeezing the breath out of them both.

Then, mercifully, they were jerked upwards again.

"I've got you!" yelled Chang, pulling them clear as the sampan righted itself and completed its turn. Blood now streamed from his ravaged hands. "How much longer can you stay up there?"

"We're fine for now!' Llewelyn lied. The pain was almost unbearable, the constricting ropes making it harder and harder to breathe. Gelert squirmed and twisted, tightening them even more.

"Please! Stay! Still!" wheezed Llewelyn. "We'll. Be. Safe. Soon!"

Gelert looked into his eyes and grew quiet, panting lightly. Llewelyn glanced past his shaggy head and watched the panorama of his predicament spinning by in the background.

The captain was smiling triumphantly.

Kung stared ahead with an expression of grim resolution.

Feiyan glanced up at him and waved. *She even smiled!*

Then the junks swung into his view, and there was the gap they were aiming for, just big enough for the small sampan to glide through. Kung held his course, eyes locked on the sanctuary of the approaching typhoon, now just a few hundred yards away.

The wind screamed, but it seemed as though everything had become silent as the tiny ship threaded its way between two stately junks. A thousand Chinese eyes on either side were fixed on Gelert, hanging tantalisingly close. The Emperor's archers fingered their bows, but dared not lift them. Their officers stood fuming, hoping and praying that the madman on the rope might slip and make a mistake.

Llewelyn nearly laughed as they passed the men they'd so successfully duped, but there was something disturbing in their collective focus on the Great Dog. Their Emperor's whim had brought an entire navy to this terrible place. *What sort of man could impose such a will on so many men?*

Then the sampan was through, clear and free.

The powerless junks fell behind.

But the danger was far from over. They still had the typhoon to face.

The looming wall of wind and waves screamed ever closer. The sampan pitched even more wildly, jerking Llewelyn's bonds tighter. Spray battered his eyes shut, but it didn't matter. In the storm they'd be safe. In the storm they were sheltered. In the storm there was hope.

Then, as they continued to spin slowly from the end of the rope, Gelert began barking. Llewelyn could feel his old friend's excitement. His tail, hanging below the bindings, was wagging madly.

"What is it, boy?" he muttered, breathless, dizzy and exhausted.

As they turned, a new boat slid into sight.

An Arab dhow burst through the gloom of the storm, its taut white triangular sail bloated by the screaming wind. There, at the prow, stood two familiar figures, one tall, one squat. Gelert barked louder, his thrashing tail making them sway wildly. The dhow was now less than a hundred yards away and closing fast. In a few seconds the two ships would collide, side on.

The taller man frantically stripped off his clothes.

Llewelyn blinked away the spray and he realised who it was. His father.

Can't be. He looks too thin. Too scared.

Llewelyn gave an exhausted laugh. *I'm soft in the head! Must be, there's Owain too!* Sure enough, standing next to his father was the old armourer, just tall enough to be able to lean over the dhow's low railings. He was calmly knocking up an arrow to his great longbow.

From his left, Llewelyn heard Captain Chang roaring, his voice cracking.

"Keep away or I'll let go!"

That's interesting, thought Llewelyn, *he's shouting in English. He can see they're not Chinese. Maybe I'm not going mad after all.*

His momentum spun him round to face the sampan again. Chang was screaming at the newcomers.

"Fall back or, on my oath, I'll drop them!" He leaned over the railings and held the rope out over the sea to make his intentions clear.

Then the arrow hit him square in the left shoulder.

At less than twenty yards range, the impact threw Chang back and pinned him to the mainmast. He released the rope, and Llewelyn and Gelert dropped.

Somehow, as they plunged toward the ocean, the captain managed to snatch hold of the rope with his right hand. It slid and twisted in his grip, shredding his already mashed palm. Flecks of blood and raw flesh sloughed onto the deck, but it was enough to arrest their fall just as Llewelyn's ankles touched the water.

The sampan tilted over, raising the yardarm and yanking them out of the sea. Llewelyn looked at the captain and witnessed the exact moment when the second broadhead impaled his right shoulder, crucifying him to the mainmast.

For a few short seconds, Chang maintained his grip on the rope. Etched with shock and agony, his face was framed by the pristine goose-feather flights of the two arrows. Slowly, he turned his head and looked at his left shoulder, then his right. Blood welled from both wounds.

"You devils!" he screamed at the on-rushing dhow. "They've only just healed!"

He slumped into unconsciousness and let go of the rope.

🦢

Llewelyn and Gelert plunged into the water just before the dhow crashed sideways into the sampan, falling between the hulls. He heard the deep thud as the two ships collided above them, and twisted round to look up into bubbling blackness. They were trapped beneath the two keels. The sea echoed with the dull splintering of wooden vessels grinding against each other. Gelert thrashed madly, clawing and kicking at him.

A growing gap of light told him that the boats were separating again, but they were sinking fast, weighed down by the heavy ropes. He sensed the cold depths of the abyss tugging at him, claiming him.

A muted splash; then strong hands grabbed the ropes that bound him to Gelert and tugged them upwards.

Abruptly, they broke the surface. Llewelyn heard shouting and the howl of the storm. As he and Gelert were dragged up the dhow's hull, the back of his head whacked repeatedly against the wooden planks, making his ears ring. They were hauled over the side railings and flung onto the sloping deck.

The dog squirmed just two inches away and vomited cold salt water into his face. There was more muffled shouting. Llewelyn's ears were full of blood and sea and puke. Someone wiped his face clean, and someone else was cutting away the binding ropes.

"It's alright, son! You're safe now!"

He opened his eyes. The storm lashed him with cold stinging spray. He glimpsed his father's gaunt, bearded face, before a bolt of lightning blinded him. The near simultaneous clap of thunder was deafening. Another huge wave caught the dhow, piling up along the angled deck and slamming Llewelyn, Gelert and their rescuers up against a bulkhead.

The inundating wave drained through the scuppers, and as his ears cleared, he heard a voice. It was Feiyan, calling from only a few yards away.

"Llewelyn! Pull in the rope!"

She said my name! Finally!

Dazed but determined, he attempted to roll into an upright position. But his efforts were too much for Gelert who snapped at him in an angry reflex.

"Llew! Calm down while we get you untied!" the King cried. A blade sawed at the ropes, which fell away and his father's strong arms enfolded him, lifting him upright.

Confused, Llewelyn looked around.

He saw Owain, dagger in hand, and Friar William, clutching at Gelert and trying to soothe him. There was the Grand Admiral and a crowd of Chinese soldiers and sailors.

What are you lot doing on an Arab dhow?

Where's Feiyan?

With his father's help, Llewelyn rose to his feet.

A mess of filthy clouds shrieked past at inhuman speed. Lightning bolts burst all around, hammering out ear-deadening claps of thunder. Rain fell so heavily it felt like river rapids, and monstrous waves pounded the foundering boat from all sides. Without warning, a crashing breaker knocked them all over again, barrelling them further up the deck in a writhing heap of limbs and rope.

Where's Feiyan?

The dhow climbed across the steep face of the next wave, the spume of seawater pouring off its tipping decks.

Llewelyn sat up and saw the sampan below in the trough. A strip of sail gave it steerage, dragging it away from him into the tempest. It too was canted at a crazy angle and looked set to capsize. For a moment his heart was in his mouth, but deep inside, he knew the tiny ship was safe.

'We make our sampans strong. Strong enough for the biggest seas.'

It righted itself and began to claw up the following wave as the dhow dropped into its trough.

Captain Chang, unconscious, was still hanging from the mainmast, transfixed by the arrows impaling his shoulders.

The rolling of the sampan flailed him against the mast like a beaten rug. Kung sat low in the cockpit, clinging to the tiller, not daring to look back. The Habasha she wolf, the otter dog, and several crew dogs barked down at him.

Gelert scurried to the railings next to Llewelyn and howled in reply.

There was Feiyan at the stern rail.

She was tying a long thin bundle to a length of rope that trailed across the ocean directly to the dhow. It was the other end of the rope Llewelyn and Gelert had been tied with.

Their end was still looped loosely around Gelert's back leg.

Llewelyn grabbed it, suddenly gripped by the hope that Feiyan wanted to pull him back to her.

The sampan now teetered above the dhow as it wallowed in the bowels of the trough. Looking down at him, Feiyan smiled, and raised the bundle she'd secured to the rope.

Then with all her strength, she threw it to him.

It arched through the howling wind and fell short into the sea.

Then the sampan was gone, swallowed into the raging sanctuary of the storm.

Panicking, Llewelyn hauled on the coarse, wet rope. The bundle at the end dragged heavily and he gasped with the effort. The swirling currents below fought him, tugging the rope from his grasp. He was too weak. He sobbed uncontrollably.

"Here, let me help." It was his father.

"No! I don't need you. Gelert, help! Pull."

The Great Dog grabbed the loose end in his teeth and began hauling it across the deck. Together, boy and dog dragged the package on board. Llewelyn fumbled with the bindings, his fingers numb with cold and exhaustion. He knew what it was before the sodden cloth peeled open.

His longbow.

The typhoon grabbed the dhow and tossed it aside. The impossible wind clawed at the triangular sail and the mainmast creaked ominously.

Crewmen everywhere rushed to take in the mainsail before it was shred to pieces or the mast snapped.

The next wave lifted the dhow high onto its crest, and there it hung for a moment, weightless, before sheering off down the other side.

"Get the dog below!" squealed the Admiral. Gelert lunged and snapped viciously at the two crewmen who attempted to grab him. One fell back, clutching a bitten, bloody hand.

Llewelyn calmed the old dog and took control.

"Keep away from him. Which way to hold?"

The crewmen pointed.

"Open the hatchway."

The sailors obeyed.

The King gawped at his son. "You can speak Chinese?"

Llewelyn was shoo-ing Gelert down the ladder as the next giant wave began to rear above the foundering vessel. He beckoned to his father, Owain and Friar William.

"Hurry!" he yelled in Welsh. "We won't last long out here!"

The three men scrambled after him, and the sailors slammed the hatchway shut just as the waved crashed over the dhow. Below deck, the din of the storm was muted and the hold was nearly dark, but when water stopped pouring through gaps in the hatch seals, the sickly light of the storm and a sudden lightning bolt gave Llewelyn a glimpse of the misery around him. Water was leaking through burst seams, adding to the knee-high slurry of shipped water and spilled cargo.

The boat corkscrewed alarmingly up the next wave and everyone was tumbled against a bulkhead.

"Brace yourselves and hold tight!" yelled Llewelyn. "We'll be alright if we can wedge ourselves into a corner."

The King wormed his way towards him.

"Oh my boy! You're safe at last! If they've hurt a hair on your head, so help me God I'll kill …"

A wrenching snap shuddered violently through the boat, followed by a terrifying creaking and screams from the Chinese crew above. Moments later, there was a thudding crash.

"The mainmast has gone!" shouted Llewelyn, "Everyone, hang on!"

The dhow bucked and lurched, then tilted sickeningly as it slewed into the trough of another wave. What might happen now was unthinkable. The tangle of fallen mast and sail was dragging the ship under the water. On deck he could hear sailors hacking at the fallen rigging with axes.

Icy fear gripped Llewelyn's heart and he held his breath. A flash of lightning showed his father wild-eyed with terror. Owain had screwed his eyes shut and seemed to be praying. Friar William clung to a thwart with one arm, the other wrapped protectively around Gelert's shoulders. Even with this help, the wolfhound was slipping and sliding, his gangly legs no match for the wildly tossing boat. He shivered with terror and stared forlornly at Llewelyn.

Friar William caught Llewelyn's eye. He shrugged bleakly, still grimly supporting Gelert. Llewelyn felt something approaching respect for the priest. He knew he must be in agony clutching nearly two hundred pounds of wolfhound.

There was more chopping from above.

Llewelyn turned to his father. "Don't worry. They'll clear the wreckage and we'll be fine!" he shouted, trying to sound reassuring.

After a cacophony of scraping wood, thrumming vibrations and a sluggish splash from outside, the dhow righted itself, twisting violently and throwing everyone to the far side of the hold. Gelert yowled with terror as he landed on top of Friar William, knocking him heavily against a bulkhead. The priest groaned and passed out.

The dhow stabilised, still in the mad grip of the storm, but the immediate crisis had passed.

"Owain, look after Gelert," ordered the King, dragging himself over to Llewelyn. "And check out the old goat while you're there. Now, let's see how you are," he shouted over the storm. "Oh my boy. What did they do to you? I was so afraid I'd lose you at the last. We have so much to talk about!"

🐾

The King felt Llewelyn's shoulders and arms and legs.

"Are you all right? What happened to your hair? You're awfully skinny!" His concern turned to anger. "Did they starve you?"

Llewelyn knew how emaciated he was, and now his chest and arms were ringed with ugly red rope burns and dark bruising. He felt weak, but seeing his father's frantic happiness lifted him.

"I'm all right," he replied. "Worry about the typhoon."

"All that matters is that I have you back. By all the Saints, Llew, those monsters led us a merry dance with you these past months, but it's over now!" he smiled, eyes moist. "You're safe. We can go home."

Llewelyn's mind was reeling. The impossibility of what had happened, that his father had followed him and found him in the middle of a typhoon on the other side of the world, was bewildering.

"How did you …? Why …?" he blurted.

The King embraced him. It felt good.

"Why? Do you think I'd let those brigands take you from me?"

"You went looking for me!"

"As soon as we knew you'd been kidnapped!" The King looked uncomfortable for a moment. "Well, it was more a matter of us tagging along with the Admiral. When he found Gelert had been stolen, we had to move fast to keep up with him. His whole army was back in the boats and on their way by dawn! Hardly any time to tell everyone what to do while we're away."

"You left Wales. For me?"

The King looked at him, baffled.

"Of course! You're my son! You're a Prince of Wales! Dafydd can look after things for a few months." He thought about that for a moment. "I'm sure everything will be fine."

"But what about the English?"

"What English?" The King laughed. "Owain, get over here and tell him about the English!"

Friar William was still unconscious, lying awkwardly in a heap. Owain left him and shuffled over, followed by Gelert. They tottered as the dhow swung into another wave, and fell onto Llewelyn and his father.

"The English?" Owain chuckled as he scrabbled upright. "Ptcha! None left. Every last one of them dead as a dormouse in a dormouse pie that's been baked, sliced, chewed up, swallowed and sh–"

"The only living English thing left in Wales after the Chinese finished with them had four legs and was wearing a saddle," interrupted the King. "It'll be years before Longshanks will be able to come against us again."

"That's if he has the stomach for it after what happened to his army!" grinned Owain. "And talking about killing the English, you saw off a few of them yourself in your travels!"

"What?" Llewelyn was mystified.

"Well, for a start, there was that fleet of theirs you destroyed!"

Llewelyn gulped. "Oh. Spain. There. Them. You saw that?"

"We saw what was left of them," said Owain. "And what a splendid sight! There they were, all burned and blinded, and clinging to what remained of their boats, and cursing the damned Prince Llewelyn of Wales. One of the survivors was bleating that they'd lost nearly three hundred men! I've never been so proud of you!"

"Yes," continued the King, "more importantly, that's how we knew we were on the right track. We were only, what? A day and a half behind you?"

Llewelyn shook his head in disbelief. He'd all but forgotten that terrible night. It seemed an age ago, but knowing now that his father had been so close was a shock. "Only a day and a half?"

"Aye. But the Admiral still didn't know which way you'd be going after that." He nodded to Friar William. "The dozy old goat over there was adamant the kidnappers would carry on south – so the Admiral had to split his fleet. Luckily, we turned left."

"Port. But how did you miss us after that? We ran into pirates."

Owain looked triumphant.

"And you did them in too!"

The King explained how they'd found the wreckage of the pirate fleet and gone ashore in search of information.

"A handful of wounded and dying scum, full of tales of …"

"A boy archer who slaughtered a hundred men!" smirked Owain, his eyes glowing at the thought of the mayhem. "And how the boy's monstrous dog herded a swarm of killer monkeys onto their ships!"

The King ruffled Gelert's head. "You did all that, did you, boy?"

The Great Dog barked happily.

That was my idea! Llewelyn thought of saying, but went on. "Our boat was damaged in the fight. We were dead in the water for three days. How did you miss us?"

"Well, we wondered why we didn't see sight nor sound of you until we reached the Holy Land," said the King, "but Kwan See told us yours was the fastest ship in his fleet. We must have passed you during the night."

Makes sense. Llewelyn almost laughed at the irony. He'd been heading for Jerusalem and a way back home, and all that time he'd been chasing his father. "So you saw the Holy Land?"

The King snorted. "From a distance! We spent the whole time beating up and down the coast looking for you. Friar William reckoned you must have been lost in a storm, but the Admiral wouldn't give up. He'd sent most of his ships back to look for you, so it was a miracle anyone was there when your kidnappers turned up. We gave chase, but by then it was getting dark."

Llewelyn grew excited. Although he'd been locked in a hold while all this cat and mouse was going on, he now remembered everything.

"And we doubled back on you, and got to shore, and the others went back to put you off our trail so that we could escape ..."

Owain looked at him oddly.

"Escape? You talk almost as if you were one of them!" he said, puzzled.

Llewelyn grew hot. He saw where this conversation might go. The enormity of his experiences began to unfold in his mind as he realised how bad falling in with his kidnappers would seem. The full truth was that he *had* been seeing himself on the side of the Jiang. He *had* been trying to escape. Willingly. The Emperor was now his enemy.

How could he even begin to tell his father that?

"Oh no. No, no, no. I was locked up in the hold," he said flustered. "Gelert was making such a racket they had to drug us to keep us quiet!" *That's true. I can tell them that.* "I was knocked out for three days!"

The King was shocked and angry.

"They drugged you? The thieving bast– ! If I ever find them ..."

"You'll find me already standing over their steaming dead bodies ..." growled Owain, equally furious.

"And just who are 'they'?" asked the King, still fuming. "The ones we dragged from the water after the battle told the Admiral nothing, no matter how much they were tortured."

"Battle? Tortured?" said Llewelyn, suddenly cold.

The King spoke with bitter admiration. "Oho! They fought us to the last. Sank three Chinese ships before we killed enough of them to be able to get on board. Of course, the Admiral was holding back for fear of harming you or Gelert. But once we learnt you weren't there, things got really brutal."

Owain grimaced. "Aye. There was only one left alive, and after the Admiral had finished with him, all that was left was his ears and his mouth. Still didn't say a word except to tell us he was only the ship's cook. He had guts, the fat little feller. I'll give him that. Well, actually he didn't. Not inside him that is. Not by the end."

The King took Llewelyn by his shoulders, a fierce gleam in his eyes.

"But you were with them," he hissed. "You'll know why they wanted Gelert, and where they're from, and where they're headed. Tell us everything, and the Admiral will hunt them down like the vermin they are ..." He was shaking Llewelyn now, gripped by vengeful wrath.

"But I, but, but, they didn't really tell me much," stammered Llewelyn, beginning to panic. *Feiyan, the captain, even Kung – I mustn't betray them!*

His rescue came in the most unexpected form.

"LEAVE HIM BE!"

It was Friar William, propping himself up on one elbow. A trickle of blood ran down from his temple. He was still groggy, but he'd lost none of his questionable authority.

"Put him down! Can't you see he's exhausted?"

The King was still wild-eyed, but caught himself.

"Yes. Yes. Of course ..." he said, relaxing and letting go of Llewelyn.

The howling of the typhoon filled the moment. For the hundredth time, the storm hurled the dhow viciously over, and a drenching slurry of water poured through the hatchway seals.

"I'm sorry, son," said the King, hugging him. "After what you've been through, you need rest. Come on, let's try to get comfortable."

It had taken three days for the sampan to ride into the typhoon, but it would take five for the crippled dhow to make it through to the other side.

It remained afloat, but without its mast it was tossed like a toy by the screaming winds and waves. The lurching motion was impossible to predict, and everyone grew steadily more bruised and battered.

Owain managed to light an oil lamp, and the King broke open some barrels of provisions. They chewed on dank strips of meat and sodden dried fruit, and sipped brackish water.

Friar William seemed more concerned with Gelert than looking after himself, taking sacks of coconut hair and making a cave for the wolfhound. The Great Dog flopped into it and lolled happily, protected for the most part while the others suffered from the buffeting.

At first, his father continued to make conversation, shouting over the howling gale. Llewelyn heard the joy in his voice, but feared that he was being probed for information. Fortunately, he didn't need to fake his weariness, and eventually the King gave up.

After his intervention, Friar William was silent, but Llewelyn knew he was watching him, brooding in the lightning-prickled gloom.

The storm continued to pummel the ship and they hunkered, dumb and helpless in the tumult. Llewelyn squeezed in next to Gelert in his nest. For a while, he was comfortable until the dog snapped in sudden pain and began furiously scratching his stubby ear with his hind leg.

Llewelyn thought he saw a tick scuttling towards him through the soggy coconut fibres. He scratched his left armpit, then his right. Soon his skin begin to crawl.

Oh no. Here they come.

Alone with his thoughts, Llewelyn grew miserable.

As he scratched, he felt the memories of his recent journeys begin to fade, replaced by a deep melancholia as they drifted further and further from his Jiang friends.

He thought about Feiyan and was bewildered to discover that he couldn't picture her face, only her eyes, blue and angry.

Perhaps it was the typhoon sucking his memories from him?

But, no. He realised abruptly that it was his father. Being with him: the King of Wales. He'd followed him halfway around the world to rescue him, and now he was going to take him home.

I should be happy. But all Llewelyn felt was hollow. He was no longer free and facing up to challenges: once again he was his father's son and heir, the Prince of Wales, dutiful, dependent and trapped.

Picking up used arrows for punishment.

He sniffed guilty tears, glad of the darkness. He wondered if he wanted go back; back to the destiny his birthright imposed on him. He'd so wanted to fight for Wales, and glory and honour, but that was now another world a million miles away.

He felt ashamed of his ingratitude and guilty about what his father would think if he knew of his doubts.

How can I make him understand? Should he tell him everything? Describe all the things he'd seen and done and why he'd done them? Why the Jiang weren't bandits, but fighting for their freedom – just like the Welsh.

Could he tell him about Feiyan? Suddenly he could see her face again. She was waving to him, about to throw him his longbow.

But Llewelyn knew the King would never forgive the Jiang for kidnapping him, and if his father knew anything about them, he'd have Friar William tell the Admiral. Once *he* knew, then so would the Emperor, and God knows what would happen then.

Nothing good.

Despair curdled his mind, and he reached into his pocket and took out Wudi's fish for comfort.

Which way is Jiang now, Wudi? Where's Feiyan?

He opened the lid. A flash of lightning illuminated the beautiful jewelled animal spinning wildly in its oil. The dhow was a broken twig caught in a melt-flood waterfall.

He looked at his father and Owain. Both were snoring loudly.

How can they sleep through this?

He felt a presence and glanced sideways. Friar William was

staring at him. Llewelyn looked away, but when he looked backed, the foul priest was still staring. Then he started to shuffle over to Gelert's coconut cave, his rancid smell wafting ahead of him.

Oh no, what does he want? He looked to his father for help, but he and Owain were dead to the world. The dog growled softly as Friar William settled himself in front of Llewelyn, peering in at him.

"What's troubling you, boy?"

"Nothing."

"Come now. You can tell me. Did they treat you badly?" But there was no sympathy in Friar William's eyes.

"Who?"

"On the junk. Did they treat you very badly?"

"No. I mean yes. Yes, I was their prisoner."

"Locked away in a hold all that time, no-one talking to you, never knowing what was going on?"

"Yes. That is right."

Friar William looked him up and down.

"And yet you learned to speak Chinese …"

"No, not really. Just a few words. Not enough to talk properly …" He petered out, realising they'd both been talking in Chinese.

"I see. You picked up 'just a few' words. Locked up. In a hold. All by yourself." Friar William's accusing gaze settled on Wudi's fish. "And did you find that 'fish' in this hold that you were locked in?"

"I, er, I suppose so …"

"I know when you're lying boy!" he snapped viciously. "Confess! You stole it from Wudi."

Llewelyn shook his head and started to deny it, but before he could speak he felt his tongue turn to ice and his throat close up.

How do you know about Wudi?

Friar William had noted his hesitation. "Well if you didn't steal it…" He laughed, his contempt quickly returning. "Don't tell me. The sentimental fool *gave* it to you?"

"Yes!"

Friar William sat back and smiled. "So, old Wudi is finally dead."

"Yes. But … how did you …?"

"Wudi had his fish for a thousand years. He would never have given it to anyone while there was a breath in his body, certainly not to a 'prisoner'. So why'd he give it to you?"

"I ... I don't know ..." Llewelyn was now trapped.

Friar William drew closer, spraying spittle in his face.

"And why did Feiyan stop to throw you your bow? What was going on there? Do I detect a *romantic dalliance?*" he leered.

Llewelyn nearly choked and he knew he was turning bright red. "No! Her? Me? No, no ..."

"Well, well, well! Chang's blue-eyed she-devil has an admirer!"

Friar William leaned in, closer still, now with more anger in his voice. Gelert heard it and growled deeply.

"You can't hide the truth from me, boy. It's clear that you fell into bed with your Jiang abductors, that you gained their trust. That you are, how can I say this ...? That you are now 'sympathetic' to their cause ..."

"No!"

"Then why are you trying to lie to me? Why else, if it isn't to cover up your betrayal of your father?"

Llewelyn's mouth opened and closed, but what could he say? The priest had backed him into the truth. Or at least part of a truth. Friar William watched him capitulate. A rare look of sympathy slithered across his face, but then it was gone.

"Well, don't worry Llewelyn, I understand the reasons for your lack of gratitude. And your secret is safe with me. In fact, I'll let you into a little secret of my own. A secret we both can share ..."

Llewelyn recoiled, but he grabbed him and pulled him closer.

"Look into my eyes boy. They're not baby blue like your darling Feiyan's, but tell me what you see ..."

Confused but transfixed, Llewelyn peered into the old man's eyes.

Close up, Friar William was even more ugly and malodourously repulsive, and Llewelyn wasn't surprised he'd never done this before. The old man's face was craggy, the wrinkles thick with dirt and flecks of dried skin. His eyelids, drooped and hooded, covered the corners of his eyes, which were thick with yellow crusting pus. But now Llewelyn saw that his eyes were pointed ovals. There, deep within filmy mucus and surrounded by bloodshot brown whites, he saw green.

Dull green irises.

A sudden flash of lightning blazed, and the green of the priest's eyes glowed brightly.

Llewelyn gasped. "You're Jiang!"

Friar William sat back, sneering.

"Well done. Ten out of ten. Go to the top of the class."

EPILOGUE

By Gelert

"What? You can't stop there!"

If Llewelyn and I have heard that said once, we've heard it said two hundred and fifty-eight times over the last seven centuries.

A problem with our story is that it's hundreds of years long. Too many glazed eyes and people nodding off have taught us that it's best to cut it up into manageable chunks, because taking on the whole thing at once is like trying to eat an elephant in one sitting. Which I've tried to several times and always failed. Never even managed to get past the trunk, and that left me feeling more bloated than a tight-fisted bloater in a 'bloaters only', all-you-can-eat free buffet. But I digress.

So now you've digested our tale so far, you might want to take a breather before you move on to the next course – 'The Dog Wars' or, as I like to call it: 'How Gelert saved everyone in the world'.

It's the story of how we went into the belly of the beast or, in modern parlance, got to 'hang with the Emp'.

Some historians have labelled that particular Emperor 'the most deranged despot of the Five Dynasties and Ten Kingdoms Period', but anyone who eats curried cat for breakfast can't be all that bad.

I joke. Even I wouldn't eat a cat. Not for breakfast, anyway.

No, as you'll see, the Emperor was one seriously messed-up bloke who thought nothing of moving the odd pesky mountain if it got in the way of a decent sunset, or butchering an entire country if he thought it was looking at him funny. Yet, I once saw him burst into tears when his four-floor Caravan Palace accidentally ran over a duck's beak (don't worry about the duck – the Emperor had his best doctors and finest goldsmiths reconstruct its face with a twenty-four carat platinum beak).

Also, in the next part of our story, you'll find out more about the repulsive Friar William, including his real Jiang name. After all, we can't keep calling him 'Friar' William – the closest he ever got to priesthood was drinking from the baptismal font.

Plus there are many more Jiang dogs to meet. Some are wonderful, some are just plain daft, but one or two have been bred for things you won't want to read about on a full stomach.

Needless to say, you haven't heard the last from Feiyan and Captain

Chang and old misery guts Kung, none of who have given up on getting hold of me (the hyenas, as Llewelyn and Feiyan suspected, deliver mixed blessings, which means a return to plan A, i.e. me).

How on earth can the Jiang breed an entire army of dogs before the Emperor twigs that something's up? Doesn't creating a new breed of dog take time? How far into the Mud Tunnels will Llewelyn have to go to find the mind-bending answer to all these questions?

And finally, you'll make the acquaintance of the Royal Court of the Jiang Kingdom. To say it's 'damaged' would be an understatement. The twisted intentions of the Jiang Queen are as black as the inside of a cow at the bottom of a coal mine at midnight in winter, if a little less smelly.

So, lots to look forward to.

Until then, it's ta-ta from us – Llewelyn has some emails to catch up on, and I have a dead seagull to roll in.

THE END

Dear Reader,

I suppose if you're still reading this far, you must be looking for more information about Llewelyn and Gelert's world.

If you google 'The Dog Hunters by David Bell', you'll find a website with all sorts of goodies about the historical background to the legend of Gelert, medieval Wales and China, plus details on how to suggest your own ideas for a new breed of Jiang dog (which could appear in the next part of the adventure).

The site includes a video trailer of the story, with spine tingling music compsed by my son Frank.

Meanwhile, I'm working on 'the Dog Army', the provisional title of the next book in the series (not 'Dog Wars' as Gelert said- really you can't trust everything he says. He's a dog, after all), and it's shaping up as something of a ripsnorter.

Meanwhile, why not do a bit of writing yourself? If you really like the book, put fingers to keyboard and review it on Amazon.

David Bell, Auckland, New Zealand, September 2013

8563951R00184

Printed in Great Britain
by Amazon.co.uk, Ltd.,
Marston Gate.